BACKSTAGE

T GEPHART

BACK STAGE
Copyright 2015 T Gephart
Published by T Gephart

ISBN-10: 09925188-5-7
ISBN-13: 978-0-9925188-5-1

Discover other titles by T Gephart at Smashwords or on Facebook, Twitter, Goodreads, or tgephart.com

This book is licensed for your personal enjoyment only. This book may not be re-sold or given away to other people. If you would like to share this book with another person, please purchase an additional copy for each recipient. If you're reading this book and did not purchase it or it was not purchased for your use only, then please return and purchase your own copy. Thank you for respecting the hard work of this author.

This book is a work of fiction. The names, characters, places and scenarios are products of the writer's imagination or have been used fictitiously and are not to be construed as real. Any resemblance to persons, living or dead, actual events, locales or organizations is entirely coincidental.

Edited by Nichole Strauss from Perfectly Publishable
Front Cover by Gianni Renda
Cover Image by Angelique Ehlers
Back Cover by Hang Le
Formatted by Max Henry of Max Effect

For Justine,

one of the strongest women I know.

It's not the end until it's the End.

@Tyghat xx

PROLOGUE

Angie

TEN YEARS AGO

GOD, HE WAS SEXY. ALL THOSE TANNED MUSCLES, POPPING OUT proudly. I had to fight the urge not to give the man a standing ovation every time I looked at him. Which was a lot. And I was thankful. Every. Single. Time.

He was different, and I'd known that from the second I'd laid eyes on him. He wasn't a boy, not like any I'd seen. It wasn't just that he was older; there was something in his face, the way he walked, that set him apart. He was a man, and he wasn't shy about showing it.

A black '72 Mercury Montego fastback had pulled up just before dusk sometime in late May. The rumble of the V8 had me at the window before the car had even been parked in front of Troy's house. And while the car had initially captured my attention, it was what stepped out of it that made me stand up and take notice. The way he strode to Troy's door was almost erotic, his movements so fluid and sure that his body screamed sex. He was so hot.

He spent the summer living with Troy and his family, and I had found a renewed sense of religion spending most of my days thanking God for the creation that was Jason Irwin. Having just separated from the Army, his hair was starting to grow out of the regulation high-and-tight, while his body was still in that be-all-you-can-be shape. I whispered my silent thank-you's to the US Government when he'd pull off his shirt.

It wasn't just his GI Joe body that had my brain feeling like it had been blended, it was the way he would talk to me when I finally stopped being a chicken-shit and introduced myself. He didn't treat me like a kid nor did he try and weasel himself into my panties like Dan. He seemed genuinely interested in what I had to say. Those times when he'd give me his attention, my world would stand still and before I could stop it, my heart wanted him more than my hormones.

The temp hadn't dipped below a hundred in four days straight, with the last days of August proving summer wouldn't give in to fall without one last fight. Which had encouraged him to be outside a lot, which is where I also seemed to be. I prayed every night the heat wave would never end. It was heaven on Earth. The heat, the night, and him.

"Angie." His voice rumbled, his eyes slowly opening.

Sleep had been near impossible. After weeks and weeks of hoping, he finally kissed me.

Except it hadn't been just a kiss.

His mouth had owned mine. His big strong hands around my head brought me in closer as his tongue teased the inside of my mouth. It was hot, my body almost combusting in the overload. I never wanted it to stop.

The flirting back and forth wasn't new. Every time we spoke, my heart thumped so loud I was convinced a marching band had taken up residence. It had been the same since the moment I saw him, getting to know him had reinforced what I had already guessed. He was perfection. Beautiful. Smart. Sexy. But there was something else, a lingering darkness that I didn't understand. He was quiet. Not rude, just held back. And damn if he wasn't a nut I wanted to crack. Last night I had gotten

BACK STAGE

that chance.

"Hey." The smile on my face threatened to split apart.

This was my favorite view. Jason Irwin lying naked beneath me, his rugged arms holding me close—those dark eyes of his giving *me* their full attention.

That kiss—the one that would forever be elevated to the best kiss of my life—didn't end with just some heavy petting. After asking me repeatedly if I was sure, he finally made love to me.

At first he seemed like he hadn't wanted to. Mumbling something about not being good enough for me. He had always been so concerned about me, so kind, but he didn't have to worry. It was *exactly* what I wanted and when I finally convinced him it was okay, he gave in.

Under the moonlight, in the backseat of his car.

It couldn't have been more perfect.

"Are you okay?" His fingers gently moved over my shoulder and down my arm.

It tickled but I didn't dare ask him to stop. I'd never ask him to stop. Not when we'd *finally* gotten together. This was going to be the start of something fantastic. I could just feel it. There were going to be so many more nights like this. Him and me. Holding each other. Loving each other.

"I'm fine," I breathed against his skin, nuzzling myself closer to his neck. Our legs were twisted within the confined space of his car, the leather sticking to parts of our skin. Did I mention how perfect it had been? It could have been a penthouse bedroom at the Waldorf Astoria and it wouldn't have been any better. His body knew exactly what to do with mine. Who knew sex could even feel like that? That I loved him, well that just made it better.

"We should probably get dressed; everyone is going to be waking up soon." His body shifted under mine, the leather creaking in protest as he moved. I didn't blame it. I wanted to protest, too.

"Yeah, we should." I fished my bra out of the pile of clothes on the floor and sat up to slide it on. "My dad is going to be heading to work in a few hours; I could make us breakfast as soon as he leaves." My smile hopefully hinted that he could repay me by taking care of dessert. It was my birthday after all, and I knew exactly how I wanted to spend my day. Naked, with Jason—in case anyone was wondering.

"That's not such a good idea." With a flicker of panic in his eyes, he threw water on whatever flames I had going on, his lack of a smile making me nervous.

"Oh?" The word had shot out of my mouth, wondering if he had something better planned. Naked on the beach could also work. It might be a bit sandy, but okay. In any case, we were still going to need to eat.

"Yeah, I think it's best if we just ... did our own thing."

He wanted to play it cool. Smart. I mean I had *just* turned eighteen and while I had no issue with the seven-year age gap, my dad would probably lose his shit. He was worried. Of course he was. We'd have to keep it a secret for a while, just until everyone got used to it. Jase moving away meant it would be easier. We could date and not have to worry about prying eyes and judgmental stares. Troy might be a little weird about it at first, being that he was usually so protective. But he had to think Jason was a decent guy if he'd invited him to stay an entire summer. Plus, once he saw how in love we were, he would come around. How could he not? We wouldn't have to mention that our first time had been in his backyard while he was blissfully asleep a few feet away. Nope, that piece of information I would take to the grave. And hopefully now Dan Evans would finally get it through his head he didn't stand a chance. Not now that I had a boyfriend.

"Sure. Did you want to meet up with me later? When the coast is clear?" My panties were next on my redress mission. Difficult, seeing Jase was still naked and not making any effort to cover up. My eyes inadvertently floated down to see his cock was very much awake and ready for me now, rather than later. The surge between my thighs concluding we were very much on the same page. This was going to be the best birthday ever.

"No, Angie. I'm leaving." He swallowed hard, shaking his head like he was finally convinced. "What happened last night was a mistake."

"Huh?"

It had been more of a sound than an actual word. My mouth no longer being controlled by my brain as I processed the words he had said. "Leaving" and "mistake" being the loudest.

"We shouldn't have done that. It wasn't smart. In any case, it won't be happening again."

It was as if a switch had been flicked, the interior of the car immediately chilling despite the sun threatening to rise at any moment. His eyes darkened, emotionless, as he threw on a T-shirt over his head. The amazing guy I had fallen in love with, gone and in his place ... someone else.

"I—I know you're moving. But we can still see each other." I purposely ignored the other part of his statement. The one where he'd said I had been a mistake.

"No." He reached down and shoved his legs into his jeans without bothering with his boxers. "We can't."

I don't understand. I wasn't sure if I had said it out loud or if it was just on a constant loop in my head. What had gone wrong?

"Hey." He looked at me, I wasn't sure if it was regret or pity in his eyes. "It's just better this way. Maybe we should just pretend it didn't happen."

"But it did happen." I blinked, wondering if it was a joke.

"Yeah, it did. But it was a mistake. You understand that, right?"

I felt like I was going to be sick. That word again. Mistake. The bile from my stomach surged uncomfortably as I scrambled to pull on my cotton, crumpled sundress. The one he had told me last night looked so hot on me. Shoes, they weren't an option as I all but threw myself from his car, the dress barely covering my skin as my feet hit the dirt.

"Yep, no biggie." I nodded, praying if there was any god at all he would help me not to cry. Not now. Not in front of him while he looked at me so impassively.

"Hey, Angie. Are you okay?" His eyes widened as my shoeless feet hit an overgrown tree root in the Harris backyard.

Pain.

The one in my foot nothing like the one that was going on in my heart. I needed to get away. Now.

"Sure. Dumb tree." *Please don't cry. Please don't cry.* My legs doing their best to keep me upright and get me out down the side path to the front of the house. "See you, thanks." My back turned before the first tear fell.

In my head, he'd call after me. Run from his car and tell me that the mistake was this stupid conversation, and not last night.

But that didn't happen.

And as I made it the short distance next door to the safety of my house, I'd heard the rumble of his V8.

I wished I'd been stronger. Asked him why. But I felt so dumb.

Dumb, that I'd been stupid enough to allow myself to be played.

Dumb, that I'd fallen in love with some guy who had only wanted to fuck me.

Dumb, that I'd fallen for the oldest trick in the book.

By the time I'd pulled my key from my pocket, his black Montego had already driven past.

He was gone.

And he had taken my heart with him.

1
Jason

PRESENT DAY

"THANK YOU NEW YORK AND GOOD NIIIGGHHHHHHT!" JAMES, OUR front man, pumped his fist in the air as the techs killed the lights, plunging the stage into darkness.

Opening night in our hometown, and the air was motherfucking electric. Two encores and fans were still chanting for "one more song", our three-hour set not long enough apparently. And damn if that shit didn't make me feel bullet proof.

"Jase! Here, dude." A towel flew through the air toward me as I stepped out from behind the keys; my hand grabbed it and slung it over a shoulder. Was going to need more than that to mop up the sweat that was pouring off me. The excitement wasn't going to wash off even *with* the shower.

"Thanks, man!" I said to no one in particular, not sure entirely which one of the roadies had been my hook-up.

My muscles ached, tightly coiled from exhaustion, but even still it would be a hard task to wipe the smile off my face.

"Fuck, that felt good." Troy toweled off his face as he fell into step beside me, our feet taking us off the stage and down the stairs. "It's been too long. Recording is one thing, but playing in front of a crowd. That shit never gets old." Big ass smile on his face was the hint he was feeling the same way I was.

"Truth, right?" Dan jogged up beside us as we made our way to the back of house area. "I don't give a shit how many times we play Madison Square Garden. Every time I get on that stage, I almost blow my load."

"Save it for your wife, asswipe; no one wants to hear about your jizz." Troy's stank-ass towel flew over my head and clocked Dan right in the mouth. He had it opened too, so that got extra points. I ignored the subsequent name-calling that erupted as a result. It was a case of the same *fuck you, asshole* I'd been hearing for the last ten years. While the others got vocal with their appreciation, I did what I always did, and kept it locked down.

Not because they weren't right on the money—that euphoric feeling of playing live for a crowd—nothing else compared. But because big, showy and emotional wasn't my thing. Not any more at least, and not because I didn't care. It was just better to keep an even keel. For me, unstable wasn't a good look. Didn't mean good things either, so I kept my shit in check. Better for everyone.

We were just five guys playing our tunes. It had always been about that. Difference now was the crowd and the venues were bigger, but if shit went down tomorrow and we were back playing a dive bar in Queens, we'd still be showing up every night and rocking its ass off.

"Awesome show guys." James clapped his hand around my neck. "This tour is going to be our best yet."

Our fearless leader was always the last one off the stage, Alex, our badass guitarist, usually leaving a second or two before him. They were our Lennon and McCartney, the drivers of the crazy train, and they usually got more time in the spotlight. None of us gave a shit, far as the rest of us where concerned, it was deserved.

BACK STAGE

It was the usual back and forth after a show. The high-fiving and us talking shop was our way of unwinding as we made it back to the dressing rooms. Roadies took care of securing the gear while security made sure we kept moving; us hanging around only made their jobs harder. They weren't assholes about it, but they made it clear that the hallway was not the place for us to get warm and fuzzy.

"Great show." Lexi Reed, our PR manager, greeted us as we rounded the corner. "Get showered and changed. There's no meet and greet tonight, but there's a few people who want to show their personal adoration." She'd barely gotten the words out when Alex put his mouth on hers. Lucky for him there would be no sexual harassment charges, being that Lexi was also his wife.

The PDA was all now par for the course with every one of the band members hooked up with a significant other. Well, all except for me, and that was more than fine as far as I was concerned. While it all worked out for them, I'd learnt my lesson early on, and I'd rather piss out razor blades than go through a relationship again. Still, I wasn't raining on anyone else's parade. Evil son of a bitch was also something I'd left in my past. The cool, calm and collected Jase version 2.0, definitely the better of the two.

A loud bang echoed through the hall; it was followed up with a piercing and vocal "motherfuuuuucckkkkkerrr!" stopping any further high-fiving and/or lip action. James looked to the door where the commotion was coming from with the same what-the-fuck look on his face as the rest of us. Seemed ground zero was our support act, *Unhinged Throttle's* dressing room.

"Hey, maybe we poke our heads in for a sec," James nodded to the door, "make sure shit isn't getting too out of control."

Wise choice, support bands had a tendency to let the excitement go to their heads, especially ones who weren't seasoned. It was like bringing a virgin to a gangbang— unpredictable, volatile and usually escalated quickly. Taking a look was definitely on the cards.

We let James take the lead as he rapped on the door a couple of times;

a loud "come on in" shouted back in response. Good sign; meant at least they were still conscious. Calling 9-1-1 on opening night would have been a buzz kill.

"What the fuck?" Alex's voice boomed across the room, the door opening to what could have been a scene from a bad movie. Two of the band members were on their knees doing lines of coke off a mirror. The gaping hole in the drywall that looked to be the same size of the reflective surface, a tip-off it hadn't been an accessory they'd walked in with.

They had company as well. Three naked girls giving *blow* of a different variety, while two other charming ladies finding an interesting use for a champagne bottle—obviously bigger fans of each other rather than the actual band.

"Hey!" Wade, the lead guitarist waved us over as the girl in his lap kept up her Dyson action. "Welcome to our kingdom. You guys want some H? It's clean, my dealer is a stand-up guy."

"Wow, didn't think when I got out of bed this morning I'd be hearing *drug dealer* and *stand-up guy* in the same sentence." Dan's eyes widened as he checked out the scene. Had to admit, he was saying what we all were thinking.

Hardcore drug use hadn't been part of the Power Station history. And while that shit was straight up reminiscent of my teenage years, thankfully I'd separated myself from those fucktards a long time ago. Most of them either in a cell or underground— I couldn't make myself give a crap either way. I was just glad it hadn't been my footnote. Which brought us to the dipshits currently in front of us.

"You losers have drugs in here? Are you motherfucking insane? There are kids on this tour." The anger rolled off James like a tidal wave. If the words that jutted from his mouth weren't enough of a clue, the bulging veins in his neck would have cleared up any misunderstanding.

"Relax dude, we're just partying." Wade held his hands up defensively, smug-ass grin on his face. "This is how we do our come down."

"You come down by getting high?" I coughed out a laugh. "Yeah

BACK STAGE

these guys are fucking geniuses."

What the poster boys for Dumbasses of the Year didn't realize was that we weren't interested in the irony. The rage kicked up to we're-going-to-bust-some-heads level as they were told to pack up their shit and get the fuck out.

Oh, and mention of the five-o made the girls who had been deep-throating suddenly take an interest in the conversation.

The motley crew of assholes got ready to clear out with Wade throwing in there, "We'll see you tomorrow," while he pushed his dick in his pants and zipped up.

It really shouldn't have needed to be said. Their contracts, crystal freaking clear. Drugs on tour equaled do not pass go, do not collect two hundred dollars. Buh-bye. It didn't matter it wasn't my woman or child that needed protecting; they were *my* family and this was a hundred percent united front. And if I got to limber up and break out some old school moves with the bastards, well that would just make the evening more interesting. My guess was the collective douchebags in front of me had never seen any real action. As for me, I'd been in more street fights than I'd cared to remember. Not that the press ever got a hold of that information. Nope, my bio was sold as an Army vet who played keys and liked to knit. The knitting thing was complete bullshit of course, but it just goes to show how nobody was taking notice. FYI, no one gives a rat's ass about the keyboard player.

"No, I don't think you understood me." James settled into an eerie calm. "You're done."

"You're firing us?" Oh look, one of the other band members, Pete, suddenly decided he wasn't mute and joined in the conversation. "You can't just fucking fire us." The unsteadiness of his voice not giving the statement the confidence he'd possibly hoped for.

"Read your contract, asshole." Alex stepped in, the edge in his voice enough to chill the room a few degrees. "I think we can all agree a piss test at this point isn't needed." His raised eyebrow dared them to prove him wrong.

What happened next I could only describe as stupid-ass shit. Because clearly you should know better than to argue with a bunch of guys who were sober and not only outweighed you in muscle, but freaking brains as well. That right there should have been an advert for an anti-drug campaign. Look kids, if the drugs don't fuck you up, the stupid shit that will come out of your mouth will finish the job.

Wade had opened his mouth, and I really didn't care much for what he had to say. The conversation had already taken too long. Cue my fist grabbing the front of his shirt and tossing him out the door while Troy threatened to go Scorsese on the other douchebags who weren't moving fast enough. And just like that, we'd pulled some abracadabra type shit. Boom—place cleared.

"We solid, big guy?" I clapped my hand around Troy's neck hoping to help him rein in some of the rage. My time with the dark side had taught me some pretty handy tricks in talking people down from the ledge. And this guy, I'd easily take a bullet for.

He shook his head, the look in his eyes enough to convince me he was exercising as much restraint as he knew how. "I don't want Megs exposed to that, especially not while she is knocked up."

"Agreed." James sunk his ass into one of the vacated chairs. "That shit doesn't go on. I'm not expecting them to be sitting around holding prayer meetings—I expected blowjobs and weed, not fucking heroin and coke."

The high we'd been on from the show took a very quick downswing; the reality of the situation hitting home. I took a seat beside James and cleared my throat. "Not to be an asshole and state the obvious, but we just fired our opening act day one of our tour. Any ideas on how we're going to play this?"

Not that I didn't concur with said firing, but tomorrow we were going to be hitting the stage again. A big gaping slot where the warm-up band should be. Going on without a pre-show was unheard of, so it was either get creative or hire some record spinner from Soho.

"Everyone decent is already booked. We can probably put out a call,

BACK STAGE

see who's around?" Dan grabbed his phone from his back pocket. His creased brow the tip-off he wasn't entirely convinced, that even with his connections, he could pull off a miracle and fill the spot.

"No, this just perfectly illustrates why we need to do this in house. It isn't just us on the road anymore. We don't need the kids finding a fucking needle 'cause some jerk-off thinks it's the 90's." Alex planted his ass beside James; Troy and Dan following suit in chairs opposite them. Well wasn't this warm and fucking cozy? Pity the situation itself blew hardcore.

"Alex is right," James agreed, "we need someone we can trust. Now would be a good time for any ideas."

"Hey what about Angie Morelli?" Troy rubbed his hand through his mohawk, the mess of crap he called hair.

Angie Morelli.

Yep, just saying her name was enough to send a chill up my spine. It had been ten years, and still not long enough. Her long, black hair and dark-brown eyes, something that had taken a while to wipe from my mind. That body. Yeah, I still remembered every curve. So freaking sweet, too. Unfortunately it wasn't only her attributes that I remembered, one of my biggest asshole moments was also front and center getting the trip down memory lane. So you would have to understand why I didn't immediately start doing backflips and welcoming her. The idea was to avoid the drama, not to give it top freaking billing.

"Dude, no. No fucking way," Dan chimed in, his words echoing exactly what was rattling around in my head.

Thank you, douchebag. An Angie reunion was bad news. There had to be someone else. Hey, was Charlie Manson out of prison yet? I mean if we were thinking up bad ideas to take on tour, we might as well put them all on the table.

"She's still playing?" James tipped his head toward Troy, taking way more interest in the topic than I would have liked. The itch to shut the conversation down danced with the need to keep my mouth shut. Delicate act. Wasn't sure which one was going to win. Honestly, it was going to be trouble either way.

"Sure is. Lexi is trying to sign her band, Black Addiction; saw them last week at a club in Brooklyn. She said they packed the house." Troy threw some more weight behind the cause. The conversation continued around me, even as the mother of all headaches took up residence in my frontal lobe.

"I saw her stuff on You Tube, they're tight." Alex nodded, the bastard not having any idea on what he was signing us up for, and I wasn't going to be neon-signing it for him either.

"C'mon! Angie?" Dan rolled his eyes, throwing his hands up in disgust. "Troy, did you snort some of Wade's nose candy before he left? She doesn't have the chops for a stadium. Besides, she hates us."

Had to admit, this was one time where I was happy for Dan to be running his mouth. Giving him a round of applause would have been too conspicuous, so I kept it on the down low, but I was a hundred percent behind his stance. The fact it wasn't me who was leading the anti-Angie movement was a fucking bonus.

"No, she hates *you*." Troy smirked. The Dan v Angie battles common knowledge.

"No, she fucking hates Jase, too."

The motherfucker had to go there. He couldn't have left it with his own reasons for not wanting her around. He had to go ahead and drag me into it.

"Hate is a pretty strong word, let's go with a strong dislike." I eased back into the chair knowing well enough that it wasn't going to be the last on the topic I was going to have to volunteer. Fucking Dan.

"Dan I understand, but why you, Jase?" Troy's raised eyebrow proving he had no idea what had happened between me and his sexy, barely legal neighbor before we'd hit the big time.

At least Dan had managed to keep a lid on it for longer than I'd ever imagined; I'd always had my suspicions that he'd spilled one time or another, but seems to be those concerns were unfounded. Who knew he had it in him. In the end, the violence was still happening. I'd just make

BACK STAGE

sure I didn't punch him above the neck, keep the SOB pretty for the fans.

"Long story." Well at least it wasn't a total lie. "Let's just say I'm not her favorite person and move on, shall we." The less I said about the subject the better. Besides, it was fucking years ago. Why the hell were we dredging it all up now?

"I heard she has a voodoo doll of you." Dan stretched out his arms, anchoring them behind his head, his grin splitting off the side of his face. "Tell me, asswipe, do you feel any stabbing pain in your cock?"

"Dude, seriously. Can we focus here?" My shut-the-fuck-up vibe via the eyeball hopefully coming in loud and clear.

So remember how we talked about Jase version 2.0? It turns out some stuff can't be wiped away even after an upgrade. A one-night-stand seemed part of this system failure. Not that I would take it back. The memory of her, and that night, worth the grief I was catching now. God, she'd been perfect. Fuck. Maybe I had snorted Wade's nose candy. Would explain the crazy talk.

Thankfully Dan's tendency to say stupid shit was enough for the band to overlook his current hard-on to bring up the past, namely mine. His comments about me, Angie, and all things to do with my cock were left ignored as they moved on to the problem of no support band. Once again, I resisted the urge to fucking applaud. Seemed someone upstairs was throwing me a Hail Mary.

My thanks to all things holy took a strong and steady nosedive as Alex sold her virtues some more. "Ain't gonna lie, someone from the old neighborhood would be a fucking godsend right now. She knows us, we know her and last I checked isn't attending AA meetings."

Awesome, was he selling the band or nominating her for sainthood? James's head action telling me he'd already made his decision.

The recon went further, with someone stalking Black Addiction's Facebook page and mentioning they were playing a bar in Long Island. Someone else chimed in suggesting we jump into our ride and put this to bed ASAP. Whose voice was whose really didn't matter. It all spelled trouble.

"Angie fucking Morelli. I can't believe we are even considering this." Dan gave it a last-ditch effort to stop the insanity.

"Dude, she will probably say no." Or at least I'd hoped she would.

"Well we can stand here with hypotheticals or we can go fucking ask. Do you not remember her back in the day? She had killer pipes and played wicked guitar. I say we at least have to consider this." Alex squared off, his no-bullshit meter running overtime.

My problem was I remembered *exactly* how she was back in the day. I remember how I was, too. Bringing that on tour. A lit match in a fireworks factory stood a better chance. And I wasn't sure if I was more worried about her or me.

"Fine, let's go fucking ask and get shot down." Dan sunk his hands into his pockets as he reluctantly planted his feet on the floor.

"Awesome, should feel like old times for you then." Troy bucked out a laugh. "Let's just go see where shit lands. And keep your mouth shut."

Yep, where shit would be *landing* would be right in my fucking lap. This night could *not* get any worse.

2

Angie

THE MONEY I WAS MAKING WAS PATHETIC. SINGING MY ASS OFF FOR an hour, working up a sweat, and I'd be lucky to cover the gas money it cost us to get to the gigs. Studio time? Ha! Only way we afforded that was courtesy of the day jobs we all were working, but I wouldn't have it any other way. On stage is when I could finally exhale, when I could finally be myself, and no amount of coin would ever be worth more than that.

"Angie, you want to go grab a burger or something?" Joey loaded the last of his kit into his beat-up Chevy Blazer.

"Nah, Pops needs me to open the shop tomorrow morning. I need to get home." The night air hit my skin. Even though I'd be jumping into my bed soon, it was going to be a while before I came down from my buzz. The crowd had been great, even more people than last time. Maybe soon we could talk Big Al into giving us a cut of the bar. We sure could use the extra cash flow if we were going to self-produce an album.

"You need a ride to your car? Where you parked?" Rusty lit up a cigarette, the blaze of the ash brightening as he inhaled. With his guitar slung around his chest and his amp in his hand, he was relegated to giving Joey a chin tip as he drove by us.

"See ya guys. My shift starts early." Max jumped into his weathered Thunderbird, tossing his bass across the backseat. Both the car and his instrument had seen better days.

"See ya." I waved, my feet restless in my boots as I stood on the side of the road and refocused on Rusty. "I'm good, just down a little ways down the road."

Rusty gave me a look over, his finger flicking ash as he glanced down the street to where I said I was parked. His hesitation a hint he wasn't sold on me walking alone. "Alrighty. Be safe." He knew better than to argue.

"Bye." I gave him a wave as he hauled his guitar and amp into his Camaro and then slid into the driver's seat. The roar of his engine muffled our goodbyes.

Walking the streets didn't scare me. I'd grown up in New York, would probably die here too. But I wasn't some tourist with a death wish—just knew my way around. Happens when you spend most of your nights around the seediest part of town. Sadly, the *Rainbow Room* wasn't looking to book a rock band with second-hand instruments and fuck-you attitude. Who knew?

There she was, my most prized possession. The glow of the streetlight hit the cherry-red curves of my '69 Corvette as I'd made my short trip down the road. Pops and I had pulled her from the junkyard and rebuilt her from the chassis up. Took us years, but was worth every single minute. The car, and the time we spent together kept us sane after mom died. Poor man had no idea what to do with a teenage girl with an attitude. It was that car and the Harris family that saved us from all-consuming grief.

A hand grabbed my shoulder as I fished for car keys in my purse. It had been a dumb move, ignoring my surroundings while I took a trip down memory lane. I should have known better.

My body swung around, throwing off the hand on my shoulder as I

BACK STAGE

faced my would-be attacker. He'd picked the wrong girl to mess with.

"Holy shit, Angie, put the gun away." Troy's eyes widened as he stared at the muzzle of my nine-millimeter. I'd flicked off the safety as I'd pulled it from my purse. The business end of my Glock pointed square at his chest.

"Troy? What are you doing here?" I lowered my gun and took my finger off the trigger. Troy Harris, my old neighbor and drummer for a now famous rock band, was not who I was expecting to see on the dark, deserted streets of Long Island. "Didn't you have a show?"

"Yeah, we did." His eyes followed my hands as I flicked the safety back on and tossed my gun back into my purse. "When did you start carrying?"

"Since always." I shrugged. Like I said, I knew my way around.

"Hey, Angie, how you doing?" James slowly walked toward us, his band of merry men following close behind him. Great. Jason fucking Irwin. I resisted the urge to reach back into my purse and palm my weapon. Not to kill him, maybe just let a bullet wiz by. Scare him a little. The thought alone made me smile.

"Well, well, it's Power Station." Did they expect me to fucking bow down before them? Not likely. "You get lost on your way home from the Garden, boys?"

Even if I hadn't grown up next door to their drummer, there weren't many people in the city who didn't know who they were. The constant rotation on the radio took care of that, the billboards promoting their current domination of nationwide stadiums, a nice exclamation point.

Their still idling SUV was parked in Big Al's parking lot not far up the road. At least I wasn't totally losing my edge; Troy's footsteps had been masked by the residual noise spewing from Al's as the last drunkards left for the night.

"We actually came out looking for you. You'd already left the bar and some guy named Eric said you wouldn't be too far. Thought we could catch up for a chat." Troy flashed me a grin, the smile a peacekeeping effort if ever I saw one.

Mental note. Punch Eric right in the kidneys for giving out information about my whereabouts. I didn't give a fuck how famous anyone was, he needed to keep his big bartending mouth shut.

"It's almost midnight." My weight shifted on my feet, my hip leaning against my 'Vette. "Last time I checked I didn't owe any of you money, what's so important?" Their impromptu visit had my interest piqued more than I cared to admit.

"Can we go out for a drink?" James offered, his head tilting toward their waiting SUV.

Was he joking? The serious look he was giving me led me to believe he wasn't, but the fact none of the other band members had said anything had me worried. Even Dan was standing there giving his best rendition of a mime. Jason had kept his eyes glued to me the whole time, despite me not even glancing his way. Peripheral vision unfortunately meant he crept into my line of sight. Damn, he still looked good. No. Fuck that. Where the hell was that gun? I need to coldcock myself for even mentally going there.

"I have an early morning, not all of us made the cover of *Rolling Stone*." My keys jingled in my hand, signaling they should probably get lost. That was a cheap shot and I knew it. They'd deserved their success and I was just annoyed. At what? Well the jury was still out.

"Give us an hour, for old times sake." Troy flashed another grin. Crap. He knew I owed his family big time for everything they'd done for Pops and me. Saying no? Not an option unless I wanted my father to disown me. Goddamit. I'd hear him out, but whatever it was, I could already tell I wasn't interested.

"Fine, an hour." Which was sixty minutes too long as far as I was concerned if Jason was going to be present. The night had been so promising, too.

"*Tuesday's* is still open, let's head there." James tilted his head to their waiting ride.

Um. No. *Not* getting in a car with them was on the top of my to-do list.

BACK STAGE

"I'll drive myself thank you very much. My 'Vette doesn't need to be on the street any longer than she already has."

"Okay, see you there." James gave me a wave as I cranked open my car door.

An hour. I could do an hour.

"What are you having?" the bartender asked the minute we'd sat down. The Power Station express arrived a few minutes after I walked in. I had opted for sitting at the bar. It was less personal than sitting at a booth.

"A double of the twenty-year-old Macallan. Neat. He's buying." I pointed squarely at Dan, barely able to contain my smile as he shot me daggers.

"I'll buy." Troy rolled his eyes as he pulled out his wallet.

"No, *he* buys." Not going to lie, it gave me an irrational sense of pleasure to annoy Dan. Sure it was childish, but at least I could get some sense of enjoyment from this ... whatever *this* was.

"For fuck's sake, here." Dan pulled out a roll of cash and peeled off a hundred and slammed it on the bar. The distaste in his voice making me smile even wider. "Give her the fucking scotch."

"Thanks." I cracked my knuckles as the bartender poured the over-priced liquor into an old school tumbler. "So, gentleman. I'm assuming you're not here to reminisce about the good old days in the 'hood." Might as well cut to the chase, we were still on the clock as far as I was concerned.

"You're right." James once again took the lead. "We have a business proposition for you."

"Yeah, thanks guys but ..." I hadn't even had a chance to give them the no-thanks-there'd-be-a-cold-day-in-hell before James cut me off.

"We want Black Addiction on the road with us. Opening act. All dates, all cities." He didn't flinch. Was he actually serious? Offering an opening slot for a stadium tour like he was asking me to split an order of chili fries? He had to be high.

"Your opening act?" Cue my mouth hitting the floor and my eyes widening to unprecedented proportions, hell even my voice sounded weird. My effort to sound cool, calm and collected taking a back seat to freaking shock. "Don't you have those assholes from Tampa on your lineup?"

Their smug smiling faces had been featured on the tour billiard, and no it wasn't a case of sour grapes. *Unhinged Throttle* were *genuine* assholes. Their drummer had once gotten into a bar fight with Rusty over a look he'd apparently given him. A look, people. That's as dumb as starting a war over a Facebook status.

Alex's mouth spread into an amused smile. He'd always been a good-looking guy and the years had definitely not hurt him. Shame I'd never been into that. "Yeah that didn't work out, we want someone else. Someone we know." His voice just as smooth as I'd remembered.

"Sorry boys, not interested in being your feel good project." My ass slid off the bar stool in one fluid movement. I wasn't, nor would I ever be, a pity fuck. Any success and adulation we had coming to us would be earned, not because of a fence line that had once been shared. My feet pointed toward the door as I got ready to give them the see-you-later. Flipping them off would have been too bratty, even for me.

"Hey, aren't you going to drink your scotch?" Dan looked at the glass of amber liquid that sat on the bar untouched.

"Please, it's almost midnight. I have to be up in six hours. I'm not a raving alcoholic." I laughed, flicking my dark hair back for good measure. "I didn't want to drink it; I just wanted you to pay for it."

"Fuck, you're still a bitch." Dan grinned, almost as if he was glad I still was.

"And you're still an asshole, so we've established not much has changed." My brow arched, daring his comeback. Our game of tit-for-tat was juvenile, but it sure beat the hell out of thinking about the guy who

BACK STAGE

was standing not more than five feet away. Despite not even throwing a greeting in my direction, his eyes had been boring holes into me since we started this little pow-wow. Another reason why I wanted to get the hell out of Dodge.

"Angie, come on. Give it some serious thought. This could open up a whole new world for you and the boys. Think of the exposure." Ever the salesman, James tried to negotiate. He didn't need to put in the effort; I knew what an opportunity like this could yield. Still—the offer—not one I wanted to consider.

"We don't need to ride anyone's coattails, thanks very much. We can do this shit on our own."

"Maybe you should let the band have a say? Instead of letting your emotions dictate your decisions." Jason unwisely opened his mouth for the first time.

Oh. My. God. Did he just accuse me of being emotional? Would he even know what the fuck that was? The man was soulless as far as I could tell. If he even tried that are-you-on-your-period bullshit, I was for real going to need to be held back. Did the motherfucker forget I had a gun? God, I'd been a dumbass when I'd gone there. Young and stupid—they were my excuses and I was sticking to them.

"My emotions?" I tried to rein it in, not wanting my *emotions* to get out of hand. "You think because I'm a woman, I'm being emotional? Head up your ass much? We have day jobs, asshole. We can't just quit and go on tour with you. Think about it. What happens after the tour, and we need to go back to our *regular* lives, pay our *regular* bills? Somehow I don't think I-played-with-Power-Station-three-months-ago will be enough to keep my lights on."

Our game of eyeball chicken continued with neither of us looking away. There was so much I wanted to do to him. Sadly, not all of it bad, and that just made me angrier.

"Okay, that's fair." Typical. James tried to diffuse the situation, ignoring the stare down Jason and I were playing. "What about you open for our next four shows, all the Garden? It won't interfere with your day jobs and we will more than make it worth your while. Gives us time to find someone else or alternatively you and the boys give us a number that will compensate for your time."

What was being offered was a chance of a lifetime. Seeking us out and telling me to give them a number was insane. No one got that lucky, certainly not girls like me. I wasn't sure if this was the break I'd be praying for, or if it would be selling my soul to the devil.

"Why us?" My head turned to James. I hadn't wanted to look away but it was going to be difficult to have a conversation *and* shoot the death glare, sadly I wasn't that talented. As far as I was concerned it wasn't conceding though, more just being polite. "There's a million dipshits out there who would kill to play with you. Why do you have a hard-on for us?"

"Because we need someone we trust," James sighed. Curiously, it seemed more than just fatigue wearing him down. Hard to believe that someone who was living their life could have problems that would lead to that kind of sigh.

Troy edged closer toward me, my feet still undecided if I was walking out the door or sticking around. "You've known us since before we made it, and never once have you tried to capitalize on that. Hell, lord knows you've got enough dirt on us from the early days, would have set you up for awhile."

"Yeah, well I'm not in the habit of selling out." And wasn't that the truth. "I'm not interested in that kind of singing."

"Which is why we want *you*. Angie, it's four shows. You hate it; you take the cash and walk. No questions asked. Worst case scenario you get to play stadiums instead of bars for a few nights and make a truck load of cash, best case you get put on the map." Troy joined James on the wear-Angie-down parade.

"Fine, but only because it's you asking me, Troy. But the band does its own thing. We play what we want." The only way I would be stepping on that stage was on our own terms.

"Your set, your rules. Complete creative control." James held up his

BACK STAGE

hands in a show of his word.

"Well ..." My eyes measured them as I looked around at each member of the band. "I guess it looks like you've got yourself an opening act."

"You won't regret this." Troy pulled me in for hug, my heartbeat already ringing in my ears as the reality of what I agreed to hit me.

"Let's hope not."

3

Jason

ANGIE MORELLI.

She hadn't changed. Well, of course she was older and displaying a hell of a lot more ink than I remembered, but she could still get me from zero to one hundred just from looking at her. The multiple piercings up her ears were new, as was the edgier wardrobe. Those doe eyes she used to look at me with were gone though. Now, those big brown eyes were filled with attitude and hate. Not that I blamed her. Still, the piss-and-vinegar routine she had going on did nothing to hide how beautiful she was. She had to have noticed me staring at her, my eyes on her the entire time. And *time* had definitely been good to her. The way she filled out that T-Shirt and jeans was definitely enough to cause a re-rack in my pants. She looked good, and not in a way I wanted to leave alone.

"So what's the story?" Troy had paid me the courtesy of waiting until after we'd dropped off Alex and James before giving me the third degree. "I know she had a crush on you back in the day, but that was some evil eye she was throwing your way." Troy's sideways glance a hint he hadn't missed the arctic chill she was blasting in my direction.

BACK STAGE

Not that she'd been trying to hide it. Hell, even the bartender felt the need to relocate to the other end of the bar, and we'd been the only people in the joint.

"Yeah Jase, what's the story?" Dan's shit-eating grin needling the situation. Unlike Troy, he *knew* the story. I'd stupidly confessed to him one drunken night early on, the guilt eating me up. And while he'd promised to take it to the grave, now it was out in the open, and he wasn't doing me any favors in trying to keep it buried. The asshole pleased that it wasn't him who was at the top of her shit list. Bad news for him was he was now located at the top of mine.

"No story. Just a misunderstanding. Not my finest moment." Yep, let's go with that. It wasn't only the stupidest thing I'd ever done but sadly, I'd kill to do it over.

Seeing her had lit a fire under my ass that I had been sure no longer existed. The stirring up of old emotions giving me a reality check. It was a knife's edge. And I wasn't just talking about the sex either. Although—yeah, let's not go there.

Well wasn't this just freaking great. My keeping-it-together shit about to be unhinged by a blast from the past. My nerves jangled with the need to get physical. The thought of having sex—not appealing, despite the hard-on I'd already worked up. Punching stuff suddenly sounded good. Wonder if Wade had checked out of his hotel yet?

"You wanna clarify that for me, brother? Angie is like a sister to me, and I'm not liking where this conversation is heading." The hard look he shot me was enough of a warning, the tone—exactly what I'd wanted to avoid.

Annnd here we go. I could dress it any way I wanted, but it was still going to be like entering RuPaul into the Miss America contest. All the fucking glitter in the world wasn't going to hide the fucking dick. In this case, the dick was me.

"Then best you stop hearing it now." Dan eased back into his seat, his grin getting even wider.

The motherfucker was enjoying himself and while he hadn't broken out the popcorn just yet, he was settling in for some payback. The karma bus had my name it and currently sitting behind the wheel was Dan fucking Evans.

"Angie and I have some history. Not all of it great."

Wow. That didn't sound bad. Not at all. Excuse me while I go kick my own fucking ass.

"Define, history." Troy's words were measured, controlled. Not good.

"I dated her once, nothing serious."

Sure, let's fucking pretend like it wasn't a monumental fuck-up on my part. Lack of judgment? Try, dumbest move I'd ever pulled. She was waaaaaaayyyyy too good for me, and like an asshole, I went there anyway. Of course the minute I came to my fucking senses, I did my best to fix the situation. Having her think she meant nothing was better than me ruining her life. Because that's what hitching your wagon to me meant.

"Translation, he fucked her." Dan piped in, freaking beaming with his addition to the conversation.

"Goddamit, Dan!" I slammed my fist on the inside of the door panel causing TJ, our driver, to turn around and give us the eye. It wasn't like me to lose my temper, but Dan talking about her being a fuck, well, she had never been a *fuck*. The bastard should be glad it wasn't my fist meeting his face.

"Fuck, dude." The loud exhale from Troy killing the silence we had going on. "When was this?"

"Before we all moved into the shady POS apartment in Harlem."

The memory had been buried but hadn't gone anywhere. I still remembered everything about that night, the way she smelled, how she smiled, the way she felt. Hardest thing I ever had to do was look at her after. Looking at myself? Try couldn't stand the sight of my own fucking face for weeks. Only thing I did right was walk away. Everything else was a fuck up for which I deserved to rot in hell.

"Wait a minute. Before we moved? She was like seventeen. I'm not liking this intel." The raised eyebrow and the tight jaw an added hint he wasn't cool with what he was hearing. No surprises. I wasn't cool with it

BACK STAGE

either.

"Nope, she was eighteen. Might have been twelve-oh-one on her birthday, but she was definitely legal."

Like it mattered either way. Legal or not, my hands should never have gone there, and yet they did. Not the nice guy everyone thought I was, because a nice guy would have regretted it. And as much as I wanted to, I couldn't make that happen.

"Jase was the gift that kept on giving." Dan tapped me on the shoulder because apparently he was done being annoying; we had to add patronizing to the mix.

"Dan, seriously stop." My fist connected with his arm. He even had the fucking balls to look surprised.

"You slept with her?" Troy's voice dripped with disappointment, and straight up I wished we didn't have to have this conversation. "How could you just sleep with her? That wasn't just some piece of ass, it's Angie."

"She wasn't a piece of ass." That control I had locked down all but splintered as I white-knuckled my fists. "She was never that."

I clocked Troy dead in the eye. "Look, I'm not proud of myself. She was sweet, and the flirting back and forth was cute, but she turned it up a little, and *cute* was no longer the word I was using to describe it."

"Keep talking."

"I swear to you, I wasn't going to go there, but it was the night before her birthday and we were drinking in your backyard."

"Okay, maybe stop talking."

She had been pure.

Not in that she'd been a virgin, as in she was untouched by the world and all its evil. I could tell just by looking in her eyes. It was like looking out on a calm lake on a warm day. The sun hitting the surface, the tiny ripples across the top. Inviting, calm and a fucking peace I'd never known could exist. It had been for that reason, in addition to me not wanting to do jail time, that I'd kept away from her for so long.

That kind of beautiful, that kind of purity, didn't belong with me—in any capacity. I knew it. I knew it every single time I was around her, and still, I wanted her. Not just sexually—although she was the hottest thing I'd ever seen—but because I wanted to feel that peace, even if it was just once. Complete dick move, selfish and fucking uncaring, but I needed it. Just to prove to myself that it was actually real.

That night, the night I caved, I'd been worn down fighting it. Talked myself into believing that all she was after was a fun night. Her mouth had been sprouting silly, drunk talk about needing a man to kiss her properly and that's all it was supposed to be. A kiss. Problem was that when I started, I couldn't stop. I didn't want to stop and figured that if I made her come hard enough it would even out the fact I was an asshole that didn't deserve to lay with her, much less have sex with her.

I used her that night—not for sex like I used other women—but for warmth. To feel the sun on my face again.

"Anyway, the reality hit the next day. Waking up with her. She was so damn sweet, dude. You knew who I was back then, that man was not for her. So as much as it made me an asshole, I told her it was a mistake and that it couldn't happen again."

"Let me guess, she didn't feel all warm and fuzzy after you slept with her and then dumped her."

"It wasn't like that." The anger surged in me again. *She was never like that.* "I never wanted to hurt her in that way, which is why I had to end it. No way did I want that for her. I'd rather her think the worst of me than *know* it. Trust me, any hurt she felt would have been a holiday compared to reality."

Troy and Dan knew my history. They'd both seen it with their own eyes. Sleeping with her had been a mistake, trying to have a relationship? We're talking fall out of biblical proportions.

"Still, dude." Troy shook his head. "This is not the kind of shit I would have expected from you. Dan, maybe. But not you."

Dan's face contorted in horror. "Why am I being dragged into this? I didn't screw her."

Mention of Dan with his hands on her, even in the hypothetical, made

BACK STAGE

me move before I even knew what I was doing. Someone as sweet as her being with him, being with *anyone* made me glad I no longer carried a gun. Irrational as it was, no one would ever be good enough for her.

"Jase, what the fuck?" Dan's eyes widened as my brain registered that my hands were gripping the front of his shirt, my teeth pitbulling at his face.

"I'm sorry." My fingers let go as my eyes flicked from Dan back to Troy. The big guy ten seconds away from getting involved. "Shit, man. I'm sorry."

"You cool?" Troy watched as I settled back into my seat. My nod doing little to convince either of us I was in fact *cool*. "Everyone needs to calm down. It's Angie. After her mom died she spent more time at my house than her own. I don't want to imagine *anyone* screwing her."

He and me both.

"All I can do is say I'm sorry. It never should have happened, but I want to be clear about one thing. I never saw her as a piece of ass. Ever. She was beautiful and sweet and I wanted to be a part of that. Yeah, I was an asshole, I'll own that, but it wasn't just means to a quick fuck for me."

If things had been different, maybe it could have worked out. Who was I kidding? It still would have ended up in flames. I was even less capable then than I was now of doing the happily shacked up thing.

"I'm not the one you should be apologizing to, dude." Troy's you-need-to-talk-to-her look transmitted loud and fucking clear.

"Yeah, well I'll go see her."

It was time I manned up and had the conversation anyway. Apologize for being a dick, let her yell at me and then hopefully we could move on. I mean, how bad could it be?

"You better."

The bell jingled as I pulled open the door. The morning commute to the *old neighborhood* hadn't been pleasant, my mind churning over thoughts like clothes in a dryer. I hadn't grown up here, but it felt more like home than Albany did. If my folks still didn't live there, I'd never go back. Even my brother and sister had shipped out. My memories of that place not pleasant. The people—I'd been trying like hell to erase from my mental space.

"Well, well, twice in twenty-four hours. I'm literally giddy from the Power Station overload." Angie scowled as she leaned up against the counter, her tits straining against the *Joe's Garage* T-shirt she was wearing. Fuck, this was going to be harder than I thought.

"Can we talk?"

Her eyes narrowed, giving me her answer before she'd opened her mouth.

"I'm at work, Jason. I haven't got time to socialize." The empty shop not convincing me she didn't have five minutes to spare. Regardless, I owed her an apology and my feet weren't going anywhere until I'd given her one.

"Hey Angie, you need me?" Joe wandered in from the connecting work bays. The rag in his hand wiped off the grease as he walked through the doorway into the office space.

"All good, Pops, just an uptight loser driving a muscle car." Angie turned to open a filing cabinet and shoved invoices into a drawer. Didn't look like an adequate filing system to me, but I wasn't about to argue.

"Hey, Jason." Joe's face spread into a smile as he put out his hand. "I haven't seen you in years. You guys did good, huh? Been awhile since you've been in the old neighborhood."

"Thanks, Joe." My hand clapped against his, returning his handshake as I gave him a nod. "Yep, it's been a while. Life has been keeping us busy."

My eyes shifted to Angie curiously. I'd half expected Joe to come at me with a tire iron not a handshake. Clearly, I hadn't been the only one who'd been keeping our past on the quiet.

BACK STAGE

"Sure, sure." He loosened his grip and glanced over at Angie. "You two kids just catching up or you need something for your Mustang?"

"No, she's great." The car I meant. Angie, not so much.

"Okay, well I'll leave you to it." He shoved the dirty rag into his pocket as he moseyed back to the doorway he'd come in from. "Don't be trusting any of those fancy city boys with the car if she needs work. You bring her here. We'll take care of it, right, sweetheart?"

"Sure, Pops." The smile she gave was for his benefit, the eye roll for mine.

He disappeared, shutting the door behind him.

"You obviously didn't tell him."

For a second I thought I saw something in her eyes other than distaste. That she had hidden our horizontal history to save us both.

"You're still alive aren't you? If he *knew,* you would be laying on the floor doing a little less breathing."

"Look Ange, I'm so—"

"Save it," she hissed, cutting me off before I'd gotten a chance to finish my sentence. "I don't give a shit. It was a lifetime ago, right? You think I've been sitting in my room crying my eyes out over you? Wow, your head is even further up your ass than I thought."

The venom was real. The hostility she was throwing today about ten times what it had been last night.

"You don't give a shit?" My head tilted as I tried to get a read on her. "But you won't let me talk either. Doesn't sound like you *don't give a shit.*"

My mission had been clear. Go, say sorry and smooth it over. Let her swear at me for a bit if necessary; hell I'd even let her take a swing if she wanted. All of it, well and truly deserved. But seeing her lie to me was something else. No matter what words were coming out of her mouth, things were most definitely not fucking fine. And that didn't sit well with me.

"You can say all the words you want, just not to me." She tried to keep her voice down, but I could tell it was a struggle. "I don't have to listen. So get back in your car and drive out of here."

Two choices.

Escalate or eject.

Any other girl and there'd have been no consideration. That big pile of drama could have stayed right where it was as I waved goodbye. Sayonara. So long. Yet my feet stayed exactly where they were. And it wasn't because she was drop-dead beautiful. It was a need in me to set things right that was of unparalleled importance. Not for the band. Not for my fucking reputation. For her.

"Angie, we need to be cool with each other."

That wasn't so much a request as it was a promise to myself.

"You want us to be cool?" Her eyes got wide like I'd said I wanted to french kiss the GTO parked out front. "We're as cool as we get, Jase. Any cooler and penguins would be starting a fucking colony."

"Noted. But your water under the bridge bullshit isn't fooling anyone."

"Don't flatter yourself. Moody bitch is my resting face. You weren't that special."

There was so much I could've said and yet what I wanted most to do was kiss that fucking mouth of hers. The exact one that had been calling me an asshole. Because clearly, not only was she right on that count, but also because I was deranged. Wanting her. Wanting this.

"We're not done here."

Another promise. And one I'd be making good on soon.

"Oh, yes we fucking well are." Her hands slammed down on the counter in between us, her chest heaving as she sucked in a breath.

"No, we're not."

My eyes locked onto hers, so much being said without even opening our mouths, and she was the first to look away.

One thing was for sure. That baggage that evidently just got FedEx'd to our doorstep was being dealt with. And as for the band, none of it would land on them. Hell, it had stopped being about the tour the minute I'd walked in.

BACK STAGE

I gave her a look over before moving to the door. Her eyes did their best to try and meet mine but for the most part, she came up empty.

My hand hesitated on the handle, my body having a hard time leaving the unfinished business. *Not now, soon*, the familiar jingle of the doorbell rang as I yanked open the door ready to leave. "See you tonight," I said, looking back one last time. Her mouth opened and closed a couple of times before she settled on flipping me off.

Well that went well.

Fire meet gasoline. Let's get cozy shall we?

The 'Stang seemed to drive itself back to my apartment, which was a bonus cause my mind was in another zip code. The purr of the engine letting me know that while we'd made it back to my apartment, I had yet to cut the ignition.

Yeah, she hadn't gotten under my skin. Not. At. All.

"What's this, an intervention?"

The Troy welcoming committee was standing by my front door as I walked out of the elevator. My suspicion, it wasn't a friendly let's-hang visit.

"Did you talk to her?" Troy didn't waste any time with the inquisition, drilling me before I'd had a chance to get my keys into my door.

"Yeah, she wasn't in a chatty mood though. Wouldn't hear my apology." I neglected to mention the other stuff. His need-to-know limited to the earlier part of the conversation.

"Well, that's a problem then." Troy followed me into my apartment, not needing an invitation.

"Troy, I've got this okay. No need to worry."

Ha! Even I sounded convinced. Good job, Irwin.

"So did she talk to you at all?" Troy parked his ass on my couch as I tossed my keys on the counter.

"Just enough to tell me she wasn't my number one fan. I believe she also mentioned my head was up my ass as well. In any case, she isn't some evil vindictive bitch who's going to sabotage the tour just to get even." My butt hit the opposite two-seater as I gave Troy the only debriefing he'd be getting.

The stuff I said about Angie pulling it together, I had absolute faith in. Confident she loved that stage more than she hated me.

"She isn't the only one I'm worried about here. That shit in the car with Dan. Haven't seen you lose your cool like that for a while. You aren't feeling nostalgic are you?"

The man sitting across from me had seen me at my worst. The whole band had. My polished, have-all-my-shit together persona was a far cry from the dude they'd first met. But those days were over. The drinking and fighting hadn't been an issue in years. And while the aggression that churned through my body hadn't left, I had found a more acceptable outlet for it.

Sex.

And what do you know. Being in a rock band meant there was plenty of that on offer. Even keyboard players got lucky. Talented fingers and all that jazz.

"Oh for fuck's sake." My lack of desire for D and M at all time high. "I'm not allowed to have a bad day? I'm fucking solid, Troy."

Trust me. No one wanted a rerun of my past less than me. That cry me a river shit had more than taken up enough of my time.

"If you say it, then I'm going to have to believe you are on the level with me. But Jase, shit changes, we talk it out. Don't think for a second I won't get involved if you don't." Troy's hard stare told me he wasn't kidding.

"Listen to me, brother, I know all this Angie stuff might seem like it's stirred the pot. But trust me on this. I'm good. Now we done sitting around in my living room like jerk offs?"

"Yeah, Yeah we're done."

4

Angie

"YOU ARE A MACHINE. YOU CAN DO THIS." THE REFLECTION THAT stared back at me wasn't so sure. No, it looked like I was going to puke my guts out. "Fuck!" I paced as my nerves got the better of me. It was just a bigger stage, nothing different. Fancier, bigger stage but still a stage. When the hell did I start getting stage fright? This wasn't me; the jangling feeling that was twisting my stomach into knots was not me. It was because of *him*, it had to be.

Seeing him again after all these years had thrown me off my game. Rattled my cage. It was the only explanation. Sure, let's put the blame squarely at the feet of Jason fucking Irwin. I liked the blame there. It felt familiar, I sure had laid more than the fair share of the blame there in the past. Not that I was jaded. Of course not. He broke my heart years ago but I wasn't bitter, I was just making sure it never happened again. EVER.

Not that there was any danger of it with him. Nope. No fucking chance. I was just mad I had to see his face again. Bring all those memories back. That's why I was so pissed off. His face.

I bounced on the balls of my feet like a prizefighter; trying to burn the extra adrenaline my adrenal gland seemed hell bent on secreting. I was over him; this shouldn't even be a problem.

So over him.

So over him it was hilarious.

I was so *not* over him.

He wasn't my first—boyfriend or sexual experience. He wasn't even my first heartbreak. Nope, that pleasure had gone to Tyler Farley. At sixteen he'd broken my hymen but had forgotten to give me an orgasm. It was horrible and messy and made me want to never do it again. But, I did and the next time wasn't so bad. Of course, after six months Tyler decided to dump me for Cindy Watts. She was a cheerleader. We weren't friends.

My poor little sixteen-year-old heart thought my world was ending when I spent those nights crying into my pillow. Little did I know the real heartbreak would come later.

Jason Irwin. That's where the real heartache lay.

Asshole extraordinaire.

Who still looked amazing.

And what the fuck was with his *we aren't done?* The guy must also be insane. Good looking and insane. Top two headers on his resume. Oh, and hot. Most definitely hot.

Great, now I was insane.

"You ready to knock them on their asses?" Rusty burst through the door without knocking, pulling me from a dangerous slide down memory mountain. I was supposed to be remembering the reasons why I hated Jason, not focusing on what his chest looked like underneath that shirt.

"I could have been naked, Rus." My attention was happily diverted to the six-foot-two blond guitarist in front of me.

"So, not like you've got anything I haven't already seen before. Plus, I know you've probably been dressed for like an hour." He shoved his hands into his worn jeans while his grin of satisfaction dared me to say that I hadn't. He wasn't wrong; I'd been dressed for over an hour and a

BACK STAGE

half.

"Not an hour." I lied; the smile on my lips spelling out how little his interruption had bothered me. "And just because you've seen me naked once before doesn't mean you get to see it again."

"I know, and I die a little each day because of it." Rusty laughed before pulling me into a hug.

Rusty wasn't just a guy and my guitarist, he was my best friend. I'm not sure if it was because I was an only child or because I'd grown up in a garage, but for the most part the whole girlie gene was missing from my DNA. High school had been a nightmare with girls assuming my interest in cars had been an angle to steal their boyfriends. Consequently, I didn't have many female friends, so when Rusty transferred in tenth grade from another school, we became tight.

Him being so good looking didn't hurt, but neither of us had ever been attracted to each other. Trust me, we'd tried to hook up in the early days, thinking being that we were such good friends the sex would be super awesome too. But it just didn't work. We both ended up laughing before he'd even gotten the condom on, quickest mood killer ever. So instead of having sex, we spent the night drinking beers he'd stolen from his dad's beer fridge, and jamming to a Foo Fighters CD.

"So, I'll ask you again." Rusty shadow boxed before raising his voice. "Are. You. Ready?"

"As ready as I'll ever be." I blew out a breath, convinced the pep talk I'd tried to give myself hadn't done shit. So much for the power of positive thought. Fuck you, *Deepak Chopra*.

"I give you gold and you give me some lukewarm meh ... yeah whatevs." Rusty's grin twitched at his outer lips. "You're not nervous are you, Angie?"

"Me? No. We play in front of eighteen or so thousand people all the time," I mused sarcastically, wondering if I should be fussing with something. Messing around with my hair wasn't going to make me feel any better.

"Well stop doing whatever it is you're doing and get excited." He leapt onto the couch and raised his arms above his head. *"What we do in life echoes in eternity."* I knew I was in trouble now he'd started quoting *Gladiator*. "We're opening for Power Station at the Madison Square Fucking Garden!" He leaned across and gave me a shake. "This is our time."

I wanted to be happy. Knowing how much this meant to him, and the rest of the band. Hell, knowing what this meant to me. "Yep, dream come true." I just wished it had been any other band. One that didn't feature Jason. Damn him, and damn me too. I hated that he still got under my skin.

"Well stop jerking off and let's do this thing. Joey's had three Red Bulls and is either going to have a heart attack or fly off the stage like Superman. I'm trying to tell him the 'gives you wings' tagline is just fucking advertising. I could use the reinforcements." He tapped me playfully on the arm.

"Give me a few minutes to get in my groove and I'll meet you stage side."

"Just don't take too long, I'm itching to plug in."

"I won't. I want this too."

Rusty gave me a quick wink and eased toward the door. "Remember, Angie. They want you, they just don't know it yet."

It had been our motto since we'd started the band. Knowing that if we could get out there and play, that's all we would need. Funny how much those words were messing with my head tonight. Maybe sometimes they didn't *want* you. Ugh. That was *so* not about the band.

"You nervous?" Troy tapped at the open door; the one Rusty had conveniently forgotten to close behind him.

"Well I wasn't until everyone started asking me. You worried, Troy? Think I'm going to make you look bad?" My arms folded across my chest as I turned to face him and smile. Where Rusty was my best friend, Troy was the big brother I'd never had. Sure, we hadn't been as close in recent years, but it didn't matter. It wasn't something that could be wiped away by time.

BACK STAGE

"Nope, I've seen you play. I know you deserve the shot." The easy smile on his face proved he wasn't worried. He'd always had faith in me, even when I didn't have any in myself.

"So this a social call?" My eyes fell toward the open doorway wondering if anyone else would be joining us or if this was just a Troy-Angie heart-to-heart.

"Yeah," Troy cleared his throat and rubbed his neck awkwardly. "So … you and Jason?"

Silence.

Well the mystery of the need for a spontaneous chat had been solved. We didn't even need the few seconds of *Jeopardy* music to get us through. How much of it he knew was still unknown, and I'd rather keep it that way. Internally I cringed; it was like your dad catching you making out in your bedroom. Not cool.

"We are sooooo not having that conversation." Like ever.

"Awesome." Troy nodded, almost looking relieved.

Yeah, let's just sweep it under the rug and forget I had sex with one of your friends, shall we.

"So you going to stand there and freak me out some more? Rusty was just in here all reciting movie lines and jumping on furniture. And Joey is probably going to need a crash cart before our first song. I'm not a hundred percent convinced you are going to want us back tomorrow." It hadn't been a smooth transition of topic, but at least we weren't talking about Jason anymore.

"Just want to make sure you know that you can come to me. You know, if you need something. I promised your dad I had your back." Troy's eyes met mine. Something uneasy flicked through those hazel pools of his, maybe concern? Responsibility?

"Troy, I'm not a little girl anymore. You left, remember? You all did. I've been doing this without you having my back for a long time."

It wasn't to make him feel bad; honestly, I just didn't need him in the same way as I did back then. I was okay with the way things were, making my own way in the world. It sure as hell made me stronger.

"Well, regardless." He didn't look away. "The offer stands."

"Thanks." His endearing words thawed my hard-ass routine. I was losing my edge tonight, all these feelings. Gah. "But can you leave now? I wasn't kidding, you standing there is freaking me out."

"Sure, I'm leaving." He laughed, pulling me into a one armed hug. "Knock 'em dead, Angie."

The door closed behind him leaving me alone in the dressing room. It's where I found the most comfort. Not having to pretend. "I am a machine. I've got this." I peered back at my reflection.

Nope, still wasn't convinced.

Faces were a blur. The lights blinding me from seeing any definition other than raised hands in the air. The noise as they chanted—deafening. Except they weren't chanting for us.

I would change that.

I'd make them love us.

The stage plunged into darkness as we moved into position. The noise got louder as the anticipation rose, and still I could hear the thumping of my own heartbeat above the crowd.

One of my hands wrapped around the mic as I peered out into the darkness, the pop of an amp signaled Rusty was ready to go. This wasn't a rehearsal. This was the real deal, and we'd finally made it to the dance.

"One, two, three, four." Joey tapped out on his sticks as a wall of fucking lights ignited above us. The sound exploded from every direction as we launched into our opening number.

There was no pretentious introduction. Fuck that. We didn't do that shit. If the crowd wanted to hear stand-up they should have gone to the *Comedy Lounge*. We were here to rock, and that was exactly what we were going to give them.

My body moved as I slipped into the familiar trance and every single

BACK STAGE

hesitation I'd had of being on the stage dissolved. It didn't matter how I'd gotten here, I deserved to be there now. It was mine to own, and I'll be damned if I was leaving any of it unclaimed. I was home.

The boys were just as electrified as I was, the energy on stage, fevered. Joey thinking he was Superman was right on the money. I was right there with him, and tonight I could fly.

One song.

That's all it took and I had the crowd eating out of our hands. I didn't care if the attention was fleeting, if it was just until they got their Power Station main course. For those forty-five minutes, they were mine. Some even knew some of the lyrics, singing them back to me by the time I'd hit the chorus. It was the ultimate high and there wasn't a drug, either natural or synthetic, that could even come close.

Then all too soon it was over.

The final note echoed from the PA as we left our instruments where they stood and waved goodbye to the crowd. And as someone killed the lights and we walked off the stage, there wasn't any doubt left. The applause that was still ringing in my ears—that had been for us.

"That was better than sex." Joey twirled his stick as he walked beside me, the grin on his face a mile wide.

"You saying that just proves you've been doing it wrong all these years." Rusty chuckled as he grabbed a towel from a roadie. "Trust me, it's better when a woman is involved, not just your hand."

"It's not better but comes a close second. Sorry Joe, I'm with Rusty on this one." Max piped in, snagging a Gatorade on his way toward us. His grin just as wide as the rest of us.

"Angie, back me up on this one. You get it, right?" Joey wasn't giving up.

"Not taking sides, boys. As far as shows, that one was pretty freaking awesome."

"Nice set." Jason stepped out, seeming to materialize from the dark. It was kind of creepy if you asked me but I was in too good of a mood to care.

"Thanks." The word slipped from my lips before I'd had a chance to substitute a fuck-you or I-don't-give-a-shit-what-you-think. He'd caught me off guard while I was feeling post-show-happy.

"Was that a smile, Angie?" A satisfied grin spread across his mouth. Jerk.

"I smile, Jason, just usually after you leave. It's less manufactured that way." Ha! See, I was back in the game, my response prompting my smile to widen.

"Yeah, most girls are left smiling after I leave." He wasn't annoyed, he was smug. "You're right, nothing manufactured about that."

Asshole.

"Well, we might get going then shall we?" Joey jerked his head toward the door making it even more awkward. Clearly he didn't want to stick around for a game of verbal tennis. "See ya, Jase. Have a good show."

"Right behind you, buddy. Later, Jase." Max followed Joey down the hall as they bailed. Lightweights, both of them.

"What about you? Have somewhere else you need to be?" Jason moved closer, giving Rusty a hard look. He seemed to enjoy the fact that my other two band mates had scattered.

"Nope, I like this vibe the two of you have going." Rusty eased back onto the heels of his feet. "It's like HBO but without the nudity. Not sure if you are going to challenge each other to a duel or a dance off. Just FYI Jase, Angie does a killer running man."

I wasn't sure who cracked first, probably Jason, both of them were laughing their asses off. Jase clapping his hand across Rusty's back. "You're okay, dude."

"Yeah, you're not bad either." Rusty—who moving forward would be known as the traitor—gave him an easy smile.

Great, my best friend and the man that I despised were falling into a weird bromance.

"Would you two like a moment to make out? I can leave if you want."

"Don't be jealous, Ange. Listen Jase, as much as I'm sure you would

BACK STAGE

enjoy it, I'm not into dating dudes. My heart just belongs to the ladies."

Seriously, we were going to be having words when I got Rusty alone.

"You can leave anytime, Rus. I think I've got it from here."

Instead of vocalizing my *displeasure*—which I'd already established I'd be doing later—I gave Rusty aka Traitor one of my death stares. He'd been around me long enough to know *the look* wasn't an idle threat.

"Fine, fine. Keep your hairy-eye ball for Jason. I'm leaving." Rusty pulled me into a hug. "I'll see you in the dressing room. See ya, man." The latter part of his goodbye for Jason's benefit.

"Later." Jason smiled as we watched Rusty leave.

Our earlier conversation hadn't been forgotten.

All that fantastic tension, his threats of not being done.

All still there.

But what I hadn't been able to achieve with my pep talk in the mirror had magically happened on stage. Jason on my care factor wasn't rating highly. Not now at least, with that buzz still coursing through my veins. I couldn't even stop the smile if I wanted to. See that's how good performing was, it was able to wipe away bad feelings. In the short term. And currently that was the only term that counted.

"He seems like a nice guy." Jason's eyes flicked from the hallway to where Rusty had disappeared. My smile possibly giving him false hope.

"He's the best guy."

Rusty was undeniably the best kind of guy, especially if we were talking about the present company. While I was happy, I wasn't delusional. And I did say that buzz was short term.

"Are you two together?" Jason tilted his head to the side as he studied my face.

Were we together? Did he mean sleeping together? The question had thrown me so much that I didn't even ask why he wanted to know. "Does it matter?"

"I guess it doesn't, I'm just curious."

There was no waver in his voice, no shrug, no hint of whether he wanted the answer to be in the positive or the negative.

It was a weird stalemate. Where I wasn't sure if his indifference upset me or I welcomed it. At least he wasn't trying to apologize anymore, hearing him say he was sorry just dug the knife in deeper. Thinking that night had meant more than it did was bad enough, having his pity … No. He wouldn't get the satisfaction.

That's why I refused to hear him out earlier. It's why I refused to enter the conversation. Yes. I was angry. Yes, I was probably bitchier than I needed to be. Yes, it was a long time ago. But I'd changed that day and there was no going back to the naïve girl.

Funny how I'd practiced this moment for years, all my insults lined up in a row ready to hurl at him and now I had not a one. Was it too much to wish for some rogue occurrence to transpire? An earthquake or a freak hurricane? Anything to give me an out. Something so it didn't look like I was running. It didn't have to be fancy. A blackout would suffice.

"Hey Jase, James was looking for you."

That random act of God I'd been praying for appeared in the form of production crew.

"Thanks, man. Tell him I'll be right there." Jase answered without moving his eyes from mine, not giving me a reprieve.

"Looks like you're being summoned. Have a good show, I've got to get changed."

The words thankfully tumbled out of my mouth. They were good words too—concise, non bitchy and not too familiar. I liked them. They made up for all the ones I couldn't formulate while I was standing there wondering if every single time I looked at him I was going to have wild mood swings.

Honestly, I'd rather not feel anything, but currently I was swaying somewhere in between stab-him-in-the-eye anger and why-did-you-break-my-heart anger. Trust me, even though anger was the common denominator, they were still very different.

"Stick around, Angie. Things have changed."

There were so many minefields in that sentence my brain couldn't compute. Did he mean tonight's show, the tour or him? Reading into it

BACK STAGE

was just plain crazy, because *whatever* he meant, didn't matter. Not to me, at least.

That girl, the one who would have cared, was gone and now I was in her place.

"You're right. Things have changed."

5

Jason

ANGIE MORELLI WAS A LOT OF THINGS: BEAUTIFUL, ANGRY, volatile *and* motherfucking hypnotic on stage. If she'd been good the last time I'd seen her perform, she blew me out of the water now. It wasn't that she could sing—she'd always had a killer set of pipes—she had a presence. The shit that you can't learn—the ability to work it and own it—she had it in spades.

So what was she going to do after this? Go back to playing grease monkey and turn her back on what she had tonight? Play some random gig in a dive bar in Butt-fuck, USA to get her thrills? Fuck that.

Her bullshit I'm-going-to-do-four-shows-and-bail deal wasn't going to fly. Not if I had anything to do with it.

Pushing the issue wasn't something I usually did. My laid back approach reaching legend status. Not because I didn't care, but because I knew there was a bigger picture. And while it was usually someone else coming up with some dumbass scheme and me sitting around watching the fireworks, my hands were rubbing together in the anticipation.

News Flash. Angie and her band were staying on the tour.

BACK STAGE

Of course she hadn't been informed yet.
We'd get to that.
Along with all the other issues.
Oh. And won't that be fun. That rumored voodoo doll was probably going to get a workout.
Did I give a shit?
Nope, not a one.

I wasn't stupid enough to think her recent thaw was going to be her regular disposition. Though I had to admit, that smile of hers, I'd forgotten how damn sweet it was. Hopefully I'd be seeing more of them. Even if those smiles weren't directed at me. Not that I wanted to see them directed at some other asshole. Yep, 'cause that made all the fucking sense in the world.

Besides, from what I could work out she was dating her guitarist. And as long as he treated her right we'd have no problems. Yeah, yeah—the fucking irony. Pot. Kettle. I'm an asshole. Let's move on.

So being that we weren't going to be BFFs anytime soon, I was going to need to enlist some help. And I wasn't above playing dirty. Not when the end justified the means. It's not like she could hate me anymore than she already did. Fuck. It. I'd take her death stares and anything else she had to throw at me if it meant giving her that happiness. Which is what she was going to get. And the first part of that was keeping her on this tour.

"Hey Rusty, you got a minute?"

Surprisingly he hadn't been too hard to find. While our original support act had taken to channeling their inner *Jane's Addiction*, Rusty, Max and Joey had been chilling with the sound engineers and lightening director at control. They'd watched our show at the desk and were shooting the breeze with our crew.

Still wasn't sold he was the right guy for her, but he seemed responsible so at the very least he had my respect. Had to wonder why he was without his girl.

Not that it was any of my business. Or at the very least *should not* have been any of my business.

"Hey Jase, isn't the stalker routine a little embarrassing for you?" He gave me a big ass grin. "I already told you we weren't making out."

The peanut gallery erupted into laughter. They were easily amused.

"Yeah, I know but you can't blame a guy for trying." I played along with his freaking rouse, not wanting to have this conversation with the rest of band in tow.

Not sure what arrangement they had but I wasn't convinced one of them wasn't going give Angie a full report. The less people knew about it the better, and given I hadn't even had a sit down with my own band, I didn't think broadcasting in front of a crowd was a smart idea. Gossip on tour spread as easily as sniffles at a kiddie daycare.

"You wanna grab a beer?" I tipped my head to the doorway, having no intention of actually drinking.

"Oh, yeah. Sure." Rusty stood up, joining me as I moved away from the group.

Responsible and not stupid. Rusty earned another nod. Still didn't mean I liked him with her.

"So aren't you supposed to be shaking babies and kissing hands or some shit like that? You going AWOL from the meet-and-greet?" Rusty wasn't wasting any time getting to the what-do-you-want. I had to hand it to him. There was no bullshit with him. I could see why he was tight with Angie.

"It was a short one, the guys have their girls and kids they were anxious to get to."

The addition of wives and offspring had dramatically changed the landscape. The fact that these additions weren't mine didn't bother me at all. I loved having the girls and the kids running around. Besides, after years on the road there were only so many sets of tits you could sign

BACK STAGE

before it all became a major snore.

"So you came to find me, should I be worried or flattered?"

Because bullshitting wasn't in my bag of tricks and I had zero inclination to add it now, I figured I'd cut to the chase. The deserted hallway served as good a venue as any to have the conversation.

"Listen, you guys were really great out there tonight. Tight sound, great vibe, low on the theatrics. It was a solid show."

"Thanks. Why am I feeling like there is a *but* coming?"

"No *but*, I was just honestly surprised. Not going to lie, I expected an unpolished bar band and assumed you guys would choke. I can admit when I'm wrong."

Me being surprised wasn't a lie. While I'd assumed Angie was going to be great, the other guys were an unknown quantity. And considering they'd had no prep time and zero lead up, the adulation I was giving them was well deserved. Not that it changed my reason for this secret squirrel meeting. And as much as I manned up when I was wrong, it was more about getting Angie locked in for rest of the gigs and less about patting them on the back.

Rusty shot me a look as he tried to work out my angle.

"Ok-ay. So. Is there somewhere we are going with this other than giving me an ego stroke? I prefer them a little lower to be honest, and by a girl, no offense."

"It's not an ego stroke, I'm just hoping you are seriously considering staying on the tour." And get your lead singer to agree, because we all knew *that* would be the deciding factor.

I'll admit I left out the last part. No point to rock the boat. Just because he seemed like a decent guy, didn't mean I immediately trusted him. In fact, I didn't trust him. And yet, we were still having this conversation so I guess I cared more about this girl than I'd first admitted.

"Is this a serious offer, or you just getting me hard for when your lawyers come to fuck me?" Rusty looked like this was the first he was hearing of it. It wasn't the fake kind of surprise either; it was a genuine I-haven't-heard-this-shit-before kind. What do you know; Angie hadn't been on the level with them.

"Wait a second, what contract did you sign?"

I pulled the pin and threw the grenade. And wait for it. Three ... two ... one.

"The one that said we were doing four shows with you. A bunch of fine print BS I didn't read, but basically unless we fucked up, we are your NYC band."

Rusty confirmed what I already assumed. Four show deal. Angie had no intention of filling the rest of the dates. Why the hell would she throw away an opportunity like that? I knew *exactly* why she'd throw away an opportunity like that. Yeah, and it wasn't sitting well with me.

"So you didn't know about our offer?"

"What offer? More cities?" Rusty's shrug more evidence that he had no idea what had been put on the table.

Angie had invited them to dinner but was only going to let them have appetizers and now here I was offering them the opportunity to stay all the way to dessert. I probably should have felt bad, going behind her back. And yet, my conscience was clear. If you wanted to get technical, I was just merely disclosing information that should have already been shared. Yeah, let's pretend like she wouldn't want to rip my balls off when she found out. Honestly, the thought of her hand on my balls made me smile. I really was a sick bastard.

"All dates, all cities. The offer was the *whole* tour."

"Huh?" Rusty's eyes got wide as I saw the mental cogs in his head ticking. "The whole thing?"

"Yes, James, Alex, Troy, they hadn't had the same reservations I'd had about you guys." I figured some backstory about how they'd came onto our radar would be helpful. Shake off some of the holy-shit that was floating around. "Lexi our—"

"Yeah, we know who Lexi is." He didn't give me a chance to finish. "She is trying to get us to sign, said she can get us a deal."

"Yeah well, *her* interest in you and Troy's recommendation had pretty much sealed the deal. Of course your performance tonight spoke for itself, they were right on the money."

"So, let's go around this one more time. The offer was for the whole enchilada but we only signed on for New York." Rusty proved he was a quick study by following right along with me. No doubt having some serious questions for his front woman/girlfriend. Not sure how I wanted *that* to go.

"Angie hadn't been as *excited* on the offer as the guys had hoped. We thought she might come around."

Oh she'd been *excited*, excited to tell us to shove it, but I didn't think that it would add anything to the argument so chose to paraphrase.

"Dude, listen. Me and you are cool, I've got no beef with you. Sure we didn't really know each other back in the day, but from what I remember you seemed like a stand-up guy. But this divide and conquer shit, isn't the way we run our band. Straight-up, what are your motives here?"

So I guess he was smarter than I thought.

"You've known Angie for a while, right?"

"Yeah, since tenth grade."

"You and her ..."

Dating? Fucking? Not sure which of the words I was looking for. Neither word seemed to want to come out of my mouth when it came to her. We'd already established that for some reason the thought of Angie and another dude poked my inner Godzilla. Seriously need a handle on that ASAP.

"Dude, please don't make me fucking punch you right now. Like for real, I know I'm a guy and stuff, but that hitting each other and other macho bullshit gives me a headache. I'm a lover not a fighter, but if you start being disrespectful about Angie I'm going to have to lay you out. I won't enjoy it, but I will fucking do it." He squared off, ready to engage if he needed. At least she wasn't dating a pussy. That was a small consolation.

"Trust me, disrespectful is the last thing I am trying to be. There's some shit that went down in our past, Angie and me. I don't want to start shit between you two if you were…a thing."

Thing was such a shitty word but what else was there? *If you two are together?* It's not like they were sharing class rings. Why the hell couldn't I just say the fucking words? Angie had every right to fuck other dudes. Why was this shit messing with my head so much?

"You worried I was going to get territorial, thinking you were going to mack on my girl?"

"Look, you don't have to worry about me trying to put the moves on your girl. Whatever happened between us is ancient history."

The chances of me putting the moves on were laughable at best. Considering she shot me death stares every time she looked at me, I'd say us getting busy were … yeah, last time I checked it still wasn't snowing in hell.

"No, Angie and I aren't dating. Never have. She's my best friend but bumping uglies isn't our thing."

Not that the new piece of info should have ranked on my give-a-shit meter one way or another, but it did. The reason why that little nugget made me smile was still a mystery but I would tuck it away for later. Like perhaps when I came to my senses and realized Angie's dating status wasn't any of my business.

"Yeah, well then maybe you can talk her around. I'm not sure why she doesn't want to take up our offer but me trying to convince her isn't going to do it."

Well wasn't that a lie if ever I heard one. Pretty sure the reason she wasn't interested was what stared at me in the face when I looked in the mirror.

"So you want me to run interference."

Bingo. The boy had skills, let's see him put them to use and convince our girl she needed to play ball. Wait? Our girl? What the fuck? *His* girl.

"I'm not saying blindside her, just maybe talk about what the tour could do for the band. Get her to think of the big picture."

My motives were pretty clear. Angie. Tour. End of story. But I could see that while Rusty wasn't dating her, they had this whole watch each other's back thing going on. The asshole in me also knew that Angie wouldn't want to disappoint her buddy either. Two birds, one stone and all that.

"You know." Rusty took a long exhale before eyeballing me. "One thing I do remember about the good ole days was the huge crush Angie had on you. Then all of a sudden, nothing. Like she just got over you. That wouldn't have anything to do with this, would it?"

Yep, it took him about ten seconds to join the dots.

"That's probably something you should ask her."

"Yeah, sure nothing shady about that answer." Rusty rolled his eyes.

"Please, just talk to her." *And maybe clue me in when you do.*

"Oh I'll talk to her, but not because you want me to."

"Whatever it takes."

6
Angie

WHILE THE BOYS HAD STUCK AROUND AFTER POWER STATION HAD finished, I had high-tailed it out of the arena. Best decision I'd ever made.

After our set, Max had recognized one of the guys who were mixing the show so we had sat at the sound desk and watched the show with the crew. Not only was it cool to see it from there, but it also meant there was zero chance of running into the band. Because running into Jason once was more than enough for one night. Who cares if he still looked like he could bench a Ford Focus? I bet he was still ripped under that shirt too. The ink he'd added since the last time also did an awesome job of making those arms look hot.

Stop.

It didn't matter how much he resembled an action figure, we were not going there. *There* was trouble. I had already been *there*, remember?

Ugh! I hated him so much.

"Hey, you know that *tune and lube* sign at the front is very distracting. I'm not sure if I should be popping my hood or looking for a happy ending." Rusty pushed open the door of the shop. The bells jingled to announce his arrival as he strode through the doorway, his eyes still a little bloodshot from the late night.

"I'm pretty sure we have a shop vac out the back, the sign below it says satisfaction is guaranteed." I couldn't help but yawn. It had been next to impossible to get sleep last night. And if I was honest with myself, it hadn't only been the buzz from the concert that had kept me tossing and turning through the early hours of the morning.

"You didn't even blink. It's not the first time you've been asked, is it?" He looked disappointed. Like anything that could come out of his mouth would shock me.

"Nope, not even close."

"So let me ask you something?"

With Rusty that *something* could have been anything. He had issues with boundaries so it very easily could have been either extremely rude or ridiculous. He'd asked me for tampons once for a nosebleed.

"Sure." I hoped this conversation wasn't going to be to out there considering we were both sleep deprived.

"Do you remember that day we went out to *Coney Island* and we rode the Cyclone until you puked?"

Ummmmm. What? I had absolutely no idea where this conversation was going.

"Yeah, of course I do. It was my eighteenth birthday, and to be fair I was hung over. I can handle my coasters thank you."

"You play it out in your head however you want to, babe, but that day your ass got owned." Rusty broke into a smile.

That day had been terrible. He had assumed it had been the half bottle of vodka I had drunk the night before that had made me sick. True, I was a lightweight back then and even a ride on the bus would have made me nauseous, but the real kicker had been something else. Like waking up beside the guy you supposedly loved and have him thank you for the good time, and leave you like you were nothing special. Gah! I pushed that bullshit away from my mind.

"Okay, so, is this a weird way of suggesting we go to Coney Island? 'Cause I have to work and I'm not really in the mood."

"I was just thinking about that day." Rus leaned up against the counter, his eyes on me as he spoke. "Thinking about the reason why I had dragged your ass to Brooklyn in the first place. You had been crying that morning about the one-night stand you'd had the night before. Older guy who you thought was into you but turned out to be an asshole. What was his name again?"

Crap. Did he know? How could he know? I never told a freaking soul. It's not like the embarrassment that I had allowed myself to be used like a groupie hadn't been enough. I didn't want anyone else to know. That would have just added to my mortification.

"Ummm. I think we decided his name was going to be asshole." I had chosen some other names for him too, but those were for my private collection. They included a lot of swear words, with so many colorful variations.

"Yeah, funny how I never made the connection between asshole-one-night-stand and you suddenly losing interest in Jason Irwin of the Power Station variety. It all kind of happened around the same time, weird huh? That's some crazy ass coincidence."

He knew.

That lying, cock-sucking spawn of evil—see, variation—must have opened his big fucking mouth.

"You deduce this theory all by yourself Sherlock Holmes or is *someone* filling your head with fanciful ideas?" *Someone* being a bastard otherwise known as Jason Irwin or Dick-face, see another variation.

"So is *that* the reason why you didn't tell me that we were offered all the dates on the tour?"

He didn't blink. His focus was locked on mine as a flicker of hurt flashed in his eyes, catching me in my lie. Sure, I could dress it up in my head as something else, omission perhaps. But in the end, I had never told any of them the whole tour was a possibility. How could I? I knew the minute I did, they would be falling over themselves wanting to sign straight on the dotted line. There would be no questions asked, and they wouldn't have even wanted to hear the reason why we shouldn't. Not that any of those reasons really made any sense, not if I was really honest.

"Rus—" I swallowed, disappointed in myself.

"Look, I'm not mad that you lied." Rusty raked his hands through his hair in frustration. "Couldn't give a fuck, and I remember how much that asshole messed with your head. I was there, watching you cry because he made you feel like a cheap slut."

I blinked at his harsh words but he hadn't been wrong. That's exactly how it had felt. "And I'll owe you for that."

"You don't owe me shit. I did it because that's what we do. We're there for each other. But, we *are* going to do this tour."

There was no hesitation in his voice. And while there was no anger either, he had made up his mind, and there wouldn't be a thing I could say that would sway him.

It was lame to even attempt to convince him otherwise, but I couldn't help myself to try. "I'm not sure that's the right decision for the band. We'd have to give up our jobs. It's not even enough time to give notice—"

"Oh come on, Angie." He interrupted me, throwing his hands up in the air for dramatics. "I sell used cars for a living. You think Archie is going to give a fuck if tomorrow he has to get some other sucker to pimp his used Chevys?"

Silence.

When I didn't answer he continued. "Yeah, and they are going to miss Max at *Staples* too. Who the hell is going to run all those print jobs? I can hear the reams of copying paper weeping now. And as for Joey, I don't even know what the fuck he does." His brow crinkled in confusion. "Does he even have a job?"

"He's a valet." Well at least he was this week. He'd been a bus boy last month, and a waiter at *TGI's* the month before.

"He's a fucking valet? Fuck me, they let him park cars? Have they seen his ride? The only straight panel on that thing is the back seat. We'd be doing them a favor by taking him."

"You practice that speech on the way over here?" I folded my arms across my chest.

"Yeah I did, was it too dramatic? It's tough to find the balance." Rusty's mouth curled into a smile.

"Nah, it was ok. Throwing in the *cheap slut* was a little harsh though. You might want to work on that for next time, go for something less offensive."

"Yeah, noted. I got caught up in the moment."

My arms relaxed as I unfurled them, my hand reaching across, needing to touch him. "I know we should do this, and I know it was so long ago." No one wanted more than I did for it to be left in the past, the memories still burning me as much as they did back then. "But he broke my heart, Rusty. I thought I loved him. I chased him around for an entire summer, and it wasn't just one sided. He encouraged it. He let me believe that he felt something toward me too, and then he slept with me. Of course once he got what he wanted he couldn't run fast enough. It really messed with my head."

More like broke me. My first boyfriend had cheated on me because I hadn't been a good lay, and then the only guy I had ever really loved screwed me and left. It didn't sell the virtues of a relationship to me, or do wonders for my self-esteem. "I know I'm being selfish, and that we should do this." *Please don't make me do this,* I wanted to beg.

"We *need* to do this, Angie. You have to make it right in your head so we can." His voice was soft, but I could tell he wouldn't be bending.

"It's the best thing for the band. I know." The words felt tight in my throat. The last thing I wanted to do was punish them for my own mistakes.

"The band?" Rus screwed up his face in disgust. "You think I'm telling you we need to do this for the band? Fuck. That. The band will do what it's going to do, and we will stand behind you, always. This is about you."

BACK STAGE

"Me?" My voice squeaked in surprise. How could it be about *me*?

"Yeah, this is about you. Middle finger in the air, giving *him* a big fuck you. He doesn't get to break you, Angie. No man is ever allowed to do that." His face became more animated as he waved his hands around. "You need to *Taylor Swift* his ass. I've got a blank space, baby."

"*Taylor Swift* his ass?" I laughed. No one else but Rusty would have been able to make me laugh at a time like this. "Rus, do you even know what that song is about? It's a fuck you about how everyone fixates on her ex-boyfriends, not at the boyfriends themselves."

"Whatever, a fuck you was extended, was it not? You're missing my point." He shrugged, with a smile added for extra effect. "You get on that stage, you show him what the hell you're made of. Hell, channel that shit into a song, the crowd will love it."

"So I'm just supposed to decimate him on stage?" Had to admit, the idea wasn't entirely bad. My smile returned at the thought of telling the world how horrible he was. It's not like I was lying—he was horrible, even if he did look delicious.

"Hells yes and we'll release it on iTunes, make a ton of money. It will make you feel better, trust me." Rusty took the idea, and as usual, ran with it.

"Making a ton of money from my buried hurt isn't going make me feel better."

"No, of course not. Showing him what a dumbass he was every night in front of thousands of people, and the *fuck you* you'll be giving him, will. The money will make *me* feel better, and I make you feel better so it gets us full circle."

"You going to draw me a diagram?" I laughed.

"If it gets us over the line."

"You've got it all figured out." I sighed. He was right. I couldn't even argue with him. I needed to move on, not to prove it to Jason, but to prove to myself that I was stronger than I thought.

"Yep, so you telling the guys or am I? We all need to quit our jobs. Oh and I'm writing the rider. We need blue M&Ms at every show, and

55

Doritos. Someone needs to make it happen." He smacked his hands together in excitement.

"I need to talk to my dad." My excitement significantly lower than Rusty's at the prospect of telling my dad I would be leaving. "I'm not sure how that's going to go."

"Talk to me about what?" Pops emerged from the work bays, his timing perfect. Or not, as the case may be.

"Hey, Pops." I forced the smile. It looked like the conversation was going to happening sooner, rather than later.

"Hey, Pops," Rusty echoed.

"Please don't call me, Pops, Rusty. It makes my ulcer flare up." He tapped Rusty across the back of the head—his usual greeting for Rus—before turning to me. "So what's on your mind, sweetheart?"

"Maybe you should go, Rus?" My head jerked toward the door, which translated into, I needed to do this alone.

"He can stay; I get the feeling he's involved." Pops eyed us cautiously.

"You know we're playing with Troy's band." A good start, but how was I going to break it to him that I would be gone for months?

"They asked you to do the rest of the tour." He answered with complete lack of surprise.

"Ummm. Yeah." The surprise that had been lacking in my father had taken up residence in me.

"So are you worried your old man can't handle himself, or are you worried I would tell you not to live your dreams?" He shot me his careful-before-answering face.

"Pops, I know you need me here and—"

"Angie, you are the most amazing kid I could have ever asked for. Your mother and I were blessed beyond measure and if she was here, God rest her soul, she would be so proud of you. But if you don't do this, I'm going to be so mad at you." He looked like he meant it too.

"Mad at me?"

"Yep, us Morellis make our dreams happen, we don't sit around

BACK STAGE

settling. My dream was to have my own shop and marry your mom. You've wanted to be on the stage since you were seven years old, it's about time you start living up to the responsibility that comes with your family name."

"Dad."

"Don't *dad* me either. You call Troy and tell him you're going."

"I love you." My eyes blinked, willing myself not to cry as I wrapped my arms around him.

"I know. I love you, too." His hand gently stroked my hair as he returned my hug.

"I love everyone." Rusty threw his arms around both of us crushing us in a group hug.

Rusty and my dad were more than just my family; they were my world. And knowing I had those two in my corner gave me the confidence to know I could do anything.

"Take care of each other, okay?" Pops warned as he shook off Rusty's affectionate embrace.

"Don't worry, Joe, I promise to look after Angie, and pull her into line if she goes all *Kayne West*."

"I'm more worried about you, Rusty." He tapped him upside the back of the head again. "Now you think we can get some work done around here before the two of you become big shots?"

"Too late for that. We're already big shots, the world is just now starting to catch up." Rusty eased back onto the heels of his feet.

"Well *big shot* how about you get out of here and go bother your own boss. Angie has work to do." Pops' voice trailed as he disappeared back into his workspace, no longer interested in Rusty's response.

"I would, but I don't work there anymore." The sheepish grin hinted he had already given his notice or had been handed his walking papers. It was a coin toss as to which.

"You resigned already?" My mouth flew open in mock horror. "What if I had said no?"

"You wouldn't have said no to me, you love me too much. Besides, I slept with Archie's daughter last week. I was on borrowed time." He laughed.

"Get out of here." I pointed to the door.

"See you at the show tonight." Rusty's feet made for the door, his hand pausing on the handle before pulling it open. "You tell James and Troy, and I'll tell the guys. And if Archie comes looking for me, tell him I've moved to Mexico."

"See ya." I waved as I watched him walk away and reached for my phone.

I could do this.

Make the call, tell Troy the good news and not freak out. Ha! Who was I kidding? The call would be the easy part; I had a whole six months to rein in my freak out. This was not going to be easy.

7

Jason

MY BUZZING PHONE BROKE THROUGH THE TUNES ON MY PLAY LIST as my feet pounded against the belt of the treadmill. I'd lost my shirt at the three-mile mark, sweat pouring off me as I sucked in air and I cut the power. This better be good, I had a few more miles before I'd burn off the mood I'd been carrying this morning.

"Yeah." I huffed into the phone, grabbing a towel that was hanging off the handle.

"Dude, are you fucking?"

I shouldn't be surprised; *Dan* and *fucking* usually came as a package deal. Still a simple *hello* would be a nice change of pace.

"I was running jack-ass. If I was fucking, I wouldn't have bothered answering the phone." I toweled off my face, reaching for a bottle of H2O.

"*Or* you would just say you were running so I wouldn't know."

Yeah, I was so not in the mood for Dan's brand of circular logic.

"Dan, it's too fucking early. What do you need?"

"Well seeing as you are asking, I really need a blowjob but Ash had to work."

I had to ask, didn't I? I tossed the sweat-filled towel over my shoulder.

"Well you won't be finding one here so you're SOL. Anything else you want to share before I hit the shower?"

"Yeah, I was actually calling for a reason. Band meeting in an hour at Troy's."

"Band meeting? Everything okay?"

"Yep, the problem of our opening act has been solved. Troy is still on the phone with Angie. Looks like her band is coming out on the road with us. You going to be able handle the daily *Resident Evil* she's going to throw your way?"

"I'll be fine." Thank fuck. I squeezed my eyes shut wondering if this was the calm before the storm. "That's good news. Really, I'm glad they agreed."

"You're glad?" Dan all but yelled into the phone. "Well that's no fucking fun. This tour is going to be difficult enough without Ash on it, I was counting on the two of you going at it for my entertainment."

"We're not going to be your source of entertainment, asshole." At least that's not what I had planned.

"She still hates you though, right?" Dan asked, the amusement evident in his voice.

"Not that I've checked recently but I'm assuming she does." I let out a sigh. It was less of an assumption and more a definite, but who is keeping score?

"Good, at least *she* hasn't let me down."

"Dan, all jokes aside. This isn't a game. You're not going to fuck with Angie, you hear me?"

"Wow, you almost sounded like you liked her." Dan laughed. "Relax, asswipe, Troy's already given me the spiel. I'm going to be a regular boy scout."

"Your words aren't filling me with confidence."

"I'll handle my end." Dan took a breath before continuing. "Hers,

BACK STAGE

I've got no control over."

"Okay, see you in sixty," I said, hoping to end the conversation. Talking about Angie with Dan, yeah ... really didn't want to go there.

"See ya. Oh, Jase?"

"Yeah?"

"You were really fucking, weren't you?" The douchebag laughed.

"Goodbye, asshole."

Well what do you know? Our boy Rusty came through after all. Who the fuck knew what he had to say to convince her. Did it matter? Not one bit.

So the part of me that liked slow and systematic torture limbered up. Because that's what I had in front of me. And fuck me if the thought didn't make me smile, because ladies with a permanent case of PMS were obviously my thing.

After a quick shower and change, I jumped into my car and headed to Troy's penthouse, the destination for our meeting.

"Hey, there you are." James pulled open the door of Troy's pad, allowing me to walk inside.

"Are you the butler?" I laughed as I strolled into the living room, Alex and Dan already situated on the couch.

"Megs has bad morning sickness, Troy's in the other room with her which is why we're doing this here. He wanted to be close by in case she needed something." James helped me play catch up.

"Yeah, good call."

We were on the same page, and Troy being all protective and shit was not an issue for any of us.

"I'll let him know everyone is here." Dan's feet hit the floor as he made for the back of the apartment.

"Hey." Troy emerged looking a little worse for wear, Dan not far behind him.

"Hey dude, Megs okay?" My chin tipped in his direction as he walked into the living room and sunk his ass into the two-seater.

"Yeah, other than being pissed at me for hovering. Apparently me wanting to be with her while she pukes isn't romantic." His tone clueing us in that despite Megs's protests, nothing much would be changing.

"In my opinion, that's as romantic as it's going to get." Dan rejoined the group, his ass sinking into the leather couch.

"I can hear you talking about me, Troy Harris." Megs slowly ambled into the room, her face pale but wearing a big ass grin.

"Good, 'cause I wasn't trying to hide it. You want anything before we start?" Troy automatically rose to his feet, his usual response when his girl walked in the room.

"For you to stop hovering." Megs waved him off, the grin hinting she knew she was fighting a losing battle.

"Maybe ask for something you actually have a chance of getting." Troy's tucked her in tight against his body before kissing her neck.

Megs rolled her eyes. "I'm fine. I'm not going to break."

So with everyone roughly assembled, and rather than jerk off anymore we decided to get this show on the road. The reason for our meeting wasn't a mystery. Neither was the reason my pulse was still racing. And it didn't have anything to do with the time I'd clocked on the treadmill earlier either.

"Okay, so Black Addiction is locked in. Full commitment, all dates. They will sign their revised contract today. Everyone cool with that? Dan? Jason?" James asked, the singling out of the two of us, no coincidence.

"They're a good fit. They owned it last night, and the crowd seemed to love them," Troy added, clearly on Team Angie.

"Yeah everyone was shitting out rainbows." Dan leaned back into his chair. "I've got no problem with it."

All eyes turned to me.

"No problem here."

Well, none that was in this room at least.

"Good, 'cause if there was going to be a problem, I'd rather hear about it now." James gave a predictable warning. The raised eyebrow clueing me in that whatever I was selling, he wasn't buying.

BACK STAGE

"Shit went down between the two of us in the past. It's over; we're fine. There will be no drama." My mouth spouted the usual bullshit. Not sure if I believed it, not that it mattered at this point.

"Awesome." James didn't smile.

He didn't believe me either.

So I'd learned a few things today.

One, we were touring with Angie's band, and two, I had suddenly developed an unexplained need to watch the support act perform.

Good work, Jase, I was now stalking her.

I was edgy, too.

My fist flexed open and shut a couple of times, my hands needing something to do while I sat in the dark. My vibe was completely off.

There had been two girls that I'd ever really cared about. One, I hoped for both our sake's, I'd never see again, and other was on the stage in front of me.

Both times I'd been stupid.

Both times I'd fucked up.

Both times I'd said I'd never go back.

But only one of those times I'd actually wanted to.

So, here I was feeding my musical appreciation. Absolutely mesmerized by the woman I was watching. Straight up voodoo shit. That had to be the reason why I couldn't look away.

Of course it had *nothing* to do with the way she looked. Those deadly curves *couldn't* be what had my attention. No, I hadn't even noticed how perfect her tits were or what a stellar job her ass did of showcasing those tight black shorts. The fact she was the perfect mix of knock-you-on-your-ass stunning and real-girl beautiful could also *not* be the reason I was sitting on a road case stage side being all Phantom-of-the-Opera.

My dick getting harder the longer I looked at her had nothing to with the fact I hadn't been laid in a while either. The opportunities hadn't changed, I could still score any night of the week. But it was my motivation that was suffering the dysfunction, not my cock.

This wasn't good.

I needed to give myself a reality check and get busy doing something else. A hobby. Possibly one that didn't involve an intervention order or require night vision goggles.

"They're pretty good." Troy parked his ass on the road case beside me. His eyes darted out to the stage, nodding his approval.

"Yep." The less that came out of my mouth the better. My need to share wasn't high being that I doubted he would embrace my new creeper status.

"So you sitting out here for a reason?"

He had waited two minutes before asking the inevitable question. My guess, it was his attempt at keeping it polite. Who says we weren't gentlemen?

"Just enjoying the show." I tipped my chin toward the stage.

Enjoying it wasn't exactly accurate. None of it was actually enjoyable, not unless you loved feeling like your nuts were in a vice. Which I must, considering Troy was giving me a hard stare and raised eyebrow combo that translated into *no, really. What the fuck are you doing here?* and I still hadn't moved.

"Jase—"

"I'm solid, dude." I cut him off knowing what was coming next.

It had been a long time since anyone had to worry about me. Since I'd come out the other end from shithead to dependable Jase. Reliable Jase. It was me who usually did the watching out for. Not the other way around. Troy's concern made me uncomfortable, and not the wearing a turtleneck kind.

"No man is an island. Just remember that."

"Yeah, and you need to stop reading fortune cookies."

Continuing the conversation took a back seat as my head whipped back around to the stage as vaguely familiar chords ripped through the

BACK STAGE

speakers. "Are they playing ...*Taylor Swift*?"

The dirtied up intro leading into the first verse snared my full attention. What the hell were we even talking about?

"Er ... like if *TSwift* and *Stone Temple Pilots* had a baby, it would sound like that." Troy was equally intrigued, his face wearing the same what-the-fuck as I was.

"Holy shit, it's "Blank Space" rocker-fied."

Angie belted out the unmistakable words of the chorus, putting any doubt to bed. It might have been someone else's tune, but she was putting her sexy-ass stamp on it. And damn if my dick wasn't suddenly becoming more interested. The heart-to-heart with Troy shelved for another day. Hopefully, never.

"It sounds bad ass if you ask me." Thankfully Troy had no idea where my mind was at, i.e. not on the fucking brilliance of the rendition.

"Totally bad ass."

Nice one, asshole. You sound like an inept moron. FYI, my hard-on could cut glass right now.

Angie's voice curled around each of the words, spitting them out with a little more venom than the original version. The heavy distortion on the guitars was also *less* sweet and *more* go-fuck-yourself, which was incredibly hot. I wasn't sure if I should be appalled or impressed that the song had me so turned on.

Who knew why they'd worked a cover into their repertoire, they hadn't played anything but originals the night before. And as far as unlikely song choices went, it was up there with shit-I-would-bet-won't-happen. It was fucking strange. Not that I was going to argue with it, because it was catchy as fuck and the crowd was eating it up with a motherfucking spoon.

I watched hypnotized as the last line of the bastardized pop song left her mouth, her lips settling into a satisfied grin as she lifted her hands in the air and signaled the end of their set, her confidence radiating off her like a nuclear detonation.

Yeah, that wasn't sexy.

Not at all.

The rest of the boys dropped their gear and moved to the center of the stage. Each of them wore the same pleased looks on their faces as they sidled up next to Angie and took a group bow to the deafening sound of applause.

"I'd say we weren't the only ones who liked it." Troy's laugh beside me reminding me I wasn't standing there solo.

It was also a good time to remind myself to pick up my damn jaw from the floor. I was sure my tongue had been spending some chill time down there, too.

It was hot. Not that I was going to mention that. The word and the sentiment a definite danger zone. As was noticing how her sweat-saturated top showed off her specular tits. Awesome, I was now a deviant as well as a stalker. Who says men can't multi-task.

"Hey!" Angie couldn't have stopped grinning even if she'd tried as she made her way backstage. "Hi, Troy." She gave him a hug before she turned to me. "Hi, loser."

Her attitude had shifted. There was no way I hadn't noticed that. Well at least now that I peeled my eyes from other parts of her body, I had. It wasn't just her smile—which was lethal all by itself—it was that she was freaking beaming.

"What's with the addition to your set list? I didn't think you did covers." I couldn't have given a rat's ass about her *colorful* greeting nor was I waiting to see if Troy was going to investigate. My curiosity at need-to-know levels.

"Rusty thought we should shake things up a little." Angie smirked at the man in question like they shared some private joke before her eyes returned to me and narrowed.

Huh? Was there something in that statement that I was supposed to decipher? I was a lot of things, but telepath wasn't one of them. Along with mind reader and chick-whisperer. All of which could have been an asset right about now.

"Well, the crowd loved it." Troy weighed in, not even hiding the fact

BACK STAGE

he'd loved it too. He alternated between slapping them on the back and shaking hands. The rest of the band loving the "awesome show" and "well done" that was being tossed their way. All except Angie who seemed to be more enjoying my reaction.

"Sounds like Rusty is a smart man." The mouth decided to get into the game.

"Keep talking, Irwin, your praise feeds into my god complex. Feel free to use more descriptive words like *motherfucking genius* and *most brilliant guitarist alive*. We're song writers, so words are our friends." His shit-eating grin almost as big as his inflated ego. Guitarists, all the fucking same.

"So can we expect more of that?" Rusty's comments completely ignored as I focused on Angie. I wasn't entirely sure what I was asking. The song? Her attitude? The fact my cock was so hard I was starting to lose feeling in my legs?

"I have a lot more where that came from." Her blood-red lips twitched into a grin.

Okay, so now I was even more confused as to what we were talking about. Not that I actually gave a shit. Nor did I care we had an audience.

"I'm looking forward to seeing it."

What the actual fuck was I saying? Was I flirting? I resisted the urge to check if I still had my balls because of the raised eyebrows it might get me, but part of me had to wonder if they weren't tucked away somewhere else.

She leaned in, each word slower than it needed to be. "Good, I think you'll enjoy it."

No seriously, what the hell were we talking about?

"I can't wait."

It was probably the most honest thing to come out of my mouth in the last twenty-four hours. I had no damn idea what I was agreeing to, except that I freaking well wanted it. Trouble? Sure, double fucking helping, right here. All my earlier thoughts about history getting a re-run were suddenly even more appealing. Which meant I was certifiable and should be committed.

"So Jase and I are going to take off, got to get ready for our set. You guys going to hang around?"

Oh yeah, Troy was still with me. Yeah, right. Had a show to play and everything. Best I shelve the crazy for a few hours.

"We're actually heading back to my place." Rusty jumped in, big smile he'd been wearing since he'd stepped off stage. "Having a few drinks with some of our friends before we get on the road. Nothing crazy, but you guys are welcome if you want to stop by."

"Thanks, dude but with Megs being pregnant, she gets tired and—"

"Yeah, sounds good. See you there."

My mouth opened and the words came out all by themselves. Boom. Like a five-year-old doing the I-want-go. My mouth and I didn't really care for the stare-down we were getting. The biggest coming from Troy and not because I'd interrupted him.

"Awesome." Rusty clapped his hands together, rubbing them with anticipation. "Let me write down my address." He grabbed a set list that had been gaffed to the wall and located a Sharpie on the floor. His barely legible scrawl printed on the page where I would be heading the minute I stepped off stage.

This was such a bad idea. The folded paper scrunched into the pocket of my pants.

"Awesome."

8

Angie

SO MY GIVING OF THE *FUCK YOU* HAD MADE ME FEEL BETTER. WELL, it had been more a singing of, rather than a giving, but the result was the same. Rusty was right. I was stronger than I thought.

I am woman, hear me roar, and all that shit.

It was great. I was great, and I might actually get through this whole tour without an addiction to anxiety meds. At least that's how I was feeling until Rusty opened his big damn mouth.

Sure, invite Jase into my safe place. Was he motherfucking insane? I wanted to kill him. The *him* was interchangeable. Rusty, Jason—blood was probably going to need to be shed.

So my plans of easing into it were tossed out the window. Rusty giving me the "it would have been rude not to extend the invitation." Yada, yada—not helping. I needed to roar god damn it. How was I supposed to roar if Jason Irwin was invading my personal space?

New plan.

My bubble was about to burst so I need to get my game face on. I had a feeling those fuck-yous I needed to be delivering were going to be after hours.

Of course Rusty seemed pleased with the latest development. He was freaking ecstatic. It was his way of escalating the process, and if we got to hang out with big shots at the same time—well wasn't that fantastic. You can only kill a person once, correct?

Rus even had the nerve to ask me if I still loved him. Pfft. Excuse me while I laugh my ass off.

Ass laughed completely off.

I am standing here with no ass because that's how much I laughed.

There was *no* way I loved him.

Not a chance.

The appreciating of his fine form was okay though. I mean, the man looked good. I hadn't suddenly developed blindness. Besides hormones clearly had nothing to do with your brain so that was totally allowed. Touching was not. I should probably remind myself of that a few more times.

So given that Rusty always said all the best stories started with regret—he had been a regular Diane Sawyer of late, digging up shit and delivering with a smile—I was ready.

Against my better judgment—the one that told me to go home—I was doing this.

Meh, who needs judgment anyway?

Famous. Last. Words.

"Angie!" Joey pulled me through the doorway as I wandered into Rusty's living room.

Some blonde I didn't recognize shoved a beer into my hand, her smile inviting conversation. She obviously didn't know my reputation for not being a people person—or my lack of ability to *chat*.

"Hey, how are you?" I nodded in her direction. See, I can be nice sometimes and I wasn't looking to cock-block anyone. Besides, I was trying on my "being nice." A practice run. It felt like wearing new shoes—tight, awkward and slightly uncomfortable. Unlike most girls, new shoes did not excite me. So the analogy was extremely apt.

BACK STAGE

"Good, I'm so happy for you guys." The mystery blonde was still there. Crap. "This is huge. I mean, it's Power Station." Her eyes widened as she said their name. It was the typical response, her voice changing tone to almost reverent proportion.

"Yeah, it sure is." Nod. Smile. Faux enthusiasm.

"Of course I knew good things would happen for you guys. You are all so talented." Her eyes floated to Joey who was currently involved in a very serious game of beer pong. I didn't believe for a second she was talking about his ability to keep time.

"Thanks." Smile. Faux enthusiasm. Nod. It was good to mix it up.

"Angie. Come do shots with me. We need to celebrate," Max hollered from the kitchen, his shirt missing in action.

"Well, bye." I waved to the nameless blonde and silently thanked Max for saving me from any more small talk. In case you hadn't guessed, it wasn't my forte.

"Ewwww, we're drinking Jäger?" The brown liquid swished in the shot glass that had just been handed to me.

"Yep, tequila is for pussies. Tonight we drink like men." He threw the liquid down his throat as a point of punctuation. His hand reached for the bottle for a refill.

"I'm not a man, Max."

"What? You're telling me now? All this time I thought you were a dude." Max's face contorted in mock horror.

"Har-Ha." My elbow jabbed him in the ribs.

"Drink." His hand edged the glass closer to my mouth in encouragement. "I've already had three, you need to catch up."

The shot burned as it went down. The herbal grassy tang coated my mouth and I wanted to gag. Yuck.

So even though I'd said I wasn't a man, apparently I needed to drink like one. Max poured shot after shot of nasty cough-medicine tasting liquor down my throat.

Honestly, give me tequila. It might be for pussies, but considering I had one of those, surely that made the drink more appropriate for me.

Although my rising blood alcohol content sure was making me feel good.

Wasn't I supposed to roar or something?

Hehehe.

That lamp was looking at me funny.

"And again!" Max's eyes glazed with enthusiasm or perhaps it was from his Jäger haze as he tried to ply me with more of the nasty, brown liquor.

"No more, just give me a beer." My limit for shots reached as I pushed Max and the offending bottle away.

My head had already started to cloud. As was probably my liver. My judgment had been gone from before I'd started to drink, so there were no surprises there.

"How he doesn't get hangovers is a mystery to me." Beth, Max's sometimes girlfriend gave me a hug.

Unlike most female company, hers was one I actually liked. Her embrace wasn't one I minded either; I generally wasn't a hugger. The feel-good juice probably played a part too.

"He goes from happy drunk to sober with no segue. It's bullshit." I hugged her back.

She flicked her short black hair out of her eyes, her smile simmering as she watched him take another shot. She got a wink back in recognition. I guess tonight they were "together".

Rusty had predictably been in his bedroom, *entertaining* a redhead from NYU. Both of them emerged an hour or so later not even trying to hide their ruffled appearance. The pleased look on her face was the other hint. By all accounts, she'd received Rusty's full service effort.

The drinking continued, as did our friends' constant congratulations and attention, which made me feel sort of weird. We were musicians, it's not like we were curing cancer. Yet somehow playing a big show had elevated us to big deals, and I wasn't so hot on the pedestal.

At some point I passed out on the couch, my legs curled up under me. My grip slowly loosened on the bottle of beer I'd been holding, waking me before I spilled any.

BACK STAGE

"Hey! There's two of you." The bottle was peeled from my hand before it had a chance to hit the floor as my eyes blinked at the body hovering above me. "And I hate both of you."

"I know you do." Jason placed my half empty bottle on the coffee table before easing back into his seat. "But the other seats are taken so you'll just have to put up with me."

He didn't even try and sound sorry. Ass.

The "fine" I huffed in response dripped with sarcasm, but I was too loaded to argue. The room was filled with bodies either dancing, passed out on the floor or occupying the limited chair space. But surely there was somewhere else he could sit, like for instance, in Staten Island.

"You really hate me, don't you?"

"Oh come on, Jason. You can't be that clueless. Don't you have a college degree?"

Ugh. I so did not want to have this conversation, and the room needed to stop spinning too. Both of those reasons contributing to my building nausea. And his sexy cologne needed to stop wafting up my nose too, that was rude.

"I should have said goodbye properly, and I should have called you. That was a dick move." He moved closer, bringing with him all that sexiness I was trying to avoid.

"Yeah, there's a lot of things that should have happened that night. Like me not fucking you." Or him not fucking me. Let's not get hung up on semantics.

"You really regret it?" His eyes did that thing where they disarmed me. I hate them. Both of his beautiful, dark eyes.

"No. Yes. No. I don't know." My mouth wouldn't behave, not sticking to the standard line we'd rehearsed. It had been a mistake; I regretted it. That's what my dumbass mouth should have said instead of babbling in indecision.

"If I remember correctly, you told me that it had been the best you'd ever had."

Of course out of everything that happened, he would remember that tiny detail. My post sex euphoria had me spilling secrets he didn't need to know.

"Well I hadn't had a lot to compare it to, the bar wasn't that high."

Lies. Even now, no one had come close, but he would never be hearing that piece of information. He could torture me and I'd still never say, which incidentally is what it felt like as he sat there watching me.

"Wow, you know how to crush an ego." The bastard smiled, not even pretending to be hurt.

"Like your ego could be crushed by lil-ole me. Crushing shit is your specialty. " *Shut up!* My brain screamed. Damn Max and his bottle of man-drink. This would not turn into another clichéd drunken confessional.

"Is that what it's all about?" His head tilted as those gorgeous eyes I hated so much stayed glued to mine. "I crushed your ego?"

No asshole, it was my heart. Thank God, I didn't say it out loud. Instead I clamped my lips shut hoping to minimize the damage.

"Angie, I'm sor—"

My hand covered his mouth. The vibrations of his voice tingled against my palm. I couldn't hear the word. Couldn't hear him tell me he was sorry. I was drunk but not enough that hearing him apologize for that night wouldn't crush me all over again. Why? Why did it still freaking hurt?

Touching him hadn't been the plan. His lips against my palm did things that confused me; it was like a memory and not one all together horrible. The familiar tug in my gut also added to the mental assault. Oh shit. As much as I wanted to, at that moment, I didn't hate him. That was not a good sign.

"Please don't. Just don't say sorry, okay?" I hadn't meant to sound so vulnerable, so small, but that is exactly what my voice sounded like. I hated it.

His eyes widened as he lowered my hand from his mouth, my fingers inadvertently interlocked with his. Great. So now my hands were against me too, my body literally rebelling.

BACK STAGE

"Okay." He nodded, and I wished I knew what he was agreeing to.

"You want more beer?" My brain scrambled for something that would get me off that couch. Yes. Drinks. Getting him a drink would give me a reason to leave without running. Because running is exactly what I felt like I was doing.

"I'm still full." His head dipped to his beer on the coffee table—the twin of the one he'd saved from my hand—a swallow or two missing from the bottle.

"Did you want to kiss me then?"

Did I just say that out loud? No, it must have been in my head. It had to have been in my head. Oh God, please let it have been in my head.

"Yes."

Fuck. I'd said it. If the yes wasn't confirmation enough, the way he was looking at me was.

"Why?"

Another thing I probably shouldn't have said but hey, why stop now?

He didn't answer, instead leaning over and brushing his lips against mine. It was slow. His touch, gentle as he moved my lips apart with his own. His tongue slowly traced the seam of my mouth, involuntarily I moaned as he nibbled on my bottom lower lip. It was my undoing.

"Yes." I wasn't sure whom I was saying it to but with the one word he moved closer, pressing my body against him as his mouth continued to invade mine. Not content with just the lip contact I was getting, I pushed him back onto the seat and straddled him, the bulge in his jeans doing little to hide the hard-on he apparently had worked up.

Still questioning my motives—and my sanity—I reached down between us and palmed him, working him with my hands. His lids lowered as a guttural "fuck" escaped through his parted lips. His body moved against my hand as I tried to reconcile what I was doing. Different parts of my brain were at war with each other as I moved my hand back up to his head and threaded my fingers through his hair.

Tension, stress, alcohol, confusion or the fact I hadn't had sex in over a month could have all been to blame. It was potluck as to why I had lowered myself onto him, using the hard-on pressing against the seam of his jeans to hit me in that sweet spot between my legs.

My brain had obviously checked out as my body took over, our mouths ending up back together. Man, he knew how to kiss. The way he pulled my head in closer was a textbook panty-melting maneuver, and he used just the right amount of tongue. If the last time we'd kissed had been good, this was off the charts. Whatever he'd been doing in those years since had obviously been working for him.

"Shit."

Like a bucket of cold water hitting my skin, my brain finally kicked in. My head snapping back as I registered what the hell I was doing i.e. making out with the enemy.

"What am *I* doing?" The question could have been asked by either of us, although I wasn't sure I wanted to know the answer. "What are *you* doing?" While my shopping list of motivators were the reasons for my mistake, he had no excuse.

"Fuck." That cold shot of reality must have hit him too. "Angie ..." There was more to that sentence, but he didn't say it.

"Okay, it was nothing. I'm drunk. I probably won't remember this in the morning." My mouth fumbled with an explanation.

I was *so* going to remember this in the morning.

"That doesn't make it better." His eyes filled with an emotion I couldn't read. Hell, in another five minutes I would have had sex with him.

On the couch.

In front of all these people.

"I'm going to be sick."

And if he still had any urge to kiss me, I'm sure talk of vomit had eradicated it. My body almost levitated in the rush to climb off him, my feet desperate to get me to a bathroom. My hands that had been so interested in playing touchy-and-feely with Jason Irwin managed to not be total assholes and slam the door behind me.

My fingers fumbled the lock closed before I made it to the toilet bowl and vomited. My body contorted in a full-body heave as I lost my battle with my stomach and threw up again.

Awesome. Perfect end to the night.

"Angie, are you okay?" Jason yelled through the door, the music doing it's best to drown him out. Just as well. At least he hadn't heard that.

"Go away," I half groaned as I turned on the faucet, my hand cupping the water and bringing it to my mouth. Never drinking with Max again. Ever.

"Angie, just open up."

Had to hand it to him, he was persistent. Of course he was about ten years too late with the concerned friend routine. The *better late than never* did not apply here.

"I'm fine." I cursed through the closed door. *Will be even better if you leave,* I finished in my head.

"I'll leave as soon as I know you are okay."

Oh, so I had said that part too. I really needed to get a better handle on my freaking mouth.

"Fuck." One hand gripped the basin to keep my balance as the other shut off the faucet. My pale, smudgy-eyed reflection looked back at me from Rusty's bathroom mirror.

"I can stand here all night," he threatened when I didn't open the door. "Nowhere else I need to be."

My eyes narrowed as I flipped him off, the door unfortunately blocking his view of seeing it.

"Flip me off all you want, I'm still standing here."

Crap, did he have x-ray vision as well?

"How did you know I was flipping you off?" I pulled open the door, figuring he wasn't going to leave until he had at least seen I was fine.

"Because you're predictable." He smiled, his hands supporting his weight on each side of the doorjamb. It showed off his biceps and his stunning ink work.

Not what I should be concentrating on.

"See, all good." I fought the urge to twirl knowing it would inevitably make me hurl. Ha. I rhymed. A small giggle escaped from my lips.

"What's funny?" Jason moved in closer, the safety of the doorway no longer being in my favor.

"Nothing. You wouldn't get it." I fumbled as I took a step back to his step forward.

"I'm not going to touch you. I just want to make sure you get home okay."

Probably a little late for the no touching thing, we could have used that twenty minutes ago.

"I said I was fine. I'll just crash here." My ass hit the sink, my backward stepping getting me no further. I hadn't been convinced there was going to be no more touching. Better to be safe than sorry.

"Here? In the bathroom?" Jason looked around, eyeing off the tub.

"No, Rusty has a guest room. It's around the back."

"Well let's get you there then." Jason stepped aside; his head jerked to the side as if to say *lead the way*.

"You're not putting me to bed, I'm not a child." Sure, put the two of us in the vicinity of a bed, that wasn't a recipe for disaster.

"Tell me, when did you start second guessing everyone's motives?" He moved closer, his arms dangerously close to mine. What happened to the not touching rule? We needed to go back to that. "And I wasn't implying you were a child, I was trying to be helpful."

Like you were when you kissed me? Yeah, thanks but I think I can take it from here. "I don't need any help. Honestly, I'm good. You can leave now."

Like you did the first time.

Please if there was a God let my mouth only have said the parts I'd meant it to.

His eyes followed the length of my body up and down, his hesitation thick in the air as he took a step back from my personal space. "Okay, I'll see you tomorrow then."

"Sure thing." My forced smile strained at the corners of my mouth as

BACK STAGE

I watched him walk toward the doorway.

Just a few more feet, keep going.

"Oh and Angie, about that kiss." He stopped, flushing any hopes I had of forgetting what we'd done down the toilet.

"It was nothing." My voice not sounding convincing, as I shrugged. I blamed the booze. "Already forgotten." Not likely.

"It won't happen again." He looked me over one last time and then thankfully—no seriously, praise the lord hallelujah—he left the room.

The breath I'd been holding slowly escaped from my lips as my body sagged against the sink.

"No, it won't."

9
Jason

WHAT THE HELL WAS THAT?

I needed my head examined.

That or some shock therapy because thinking about kissing her was one thing, following through, something else.

Dumb move going to Rusty's afterparty last night. Complete rookie mistake. Clearly I'd been thinking with my dick because going to see her was asking for trouble. Yet, there I went. Straight off stage, did our hello-how-are-yas with the fans and then I jetted out the door.

It wasn't even a debate, and it fucking well should have been. What was even worse was that I'd lied about it.

Troy had been anxious to get Megs home, standard. She could tell him she was okay until she was blue in the face, but she looked pale and Troy was locked on target. He had the caveman bullshit jacked-up to eleven. So the two of them bailed the minute the official BS was over. James, Hannah, along with Power Station's second string Noah and their kid on the block, Jesse, left soon after. Alex, Lexi and mini Lexi, aka Grace, hung around a little longer but not by much. Which left me

BACK STAGE

kicking it backstage with Dan and Ash. Cue my lame excuse of being tired when they invited me to go hang with them.

It hadn't even been convincing and still neither of them suspected anything. Such was the trust they had in me. They just smiled, told me to go get some sleep and waved me goodbye. I should've felt bad, but instead I got in my car and went the one place I knew I shouldn't. To see Angie.

She was like a fucking Rubix cube. I wasn't even asking why anymore, it was enough to know that no matter how scrambled the puzzle was, I had to solve it. And that shit with the song—pulling out a *Taylor Swift* cover—that just made it more interesting.

Of course by the time I'd made it to the Bronx, the small get-together had gotten messy. It was a typical Saturday night in the old neighborhood. Even if they hadn't been doing the farewell thing, there still would've been half a dozen cars parked on the lawn and wall-to-wall people on the inside. Much like the night before we'd left. The night Angie and I had ... yeah so much for ancient history.

So, we'd established that I hadn't been thinking. Add to that a beautiful woman I'd never been able to resist, and we ended up reminiscing—with our tongues.

Fuck.

Well, at least it hadn't gotten *that* far because that's exactly where it had been heading. Her hand worked my cock like she was trying to get the genie out of a bottle; any conscious thought I had did an *Elvis,* and left the building.

Just a few more miles.

Right. I could run to Cleveland, and I'd still not have my mind right.

The T-shirt I'd stripped off thirty minutes ago multitasked as a towel. I used it to mop up the sweat off my face as I sucked air in and out of my lungs. My legs not getting anywhere close to the burn I needed to feel.

The buzz from my front door cut through the whirl of the treadmill, my stride thrown off by the knocking accompaniment. My feet hit the side guards as the belt kept moving, and I cursed the asshole who was on the other side of the door. My legs were slightly unsteady as I made my way to the source of the disturbance. It wasn't going to be a friendly greeting.

"Angie?"

My eyes flew open to match my mouth's display of surprise. That was followed up by my head flipping around the doorway to see if anyone else was in tow. "You're alone? How did you know where I lived?"

She nodded as she moved through the doorway and into my apartment. "Yep, just me. And I asked Troy; he had no problem telling me where I could find you. Seemed only fair seeing as you knew where I lived." My mind loitered in the hallway as I tried to reconcile the what-the-fuck.

Angie looked all kinds of fine as she strode in, my dick instantly taking an interest. Her jet-black hair was pulled back from her face, which was without the usual dark eye makeup. She looked better without it. The multiple studs down either side of her ears catching the light as she turned her head. The blue jeans she was wearing clung to her body like they'd been painted on, and her lotus tats stretching the length of her right arm peeked out from her faded *Nine Inch Nails* T-shirt. All put together, it cemented one hell of a vibe—sexy as hell.

She was the last person I expected to be showing up on my doorstep any time soon. And by any time soon, I meant *never*.

"Wow, you really are Captain America underneath the shirt." Angie's eyes widened as she glared at my bare chest. "Still *Army Strong*, I see."

PT five days a week had been a habit even after I hung up my uniform. Working out was as much part of my routine as was brushing my teeth. I wasn't huge, but I could hold my own.

"I wasn't expecting company. I run to clear my head."

Perspective was easy to come by when you had to slow down and concentrate on your body. Simple things, like breathing, makes all the worrying about trivial bullshit fall away. And if there was one day I needed to run, today was it.

BACK STAGE

"Well, judging by that," she waved her hands in front of her, "you've got a lot on your mind." Her lips twitched into a slight smile. She hadn't been quick enough to hide it before resuming her usual death glare. It's the look she usually gave me. The one I was most familiar with.

As much as I enjoyed seeing her smile—it made a change from the usual venom she had for me—I was still no closer to knowing why she was here, in my apartment.

"So you here to check out my suitability for *Armani's* new underwear campaign, or was there something I can get you?"

Obviously there was a point; the sooner we got to it the better. Besides, the longer I looked at her the greater chance of having a repeat of last night. Those lips were so fucking inviting I had to nail my feet to the floor. Did I mention how fucking hot she looked?

"You should totally do the underwear thing. Bieber had a billboard, so being an ass obviously isn't a deal breaker." Another smile. This time she didn't try and hide it.

"Nice backhanded compliment." My grin matched hers. "Who says singing is your only talent."

"I can also play guitar." Her smile got wider. "The bitch thing is just a hobby."

"Of which you excel at when I'm around." My feet inched forward, bringing me to stand directly in front of her. Nothing like tempting fate. It was like jumping out of a plane and then checking to see you had the parachute.

"What can I say? You bring out the best in me."

Yeah, not even going to pretend that she wasn't giving me a hard-on from hell. It didn't even make sense. Clearly she was telling me she didn't like me and yet here we were.

"You want to go back and forth some more, or we going to get to the point of why you're here?"

Before I take you to my bed and we can work out our differences there.

Her chest rose as she took a breath. "After you left, I started thinking."

"Not sure you were in any condition to have any conscious thoughts." She could barely stand; not sure much actual *thinking* had gone down.

"Oh shut up, Jason, I wasn't *that* drunk." Her death glare was back with a vengeance.

"Drunk enough to throw up."

The taste of Jäger and beer had been on her breath when I'd kissed her, and the fact that she'd let me was also a hint she was far from sober.

"It was kissing you that made me puke, *not* the booze."

I could barely contain my fucking grin. "Wow, Angie. That's two for two where you've gone zero to bitch in three seconds."

"You interrupted me." This time it was a death glare/smile combo.

"Go on." I folded my arms across my chest, waiting to see how this was going to play out.

"So I was thinking," she repeated, her game clearly off.

"Yes you mentioned that." I leaned up against the back of my couch, settling in for what was no doubt going to be a hell of a story.

"Can you put on a goddamn shirt or something? I feel like I've stumbled into *Nick Bateman's* Instagram."

"Give me a second." I grabbed a sweatshirt that had been hanging across the back end of my couch and shoved it over my head. Not ideal but it would do. I tried to not enjoy that my being half naked threw her off her game. Because that would make me an even bigger dick, wouldn't it. Not to mention I'd rather be taking clothes off rather than adding them. Looks like she wasn't the only one losing her trail of thought. "Alright. You were thinking …" My head nodded waiting for her to continue.

"Are you gay?"

Huh? Did she just ask me if I was… gay?

"Are you high?" That casual leaning I had going on no longer worked for me as I straightened back onto my feet.

"No, I'm not trying to be a wiseass, I mean it kind of fits."

Holy shit, she was serious. I had to fight the urge to show her how *not*

BACK STAGE

gay I was.

"What the hell are you talking about? *It kind of fits.*"

She shifted uncomfortably in place before meeting my eyes. "So, that summer you were at Troy's, I didn't see you date anyone. Girls were throwing themselves at you, but you didn't do anything."

"I think I recall doing *something* with you that would disprove your theory."

Maybe I was mistaken, but I kind of thought the sex we'd had in the backseat of my car qualified for something.

"We had sex *once* and then you ran like a bat out of hell. A gay guy can sleep with a woman and it means no more than a straight woman sleeping with another woman. It doesn't mean anything. Hard-ons can be a physical response."

Well fuck, she had actually sold herself on this theory.

Like, she'd actually given it some thought. A plus B equaled I liked to suck dick.

"I assure you, I'm not gay."

I would have loved to have seen the thought process. The one where she forgot how many times I made her come. That, and the fact I'd had been ready to do it again last night. Because clearly that didn't sell my position on whether or not I preferred pussy. Her fucking extrapolation so freaking funny, it didn't even offend me. Proving her wrong, still very much on the table.

"I've rarely seen you linked to anyone." She took a breath before qualifying. "Like online. James was with Hannah for like forever so he was out. Alex and Dan, those two were all over the internet the whole damn time until they found their significant others. Even Troy, who was super discreet, couldn't escape the limelight. You? There was one mention of a chick you were seeing long distance but never any photos. Did she even exist? Oh, wait? Was she your beard? And Rusty said you were being really friendly to him."

"I was wrong. You aren't high, you are motherfucking insane."

Wow.

No idea.

She honestly had no fucking clue.

"You can tell me." Her voice softened for the first time since our reconnection. "Honestly, it would explain a lot."

She was actually being sympathetic. Like I had been stuffed all this time in a closet with a dildo up my ass. Let me be clear. Gay, straight, bi, whatever. I gave zero fucks—yeah, the word choice completely intentional—on anyone else's sexual orientation. They could fuck whom they wanted, as much as they wanted and they could all skip into the sunset.

My preference was one way—my dick in a woman. *Where* in the woman was the only part that was open for debate. There wasn't any other gray area. Not a *maybe let's experiment*. Not an *excuse me sir, can I lick your balls?*

"I'm sorry I slept with you and left you. Like I said, it was a dick move, but it wasn't because I was gay, it was because I was an asshole." And I was a coward, but I chose to leave that bit out.

"Rusty is a cool guy but I don't want to fuck him. The lack of girls in the press is partly because I'm the freaking keyboard player and no one gives a shit, and partly because I don't date women who are looking to land a role in *The Real Housewives of New York*."

"Oh." Her face vacant of emotion.

"Look, I don't do relationships. I know some guys say that, but I've tried and every single time is more miserable than the last. I do casual hook ups but don't flash it around. I'm with them and then I leave. It's just the way I'm wired."

Not that it had always been that way, but it had been for a very long time. If it wasn't broke don't fix it, and as far as women were concerned this was the only way it worked for me. Everyone assumed it was Dan who was biggest manwhore, but they had no idea. He just ran his mouth about it, I didn't. Plus, I was careful about the women I chose. If they looked like they were angling for a feature in *Billboard Magazine*, I'd leave them to him. He could have all the publicity he wanted while I

BACK STAGE

found someone who would rather fuck than have her picture in the paper.

"But what about the girl, the one you were seeing?"

Angie had obviously heard about the girl I tried to do normal with a couple of years ago.

"Erin." That was the name of my failed foray back into relationship land. She was a cutie. We met at a show but actually wasn't a fan, and what started as one of my planned hook-ups went pear-shaped when she thought it meant more. It had been a while since I'd done the girlfriend thing so I thought I'd give it a try. Shouldn't have bothered. It didn't end well.

"Erin." Angie repeated it back; it felt weird hearing that name on her lips. Almost like it was dirty. It wasn't like what we'd had. I had been with Erin because I felt obligated; I'd been with Angie because I couldn't stop myself from *not* being with her.

"Honestly, I was only with her because I figured it was something I should be doing. We should never have gotten together. It's not that I didn't like her, she was a sweet girl but she wanted things from me that I couldn't give her. Besides, she lived in fucking Pennsylvania, it never would have worked out."

Webcam dating didn't interest me, nor did jerking myself off with phone sex. It was more work than pleasure. I ended it as soon as I was able to.

"Because she's a *Steeler's* fan, right? I don't blame you, I never got that *Terrible Towel* thing either." A slight smile ghosted on her lips, it was the first one she'd given me since the whole are-you-gay discussion had begun.

"No, she didn't even like football."

"Well it's a good thing you dumped her then." Angie straightened, and I realized I hadn't even asked her to sit down. We'd been standing the whole time and I felt if I asked her to sit now it would probably be inviting trouble. I guess we'd be standing a little longer.

"Yeah, maybe."

Yes, definitely, but not because she didn't like football, because she

87

wanted a boyfriend and I wanted sex without commitment.

"So you like women then." It wasn't a question, more a confirmation of the fact that I was very much into pussy and not cock.

"Yes, very much so." And often, just not with the attachment and dating after.

"Just casual hook ups."

"Yes, generally. It works."

This conversation was not one I wanted to be having. My bed was my business and no one else needed to hear about it. It wasn't for bragging rights. Not even the band knew the full extent of my extracurricular activities. They'd seen me with a girl or two, but for the most part it was kept on the down low. Like I said, Dan took the heat off for a lot of years.

"Do you know them? Like, know their names?"

Well, wasn't that the question of the century. It actually helped if I didn't know them too well, made it easier. I'd never paid for sex but that line of who was a whore wasn't always clear. They weren't prostitutes, but who was I to question their lifestyle, especially when I was doing what I was doing.

"Sometimes. Not always. They knew what they were getting themselves in to. I don't pretend it's going to be more than it is."

She flinched. Not a lot, but enough for me to notice. Obviously, not the answer she'd expected. Maybe the truth disgusted her, not that I blamed her. My reality was no fucking fairytale.

"Well I guess I know then." Her eyes shot down to the floor before coming back to me. "Thanks."

Any progress the two of us had made went right out the window. I felt the chill coming off her as her invisible wall went up.

"Know what?" I asked.

That I was an asshole? That I fucked around? That I was a complete commitment-phobe? Obviously, she was disgusted.

"Know ..." She hesitated before continuing. "That you're not gay."

"Don't lie, Angie. What were you going to say?"

BACK STAGE

It wasn't like her to bite her tongue; it made me uneasy. I'd rather have her say it to my face. It's not like it wouldn't be something I hadn't already said to myself.

"It doesn't matter." She shot down any further hope for discussion as she made for the door. "I should go. Rusty wants to go through another song for tonight."

"A new cover?" It was a cheap shot but I hoped if I changed the subject I could get her to stay a little longer. I just needed more time. Time to work her out.

"Yes." She tried to smile but didn't quite pull it off.

"I'll look forward to it." Lord knows I'd be sitting there watching like I had the last couple of nights, no need to pretend like I wasn't.

"Yeah, whatever." She grabbed at the doorknob and yanked it open. Her back faced me as I watched her about to leave.

"Angie, did you really think I was gay?"

She took a deep breath but didn't turn around. "No."

She stayed still in her spot as I walked up behind her and whispered in her ear. "Are you going to tell me what you're holding back?"

"No," she whispered back.

"You should go then."

"I know. I'm going."

Her feet moved and then she was gone, the door slamming behind her.

'10

Angie

WHAT JASON HAD SAID RIPPED RIGHT THROUGH ME.
Casual hook ups.
He didn't do relationships.
Sex with lots of different women.
It's what worked.
Sex with me, didn't.

Well, he hadn't said that but that's what he meant. What did he say about his ex girlfriend? She was sweet but wanted things he couldn't give her. Is that what he'd thought about me? At least he hadn't run out on *her*. I wonder which was worse, knowing or not, that it had all been a farce. It's not like I could ask her. Not sure I wanted to know the answer.

What I didn't understand was he said they all—the hordes of women, okay maybe I was exaggerating—knew what they were getting into. I hadn't. At no time did he ever imply it was just sex, well I guess he did when he told me it was a mistake and left, but that was after the fact. He didn't get to change the rules after; that was not fair.

Perhaps I'd missed the briefing before, the one he obviously gave to

BACK STAGE

these women who had no problem screwing him and not getting attached. That had been my bad, I guess. I got attached.

"Hey, you solid? You're not still hung over are you?" Rusty burst through the dressing room door. Once again he hadn't knocked. Once again, I had been dressed hours ago.

"Don't you ever knock? And no, I'm not still hung over." If I hadn't been sober before, my candid little chat with Jase earlier sure had taken care of that.

"Knocking is for strangers. I'm family." Rusty took a seat beside my illuminated makeup mirror. "You sure you want to do *that* song tonight?"

"Yeah, I ran through it today. Just make sure the band is tight, I've got the rest covered." It was most definitely the song I wanted to sing. Years later than I should have, but at least I was getting the opportunity now.

"The band has it covered, I meant the *words*, dude." His raised eyebrow hinted at his concern.

"Did you just call me, dude?" I punched him in the arm trying to lighten the mood. Changing my mind wasn't an option.

"I call everyone, dude." Rusty barked out a laugh.

"And here I was thinking I was special."

"Stop avoiding." He knew exactly what I was doing, and he called me on it. "The song."

"It's the one that I'm singing so it would be in the band's interest to be the one that you play."

There was probably a better song out there—one that better expressed my feelings—but not one I could learn in a few hours.

Closure. That's what it was about. And this felt like the best way to do it, because despite my tough exterior, I wasn't that tough. But that was my secret, and Jason or anyone else didn't need to know it.

Rusty continued his rant on my song choice, threatening to *play the fuck out of it*. Not sure that was going to be possible but it was a conversation I was more comfortable having while I finished applying my makeup and smoothed on the finishing touches.

It would have been so much easier if he had only been gay, if that had been the reason. It must have been my alcoholic delusions—trying to make sense of it—that convinced me it was even a possibility. My stupid brain pairing together his lack of arm candy reported in the press and the hope that it was *all* women that were the problem. But nope, he was straight and just not interested. Wishful thinking hadn't helped me up to this point. Not to mention how stupid the idea seemed in the light of day, while I was sober.

Never. Drinking. Again.

"So rumor is, you made out with Jase last night." He eyed me hard while I blotted my lips with a tissue. "The whole *fuck you* thing doesn't work if you kiss him later. Sends mixed messages."

"And where did you hear this rumor?" The tissue was tossed into the trash as I turned to face him, wondering which snitch had turned me in. It could have been anyone. Traitors, the lot of them.

"From the fifty people who saw you with your tongue down his throat."

He was right; we hadn't been discreet. Funny how I was more annoyed about getting caught rather than actually kissing him, yeah that's not telling at all.

"It was nothing, I was drunk. I get friendly when I drink." Not a lie, I do get very touchy-feely after a few beers. I hugged Beth remember, and I was nice to that other girl, too. See, just friendly. "Besides, how many girls did you make out with last night huh? A little late to be throwing stones."

"I made out with three girls, and each time it was a beautiful thing." He smiled at the memory. "Just make sure you know what you are doing, Angie. You want to kiss him, do it. Hell, sleep with him if it will make you feel better. But do it with your eyes open this time."

It wasn't necessary, my eyes were well and truly open this time but I appreciated Rusty being a friend. At least someone was thinking out of the two of us. Obviously last night, it hadn't been me.

BACK STAGE

"I'm not going to sleep with him." Not that there was even the slightest chance. "I asked him if he was gay."

"What? You asked Power Station Jase if he was gay?" Rusty erupted into laugher. "Oh my God, I can't breath." He doubled over as he continued giggling his ass off. "Seriously, I wonder if there's oxygen around." And still the laughter continued. "Oh fuck, that was awesome. I wish I had've been there. Damn, girl, you're killing me."

"I'm glad you are amused." I popped him in the arm. It wasn't *that* funny and had made more sense to me this morning. Not so much now.

"Of course I'm amused, who asks someone they actually have *had* sex with if they are gay. Unless they sucked, which from all accounts he didn't." He wiped the tears from his eyes.

"How do you know he didn't suck, I never spoke about the sex."

Jase had been great. Out of this world phenomenal, but pretty sure I never mentioned it. I'd been too devastated, lots of crying. Proclamations of a broken heart a-plenty but I can almost guarantee his prowess as a lover took a backseat to how much I hated him. Asshole was thrown around a lot. Talk of great sex, not so much.

"Because *if* he sucked, sweetheart, you would have been happy to see him leave. Love him or not, life's too short for bad sex. And you had your fill with Taylor Limp-dick."

"His name was Tyler." A chuckle escaped my lips.

"Yet notice how you didn't correct me on his last name."

"Touché."

"So you asked the guy if he prefers dick. How did he take it?"

Yeah, not my finest moment. It had definitely sounded better in my head on the drive over. When I was living in my fantasy world of, maybe it wasn't me, maybe it was all women. I should have quit while I was ahead.

"Oh, he set me straight by explaining to me not only is he *not* gay, but he has meaningless sex with lots of different women. He doesn't do relationships. Could have used that memo *before* he'd had sex with me." Or alternatively had sex with me *before* I fell in love with him. Not sure it would have changed much, not that it mattered now.

"So you know then."

"Yep, I know."

Known that I had just been another vagina. Nothing special. Even worse, less than special, because no sooner had he fucked me, had he given me my walking papers. It had always been a suspicion, one that twisted and turned in my head. It was the reason I swore never to give my heart again, not fully. But to have it confirmed was something else entirely. That cut went deep. So glad to have that new level of awareness—not.

"You wanna say that out loud?"

"Rusty, don't."

I couldn't say the words. It would make it that much more real. Make me feel that much more stupid. No. Words weren't needed. My heart ached enough without them.

"Fine, sing your damn song tonight then." Rusty wrapped his arms around me. "But I strongly recommend you don't kiss him. Kiss someone else."

"Yeah, maybe I will."

"Wow, you guys were fantastic."

Our backstage crowd had grown to include not only Power Station but also some of their wives. Ashlyn and Megs, Dan and Troy's ladies, were the newest additions.

"That N'Sync song sounded crazy good. I loved it." Ashlyn, the redhead whose last name she shared with Dan, threw her arms around me in a hug.

Great. I wasn't good with touching when I was sober, although Ashlyn didn't seem to have the same trouble as she beamed at me. Rusty and the boys wandered off, leaving me to accept the adulation on my

BACK STAGE

own. Bastards.

"Thanks." My hands awkwardly tapped her on the back, not knowing exactly what to do here. "Who didn't love that song, right?"

"I know. Can you imagine if that was written about you? Hey, I loved you but I'm kicking your ass to the curb and leaving. Kind of the ultimate fuck you."

Wow. She had got it. That was exactly what the song was about and even though she hadn't been my intended audience, I was glad at least someone saw my genius.

"Yeah, that sounded great." Megan aka Megs aka Mrs. Troy took her turn in giving me unsolicited affection, she received the same stiff-arm tap, tap I'd given Ash.

The two ladies, as well as being married to their rock star husbands, were also best friends. Oh and totally welcoming, didn't even look at me funny once or ask me why I had so many tattoos. Plus neither had accused me of trying to sleep with their husbands either. It was almost too normal. Could these women actually … like me?

Of course the song they were referring to was *N'Sync's* "Bye, Bye, Bye." The message of the song, as Ash had so appropriately put it, was I love you but I'm kicking your ass to the curb. See ya. Full stop.

"Well, well, Angie. You seemed to have won over some new fans." Troy planted a kiss on his pregnant wife, which of course had her wriggling with delight. Which was not surprising considering the few times I had seen her, she seemed to be in a perpetual state of happiness. I wasn't sure she had another mood. Oh and she called her husband by his whole name, kind of adorable but mostly weird.

"Don't give her a head swell." Dan snuck up behind his significant other, Ash. "We need for her head to be able to get through the door." He not so subtly kissed her neck.

Those Power Station men did that a lot, PDA's I mean. It was as if they had decided everyone needed to be aware of how loved up they were. I wasn't sure if it was sad or sweet. Perhaps we should be breaking out in the song, "Can you feel the love tonight."

Everyone laughed.

Crap. How much of that had I said out loud? I needed to keep better track of my mouth.

"Just the part about *The Lion King*, and they are laughing because I'd said the same thing at Dan and Ash's wedding. Strange coincidence." Jason materialized from the darkness.

While making out with wives was what the other band members did, appearing from the shadows was Jason's usual trick. "I'm assuming you hadn't meant to say it. Or the bit about needing to keep better track of your mouth."

"Yeah. Sorry. No disrespect intended."

While I didn't care for Jason's opinion, I wasn't deliberately going out of my way to be a bitch. I know that's what people generally thought, my appearance and general attitude not really soft around the edges, but part of that was insecurity. Rudeness wasn't attractive and not something I wanted to be known for, even if in the past that was what I had usually come to expect from other girls. I assumed my newfound hug buddies would make the regular assumptions about me, that I was a whore or something. Then hate me, and warn me off their men.

"None, taken." Ash shrugged, her smile still sincere.

Wow. Maybe she wasn't going to automatically dislike me.

Both Ash and Megs were stunningly beautiful, confident and educated. Sassy too and it was hard not to be awed in their presence. They seemed so well put together, I on the other hand, was not. My mom had been like them. Classically beautiful, smart and so kind that I'd wondered if she hadn't been an angel all along. Sometimes I thought if she'd been around longer things would have been different. If maybe some of that might have hopefully rubbed off on me. Instead of me being, well ... me.

"You guys let her off the hook too easily. I would have totally made her sweat it out a little longer," Dan unhelpfully added.

"Oh hush, Dan. Don't be an ass." Ash elbowed Dan in the ribs.

She didn't take his shit either. I actually really like this girl.

BACK STAGE

"Thanks, I like you, too." Ash giggled.

"Yeah, I should probably go now before I embarrass myself further." I prayed the floor under me would swallow me as I resolved to staple my mouth freaking shut.

"No, hang out with us." Megs grabbed my arm, her smile just as warm as her friend's had been. "It will be fun. Say whatever you want, we don't care."

"Exactly, and Megs has a tendency to let her mouth fly so we're totally used to it." Ash laughed, Megs nodded, not even trying to disprove her statement.

They were being nice, and seeming so welcoming of me. Not mean or judgmental, like they were actually interested in getting to know who I was. Which was completely unexpected, because along with never giving my heart away again, I'd assumed I'd never have that. Even going so far as telling myself I didn't need them—girlfriends. But, it was really kind of cool. I wondered if this is what sisterhood felt like. Sort of like peeing in the pool, I felt completely weird doing it but I really liked the warm feeling it gave me.

"C'mon Dan and Jase, we're on in ten. Ladies, we'll see you after the show." Troy said his goodbyes and rounded up the troops, all with his arms still around Megs. "You need anything?" The last bit was only for her.

He was being so incredibly sweet, even a non-believer like me couldn't help but be sucked into a sappy awww-aren't-they-just-adorable. Thankfully this time my mouth had stayed shut.

"Troy Harris, I'm fine. Go." Her small frame comically pushed him toward the stage exit. Dan laughed as he kissed Ash goodbye and made his way out.

"By the way, I love this new T-shirt with the arms cut off." Megs ran her hands suggestively over his biceps. "It's freaking sexy, you're so getting laid tonight."

"Yeah, not what you want to say to me, Megs, right before getting on stage." Troy's voice rumbled as he slowly edged her toward the back wall.

Ummmm. Hello. We're still here. Please don't have sex in front of us.

"I'm pregnant. I've got no control over it." She didn't even seem the slightest bit sorry. The smile she wore a hint that she enjoyed seeing him all revved up. "Go smack stuff, and then come back to me."

"Okay, I'll just be over here." I sidestepped a little and gave them their privacy. Well as much as they were going to be getting with a bunch of other people milling around. But I figured some pretty showy kisses were bound to happen before Troy got out the door, and I didn't need to see that.

"You're a popular girl."

Oh look, Jason was still here. Awesome.

"Oh, I'm sure I'm just a novelty. But they seem really nice."

All true. I wasn't sure how long their fascination with me would last but I was glad I was able to survive the small talk and not sound moronic. Chit-chat was not something I excelled in and I really did think both Megs and Ash were great.

"They are. Both those girls are sweethearts. Honest, loyal and genuine." His eyes didn't move from mine as he rattled off the remarkable attributes of his band mates' wives.

Jase also forgot to mention beautiful, which both of them were. "Looks like they won the wife lotto. Lucky them." Which explained the fixed state of happy their husbands seemed to be in.

Had me wondering why he would choose his sex with no strings lifestyle when he saw what he could have. Surely, it couldn't feel the same. It was the first time I actually felt a little sorry for him.

"Yep, lucky them." Jase moved closer, his big body dominating the space. "Interesting song choice." The direction of the conversation took a sharp left turn.

Avoidance, or he was just done with the other conversation? It seemed really sudden to be talking about one thing and then, boom, something else. Still I needed to remind myself that Jason Irwin was not a riddle that I needed to solve.

BACK STAGE

"Oh it's a classic, you know. We just jazzed it up. JT is a crowd pleaser."

I followed his lead, moving the conversation to a place that was probably safer—music, songs, my finales etc. The appropriateness of the song's message didn't get a mention sadly, but I secretively hoped he'd been around when Ash was making her observations. Probably not—such a shame.

"Yeah, is there a pattern to these covers? Or just random songs? You have to admit, your choices are a little left of center."

It felt like a fishing expedition, like he knew there was *something* there but he hadn't worked it out. The songs almost too random to be accidental choices. Well, I sure as hell wasn't going to tell him. Oh, no. My odes to him could be like a little treasure hunt. Eventually the penny would drop.

"We like left of center."

Really, what was center anyway? Clearly I was the last person you should be asking because despite everything I knew, deep down, I felt like I was fighting a losing battle. The one where I told myself I was over him.

"I guess I'll have to wait and see tomorrow's song. Last show in New York before we hit the road."

"Looking forward to it."

So not looking forward to it.

"Jase, don't you have somewhere to be? Stop crowding, Angie." Megs had obviously freed herself from Troy, the latter having already disappeared. "Ash and I found her first."

Oh how wrong she was, Jason had most definitely found me first, but I was thankful for the reprieve. All these warm feelings, I could feel myself softening. Just a few more minutes and I probably would have jumped into his lap. So much for my *I am never going to kiss him again*. My lips had happily screwed me over by spewing every single thought that had passed through my head; they would just as surely betray me when it came to kissing. The bastards would probably welcome it.

"Bye ladies. Enjoy the show." Jason said *ladies*, but he was only looking at me. Totally sexy move too because we'd already established what his eyes did to me and why I hated them. The reason—in case it was unclear—being the things they did to my girlie parts.

"See ya, Jase."

"Bye, Jase."

Megs and Ash took their turns in saying their farewells. Their excitement bubbling as they turned to me. I had no idea what their plans were, honestly didn't care. Whatever they were, they had to be safer than standing here with him.

"Bye." I shoved as much confidence into my voice as I could. Bye, bye, bye. I repeated in my head as my mind floated over the lyrics I had just sung.

He smiled—something else of his that I hated—and then disappeared down one of the narrow corridors.

"Let's go grab a place to watch the show, okay?" Ash's head tilted toward the mostly deserted hallway.

"Sure." I shrugged; with my band AWOL I didn't have any other plans.

"Great." Megs slung an arm around me. This time, I didn't mind the touching so much. "We're going to have an awesome night."

"We so are."

A nervous laugh escaped from my throat. This was a new start, a way to break away from my past—all of it. There was no going back. Goodbyes had been said, I was moving on and Jason could have as many casual hook ups as he wanted. In fact, I'd have a few of my own. This tour would not be my undoing. Finally, I felt free.

11
Jason

"WOMANIZER" BY *BRITNEY SPEARS*.

That had been the next night's song choice. And I knew for a fact she couldn't stand Britney. And it wasn't a coincidence that she had just learned about my colorful dating history and, there you go—a song about a man who couldn't keep it in his pants.

I'd had my suspicions about the random additions to their set list. First I thought it was the band trying to be edgy, an unpredicted tune mashed up with some distortion and heavy beats giving the crowd a we-aren't-a-one-trick-pony.

Wrong. While they had proved they could pull a Top 40 high-rotation song and inject it with some rock, I highly doubted that had been their motivator. I'd say the reason was more on par with what Ash had said after the *N'Sync* performance. A big, loud, fuck you. Womanizer. Well that was the smoking gun.

Was I offended? Not even close. I was intrigued beyond fucking measure.

I assumed Angie was leading the parade on the musical vendetta. The sly smile she wore thinking I hadn't clued up was almost adorable. But I wasn't that stupid. She could have left smaller breadcrumbs and I *still* would have found the trail. The fact that it pleased me wasn't right. It shouldn't please me, it should fucking horrify me. But in my twisted mind that connection was better than none. Give me a minute while I go book some therapy.

That she still hated me, or that she thought of me, was the variable. And it was a coin toss as to which of those was the one I was hoping for. She had every right to hate me; we'd already established I had been less than a gentleman. That she still thought of me; well wasn't I the sick bastard who strangely got off on that.

With New York done and dusted we'd headed to Boston. The plane ride had shown me another side to her. She seemed different, more relaxed on the short flight. Like we'd entered into a silent truce. Except for at night on stage when I was sure to get the usual burn she planned on serving up. And wasn't I just looking forward to it more than I should.

Ash reuniting with her family in her hometown was pretty sweet. While Lexi and Hannah we're on the tour for the long haul, Megs and Ash were temps. They'd join us when they could, which would be for the next two weeks before they scaled it back to weekends. Both of them had clocks to punch and jobs to be at, so following around their men on tour wasn't in the cards. Plus Megs was expecting, it was only a matter of time before her doc pulled the plug and stopped her flying altogether. That was going to be a fun day, Troy probably not going to do well with the separation.

Knowing that I was the only one who didn't have an entourage might have made another dude sad, especially seeing how happy everyone else was. But I'd resigned myself to fate a long time ago. That part of the story wasn't destined for me, and I was okay with that.

"Why don't yer drink a real beer." Ash's dad laughed as he shoved a pint of the thick brown draft he'd just pulled in front of me. Guinness. Somehow I didn't think anyone was going to be asking for *Miller Lite*.

"Thanks, Finton." I lifted my glass. "For the beer, and the hospitality."

BACK STAGE

"Pleasure." His Irish accent causing the words to lilt. "Anything for my baby girl." He shot Ash a proud grin as he mopped up the bar. His baby girl doing a fine job of proving no matter how long it had been since she'd pulled a beer, she still had what it took.

"Babe, you are turning me on right now." Dan leaned not so subtly forward in his bar stool. "Watching you do that with your hand is giving me such a hard-on."

"Dan." She didn't skip a beat as she pulled another glass. "My dad is right there." Her eyes darted to the man who had closed up shop so we could have a private reception. He probably hadn't heard Dan but the vibe he was throwing off was unmistakable, like a cat in fucking heat. No one needed to see it, especially not Ashlyn's dad.

"Keep it in your pants, lover boy." Alex gave him a friendly slap across the back. "The kids don't need to see you dry humping a bar stool." His glance shot to Lexi, who was sitting with Hannah and the collective of rug rats. The mountain of toys, coloring shit and other crap covering the table they were seated around. It was the only time the kids were probably going to be in a bar.

"The kids love their Uncle Dan, don't you kids?" Dan turned his attention to the little people who proved how smart they already were by ignoring him. Their heads buried in whatever activity that was dominating their little minds. "Not cool, children." Dan shook his head. "I'll remember this when your parents piss you off and you want to run away to Uncle Dan's."

"God, help us if that happens." James laughed, throwing back what was left of his beer. "Or when there is a little version of him running around."

"Nah, Ash has superior DNA, it will override Dan's. Their kids are safe," Troy chimed in, taking a sip from his glass. His drink, an iced tea; keeping his wife company with the alcohol avoid.

"Hi, sorry we're late." Angie walked through the side door, her long hair floating around her shoulders as she stepped into the room. She was wearing a skirt for a change; her tanned legs getting lots of view time given the length of the hem. Wow. I didn't know who the designer was, but I suddenly felt the need to write them a thank-you.

Ash's mom ushered the rest of *Black Addiction* through. Not that I gave a shit, my attention still locked on to Angie. "The cab drivers here are freaking crazy." She shot a look toward Ash's dad who was smiling. "No offense."

"Nah. None taken. The cab drivers are crazy. Take a seat." He nodded to the collection of empty tables. "We'll get yah fed soon enough." The hospitality extended to dinner and chill time for all of us at *Murphy's Irish Tavern*.

She gave him a smile that would no doubt melt his damn heart, her dark eyes scanning the room before taking a seat. My eyes shifted to the curve of her thighs, her hem riding up a little and exposed more skin as she sat. Got me thinking about what was in between them. Damn. I needed to focus, and probably get laid at some point.

And while the rest of her band sunk their asses into chairs as well, none of them held my attention like she had. The conversation flowed easy. And it turns out that they weren't only a good support band, but they were polite bastards too, remembering their pleases and thank yous, charming Ash's parents.

Max, their bass player, confessed to being a Red Sox fan, which had Ash's dad almost blow his load. Ash stirred the pot a little more by smiling at the bass player that wasn't her own, which earned the poor bastard some heated stares from Dan.

"Hey, Pa, you need a hand?"

A diagram of the family tree wasn't needed to assume that the dude who wandered in was Ash's brother. Besides the obvious of addressing his old man, the family resemblance was also pretty hard to miss.

"Liam!" Ash squealed, hugging the guy within an inch of his life. "Everyone this is my brother, Liam."

I'm sure I'd probably met him at the wedding, but obviously the introduction hadn't been memorable.

"Hey everyone." He gave us all a wave, his smile getting a little wider

BACK STAGE

when his eyes settled on Angie. Bastard didn't even try and hide the fact he was scoping her out. Just stood there smiling like a douchebag with his dick in his hand.

Knowing I had no claim to her didn't make me any less edgy. We'd been through it before—none of my business, and yet there I was, wondering which fingernail I'd rip off first if he laid a hand on her. The guy was an easy read too, his attention not shifting since he entered the room. The big ass grin plastered on his face further proved where his interests lay. And they weren't on helping his *Pa*.

Angie should date. Of course she should. And she could be with anyone she wanted—just not this guy. He was probably a decent guy, truth is I knew jack about him. Except that he wanted to fuck her. That part was plainly obvious. Which of course made me instantly dislike him.

Rough introductions were made by Ash with hellos and how-you-doings being thrown at the guy as he settled in with the group; the dick taking a seat right next Angie despite his dad telling him his help wasn't required. Not obvious at all, asshole. He immediately climbed to the top of my shit list.

"So you are musicians?" Dickhead asked. The fact I knew his name was Liam meant very little to me.

"Some of us, some not so much." Dan grinned at Max, answering his brother-in-law.

"It's two bands," Ash pitched in given that Dan's explanation hadn't been adequate. "Angie, Rusty, Max and Joey are in Black Addiction. They are Power Station's support for this tour."

"And what do you play?" Loser turned his head toward Angie in what I can only assume was an attempt to flirt. Newsflash. He sucked at it.

"I sing and play guitar."

Thankfully she didn't seem to be swallowing his bullshit line, the information that she gave him stock standard and without any extra attention. Had to admit, that was the only part of the exchange I was actually enjoying.

Apart from the obvious train wreck that was poor Liam Murphy's attempt at seduction, the room hummed with conversation. The others got pulled into one exchange or another, bullshit chatter filling the air. I, on the other hand, was curious to see how our resident Casanova was going to play this out. My eyes and ears trained on them both.

"I'm sure we'll be seeing you headlining your own tour soon." Liam's fingers drummed nervously on the table.

Clueless. I almost felt sorry for the guy. He was fucking drowning in a sea of no-fucking-idea and Angie hadn't so much as given him a second look. It made me want to laugh, my body finally relaxing in the seat as I watched him fight a losing battle.

"We'd need to be signed and have recorded an album before that can happen. It's a long way off. But thanks." The brush off was gentle—who knew she had it in her—as Angie shifted uncomfortably in her chair. She really wasn't into him. A celebratory drink was definitely in the cards, my glass raised toward my smirk as I took another drink.

"Liam, Riley's here." Ash's dad gave the poor douche an out, the sound of footsteps coming toward the bar from the direction of the kitchen.

"Shit, I forgot we were supposed to hang." The disappointment on his face was real, as was my utter freaking delight.

"Hey, you ready to go?" A dude who was around the same height as Alex, strolled through the door. "Hell, man, didn't realize you had company." The new guy peeled the ball cap off of his head, and shoved it into the back of his jeans.

"Hi, Riley," Ash and Megs sung out at the same time. Seemed like the new guy had a fan club.

"Hey, Ash, didn't realize you were home, doll. Let me get your loser brother out of your hair." He shot Ash a wink, Dan stiffened beside me at the mention of the word *doll*. I guess it wasn't a good night for either of us.

"Ry, you wanna stick around? Pull up a chair and chill for a while." Liam gave his buddy the subtle head tip toward Angie, in what I can only assume was some fucked up bro-signal that he was trying to put the moves on. I'd seen Tibetan Monks with more game.

The new guy—Riley, another name I gave zero fucks in knowing—rolled his eyes before he took a few steps closer to where his buddy was situated.

"I'm Riley." He offered Angie a handshake, not waiting for an introduction. "You want me to get rid of him for you?"

Angie laughed, a real one this time, not of the lame variety she'd been giving Liam. I didn't like it.

"It's fine. I'm Angie, by the way."

All that interest she hadn't shown the first guy was directed at the feet of this one. Me wanting Liam to disappear had been premature. He wasn't the enemy; no he was the harmless decoy. Riley—I really hated saying the asshole's name—not only had Angie's attention but didn't suffer from the same deer-in-headlights his friend had been struck down with.

"Nice to meet you, Angie." Douchebag number two flashed her a grin like he was auditioning for a toothpaste commercial. "I'd love to stay and chat but we have a hot date with … exactly what could we be pretending to do tonight that might sound cool?" He looked to his clueless friend who answered with a shrug.

She laughed.

And it really, really pissed me off.

Not because her head was thrown back as she enjoyed whatever bullshit was spilling from his mouth, but that I was rationally trying to justify punching the asshole in the face.

The reasons didn't even make fucking sense. We'd established that we were barely even friends. Yet, here I was, my fist ready to get busy on the asshole's face as I watched him put the moves on my girl.

Wow. Dangerous territory. She wasn't *my* girl. I didn't have a girl, and if I did I'm pretty sure the shit I'd pulled years ago guaranteed Angie wouldn't be in a hurry to fill the role. I couldn't just flip the script now. I'd made my choices. And it was better for both of us, both then and now. *Remember the reasons, asshole.* Remember *why you don't do relationships.*

The noise of the room resumed as conversations picked up from where they'd left off. Power Station and Black Addiction settled into what seemed like a relaxed night of not much happening, which is exactly what had been the plan. It also became clear that douche one and douche two would also not be leaving. No one else seemed to have a problem except for me, if the motherfucking easy vibe was anything to go by.

"Hey, you cool?" Troy had ninja'd himself onto the bar stool beside me. It could have been a circus of monkeys and I'd probably still been surprised, my attention too locked onto Angie to notice. The feeling made me uncomfortable, as did the heat prickling at my neck. Animosity I had no business feeling was setting up and taking residence.

"Yeah, I was actually just thinking the about time we all got together. Back in Montreal."

Well not so much the city but more as to why I ended up in the Great White North. It was the same reason why I wouldn't tangle with that whole love game bullshit, and the same reason why I'd known I'd screwed up after Angie. No matter how much distance and time passes, there are some things you just can't outrun.

"Montreal? Fuck, dude. That was an eternity ago. That hockey game changed the band lineup forever."

"I'd say it was more the bar fight than the hockey game."

"Right? Holy shit, that was a good time. Dan had a black eye for days."

"He probably shouldn't have asked the goalie's girlfriend for a blowjob."

We both laughed. Just as we had after the fight, which not only served as our introduction but changed things for all of us.

Back then Power Station was a foursome, still finding their feet. No deals, no labels, just the music. James had managed to secure them a gig across the border, which made for a nice addition to their resumes—

BACK STAGE

international gig. The fact the Rangers were playing that weekend had sweetened the pot, hell they would have played that shitty sports bar for free. My reasons for being there were very different.

Traveling alone, in the hopes of getting so drunk I'd forget the misery I'd left back in Albany, I'd found myself in the very same bar. Dan's mouth had got him to trouble; something that I would later learn was typical and expected.

Jumping into the fight wasn't something I thought about. In fact, it had been the exact opposite. I hadn't been thinking. But taking a right hook to the jaw beat the hell out of sitting in that seedy, worn booth alone feeling sorry for myself. And at that point, the reason to get up was as good as any. My assist helped even out the numbers between Canadians and Americans. I didn't even care why I was hitting people or getting hit, it just felt fucking fantastic to not be dealing with the messed up slide show I had repeating in my head. The conversation we'd had after, while icing up and swapping names, was when shit turned out to be a game changer.

Their band had been good, even in my half-hammered state I'd seen it a mile away. They just need something else—me. Who even remembered whose idea it had been, but it wasn't much of a discussion in any case. We'd all sobered up and drove back to New York, where I was crashing at Troy's till we got our plan for greatness sorted. I didn't even go home to say goodbye. There was no need and my folks more than understanding of the whys, shipped my shit to Troy's address the week after.

"So what's got you thinking about that? Getting sentimental in your old age?" Troy's sideways glance concerned about where this was leading. It had been a while since we'd taken that stroll down memory lane.

"Watch it asshole, I'm not yelling at the kids to get off my lawn just yet." It had also been a while since the three years I had on them came up in discussion. Still, it was all about the classics tonight it seemed.

"Probably because you can't hear them, maybe turn the hearing aid up. How old are you now? Forty-five? Fifty?" The bastard laughed, thoroughly enjoying himself.

"Thirty-five and I could still out run all of you every day of the week and twice on Sunday."

"No doubt." Troy nodded, the look on his face easing away from yanking my chain to respect. "You got something on your mind, brother?"

Ha. Where to even start on what was on my mind? So many scrambled, messed up thoughts, and they all were given birth to by the same fucking woman.

"Em."

Just saying her name made me want to glass myself in the face. The goddamn hate and rage that those two fucking letters came with, it was a dangerous place to be.

Not the same kind that I was in when I thought of Angie. No, while that had the capacity to make me act irresponsible and make bad decisions, it wasn't the kind that was going to see me doing jail time. Which is exactly where I would have ended up if I hadn't have left Em and my hometown behind. The band, it had been more than just a gig. It had saved my life. Saved me from a road that there would be no coming back from, and that's why I'd take a bullet of any of them.

"Not a name I hoped to be hearing." Troy's lowered voice kept our conversation tight between us. Best we didn't do a show-and-tell, especially not here.

Yeah, not a name I wanted to be saying either. But no amount of booze, women, time or fucking distance would ever jack that evil bitch from my mind. Like a motherfucking scab that could be picked off at a moment's notice and open the festering wound. There weren't many people that I hated; in fact that list was reserved for just one. Her.

"The flashback isn't intentional and my feelings of zen aren't cutting it tonight." Even Mother Teresa would have had her work cut out for her. Em, was pure evil and if the devil hadn't claimed her as his own it was because even *he* didn't trust her.

BACK STAGE

"Fuck," Troy warned, not even trying to hide the concern in his eyes. He knew how quickly it could go bad. "She's not worth it, Jase. Don't get pulled back in."

"Trust me, not going there." Not unless I was willing to give up everything I'd worked for in the time between leaving her and now, and I sure as shit was not giving her that satisfaction. The bitch had taken enough.

"You better not be. Seriously, Jase. Don't go there."

He knew. Knew where the road would lead, had seen it first hand as I busted some asshole's nose for no fucking good reason other than I was itching to get into a fight. Because of her, because of what she'd done, and because of what I had become in the aftermath.

My gaze flicked over to Angie and I felt like I was going to be sick. Her beautiful eyes sparkling as she enjoyed the fuckwit putting on his lame-ass moves. And so she should. At least he was being honest with her, not like I had been. I hadn't even been fucking honest with myself that night, fooling myself that I could sleep with her and shit would all be okay. Right, and we all lived in fantasyland where leprechauns sat on buckets of gold and assholes like me didn't use a sweet girl like her.

That's what it had been, no point pretending like it wasn't. I'd wanted her and I took her, not even giving the consequences a second thought. Her feelings, they'd also been on the backburner because if I'd given half a fuck about anyone but myself, I would have gone and screwed someone else. Anyone else but her. Yet, here we were.

"Hey, do you think anyone would care if I bailed? I know we were supposed to be doing the hanging-as-a-band shit tonight, but I really want to get out of here." Not just to get this twisted stench of misery off me, but also to stop me from having to watch Angie score. Both primed to push me over the edge.

"Do not call her." Troy grabbed my arm as I got up to leave.

"I won't, trust me. I promise you, I'm not stupid enough to make that same mistake twice." I'd rather cut my own dick off than see or speak to her again.

"Then go do whatever it is you need to do to get your head right. I'll handle the Q and A if anyone sticks their nose in." Troy gave a slow nod, giving me my out.

"Thanks." I met his eyes and nodded. I wasn't just thanking him for this. It was more. Much, much more.

"All good, brother."

"See ya."

No one noticed me leaving; they didn't even look up. The conversations had balled together to become a big amount of white noise.

It wasn't just about Em, although she was the springboard. I needed out, in a big way.

Troy was right about one thing; I needed my head right. That shit getting revisited wouldn't help anyone, least of all me. It was done and buried. *Move on, asshole.* Which is exactly what I intended to do.

Waiting outside was our driver—not TJ the guy who usually ferried us around—Jake, the dude we took on tour with us. The ex-seal also doubled as security. It was a pain in the ass but that was our life now, so rather than pissing and moaning about it, I just accepted it.

"G'evening, Sir." Jake stood to attention as soon as my boots hit the outside sidewalk. Though I doubted he'd been chilling even before I'd appeared. Old habits died hard, and despite this guy leaving the Navy a long time ago, he was still rocking *the service before self* mentality.

"Dude, it's just us. You can lose the sir."

"Sorry, s—" He caught himself for finishing. "I'm working on it."

He held the door open of the blacked-out SUV and waited for me to get inside before swinging around to the driver's side and climbing in himself. "Where do you want to go?"

"Drive around a little. Maybe find some company."

Yeah, 'cause sex is always the answer. Great. I really was a motherfucking asshole. Well, I might as well not fight the tide; it's probably the reason why I was in this damn mess in the first place, trying to be something that I wasn't. I wasn't boyfriend material. I fucked and I left, that is what I had told Angie so why I was trying to pretend that's not

BACK STAGE

what I was going to continue to do was beyond me. Best I set things back to the way they needed to be and the sooner, the better.

'12 Angie

Riley was sweet, as was Ash's brother Liam, but there was no way I would be hooking up with either of them. How could I even go there? Nope, I need more degrees of separation than that. Pity, because Riley was good looking. My future self will thank me when I'm not doing the walk of shame tomorrow and having to look Ash in the eye. It would be too weird, even for me.

"Crap, my phone is completely dead." Stupidly I shook it like it would suddenly spring back to life. Predictably the red flashing battery icon didn't change, with the last gasp of juice evaporating and the screen shutting down. Awesome.

"You need a phone, Angie? Here use mine." Riley pulled his iPhone from his pocket and placed it on the table. His smile telling me he was offering me more than just the use of his minutes.

"Thanks, but I was actually looking to email my dad." It had been less than twenty-four hours since I'd left New York, and while my brain told me he was a grown man capable of looking after himself, I still worried. It was the good Catholic, Italian upbringing unfortunately. Here, have a side of guilt with your lasagna.

"Hey, Angie. You need something?" Troy lifted his head from the other end of the table, his concern working overtime between keeping tabs on me and fussing over his knocked-up wife. Megs looked thankful that he found a new target, the smile she directed at me hinting we were both in for a long haul.

"Yeah, I just wanted to email my dad, but my phone died. The battery life is a joke." I shoved the phone back onto the table; it's not like it was any use to me anyway in its current state. "It's just this nightly thing. Keeping an eye on him. I haven't left him alone before; I just like to check he hasn't burnt the house down or forgotten how to program the DVR. It's lame."

"It's not lame, I'm sure he appreciates knowing you are okay. Can't be easy for him, you being so far from home." Megs gently rubbed her small but growing bump. Troy followed up with a nod.

"Yeah, well it's going to take a while for this stupid thing to charge. I should probably head back to the hotel." I started gathering my things and wondering if it would be cool if I snagged the use of one of their drivers. They had two after all, and it's not like I'd keep him occupied for long. The idea of getting into another cab and playing Russian roulette wasn't ranking high on the way I wanted to spend my evening.

"We have a computer in the office you can use?" Ash offered, her chair shifting back as she moved to get up.

"It's cool, I should be getting back anyway." The attention everyone was suddenly paying me, making me uncomfortable. No need to get excited people, just let me slink off and send the email. "Besides, I want to go over a song. It's new."

"I chose it," Rusty unhelpfully added, his fork waving in the air as he finished his second serving of dessert. The man could eat anything he wanted and still not get fat. He really did have such a charmed life.

"You want to use my laptop? It's hooked up to the Wi-Fi in my room. Just get Brad to take you back and send your email from there. Saves you waiting for your phone to charge. Megs wants to hang with Ash a little longer before we head back. Let me just grab my key." Troy reached into his pocket and pulled out the small credit card-sized plastic keycard.

"It's okay, I don't want to put you out. Besides, as soon as I plug in, it will power up enough to use." Seriously, could everyone go back to their pie and not worry about me?

"Yeah, but didn't you want to go over a song as well? Just let the freaking thing charge properly. It's a computer, Angie, no big deal. Here's my room key. Jase, Dan and I are on the top floor. Just use the keycard to get access to our floor and in the shared living area is the desk. It's sitting right on top." Troy extended his hand, the plastic keycard in it waiting for me to take it.

"Are you sure? Won't someone be up there?"

It hadn't escaped my attention that he had listed the occupants of that particular floor. Himself and Megs, Dan and Ash, annnnnnnd Jason. Who at some point before we'd even eaten dinner had slipped out and was currently MIA. Not that I was worried, I mean it was none of my business, he could be doing anything he wanted, and I so would not care.

Not at all.

Not in the slightest.

Just as long as he wasn't there.

I could still not care and not want to be alone in a room with him. That still counted. Well it did in my book, and my book was the only one that mattered.

"Jase is off somewhere, and the rest of us are here, so you're good. Trust me, no one is up there. Do what you need to do and then leave the key on the desk. We'll use Dan's when we want access."

He had been very non-committal about Jason's whereabouts. *Somewhere* was not a place. In fact it was the absence of a place and not where you'd want a member of your band to be, especially if they were famous. Surely their record label had them all micro-chipped or tagged or whatever. So either Troy knew, and didn't want to say, which was completely plausible—we'd already established it was none of my business—or he genuinely didn't know, which you had to wonder why

BACK STAGE

he wasn't more worried.

Not my problem. Well, that's what I told myself as I grabbed the key from Troy and got ready to leave.

"Thanks, Troy. I owe you."

"Let's say you coming on tour with us made us even." He gave me a smile and went back to the conversation at the table, his arm slung back around Megs.

I gave everyone a wave and "see ya" as I made my way to the door, Riley offering to "walk me out," I guess in case I got lost. It was a complicated journey, the ten-foot straight shot to the door.

"So you're going?" Riley asked, making an exaggerated puppy dog expression in what I can only assume was a show of disappointment.

"Yeah, I have stuff to do." *Email my dad, learn a song and not have sex with you.* "It was cool meeting you though; if you are ever in New York you should look me up." *Oh please don't look me up, why did I say that?* "Um ... So ..."

I wasn't sure whether I should wave, offer him a handshake or a hug. High five? Did I mention how bad I was at small talk? I literally sucked.

"It was good meeting you, too." He pulled me in for a hug, solving the what-do-we-do problem. I still wasn't sold. Too much touching and I'd already established how I felt about strangers touching me.

"Alrighty. See ya." Clutching Troy's keycard and my dead phone as I gave Riley a friendly tap on the back and made my way to the waiting SUV. There was only one still parked beside the pub. The other one probably wherever Jase had disappeared to. The magical land of *somewhere*, no doubt. At least I wouldn't be running into him. Definitely a positive.

Brad, the driver who took me back to the hotel, didn't speak. Not unless you counted his nods and grunts as communication. In any case, I was happy to not have to make small talk. Plus he looked liked he ate a side of beef at every meal—there's huge, and then there was the whole fuck-are-you-a-person-or-a-planet mystery—when was the last time anyone saw the Incredible Hulk? Are we sure he isn't moonlighting as

Power Station's security? I'd say it would be foolish to completely discount the theory.

As the elevator doors opened on the floor the trio's rooms were situated on, it was clear how different their suites were from ours. Our hotel rooms were lush, stunning even, but this was something else. It was like our rooms, only on steroids.

A huge shared space stretched out in front of me. The three large wooden doors to the penthouse rooms decorated the periphery, past all the expensive furniture and obscenely large flat screen television.

In addition to the television—or time traveling portal, it really could be either—were two huge leather couches, a massive mahogany desk and an office chair. Thankfully the laptop was where Troy had promised, sitting on the desk. That meant I didn't have to snoop around in bedrooms. Because that would have been bad, right? I had no interest in seeing where Jason slept, or what his personal space looked like. Being in his apartment had been bad enough; I mean his bedroom, even if it were just a temporary one would be bad news, right?

No.

I'm not looking. No reason to. I'm sending my email, downloading my song notes, and getting the hell out of here. Focus. This wasn't a reconnaissance mission.

I fired up the notebook, the screen illuminating as it came to life. Thankfully I was able to log in as a guest without the password, seeing I hadn't bothered to ask what it was. The flashy *Dell* was so much fancier than the archaic piece of shit I used at home.

As I sat at the desk in front of the computer, I felt like I was somehow breaking and entering. Out of place. I knew I had Troy's permission, but I couldn't shake the feeling that I didn't belong. Maybe it was the excessive luxury of the room, or perhaps the state of the art computer, but it reminded me that this was not in fact my life. It was an altered reality, a ride at an amusement park. As awesome as it felt, it would inevitably end and we'd have to get off the Ferris wheel and go back home.

BACK STAGE

My fingers clicked away at the keys as I quickly logged into my email account and accessed my inbox. The message I composed was short and to the point. After all, I had mapped it out in my head on the ride over. Get in, reassure my dad all was fine, ask him how he was doing, send the thing, and get the hell out of their room. Simple. Or so was my plan.

However, nothing in my life is ever simple. I powered down the computer not even bothering to download my music notes, deciding to work off my phone once it was charged. And with my email happily sailing away in cyber space, I became suddenly curious what the bedrooms looked like. I mean, if this was the shared space, I imagined the bedrooms would be pretty spectacular. It wouldn't hurt to look; I would definitely not touch anything. I didn't even have to go all the way in, just poke my head through the door. What's the harm?

Holy shit.

The room was impressive. Well as much of it as I could see from the door. I wasn't tempting fate and going all the way in. That would be taking it too far right? I mean, I didn't even know whose room it was.

It was while I was justifying my argument that I heard the elevator ping, announcing the arrival of a guest. Who the hell was that? Housekeeping? Staff? Security? Was there some hidden security cameras and they'd seen me going where I shouldn't? I'd barely stepped into the room. Crap. I should have just left.

And for no good reason, I panicked.

I could have just quickly shut the bedroom door, sat at the desk like I had been five minutes earlier. But no, I had to act like I had been robbing the place, disregarding that I had a key *and* a reason to be there as I crawled under the desk and hid.

It was a stupid instinct, that instead of just waiting to see who it was, I was now crouching low like an idiot, in the tiny space.

Carefully my hands circled my knees and clutched them closer to my body, my effort to hide myself being taken very seriously.

Not that I'd have an excuse for being under the desk if I ended up being caught. Other than me being an idiot. Which would be the truth in this instance.

Footsteps.

My ears strained against the wooden panel of the desk. It was hard to hear anything, with the thing not being some MDF wannabe from Ikea; it was solid. Possibly antique. I had no idea why I was surprised.

The door opened. Then shut really quickly. The sound of heels and men's shoes clicked on the floorboards. There were definitely two people in the room.

"Jason," a female voice giggled, "I'm so turned on right now."

Great. Not only was it the person I least wanted to see, but he also had company. The giggling annoying variety.

"Yeah? I haven't even done anything yet." His voice was low, dark—a rumble.

Whether or not he'd touched her, I could see where giggling, annoying groupie—I didn't know she was a groupie, I'm assuming—was going with *that*. He had that sexy shit locked down.

Not that he held that power over me anymore. No, of course not.

"Don't you believe me?" More giggling. "Why don't you let me show you how wet I am."

Excuse me while I puke. Seriously, why do girls talk like that? Like he doesn't know what a wet pussy feels like? I'm sure, honey, he knows exactly what it feels like; he doesn't need a guided tour. And another thing, dressing it up like a treasure hunt doesn't make you sound sultry, it makes you sound like a fucking pirate. *Argh, follow me trail to where X marks the wet spot.* I will never understand how guys got turned on by that. Obviously now was probably *not* a good time to ask.

"Hmm, you are wet."

Hold the phone people, the man was a genius. He was also an asshole and I hated him even more. You know, in case I needed more of a reason, listening to him be with a girl would do it. Ignore the fact I didn't want to sleep him and the man obviously wasn't going to stop having sex. *Shut up logic, you have no place here.*

"Oh, yeah. Touch me like that."

BACK STAGE

There wasn't a need for me to actually see what was going on, the moaning and the rustling of clothes was enough of a tip-off. My earlier idea of hiding was even dumber than I first thought. I might be hunkered down for a while. This was so going to suck.

"Like this?" he asked, clearly needing the treasure map that I had stupidly said men didn't need. Oh look, it was a fucking expedition. I was literally shaking my head and rolling my eyes at the same time. It was a talent.

"Yes. Yes. Oh, yes." The giggles had stopped, however the annoying hadn't. It was just breathier now. Elongating every syllable. My hand clapped around my mouth as I forced myself not to yell, "Oh please."

"Or is this better?"

Was he fingering her or was it an experiment? It still wasn't clear.

"Holy fuck. Yes. Yes, like that."

She obviously liked it, whatever it was he was doing.

"Are you sure? Maybe you'd prefer this."

Seriously? Just fucking *do* whatever it was you were doing before and move things along. I'm getting a cramp in my thigh. Oh and P.S. I hope she has crabs.

"Oh God, you are going to make me come."

Thank God. Let's wrap it up, lady.

"No, you aren't. Not yet."

What do you mean no she isn't? Why the hell not? Just give her the fucking orgasm.

"Jason, oh God. I'm going to come."

Lady, I'm thinking you might have to take care of it yourself. Just reach down there and give him a hand. And I'm talking literally.

"But I haven't done this yet."

No one likes a show off, Jason. I hope she has crabs and herpes.

"Ah, ah, ah. I'm going to come."

I'm yet to be convinced, you said you were before and you let me down. Let's not get too excited.

"So do you want me to stop?"

YES! For fuck's sake just either make her come or give her a vibrator. I can't stand it any longer. Oh, and in addition to the crabs and herpes I hoped she had originally, could we add a yeast infection? I mean, if I'm allowed to have a list, why not.

"No, no. Don't stop. I want to come. I want to come."

Trust me, we all want the same thing, lady.

"Like this?"

Jesus, I hated him. Like hate of epic proportions. Her too, whomever she was.

So. Much. Hate.

"Yes, I want to come, please."

Honestly, I don't blame her for begging. At this point I was too. For what? Well, who the hell knew? A pair of noise-cancelling headphones would be a good start, followed by some chiropractic care for this crick in my neck I was developing. Oh, and the last twenty minutes or so of my life back.

"What about if I do this?"

Please make it stop. Please make it stop. Was he a sadist? Why won't it stop?

"Oh. Oh. Oh."

"Oh for fuck's sake, make her come already!"

It was supposed to be a thought, I'd had a lot of those through the course of this craptastic experience and yet, somewhere between my mind and my mouth something must have gone wrong. Because, instead of it being harmless internal dialogue, of which I'd had plenty, those words leapt out of my mouth and had announced themselves.

It was quiet.

Really, really quiet.

No annoying giggling, no moaning, no threats of *coming*.

Nothing.

Crap.

"Angie?" Jason's sexy voice was gone and in its place was his what-the-fuck voice. I'd heard it a few times in the last few days so I knew it

BACK STAGE

was him, even without looking, or the fact that his fuck-buddy had said his name fifteen times. Okay, maybe it was only ten. Whatever, she'd said it a lot.

"Heeeeyyyyy." I slowly rose to my feet, brushing myself off as I stood. Pins and needles shot up my leg, the lack of circulation from being curled underneath my body making them feel tingly. "Sorry, didn't mean to interrupt." My lips spread into a forced and probably freaky looking smile.

Really, it's not like there was an etiquette guide for it. I was totally winging it.

Jason's hand shifted from the front of *I'm-coming's* jeans. The look on her face, priceless. That elusive orgasm probably was going to be a while. It's okay though, because given the way things were going, it hadn't been a sure thing anyway.

"Who is she?" The eye daggers she shot me enough of a clue I wasn't going to be winning any fans here. It was only fair though seeing as I had wished the crabs, herpes and yeast infection on her. Although her disliking me wasn't going to have me losing any sleep.

"A friend." Jason answered before I'd gotten the chance. His face, unreadable.

"Actually, I'm not really."

We were so far from *friends* it was laughable he'd even call me that. We were the opposite of friends, we were frenemies. Who'd had sex once and now hated each other. And wished evil fungal infections ... oh wait, that was probably just me who wished that.

"Okay, well. I'm not really into girls. So. Um. Can she leave already?"

She didn't bother to address me, my existence meaningless to her, as she turned her attention back to Jason. Her hands scrunched tight around his t-shirt.

She could hold onto him all she wanted, that orgasm I'd robbed from her wasn't coming back. At least not in the short term.

His eyes stayed locked on mine, ignoring her clawing hands.

"Did you need something, Angie?"

He said the words slowly, letting each one settle.

"No, no I'll let you two get back to it. Seems like you have your hands full."

Or at least he had, and there was no way I'd be sitting through another round of *that*. No, no, no. *Get your shit, get out the door and go scrub your ears with bleach.* And, I was going to need about five gallons of ice cream as well to deal with the truckload of emotions I had going on.

"Jason." Ms. I'm-going-to-come-or-maybe-I-wont pulled at his shirt again. In case he forget she was hanging there, or maybe it was a prompt to remind him he had unfinished business.

"Why are you here?" He completely ignored her, his eyes following me as I moved further away from the desk and closer toward the door.

"Did you hear me? Hello?" She was getting impatient, I think she actually stomped her foot.

"No one was supposed to be up here." Why the hell was I justifying myself? Troy had given me his key; I hadn't broken in. And, I was not the one who was trying to satisfy my screwed up need for a casual hook up. Oh, that's right, because I don't do that. I actually have to *know* the person before I let them into my vagina.

"Are you just going to ignore me? I'm right here." She sounded mad, she was probably mad.

"I'm sorry, Kristen. Why don't I give you a call later?" *What do you know, he knew her name.* Jase turned to face her for the first time since he removed his hands from down her pants.

"But. But. I thought—" She tried to argue, and what she was going to pick as her selling point I had no idea. *I thought you were going to make me come? Have sex with me? Love me, and stick around?* No, I was the only idiot who'd have thought the last one. Even *Kristen* wasn't that stupid.

"Yep, great. Talk soon." He didn't give her chance for any further discussion. In fact he didn't give her the chance for anything, and all but pushed her out the door.

BACK STAGE

"Call me." The words were cut short by the slamming door in her face.

It was a stand off.

The two of us on opposite sides of the room. Neither of us saying a word.

And I knew I shouldn't have looked down, but my eyes had a mind of their own as they followed the lines of his body down. To his crotch, and where his very hard cock was still straining against his jeans.

"See something you like?"

I'd been busted. Not only had it been mortifying enough to have to been caught hiding under a freaking desk while he *dated* some girl, he'd now caught me staring at his pants. And not in a way that was anywhere near innocent.

"No. Been there, done that and got the t-shirt. Thanks for the offer though."

Well at least I could count on my mouth to get with the program. For better or worse, if I was thinking it, I was probably going to be saying it and in this instance I totally approved of my verbal spillage.

"I know you hate me." He was back to the measured words, and the low rumbly sexy voice.

"Wow, you really are smart. Here I was thinking that college education was nothing more than a fancy paper." I folded my arms tightly across my chest, my mood confused.

"But I also know how good it was when we were together." He moved closer.

"And now you're back to dumb again. That night was nothing. I faked it the whole time." Of course that wasn't even close to being true but I wouldn't give him the satisfaction. Even if it meant tarnishing the memory. It's not like it had meant anything to him and for me, it was just a reminder of heartache. Who cared if I tore it to shreds.

"Lie if it makes you feel better, the way you came—on my mouth, on my hand, on my cock—you couldn't have faked that." He was right. None of those times had I faked it, and he knew that.

"Maybe I'm that good of an actress? I was still nice back then, and didn't want to hurt your feelings." I *had* been nice back then. It was before he'd ripped out my heart. Before I knew people did that, before I'd opened my freaking eyes.

He had moved. His feet had progressively walked him to directly in front of me, where he now stood. Still. There.

"I'm pretty sure it was you I was having sex with, and not Meryl Streep." His voice was sharp. Like a ruler slapping a desk and he wasn't letting me off the hook.

"I was easily impressed, and my inexperience worked in your favor." As much as I wanted to, I did not move back. I didn't filch and I didn't run. I stood my ground, playing our stupid game of verbal ping-pong.

"Bullshit, I bet I could make you come just as hard now." *Whoa! What?*

"Dumb and delusional. Sadly, it doesn't make you more appealing." I'd snapped back so fast, I'd almost not heard the words.

Silence.

He didn't respond which annoyed me. It was his turn to say something, why didn't he say it? He always had a comeback, there would be no way he'd let me have the last word.

And I waited. Nothing.

Instead his mouth stayed tight, his jaw clenched, as his dark brown eyes studied me. Their path travelled over every inch of my body so that I felt naked. Exposed.

"What? Why are you looking at me like that?" I demanded, my voice not as confident as I would have liked.

"How am I looking at you?" He tilted his head to the side, a slow smile working at the edges of his lips.

"Like—Like you want to eat me."

"I'd love to *eat* you." His smile got wider.

"That's not what I meant."

"No, but it's what *I* meant."

The oxygen from the room seemed to have evaporated. Poof! Gone. It was like being in a big black hole, a vacuum. There had to be a plausible explanation as to why I could no longer breathe. It wasn't just my lungs that were having difficulty trying to function, it was my brain too. Sound had also gone to wherever the air had disappeared to as the silence deafened me.

I tried to remind myself how much I hated the man in front of me as my body had kicked into autopilot. Those words he said were making me respond in a way I was not comfortable with. A way I knew he wanted. A way he would enjoy.

And I couldn't stop it because despite what I told myself, my feelings for this guy were so freaking twisted he still turned me on.

Fuck biology and its chemical reactions.

"That is not happening." Oh, thank God I didn't just strip down and offer myself to him. Ain't going to lie, it could have gone either way.

"You don't sound so sure."

"I'm positive. Like I would go there anyway. You were just about to have sexy time with someone else."

"But I didn't, and now here we are."

"I'm not the alternate, Jason."

"You *never* were the alternate, Angie."

"Stop. Stop talking." My body shook all over.

What did he mean; I was never the alternate? I was never his first choice either.

"Ask me why I was with that girl." He lowered his head so his face was inches from mine. Too close. Way too close.

"No, I don't give a fuck."

"I was with her because I haven't had sex since the first night I saw you again. I can't function, Angie. It is way beyond fucked up. I want you, and I know I can't have you. And I have had a raging hard-on I can't seem to get rid of." His nose skated against the length of mine. I'd never heard the pain before. The underlying ache in his words, not that it could change what he did. Or where we were now.

"Am I supposed to be flattered?"

"No, you should be disgusted and you should leave." His mouth moved to beside my ear, his voice lowering to a whisper. "Why aren't you leaving, Angie?"

"I am." I nodded, knowing I needed to leave.

"Your feet haven't moved."

"They will."

"They better."

There was a snap. Like a band inside of me breaking and flicking me back, my body recovering before I lost my footing. And by some miracle in what I can only think confirms the existence of God, my feet moved toward the door and took me out of that room, my hands also worked as part of the team and shut the door behind me.

My head pounded in time with my accelerated heartbeat. I was confused, turned on and disgusted, and I had no idea which emotion would end up dominating. How could I want him after hearing that? There was something wrong with me. There had to be. Only some sick, twisted or deranged pervert would want that. And yet if I hadn't walked out that door I know I would have gone there. Why? Because all the messed up feelings swirling around were driving me insane and I just wanted to feel good, even for a while. Even if it was the wrong kind of good. Which is why I left. Which is why I needed to go far away from him. Which is why I was standing outside his door wanting to go back in.

Leave, Angie. Put your damn feet one in front of the other and walk away.

So I did.

And then I was gone.

'13

Jason

ANGIE SEEING THAT WAS NOT PART OF THE PLAN. NOT THAT IT should've mattered, she could screw whoever she wanted and so could I, but I was better than that. More careful. More discreet. And usually I was. This time, I hadn't given a shit. It wasn't like me. I wasn't Dan, even though I'd probably slept with twice the number of women he had.

She should never have been there.

The reasons of how it came to pass were still a mystery. I stared at my reflection in the bathroom mirror while the water ran over my hands. The temperature so hot I wasn't sure I wasn't going to be rocking third degree burns. The messed up situation echoed in my head as I cut the water, toweled off and went back to the living room. Why the hell did she have to be in the fucking room? I would have assumed she'd been tied up with one of the douchebags. It looked like that's where it was heading.

Yeah, I was going to need a drink. And not a beer.

The bar fridge offered a bunch of options, all of them tiny. Still a drink was a drink, so I opted for the scotch. I opened the bottle and threw it back, the need for a glass non-existent; the damn thing was barely bigger than a swallow.

The burn down my throat felt nice but didn't last long; it also wasn't even close to making a dent in what I needed. There was always the gym, running it out had always been my go-to solution. Well, *that* or sex, and seeing as sex was not going to happen, a run was probably the best option.

Not that my dick understood. No, I was still rock solid. And it hadn't been from Kristen, not even fucking close.

As I toed-off my boots and stripped off my shirt, I figured the run probably wasn't the best idea. Drinking and exercising, not a good mix. Not unless you were on *The Jersey Shore.* Of which I wasn't. So I guess that was out for the night too.

The next bottle I snagged was bourbon, because that was smart. I figured might as well mix it up, it's not like I gave a shit as long as I could continue drinking. Which I was going to have to stop the minute I exhausted my supply of tiny bottles.

This was so fucked up. Downing liquor like I was Ozzy Osborne. Any minute the assholes from *VH1's Behind the Music* were going to bust through the door to interview me about my fall from grace. Might as well make the fall epic, go hard or go fucking home.

My ass sunk into the leather couch, the one near the desk Angie had jack-in-a-boxed out from, and I picked up the phone. My fingers hit the call button, the one that would connect me to room service.

"Good evening. This is Claire, how can I help you?" A sweet, bright voice answered.

My fingers squeezed against the bridge of my nose, the pressure building in my head. I didn't want sweet, *sweet* had just walked out the damn door, so the reminder was just an irritation I didn't want.

"Yeah, I want a real bottle of bourbon. Not this shit in the mini bar." My voice was harder than it needed to be. And yet I couldn't make myself give a shit, such was the intensity of my jacked-up mood. *Fuck you, Em.* I flipped off the air as I apparently started to lose my mind.

BACK STAGE

'Cause that's what sane people do, tell a memory to go fuck itself. Seriously losing my grip.

"Sir?" Sweet-voice Claire called me to attention. Her tone hinting that she'd asked something. She'd probably asked if I wanted a pair of forceps to pull my head out of my ass. Valid question.

"Sorry, what was that?" I asked, trying to keep the bite on the sidelines. It wasn't her fault she'd drawn the short straw and been on the other end of the phone.

"I asked if *Maker's Mark* would be acceptable."

Of course that's what she'd ask, because it would make sense that she would want to clarify my order. What any normal person would assume. Pity no one in the room was currently flying the normal flag.

"Yes, send it up." I resisted the urge to ask for a bottle of Grey Goose as a chaser. Probably over kill, I wasn't an alcoholic despite my fucked-up behavior.

"Sir, might I suggest something from our extensive menu."

Nice. She hadn't apparently got the memo about me not needing a voice of reason. Or a burger and fries. Both which I hadn't ordered.

"No food, just the bourbon, and I'll take it without the side judgment as well." I really was an asshole. Not sure how anyone thought otherwise.

"Sir, I wasn't implying ... I'm sorry. Of course, right away."

The call ended and I tossed the phone onto the desk, not bothering to hang it back on the base. It's one of the things I had marked on my list of don't-give-a-fuck.

The knock at the door came pretty quick, which was just as well because I was all geared to drink myself into oblivion. Putting it off was more an inconvenience than anything; so the sooner I got started, the better.

I yanked the door open, ready to get my party for one started.
Motherfucker.

"Angie, what are you doing here? You need to go."

She could not be here, especially not now.

"No." She didn't even flinch, her hands on her hips, the same fuck-you she usually gave to me.

"What the hell did you say to me?"

"I said *no*, Jason. I'm sure it's been a while since you've heard it but I don't give a fuck it's not what you want to hear."

Well then, she had my attention.

She moved forward and I hoped she didn't trip on my jaw as she passed through the doorway and walked into the suite.

"Do you still want to have sex with me?" She moved closer, her breath hot on my face as she leaned into me. No booze that I could smell. At least one of us was sober.

Wait a minute, how many of those little bottles did I drink?

"Yes." The word was out of my mouth before I had a chance to stop it. Me being honorable tonight wasn't going to happen.

"Why?" Her eyes nailed me, and I had to concentrate to stay upright.

"Because you're beautiful, and I can't seem to stop myself from wanting you."

"Okay." She nodded once, her hands still planted on her hips.

"What exactly are you saying okay to?" The instructions would be good right about now. I'd already said I wasn't a chick-whisperer.

"To have sex." No blushing, no blinking, no flick of the hair. Her eyes on me and she was dead serious.

"Woooahhhhhh. Did you not tell me how much you couldn't stand me?"

"I think I also mentioned hate."

"So why the hell are you agreeing to sex?" This had to be a trap. Any minute she was going to whip out a machete and slice my balls off. Or my dick. Maybe both. I'm sure she already had the plaque picked to have them mounted.

"Because I want to, and this time at least I know that all I am getting is a fuck. There is something freeing about knowing where you stand." She moved closer, the familiar smell of her shampoo invading my nose. Any chance I had of saying no to her was slipping away.

BACK STAGE

"Angie, trust me. You do not want this."

Translation, we are both going to regret this in the morning and this time around I can't get in my fucking car and drive away.

"How about you don't tell *me* what I do or do not want, and take off your damn jeans and do what we both are so desperate to do."

Well I guess some things had changed. Her mouth, for one. Not that I was complaining. It was completely fucking hot.

"This is a bad idea." Actually, in the history of bad ideas, right here was numero uno.

"I know, and I don't care."

She slammed her mouth on mine, her tits pushing against me. Her hands, they were on a downward trip as they slid down my back and grabbed my ass. She was angry and aggressive, and I was so turned on my balls ached.

"Angie." My hand fisted her hair as my tongue explored her mouth. She tasted so fucking amazing, I wasn't sure I'd ever be able to stop.

"Shut up." Her teeth bit down on my lower lip as she pushed me back. The sting of pain smacked my mouth, followed by the slight coppery taste of blood.

"You fucking bit me?" My hand grabbed a handful of her hair and pulled her lips from mine, her eyes jacked-up on lust and rage.

"You deserved it. You were talking too much and if we're just fucking, there doesn't need to be any small-talk." She smirked, licking her lips with freaking satisfaction.

"You want to be fucked? Is that why you're here?" I kept her hair wrapped around my hand as I pulled her head further back, giving me access to her neck. Her pulse hammered away underneath the olive skin.

"Uh-uh." She struggled to nod, my grip on her hair keeping her head from moving.

"You better know what you are signing up for, Angie, because I'm beyond the point of stopping."

"Then stop being a pussy, and give me your cock."

Control went out the window. My hands, my mouth, they were clawing at her like I was a savage. I *was* a savage, my fucking need for her so off the chain that I wasn't sure I wasn't going to stroke out.

That bullshit top she'd been wearing, the one that curved around her tits within an inch of their life was in my hand and torn from her body. I didn't even give a shit I'd literally ripped her clothes off. It was in my way and I needed her naked. Her beautiful tits heaved up and down in her lacey black bra as I reached down to her ass and yanked at the zip of her tight black skirt. My concern for its welfare also did not rank highly.

She was so hot I couldn't think straight, her skirt dropped down to her ankles and gave me a better look at all her marked skin. She hadn't been afraid of the pain. The color stretched not only up and down her arms, but also across her ribs and down her hips. It was beyond stunning; it was the most beautiful thing I'd ever seen.

The ice bucket moment came just as I'd snapped her bra from her chest. The shredded material still in my hand as the knock at the door happened.

Fuck.

She stopped and grabbed my face. "That better not be a fucking booty call, Jason."

That thing I'd discussed earlier, about her cutting off my balls, she had a look that spelled out the desire to do just that.

"It's room service, I ordered bourbon before you got here."

My brilliant idea, not so fucking awesome now. Who needed a drink anyway, I'd take my high in the form of the smoking, hot woman in front of me.

"Give me a second." My hand reluctantly dropped her damaged bra and I made for the door. It was more than just an interruption. It was a wake-up call. One that I had no doubt she would take. Which was going to be a problem, because letting her walk out of my door tonight was not going to be easy.

"Hey." I cracked open the door, my body blocking the view of the interior of the room.

"Hi, just delivering your drink, sir." Some glorified bell-hop stood

BACK STAGE

beside a silver cart, the *Maker's Mark* sitting on top with a bucket of ice and a couple of tumblers.

"Just leave it there." I reached into my back pocket and pulled out a tip. "I'll grab it in a minute."

"Of course, sir." Was what he said, but his face read differently. More like the man was questioning my sanity for leaving a bottle of booze out in the hall and why I wasn't giving him access to my room.

All valid.

He took his suspicions and wisely didn't ask questions, turning around and heading toward the elevator. The cart being pulled into the room with one hand while I held the door ajar with the other.

Angie was probably getting her clothes back on and getting ready to bail at that very moment but there wasn't a chance anyone was getting the opportunity to look at her while she did it.

Nope, not a chance in hell.

"*Maker's*, nice choice." She wandered over to the cart and picked up a couple cubes of ice and tossed them into a glass. "I hate *Jack Daniel's*."

Not only was she *not* dressed, her tits still on display, but she'd lost her panties as well. Her body, naked, except for the obscene pair of black heels she'd walked in with.

"You're naked." My hands cracked the red wax as I twisted the cap off the bottle.

Her hand tilted her ice filled glass toward me. "Yep."

"So, that last minute time out didn't change your mind?" The amber liquid poured out of the bottle, filling her glass.

"Nope." Her mouth popped off the P before she raised the glass to her lips and took a drink.

My fingers wrapped around the glass and stole it from her hand, not bothering to pour my own. "I like you like this." I took a mouthful, as my eyes steamrolled over the curves of her body. My dick punched out against the zip of my jeans in a show of unanimous appreciation.

"Well, unless you expect me to fuck myself." She didn't even bother covering her tits, her tight pink nipples waiting for me to lick them as she pulled the glass from my hand. "You're going to have to get naked too." She took another mouthful before putting the glass down on the cart. "And unlike your last little *friend,* I'm going to need something more than just your hand to get me off."

My mouth slammed against hers, the taste of bourbon and possibly regret, feeding me as I grabbed her ass and hauled her against my erection.

"That feel like enough of a *something* for you?"

I didn't give her a chance to answer, instead lifting her off the ground and wrapping her legs around my waist. The resistance she offered, non-existent.

As much as I wanted to unzip my jeans and plunge my cock into her right there, the fact we hadn't made it to my room yet was a problem. The shared space of our penthouse apartment, not a suitable location for it to all go down.

"Jase." Her lips sucked at my throat as I opened the door to my bedroom, kicking it shut after we'd walked through the doorway.

"I didn't think you wanted an audience and they're going to be back soon." There was no need to clarify the *they.* I'd been surprised *they* hadn't arrived already. Saying hi to Troy, Dan and their ladies while my cock was buried inside Angie wouldn't have gone down too well. Especially not with Troy. Best the big guy didn't know, because me not having her tonight wasn't an option.

"These need to be off." Angie grabbed at my jeans as I tossed her onto the mattress, my body joining hers on the bed.

She wasn't gentle, her fingers clawing at the denim in a bid to get them down. Her short fingernails my saving grace, with the abrasions on my thighs being nothing more than a few red scratches. The sting of it juicing me up more.

My boxers were the next thing to go, her hands giving me an assist while mine were otherwise occupied. I couldn't get enough, my fingers on her skin setting me on fire. It was a deep fucked-up need to touch every single inch and I felt completely out of control. My hand snaked down between her legs as I sunk two fingers into her hot, wet core.

She moaned against my mouth, which I'd been keeping busy kissing her lips before migrating south to her tits, my teeth gently biting her nipples. The noises she made threatening to make me blow my load before we'd even got to the actual sex.

It was too much.

Wishing there was another way to get a rubber without needing to stop touching her, I cursed out a breath as I reached into my nightstand and pulled out a condom. My intention of making her come with my hand or my mouth first, no longer working for me. I'd do it later, and I would make it worth her while but if I didn't fuck her right now, I was going to lose my damn mind. And probably the use of my cock, which had gotten so hard, it was actually starting to hurt.

I sheathed my dick in the condom, my hand smoothing the latex down the length of my shaft. Her body jacked up off the mattress in protest, her legs kicking open to reveal the slickness between them. It was beautiful, seeing her so wet and ready for what I was about to give her, I needed a second just to look. She took advantage of my distraction by reaching her hand down between us, palming my cock and giving me a stroke. I needed to fuck her. Like, yesterday.

"This is probably going to be faster than I want." I smacked her ass as I gained control of her legs. "But we can do slow later."

"Fuck. Me." The words jutted out through her gritted teeth.

And I'll be damned if that isn't exactly what I intended to do.

While one of my hands peeled hers from my cock, the other one held my dick steady while I drove into her in one swift movement. Smothering her body so completely I wasn't sure I wasn't crushing her.

"Agh!" Her hands griped my shoulders as her body tensed, her pussy gripping me tight like a vice. Her tits pressed hard against my chest.

"I thought you said you wanted to be fucked?" I drove into her again, this time her body easing up on the resistance, the slide of my dick getting easier with each thrust.

Her head thrashed back against the pillow as I slowly picked up momentum. "Yes." She screamed biting against my shoulder. "Harder."

That sweet eighteen-year-old I'd had in the back of my car was not the same girl I was currently screwing. She was different, and it wasn't just her body that had changed, it was her whole attitude.

She grabbed my ass, pulling me deeper into her. Her hips lifting to meet each thrust, pushing me right where I needed to be. I couldn't have talked even if I'd wanted to, our verbal exchange limited to primal noises. The need to be with her was so intense I thought I might actually blackout.

"Oh God," she screamed as her body finally gave in, her pussy milking me as she came hard underneath me. Her body shook as she took all of me, the pulsing against my shaft undoing any hope I had of trying to make it last.

"Fuck." It felt like every single nerve ending simultaneously exploded as my body tensed, my load filling her as I panted against her throat.

Fuck.

Both literally and figuratively, we were fucked.

And it had been so, so good.

"Angie?" My tongue traced the length of her jaw, more hungry for her than before. There was no way I wasn't going to do that again. "Are you okay?"

"Just give me a minute." Her eyelids slowly cracked open as I eased off her, another tremble shaking her body. "It's just been a while." Her satisfied smile enough validation that it had been just as good for her.

"Since you've had sex, or since you came like that?" I wasn't sure which answer I was hoping to hear, either one making me feel fucking awesome. I slowly eased my semi-hard dick out of her—the bastard already limbering up for round two. The discarding of the used condom was a necessary evil but I took care of it quickly so I could climb back into bed and continue the conversation. Her body curled up against mine the minute my back had hit the mattress.

"Oh I can come like that anytime I want, it just usually takes a lot of

BACK STAGE

work and a man isn't involved." Her fingers traced the grooves of my chest, slithering down to my abs.

I bucked out a laugh. "Well then you've been sleeping with the wrong kind of men."

"Yeah, it seems to be a habit for me."

She didn't smile; the lighthearted tone of the conversation taking a dive. That satisfied glow she'd had plastered on her face was also MIA with my stupid attempt at a joke, sounding like a personal taunt.

"I didn't mean it like that." Could we rewind ten seconds so I could pull my foot out of my mouth?

"Actually, that's exactly how you meant it." Her eyes nailed me in a way that was not going to let me off the hook. "But it's okay, the *wrong guy* usually gives the better orgasms."

Bravo. Another backhanded compliment courtesy of Angie Morelli. It was really impressive how good she was at it. Almost made me want to beg for more.

"Is that why you're here, using me so you don't have to masturbate?" *Because straight up, that would not be a problem for me.*

"Yes, that's why I'm here."

If she was on the level with me or not, I had no idea. The let's-just-fuck routine, a complete one-eighty from where we'd both been twenty-four hours ago. Surely no one does that. She hated me; she'd even said so. Who has sex with someone they didn't like? It made zero fucking sense.

"What are you thinking about?" She moved closer against me, her lips kissing my neck. And as much as this didn't make sense, I would rather die than ask her to stop.

"That I generally don't have sex with people who hate me. I'd like to avoid the whole being-smothered-in-my-sleep thing. Call me sensitive."

In all honesty, I couldn't say that if she did give my face some pillow action while I was catching some z's that I wouldn't have gone happy. That alone should have been enough of a warning to prove how bad of an idea this whole *scenario* was. But my dick, it seemed, had a death wish.

Her face broke into an amused grin as she commenced laughing her ass off. "You think this was some sneaky diversionary tactic to try to kill you? Oh my god, that's hysterical. I'm a musician not a CIA operative. And how conceited are you? No man would ever be worth jail time."

"Good." My hand slowly slid down between her legs. "Now, get on your knees and let me do that again."

14

Angie

THIS TIME, I WAS THE ONE WHO LEFT.

It was two in the morning, or so said the obnoxious clock beside Jase's bed. Its stupid illuminated face taunted me, singing out with judgment, "Well done dumbass, you just slept with the enemy."

I'd never intended to stay. Sleeping over had never been part of the plan. Hell, fucking him had never been part of the plan, but that's exactly what happened. My big plan went right out the window when I saw him and before I knew it, I had convinced myself that this was the right thing to do. It wasn't beautiful or romantic, there were no whispered *I love yous* and there sure as hell wasn't any slow seduction. It was erotic and rough; both of us primed for explosion, which is exactly what we got. Sex. We weren't making love. It was pure unrestrained sex.

What the hell had I been thinking?

Anger.

That was the only explanation as to why I would sleep with a guy who was just about to sleep with someone else. Who does that? Who decides that they are happy to be the next one in line? That had never been me. I should be disgusted. I should be sitting in a shower so hot it peels the top layer of skin from my body. Because that's the way I'd felt the first time I'd slept with Jason. Or at least, how I'd felt the next day.

Rage. Which was like anger but amplified, so at least I was consistent. That is why my dumbass self decided that the only hope I had of getting over Jason was doing exactly what he'd done to me. Use him for sex, but this time, on my terms. Taking back the control.

It made more sense in my head.

Mind blowing sex—which is what we'd had the last time, so I was hoping that hadn't been a one-time deal—then out the door. Only this time, I would be the one walking.

But all the good intentions in the world couldn't fight the all-consuming fatigue I'd felt after. Screwing him *one time* and bailing hadn't played out quite like I planned, oh no, with neither of us satisfied after just a taste. And the sex, was indescribable.

Maybe it was because we had been avoiding each other for so long, maybe it was because I was so angry, but that great sex we'd had all those years ago was like a watered down *Kool-Aid* version of what we'd just had. I'd never been fucked like that. My body actually ached. At least I could skip the gym tomorrow, lord knows riding Jason Irwin burnt more calories than the elliptical.

So when my eyes couldn't stay open a minute longer, I rested my head on the pillow allowing myself a twenty to thirty minute nap. No harm in that. And then I would wake up refreshed from my power nap and walk my ass out the door. All in-your-face, just as I had planned.

I wasn't supposed to stay the night.

Panic woke me. Or maybe it had been the fact I was dying from an obscenely high core temperature. Probably the latter given that Jason's arms and legs tangled around mine were making me feel like I was in a hot dude cocoon. It might have been pleasant if there hadn't been a history. One where I had fantasized about systematically removing all his internal organs starting with his heart. More to see if he had one. Which I assumed he did because I could feel it sarcastically beating against my back. Ugh.

Being awake presented new problems, ones I hadn't had to face while I had been blissfully ignorant in dreamland. My escape was the most pressing issue and how the hell I was going to unravel myself from Mr. Big Cock.

Of course that wasn't his real name, but honestly I'd forgotten how impressive it was. Not that I had actually looked at it the first time, I had been too excited that he was finally going to sleep with me, nervous too and the vodka I'd had hadn't helped either. Then, in between then and now was the flood of *average dick* I had been subjected to. Nothing noteworthy, that's for sure. All of which contributed to diluting the memory of *it*. Which was such a shame because it really was spectacular in all its pink perfect glory. Which is why I thought up that little term of endearment.

While he impaled me.
With his h-u-g-e cock.
Repeatedly.
Expertly.
Amazingly.
It had not been a problem for me at all.
The problem *was*, getting out and getting gone.

It started off slow. More like a little shimmy of my shoulder to see if my moving would wake him.

It didn't.

Which meant I was able to graduate to wriggle, freeing the upper part of my body from his huge arms. Seriously, the man was tall, he had the wingspan of an albatross; this was not an easy feat.

Still sleeping. Thank you, Jesus.

Next were the legs, this carried a nine-point-eight difficulty rating because his leg was actually hooked around mine. Oh and his cock was hard and pressing into my hip, which meant I had to focus on the task at hand instead of leaning down and giving him a blowjob. Because that would be helpful—not.

Success. I had wiggled, duked and jived my way out of the spoon-of-death, and had gently been able to lower my feet to the floor. My prayers to the gods of good times continued to allow me my walk of shame uninterrupted. *Please do not wake up.*

Thankfully, he didn't.

Other problems, which presented themselves later, were the state of my clothes. Or should I say, the lack of my clothes. The cute top I had been wearing—torn in half. My pretty black Victoria Secret's bra—toast. My black skirt—a busted out zipper, and a split down the center seam. Oh look, my panties were still in one piece. And I found both my shoes. Wow, there was a silver lining after all. Unfortunately I was not a showgirl in Vegas, which meant my useable items did not an outfit make. Shit!

As quiet as I was able—which was difficult being I was uttering the word *fuck* under my breath repeatedly—I cracked open one of the closets and prayed the man had something I could wear. Like a damn designer dress, worth a few hundred dollars to make up for the clothes he just destroyed. Asshole.

Sadly his closet was not lined with anything other than jeans, shirts, T-shirts and other *man* apparel, so I settled for a T-shirt that was about ten sizes to big that very elegantly said "I Don't Give a Fuck." The irony. Ha. Ha. Ha. I was so freaking funny. The bottoms were a problem. Maybe I could pretend the T-shirt was a dress? It was long enough. Except my room was situated ten floors below the one I was on. Which meant walking out of here, getting into an elevator and—yeah not going to work.

I begrudgingly threw on a pair of his sweatpants as well. Fucking ridiculous. Even with the drawstring pulled as tight as I could, they'd barely stayed up. Sure, that wasn't obvious that I had no clothes. Well at least I wasn't naked. See that's twice with the silver lining. So much optimism I thought I might choke. Which is exactly what I needed to do to myself as soon as I left this room.

With my heels in my hand, and hoping I hadn't pushed my luck with my *Fashion Police* critique, I crept out of Jason's room and into the living area. He slept right through it. Didn't even move a muscle. His sleeping like a stone really was an occupational hazard, and should be addressed however. I could have robbed him blind. The clothes I had taken didn't count as stealing though; they were restitution.

Yes! Home free, baby. With Jase's door shut securely behind me all I needed to do was walk across the large, dimly lit living room and I was in the clear. Thank you Jesus, it was easier than I thought. Oh, apart from having to pull a Houdini to escape his bed, and the improv on the wardrobe. Who was I kidding? Just get the hell out while the getting was good.

"Angie?"

Crap. So much for a clean getaway.

"Hey, I thought it was you." Megs lifted herself off the couch and strode closer toward me, obviously needing a front row seat to my mortification.

"Hi." One of my hands did a lame wave while the other, still holding my shoes, also held up my pants. I mean Jason's pants. Ha. I had literally gotten into his pants. More irony. My lips spread into a smile before I could stop them.

"Um. So, interesting shirt." Her eyes dipped down and gave me an all-over inspection, the edges of her lips twitching with amusement.

"I had an accident and needed to borrow something of Jason's." Lame. I didn't know why I even tried.

"Did your accident involve a penis?" Megs bit her lip as her grin widened.

"Huh? What?" I scoffed, trying to sound surprised and indignant. No one was fooled.

"There's a condom wrapper in your hair." Her fingers gently reached into my hair and pulled the foil *Trojan* packet that had seen fit to lodge itself there. I officially hated the universe. Fuck you very much, Jason Irwin.

"Oh. That. Well. We had sex."

She really didn't need the confirmation. No one was that stupid. Except for Jason, who should have had a better system for trash disposal. Another reason why I should hate him.

"Cool. So, you want some ice cream?" She didn't miss a beat, just lifted the tub in her hands, completely cool and unaffected. "I couldn't sleep. Heartburn is a bitch. The stupid book I'm reading said ice cream is supposed to help but I think it's just some bullshit old wives tale. I'm totally going to have an ass the size of Texas. I don't even care." She laughed flipping open the lid and waved her spoon.

Where the hell was I? Was I hallucinating this? Who has these kinds of conversations? Did I miss the part where she gave me judgey eyes, which usually complemented the you-are-such-a-whore scowl? And ice cream? This was just too crazy.

"I'm sorry, what?" Yeah, because all of that conversation couldn't have just happened like it did. I must have knocked my head one too many times on the headboard. It's not like it couldn't be a possibility.

"Ice cream." She said the words slowly and looked around for a spare spoon. "It's vanilla, so not that exciting but we can call and get—"

"No, I got that. About the ice cream. I mean, I just told you I slept with Jase. We had sex." It didn't sound any less shady the second time, not sure why I was pushing the issue.

"Oh, sorry. Did you want to talk about it? Was he an asshole? Do you want me to wake Troy? He can yell at him if you like."

"No. God, No." Wasn't sure exactly what I was saying no to, probably to all of it. Especially the part where she told Troy, that part deserved a big N to the Oh. "I'm not used to people being so—" What was the word? "Nice to me."

"Why wouldn't I be nice? Troy's told me all about you, and if you are important to him, you're important to me. Besides, don't let this normal exterior fool you, I am completely crazy underneath so I'm in no position to judge anyone. Unless they are wearing bad shoes. Then they are kind of opening themselves up for it. People who wear nice clothes and then skimp on the shoes can't be trusted. I guarantee you, they're hiding something." She had barely taken a breath.

"Wow, you are crazy, and I really like that." And best of all, it had taken some of the weirdness out of the situation. The one where I was standing in the shared living space of Troy, Dan and Jason, wearing clothes I had *borrowed* from the man I'd just slept with. And then left.

"Aw, thanks. Do you want to borrow some clothes? All my stuff is maternity but I'm sure we can ask Ash for something." She moved toward her cell, which was lying on an end table. Her offer to *ask Ash* probably involved waking her, which wasn't ideal. There was no need for anyone else to get drawn into the circus of crazy.

"No it's fine. I'm just going to go down to my room. I'm sure he won't miss them." My hands gripped the sweatpants tight, hoping I could just get to my room without having to make any more post-sex confessionals *or* flashing my ass. Hopefully achieving both was not out of the realm of possibility.

"Alrighty then. Have a good night." Megs waved her spoon in lieu of her hand. Her quest for ice cream more important than my undignified slink to the door.

My hand hesitated on the doorknob, looking over my shoulder before I left. "Thanks, Megs. It was really nice talking to you. Oh and please don't tell Troy. I'm a big girl, I can handle myself."

The one heart-to-heart Troy and I had shared about Jason was more than enough. Me, telling him I'd slept with Jase again, would not be happening. Ever.

"Sure, sure. No problem. And if you ever need anything, you can talk to me if you want. It doesn't have to go any further." She gave me a warm smile. Maybe I could actually have some female friends and it be okay. Ash and Megs both seemed so genuine.

"Thanks. Bye." I gave her a smile on account my hands were occupied, the door, my shoes and the saga of Jase's pants—a wave wasn't happening.

"Bye," she mumbled, her mouth full of vanilla. The door closed behind me to the view of another spoon wave.

Bed. I need a bed. This time, it had better be my own.

"'Promiscuous' by *Nelly Furtado* does not sound like a fuck you song, Angie." Rusty had walked into my hotel room all guns blazing. The text message with our new song suggestion that I'd sent in the early hours of the morning had obviously been received.

"I like the song," I yawned, my mind and body still tired from last night. No amount of sleep was going to change that. "I think it would be a good addition to the set." And give a clear message, which is exactly why I wanted to sing it.

"Firstly, it's a two person song." He sat himself on the small sofa opposite the queen size bed. Our allocated rooms were tiny compared to the Power Station suite I had the pleasure of seeing. "So unless you're planning on doing the half-half thing and flipping around on stage like a flapjack, I'm assuming you're going to need me to do *Timbaland's* part. Secondly, I thought we agreed we were doing the *Beastie Boy's* "Hey, Fuck You." I mean, it doesn't get more prefect than that, it actually says fuck you in the title."

We had agreed to do the Beastie Boy's song, both of us laughing hysterically at how perfect it would be. And it had been, even some of the lines were appropriate. Except then things changed and it wasn't what I wanted to say anymore.

"Rus, I did something bad."

Rusty blew out a long, slow breath and then stood up. "Give me a second to grab a shovel, and change my kicks. I just got these and I don't want to get them dirty." He pointed to his new boots, no doubt purchased with the sizeable advance we had all received.

"You don't need a shovel. I haven't killed anyone." Not unless you counted my common sense in which case, that was most definitely in need of a burial.

"The shovel is to beat you over the head." He rolled his eyes. "The song. You've either gone *there* or are going *there*. And in case there is any doubt as to where *there* is, it's the fucking keyboard player for the band who is paying our ticket right now. And, he's already broken your heart once before." He shoved his hand through his hair for good measure. "So much *bad* in the situation, even I'm washing my hands of it.

"You are such a drama queen, you know that? I went there, but it's different now. I know what I'm getting into." I could totally handle Jason this time around. No feelings involved at all. Unless you counted the sexual ones that still tingled in morning at the mention of his name, but they did not count at all.

"Same thing is going to happen." He gave me a hard stare. "I don't even need a magic eight ball. It's going to end the same way it started. Badly."

His feelings were clear. And I probably wasn't going to get his support, but I had already made the decision. Good or bad, it was my mistake to make. Again.

"I slept with him, and you know what, I am not in love with him anymore. It was like hitting the release valve. Maybe I had only thought I was in love with him back then, I was young. It's not like people end up with the same person they were in love with when they were eighteen. Maybe it was just a crush, and him leaving had hurt me so bad because I was confused and he made me feel used. And that's the hurt I was feeling. Not love. I don't know. I just know that I don't feel that way anymore. I don't love him. I don't need him to love me back. And I got that by being with him and seeing that it was just sex between us. Which is okay, if both parties are aware of it."

As crazy as it or I sounded, everything I said to Rusty was the truth. I didn't feel that way anymore. The love that I may have felt, that had been over a long time ago. This was different. I was different. This time around, I was okay with just having his body. And what a fine body it was.

"Sounds to me like you plan on doing it more than once." Rusty's question was one I had already asked myself. Did it still count as walking away if I requested a repeat performance? He hadn't called me this morning. There was no banging on my door demanding to know why I had left. Not even a note delivered by one of his *people* demanding his clothes back. FYI he wasn't getting the T-shirt back, I'd pretty much decided it was my new sleep shirt.

"Would it be so bad? We actually had fun and look, I'm fine." I twirled in an effort to demonstrate how fine I was, in case my big cheesy grin wasn't enough. "I bit him." The memory made the grin even wider.

"Ew. I don't want to hear your kinky vampire fantasies." Rusty held up his hands, our show-and-tell over already.

"Are you worried I'll turn?" Not that I was in any danger of me going all *Jolie* and wearing a vial of blood around my neck, unless the vampires looked like those dudes from *True Blood*.

"Nah, you're Italian. You guys eat too much garlic to worry about that," he said seriously, like vampires existed and if they did, there was a danger of me becoming one.

"You're so weird. It's a good thing I love you." I threw my arms around him and pulled him in for a hug. He was the one person who I could get touchy- feely with and it not feel weird. Although if I was going to continue this Jase thing, that was probably going to have to change.

"And I love you too. Even if you are going to make the most epic mistake of all mankind." He hugged me back.

"Thanks, Rusty." For always being there, I finished off in my head. See, I had the perfect relationship, we just didn't have sex and if I could fill that void with Jase, then it might just be the perfect solution.

"Alright, now let's learn your fucking song."

15

Jason

PROMISCUOUS.

The song, I meant. Angie and Rusty had duo-ed tonight, the crowd once again loving their take on the *Nelly Furtado* tune. And damn if it didn't send a shiver down to my balls hearing her tease me with every lyric. The roll of her hips enough to make me blow my load. Hell, there wasn't a man in the audience that wouldn't have gone home with her tonight, including yours truly.

That sweet girl I'd first met—the one who had been all shy about touching my cock—gone. In her place was a straight up sex bomb that blew my mind. If her body hadn't been lethal enough, the fucking attitude on her tipped it into a hazard level that there was no coming back from. I wasn't sure if I should be thankful she hadn't left more claw marks on my back or praying I'd get another chance. Intense didn't even come close. It was like waving a lit match in a barrel of gunpowder, unstable with the blast capacity guaranteed to level a city block. And fuck me if I didn't want to be there for that fucking detonation.

The whole-bad-idea shit my brain had been preaching since the first minute I laid eyes on her was null and void. I didn't care if I ended up in a freaking ditch—no doubt at her doing—it would be fucking worth it. There was zero chance of me heeding those alarm bells as I put myself once again on a crash course with fucking disaster.

Angie had ghosted at some point through the night. I'd woken up to a neat pile of her torn clothes on the side of my bed where *she* had previously been. She would have no doubt been pissed; cussing me out for ruining her clothes, and the smile automatically crept across my face. Missing it had been the only part of *that* situation which had sucked. Just her calling me an asshole was enough to get me hard, and fuck me if that wasn't messed up. Maybe all those years of screwing around had made me depraved? As long as I didn't start needing to start jamming electrodes to my balls just to get off I guess it wasn't too bad. Besides, normal was relative and there wasn't a lot of run-of-the-mill hanging around where I was currently kicking it.

"Hi Jason, I'm a massive fan." Some random girl flung her arms around me, her hands getting cozy with my back. It was the usual backstage routine, meeting people after the show. Usually I had no problem with it—I loved meeting the fans—tonight, not so much. Her body pressed tight against mine spelling out exactly what kind of *fan* she was. "Wow, you are like really fit," she mumbled as her head rested on my chest.

"Thanks. I like to run." I smiled back, already sick of this dog and pony show we had to do. I gave her arms a subtle yank as I peeled her off me, her brown hair flicking down across her hazel eyes. She was pretty, I'll give her that, but I had no interest in getting any more *appreciation* other than the hug she seemed hell bent on making linger. "What did you say your name was?"

"Shelley." She pushed out her tits proudly, probably hoping that would get her more attention. Not likely, considering my head was with a dark haired, dark eyed singer who I hadn't seen since she'd left the stage.

"Awesome, Shelley. Glad you enjoyed the show. Have you met the rest of the band?" My eyes darted to the others, each of them engaged in some other conversation or posing for a photo. Great.

Not sure why I was trying to palm her off, it's not like any of the others were going to give poor Shelley what she was after. Of course I was speculating that the kind of autograph she wanted was one where my cock signed her pussy, but given that her hand was now squeezing my ass, I'd say it was a fairly safe assessment.

"I have." She grinned. "You're my favorite." Her nose scrunched up in what I'm assuming was supposed to be adorable but mainly just looked like she was about to sneeze.

"Well thanks," I said with as much enthusiasm as I could without adding sarcasm, hoping I didn't roll my eyes. "Did you want a photo?"

"Actually ..." She bit her lip as her sentence was left trailing.

Here we go, the initiation of the conversation that would end with *do you want to fuck?* Surprising how many variations there were ranging from hey-let's-go-get-a-drink or I've-never-done-this-before-but ... and yet the end result was always the same.

"Hey, man, you cool to do a group photo?" Alex's hand tapped me on the shoulder.

I could have kissed the man, which was saying something seeing I didn't share lip action with dudes. His well-timed interruption saved me from having to listen to Shelley's bumbling attempt at trying to get me in the sack.

"Yeah, sure. Sorry, Shelley. You want me to sign anything?"

"Um. No. That's okay." Her face pinked with embarrassment, perhaps having second thoughts about what she was about to ask. "Maybe some other time."

"No problem. Thanks for coming out and seeing us. It was great meeting you." The standard goodbye fell out of my mouth with very little effort. I threw in a smile at the end to soften the blow.

"Bye." She reached up and gave me a kiss in what seemed like a last ditch surge of courage. Her lips off mine almost as quickly as they'd been on. She was definitely the I've-never-done-this-before girl, her smile almost splitting off her face as she scrambled back to a group of girls I assumed were her friends.

"Nice girl." Alex lifted his brow, the group giggling as they looked back at us, getting his attention. I'm sure the kiss was the topic of conversation, all one point five seconds of it.

"Yeah, thanks for that. I wasn't feeling it." My hand reached up to my neck and rubbed out a knot.

The gig tonight had been great. The energy was easy to feed off, and I had been a little more enthusiastic with my playing, hoping Angie had hung back and watched. Not sure if that made me pathetic or perverted—neither of them favorable.

"No problem. We've got a few more photos then we can bail." Alex tipped his chin to James who rounded up the rest of the guys. Troy and Dan joined us as we lined up ready for the happy snaps.

"So do you think Rusty is doing Angie?" Dan muttered under his breath as flashes from both professional cameras and smartphones started rapidly firing at us.

"Dan, seriously man," Troy managed to hiss out through his forced grin, the crowd in front of us having no idea what conversation was taking place.

The photographers took turns in calling to us to face their direction.

"Over here, guys."

Smile.

"Look this way please."

Smile.

"Did you see them on stage tonight?" Dan briefly broke formation, turning to Troy and smirking. "He is strumming more than just his fret board, I guarantee it."

"Can you just shut up and smile already?" I gritted out through my clenched jaw, hoping I was still maintaining a stupid grin.

Rusty was *not* doing Angie, that much I knew. But whether or not she was doing someone else was always a possibility. We sure as hell weren't dating, and I doubted a girl like that would be single for long. Not that I thought she would mess around on a dude if she was with someone. Still the prospect didn't make me feel warm and tingly thinking about it, that was for sure.

"Fine, but you know I'm right." He faced the group, big grin on his mug.

"Whatever, Dan." Troy elbowed him in the ribs as we took the last few shots.

"Thanks everyone." Lexi motioned everyone to the door, giving them a gentle that's-all-folks and directed them out of the room. Shelley gave me one last lingering wave before disappearing with the rest of the crowd.

"Daddy!" Grace ran into the room and launched herself at Alex, the big guy scooping her up into his arms. Not sure which of them more pleased to see each other, both of them wearing matching grins.

The room that had been emptied of fans, filled up with significant others. The guys gave their girls all kinds of attention while the kids ran around—their late afternoon naps meaning they were still up and pumped. It didn't bother me, I was happy they had all carved out their little slice of happiness, it just wasn't what I wanted for myself.

"Hey, Jase. You have a sore neck?" Megs nodded to my hand that unconsciously found its way back to the base of my skull. The tension build up not all entirely physical.

"Yeah, just a little tight." I flexed my head from left to right for good measure. Nope, none of it did any good.

"Was it the way you slept?" Megs gave me an overly enthusiastic smirk with a raised eyebrow for good measure. Maybe we'd been louder than I thought; noise control wasn't really where my mind had been. Not after I'd seen Angie naked. All the inked skin, and her perfect tits and ass. Yeah, you could have set fire to the bed and I probably still wouldn't have noticed.

"Yeah. Possible."

Definitely felt liked she knew more. Megs was a great girl, super sweet, but as far as being able to keep a poker face, she sucked. I mean seriously bad.

"Something you want to ask me, Megs?" No point in stringing it along.

"No, not really." The smile she was rocking told me otherwise.

"Hey." Troy wrapped his arms around her, his usual routine whenever she was close by.

"Troy Harris, I was trying to have a conversation." She pouted, nowhere near as annoyed as she was pretending to be. "Jason must have slept funny last night. He has a sore neck." The smile was back, as was my belief that she knew something.

"Oh yeah? Troy asked, kissing his wife, showing no interest in my nocturnal habits. "Poor Jase," he said with zero sympathy, shooting me a wink.

"Must have been that girl he brought home. What was with that? Not usually your thing." Dan weighed in, Ash smiling by his side. Whatever Megs knew, she'd shared it with her best friend. That much was clear.

"What is with everyone today? When did you all get so interested in me?" I deflected, thinking everyone needed to find another pet project other than my love life.

"Does Uncle Jase have a girlfriend?" Noah asked, obviously the kid picking up parts of the conversation. Awesome. Even the kids were against me. Fucking perfect.

"On that note, we might get the kidos to bed." James hauled his son up onto his shoulders ending the conversation. Hannah cradled a sleeping Jesse in her arms and was already heading toward the door.

"See you everyone." Lexi waved as she made for the exit, her interest more on getting her family back to the hotel rather than finding out who had been my bed partner. Alex and Grace followed close behind.

"Okay, so they're gone. Who was she?" Dan was back on the attack. I swear he was worse than an old woman. His interest nothing new, but somewhat irritating.

"None of your business." Was as much as he was going to get. At least for now.

"Screw who you want, just don't marry her yet. I've got ten G's riding on you waiting six months. And while I'm all for your happiness, Troy doesn't need any more of my money." The bastard grinned, his true motivation shining though.

"Dan, you can shove your ten grand. There is no way in hell I'm getting married in the next six years, let alone the next six months."

Or ever, which was more to the point. No fucking way. I'd rather pull my fingernails out one by one than get hitched.

"Famous last words," Dan laughed. "Just make sure whatever tail you're screwing doesn't get her claws in for the time being. That's all I'm asking. Be a team player."

"For fuck's sake. This is why I don't bring girls home." I ran my hands through my hair, wondering if the asshole was baiting me intentionally. Probably not. Dan wasn't that smart.

"You cool, brother?" Troy laughed, noticing my game was off. Not so long ago it had been his inability to get his act together that had been the talking point. He too was enjoying this shit a little too much.

"Yep. Laugh all you want, but you aren't getting dick out of me."

Megs laughed, as did Ashlyn. And I don't think it was over my use of the word *dick*. They'd both had seen plenty considering their husbands could barely keep their hands off them. The fact one of them was knocked up, evidence enough.

"Spill it, Megs Harris. And don't pretend like you don't have something to say." I eyeballed her, knowing she was close to breaking.

Out of the two of them—Ash and Megs—she was the weakest link, and the sooner we got it over with, the better. I assumed this was where she said she heard something last night. Those moans on both sides had been well and truly earned. Whatever. If they were looking to embarrass me then they were going to be waiting a while.

"I saw her. This morning. Coming out of your room. I'm sorry." She shot me a pained look of apology. Seems it wasn't speculation she'd been hiding after all. More like insider knowledge.

Fuck.

Yep, did not want to have this conversation.

"Who did you see, Megs?" Troy asked, his eyes looking between us for an answer.

"She saw Angie," I volunteered, knowing one way or another they were bound to find out. It's not like shit stayed under wraps in this band for long anyway. Worst group of people ever to try and keep a secret from. Their track record, fucking horrible.

"Ha, very funny asswipe. She hates you, there's a better chance of me sleeping with her than you." Dan folded his arms across his chest smugly.

"Dan!" Ashlyn shot back, not impressed by her husband's analysis. No one dug a hole like Dan. He really had a talent for that shit.

"No I didn't mean I would, I just mean probabilities." He tried to justify himself and reassure Ash. "Which would be zero. So her sleeping with Jase would be less than zero."

A few days ago, I might have agreed with him. Now. Well weren't we just a fucking example of never say never.

"Well then there must be some crazy quantum mechanics at work because that negative probability happened, asshole."

And there it was. The admission—for everyone to see. Whether or not Angie or I had wanted anyone to know was no longer relevant, because guess what? They fucking knew now. And I wasn't ashamed of it either. She and I had wanted the same thing, which is exactly what we got.

"What. The. Fuck." Dan paused between each word, with a look of complete disbelief. The are-you-serious vibe also coming from Troy.

"Don't start." My head shook as I went on the offensive. "And Troy before you go all losing your shit, no one took advantage of anyone. It was completely consensual."

"As long as you both know what you're doing, I'll keep out of it." The eyeball that came with it warning that his keeping-out was contingent on shit not going bad. Predictable.

"We're good. Trust me."

My words were solid but I wasn't sold, in fact I had no freaking idea what the hell I was doing. And as for us being *good*, another assumption that was made without evidence. Who knew where Angie would land on the whole situation. One thing was for sure, I was going to find out.

"Okay, new bet." Dan rubbed his hands together, shit eating grin back on his face. "Double or nothing says Angie kills him in his sleep."

Well that was fun.

Still, not as bad as I'd assumed it would have gone down. Even Troy had kept the warnings to a minimal, well for now at least.

Ash and Megs—those two were going to be trouble. I could already see how freaking pleased they were. They'd been hell bent on hooking me up with someone for god knows how long. My solo routine the reason for most of the grief they threw my way. Of course they were probably reading more into it than there was, i.e. Angie and I weren't looking to buy matching bath towels anytime soon. But if it got them off my ass and quelled the why-don't-you-have-a-girlfriend discussion, then that was just a bonus. Who knew if Angie was even interested in a repeat. Let alone an extended performance.

"You lost, asshole?" The devil herself stepped out from the shadows. She was alone and looking more incredible than the last time I saw her. Her dark hair loose but pinned away from her face, her body barely covered by a tight, black dress.

"I could say the same for you. Your set finished hours ago."

The rest of the band had left, grabbing a ride back to the hotel, but I liked to hang back at the venue after the show a little sometimes. Like the running, it gave me a reality check of sorts, and if ever I needed one, it was tonight.

"I was watching you." She moved closer, her body showing a dangerous amount of exposed skin.

The area we were in was secluded, filled with road cases that would soon be loaded onto a truck for our next gig. The roadies were too preoccupied with tearing down the stage to be worried about shit they'd already packed away.

"Really. You channeling your inner stalker?" My smile was automatic as was my feet moving closer toward her.

"Yeah. Figured you watched me, it's only fair." She shrugged, the smile tugging at her lips. And God help me if that smile didn't make me want to take her right here.

"So you left this morning without saying goodbye." I tilted her chin toward me, my eyes locked onto hers.

"I didn't realize we did goodbyes, sorry. Was just following your lead." She squared off her shoulders without even a hint of apology. It was so fucking hot.

"Well, in the future I think you should say goodbye." I moved my mouth inches away from hers.

"Who said there was going to be a future?" She smiled, like she knew exactly what she was doing.

My lips crushed down on hers answering her question. My tongue invading her mouth as my hands hauled her body onto mine. I had no desire to be gentle; with the need to feel her more desperate than the last time I'd been with her. My cock was already straining against the seam of my jeans, begging to get out.

"Just so we're clear, just because I'm having sex with you doesn't mean I like you." Angie's hand moved down my back and grabbed at my ass, her body rubbing against me as I continued to kiss her.

"Good, I'm glad you don't like me. You shouldn't. I'm not a nice person." I pulled my lips away from her mouth long enough to answer. Her beautiful eyes giving me the all clear as I moved one of my hands up her thigh. My fingers teased the edges of her panties, while my lips sucked hard at her neck.

"I like that." She arched her neck back, giving me better access.

"Just as well. Because I like doing it to you," I mumbled against her throat as my fingers got bored playing with her panties and sunk into her pussy.

BACK STAGE

"Fuck," She gritted out, her eyes flying open as I stretched her out with another finger. The fabric of her underwear strained against my hand.

"Is that what you want? Me to fuck you?" My thumb joined my fingers, circling her clit while I pumped into her. She was so wet and ready.

"No, this time I'm fucking you." She pushed me back, my body hitting a wall of road cases as she attacked me with her lips.

Her hands pulled at my T-shirt as her tongue plunged into my mouth. Whatever she was doing, she wasn't playing as she shoved me harder against the metal boxes.

"Get it off," She ordered, my T-shirt obviously offending her as she moved her attention to undoing my jeans.

"You know, this isn't exactly private?" My mouth shot out, our location far from ideal. "Anyone could walk in here at any time. There are over a hundred people roaming these halls." The sound of footsteps echoed not more than a hundred feet away, as did the voices of rowdy men who'd kill to be where I was. Not that I'd ever give them a chance.

"Are you shy, Jason? Because I'm not." She stepped back and slid off the tight black dress she'd been wearing, her body completely exposed except for that pair of lace panties I'd been playing with. No bra, her tits standing proudly. And so they should, they were absolutely spectacular.

"No, I'm not shy." My eyes didn't leave hers as I pulled off my shirt, and I kicked off my boots. My dick screamed for attention as I stepped out of my jeans and stripped off my boxer shorts.

"Nice." She glanced down at my hard-on, her lips spreading into a grin.

"If you want *nice*, sweetheart, then you're with the wrong person."

I wasn't sure if it was her or me who moved first, both of our bodies crashing into one another as our mouths got busy. My hands pulled at her panties, determined to strip the last barrier between us.

"Don't rip them, asshole, you still owe me for the rest of my stuff you ruined," she warned as her fingers gripped tight against my skin.

I couldn't help it.

The shredded panties were tossed aside the minute I'd torn them from her body. It was her fault, her telling me not to just made me want to even more. Sure it was twisted logic but that's the way we operated, and there was no way I was backing down from a dare. Her threats and venom just served to turn me on more.

If she was genuinely mad, she didn't show it, her hands stroking my shaft as I once again attacked her mouth. The need to be in her had me so crazy I could no longer think straight.

Her promise to be the one doing the fucking wasn't an idle threat, taking control, her hands wrapping around my cock as she ordered me to "lay down."

Every single time I'd had sex, it had been me calling the shots. Not because I was a sexist asshole, but because that's just the way I liked it. I liked the control to watch a woman unravel underneath me, knowing it was me who put that satisfied look on her face. And I liked sex. The feeling of freedom after just having blown your load was addictive. In that moment, nothing else existed. No problems, just two people making themselves feel good.

Giving up the control—even if it was just for now—was not something I was comfortable with. I'd rather walk my naked ass out in front of all those roadies and ask one of them to jerk me off, that's how much I wasn't down with it. But with Angie, there was something about her that I just couldn't say no to. If she wanted me to lie on the floor and call me an asshole then I'd probably thank her for the privilege. Sure, that wasn't messed up at all.

And that's exactly what I did. Metal cut into my back as I laid on the rolling cases, her hands tight around my wrists as she climbed on top and straddled me. I had no idea what she was going to do. Her hands were probably going to need to let mine go if she was hoping to move this past just rubbing my junk against her pussy, but I didn't ask. I was mesmerized by her.

"Don't move," she warned as she let go, her fingers tracing the lines of my torso as they moved down my body. Her lips followed where her hands had been, kissing and licking their path. My body rose to meet her lips half way in a show of appreciation. "Don't move." She nipped at my abs, her teeth grazing my skin, my punishment for not following her instructions.

"You're not making it easy for me." My neck craned off the case just in time to see her beautiful lips take my cock into her mouth. "Fuck."

I didn't care how loud I'd yelled it. In fact, there wasn't a lot that could have been more important other than what she was doing. She could have asked me for my bank account details and the deed to my apartment and I would've asked her where I needed to sign. As long as she kept doing exactly what she was doing, her tongue expertly working every inch of me.

"Jason." She hissed as I pulled my cock from her mouth, my hand around her hair. I'd taken as many orders as I was going to, and I'd done the lay still bullshit long enough.

"You wanna punish me, Angie, go right ahead. But I need to be in you."

"You want me, Jason?" She shuffled back up to her knees—which would no doubt be sporting road rash after we were done—and placed each one of her legs on either side of my thighs. "You want this?" she asked again, her hand snaking around her tits then down in between her legs.

"Yes. I want you."

"Then take me."

In a moment of freaking clarity my brain finally kicked it. No way was I doing this without protection. Not even if it meant my balls were going to explode because I was so turned on.

"Angie, I need a rubber."

"Well look what I happened to have?" She reached into her hair and pulled out one of the pins, the condom that had been tucked away up there, now visible. "I'm like a regular girl scout." Her satisfied grin lit up her beautiful eyes as she fished out the foil packet and held it proudly.

"Well thank fuck you aren't selling me cookies."

I snatched the condom from her hand, tearing the wrapper open with my teeth before rolling it down along my length. We could commend her brilliant prior planning later; right now I didn't think either of us was interested in anything that didn't involve us getting busy. And I needed her more than I needed my next breath.

She barely let me get the thing on when she sunk down on me, my cock sliding into her and stretching her out. She wasn't full ready, the fit tight, not that it seemed to stop her.

"Angie." Her name was like a fucking curse. I said it over and over again as any control I'd had went out the window as freaking want took over. I grabbed her ass and pistoned hard against her, unable to stop.

"Yes," she screamed, her teeth sinking into my shoulder as I felt her come hard against me. That sensation alone was enough to finish me as I exploded into her, my breathing like an out of control freight train about to derail.

"You're crazy." I panted against her neck, her body still shaking slightly on mine.

My good mood immediately flipped to pissed off after seeing her beautiful skin marked by the red scratches our little exercise had caused. "Shit, did I hurt you?"

"Don't flatter yourself," she laughed. "It's going to take a lot more than that to hurt me."

God I hoped she was right, because hurting her was the last thing I wanted to do and selfishly I knew I wasn't going to be able to stop.

"Just promise me you'll tell me if I do." And I wasn't talking about the grazes on her knees.

"Fine, Jason." I didn't need to see her to know she was rolling her eyes. "I promise."

'16

Angie

Last night had been insane. My behavior crazy, and yet I regretted nothing. It had been out of character, but not in the way that most people would think.

I wasn't a whore, but meaningless sex was pretty much the only sex I had. No, it wasn't as horrible as it sounded; it was actually better that way. Considering the few times I had done it for the "right" reasons the guy left, I'd say my way was healthier. At least there were no surprises. That didn't mean I slept with just anyone, and of course I had boyfriends, it just wasn't lovey-dovey. I wasn't looking for that beautiful love. Because don't they always leave? Even if it's perfect, someone always has to go. My dad had loved my mom like no other love I'd seen, and she'd been taken too. I knew it wasn't the same thing, but he'd never found anyone else.

Two people. That perfect love. Someone was going to have to go, one way or another.

That's why meaningless sex was best, except meaningless should be emotionless too. And with Jason, it wasn't.

Anger—emotion
Hurt—emotion
Revenge—emotion
Lust—emotion

Did I need to go on? It didn't matter they weren't good emotions; they were there nonetheless.

As long as I kept them in check, it would be okay. Well at least that's what my vagina was telling my head because she didn't want happy time to end. And no one made *her* happy like Jason did.

I knew he watched me perform, I felt his eyes on me as I sang and I liked it. The thrill that he was there in the wings was almost as big a rush as being on stage. He hadn't worked it out yet—my game of musical clues still being unappreciated for its full genius—but every time I sang that final last song, I loved it just a little bit more.

"Hey." I poked him, not quite believing he'd spent the night. "It's morning, you should probably leave."

"Screw that, it's early." He rolled onto his side, taking me with him. My body tucked next to his. He had a habit of doing that as I'd come to find out. Holding me throughout the night. Funny, I'd never have pegged him for much of a cuddler. Wonders will never cease.

"Well, you should be in your bed, not mine."

We'd been careless. Part of the thrill was the dancing with danger, the prospect of getting caught. The sex backstage, I have no explanation for. Perhaps some sex fiend had momentarily possessed my body? While I wasn't the poster woman for missionary sex, I'd never been so reckless and brazen. But I'd been inspired to let go and jump. So I did.

"They know, Angie. Don't worry about it." He yawned without opening his eyes. His lips kissed my neck as he tried to go back to sleep.

Unlike our previous nights together, no one had left this time.

By some freak of fortune, our wild sex on the road cases had gone undetected, which was reason to celebrate. Our choice of celebration was easy—more sex. This time with less metal gouging into my skin, and less chance of giving some random roadie free material for his spank bank.

BACK STAGE

So we moved our party of two to my room, where there was less chance of running into pregnant wives of other band mates. Speaking of which.

"Megs?"

"She hinted. I confirmed. No one cares. It's not like we're dating." Jason's hand travelled up my body, resting on my breast. I felt his smile against my skin.

I liked it. His smile, and his touch.

"True. I wouldn't be stupid enough to date you." I tried unsuccessfully to wiggle out of his hold. God, he was strong. He must lift weights in addition to the running. I silently praised his dedication to fitness, not willing to give him the satisfaction of actually praising him.

"Well seeing as you woke me." With a twist of his arm he'd effortlessly flipped me onto my back so I was facing him. Yep, definitely lifted weights. "We should probably talk about something."

"I thought we didn't have to talk. The whole not dating thing we had going for us."

Besides now I was facing him, I really didn't want to talk. Unless by talking he meant kissing me, which I was totally on board with. And that wasn't as sappy as it sounded, because I didn't mean I wanted him to kiss me on my mouth.

"Are you seeing anyone?"

Not what I thought he was going to ask me. I'd assumed it would be more something along the lines of *so what's your stance on anal* and not *do you currently have a boyfriend.*

I should've been offended by the question and what it implied. That he thought I could possibly cheat on someone I was dating, but really what kind of girl was I? Having sex with a guy I repeatedly said I couldn't stand, sometimes in public places. Not the kind that you'd expect to be sitting in church on Sunday. Maybe someone who fucked around?

Something in his voice also stopped me from calling him an offensive asshole. Like maybe there wasn't more to the question than what he was actually asking.

"Don't you think you should have asked me that *before* you had sex with me?"

"You didn't mention a boyfriend, but I wanted to be sure." His fingers moved my hair out of my eyes.

Well, he had asked me. Sort of. When he wanted to know about Rusty. Which made no sense then, because … well who cared. Now, it just made me curious as to why.

"Was that something you were worried about?"

"No. I mean I wouldn't have gone there if I thought you were with someone. That's not something I'd be part of."

We all know that when it came to insulting Jason Irwin, I wasn't shy. Remember I had all those lovely names for him, tucked away just waiting for me to blow off the dust. But this conversation was not one of an asshole.

His voice lacked the sarcasm for that. There was no fake smile, or flirty eyes. Nothing even remotely asshole-ish. What we had instead was the makings of a serious conversation where two adult people spoke and didn't dissolve into name-calling or obscenities.

While one part of my brain figured this was going to add some serious complications to the meaningless sex rule, the other part wanted to go a little deeper.

"Infidelity?"

It was a word I was familiar with. I'd been on the receiving end and felt its hurt.

"Yes. I want no part of that." He answered with no hesitation.

While I admired his respect for the institution of relationships, it was kind of at odds with the rest of his philosophies. The ones that had him sleeping with people i.e. me, and then leaving without a second thought, or the ones that let him have sex with numerous people he didn't really care about.

I guess I sort of fell into both of those categories.

"But you said it yourself, you don't date. So what does it matter?"

It was supposed to be another thought. Like the others I'd had while trying to figure him out, but stupidly, my mouth opened and the words just fell out. Just like that. There they were. Me asking things I wanted to know but really had no business asking.

"It matters to me." His brown eyes locked on mine, and for a tiny second I remembered exactly how easy it was to fall in love with him. That flicker of vulnerability. Kindness. It was there, but very well hidden.

Thankfully, it was in the very next second that I remembered why I shouldn't, and no longer loved him.

"Do you ask all those other girls? Make sure they weren't cheating?"

"Every single one. Some try and lie, but there is usually a tell, not many people can do it convincingly. If I have any doubts, I don't."

"A whore with a conscience."

It sounded so insensitive, but I hadn't meant it like that. Once again, my big mouth just spilled the thought with zero filter. But I was caught off guard, not only by the conversation, but his honesty. This was a new place we found ourselves in.

"Yes, a whore with a conscience." He laughed, not offended. He probably should have been. I really wasn't in any position to call anyone a whore; there was no way I was going to be able to wear white on my wedding day convincingly.

"So, while you aren't dating people *but* sleeping with them ... Do you sleep with other people?" My mouth spewed out a jumble of words that didn't constitute a sentence by anyone's standards. "I mean, is it one night stands generally or are there times where you continue to sleep with the same person?"

Better, but I hated how vulnerable it made me sound. Because what I really was asking was, so what exactly are *we* doing and do you plan on having sex with *me* only to go have sex with someone else?

The more I thought about it, the more I didn't feel good about myself. I was breaking my own rules. Those damn emotions poking their head around where they didn't belong.

"Are you asking me if I plan on sleeping with other people while I'm sleeping with you?" He waded through my stumbling mess of words and knew exactly what I was asking. He was so smart. I hated how all together he seemed to have it. It just shone a mirror on my shortcomings.

"Yes, I know you think I'm a freak." Which given what I'd displayed recently wasn't too far from the truth. "But I'm not great with sharing."

If he was being honest, then I would be too. I wanted to have sex with him again. I loved that while I was with him I wasn't thinking too deeply, that my body just let go. Maybe it's because I didn't need to impress him, maybe it's 'cause he'd seen it all before. But there was a freedom that came with the sex, and the things he did to my body. And that's what I wanted.

"You know," Jason laughed. "You and Dan are a lot more alike than you think."

"Please don't compare me to him." I recoiled in horror. "He's a social moron with a constant boner. I'm nothing like him."

"I meant your inability to share." He stopped laughing, his finger tracing the line of my jaw. God, he was smooth. "I take it by your question you might like to do this again?"

"Well I'd hoped that wasn't the last time I was ever going to have sex." This time it was my turn to laugh. Nervously, I might add. "It was good but certainly not good enough for me to slap an eviction notice on my vagina."

I was flat out lying. It had been *that* good.

"With me. Did you want to have sex again with me?"

There was that smooth, hot combination that he seemed to throw at me like a one, two punch. Not even taking into account the sex—which was out-freaking-standing—I knew I'd want more.

"Sure, I guess. I mean, if there was nothing better to do." I lied again. Not willing to admit that I was that easy. Gah. I hated him.

"No, Angie. Without the attitude." I guess he didn't find my off-the-cuff answer as amusing as it had been intended. "If this isn't something you're into then I'll stay away."

Was I into it? Yes, and probably more than I should be. But all that rationality that existed in the world wasn't around at present. It was probably dealing with other people, who it probably would have stood a better chance with. Crazy is who we were in bed with. Both of us. Because only crazy people sleep with someone they had a past with.

"Yes, it's what I want."

Jason Irwin was a lot of things—sexy, smart, and intense. He was *not* romantic, sensitive boyfriend material, in other words, he was not *Ryan Gosling*. Girls were not lining up with their boxes of Kleenex ready to declare their undying love, no matter how badass his abs were. Which they were—he could totally give RyGos a run for his money. And the tattoos. Ryan was too clean cut for my liking, but that was just my personal preference. But seeing as I wasn't going to be declaring my undying love for anyone, I was okay with that.

And I wasn't delusional. No relationship. He'd been clear about that from the start.

Eyes wide open.

It was a *Hey I like sex and you like sex, so lets have sex together. Yippee.* But without the messy *feelings* that could make the sex less pleasurable. And when I was sick of him—which eventually I would be—I could just walk away, vindicated.

And I *could* walk away.

"Hey, where did you go? What are you thinking about?"

He waved his hand in front of my face, pulling me back to the present. I didn't even blink, my mouth doing what it usually did, flicking on autopilot.

"Plotting your demise. I just need to figure out a way to keep your penis viable."

"This is a long ass list, Angie." Max scanned the length of the page in front of him. "You want us to learn all these songs?"

"Yep. Let's have some fun with them. Who knows when else we'll get the chance to play stadiums."

I had amused myself greatly choosing the next few musical clues in the game of *fuck you Jason Irwin*. Except it wasn't so much fuck you any more, it was like an aural treasure hunt. The songs reflecting the many moods he seemed to evoke: angry, sexy, and I'm-going-to-fuck-your-shit up. I really was a ray of sunshine.

"This list looks like it's drunk." Joey twirled his stick, while randomly hitting the base drum. It was a drummer thing, I didn't question. "Are we a rock band or auditioning for a fucking Vegas lounge show?"

"I can already smell the fourteen-ninety-nine buffet." Max laughed.

"Gentlemen, where is your sense of adventure?" Rusty clapped his hands dramatically. He was late but no one had seemed to mind. "Let Angie stretch her pipes on the musical diversity, poor girl is trying to impress her new boyfriend."

"Rusty." I threw a guitar pick at him, hoping none of the crew walking around were paying us any attention. If they'd heard what was being talked about no one seemed to care. I'm sure shadier stuff went down on tour. Like public sex displays … oh wait. Yeah.

"What new boyfriend?" Max stopped scanning the list.

"Angie, has a boyfriend?" Joey chimed in just as interested.

My hopes of keeping my *arrangement* under wraps vanished before my eyes with both the guys looking to Rusty for answers. He had already displayed his inability to keep his mouth shut. I needed a more discreet best friend.

"Oops. I've said too much." Rusty clutched his chest, screwing his face up in mock horror. The smirk he was struggling to hide a dead giveaway it wasn't just a slip of the tongue. "Sorry. We were not talking about *it*." The "it" whispered for effect. Killing him wasn't completely off the table.

"He's not my *boyfriend*," I started to explain, knowing Rusty would just make it worse if I left it up to him. "But I'm sorta *seeing* Jason."

I wasn't sure of what word to use. *Dating* was out. *Fucking* sounded way too crude. *Sleeping with*—yeah still not much better. So *seeing* it was. FYI the English language sucked, we needed more words to describe people we were involved with that we weren't emotionally attached with. Something like, funfriend or pleasurepal, right 'cause that didn't sound like a cheesy blow up sex doll or a bad porno.

"She means she's seeing him *naked*," Rusty clarified, as his stupid ass grin got wider. He was enjoying this way too much; we needed to find Rusty a girl. Someone to distract him so he didn't have to be so interested in my life. Hopefully a fan girl who'd tie him to a bed and gag him.

My best eye daggers were fired in his direction as I folded my arms across my chest. Oh, he was history the moment *he* started dating, as I mentally tucked away this memory for future revenge. H-i-s-t-o-r-y. I was Italian; the whole vendetta thing was hard-wired to my DNA. Horsehead in your bed anyone? "I hate you, Rusty."

"Is that like you *hate* Jason?" Rusty continued to laugh, oblivious to my plots for my revenge. "Does that mean you're going to want to see me naked too?" He wrapped his arms around me, his guitar hitting me in the ass as he gave me an awkward backward hug. "I'll strip for you, babe, no problem, but we don't want Max and Joey feeling inadequate."

"Does he mean inadequate in that he thinks his dick is bigger than mine, because I'm positive microscopic is *smaller* than ridiculously huge." Joey completely disregarded the issue of Jason, his attention diverted by a stab at his manhood. Boys. Every single one of them was packing a twelve inch penis in their own minds.

"Tell yourself whatever you need to, Joey—"

"Can we stop talking about dicks for a second here and focus?" I interrupted Rusty before the conversation degenerated into a need to *contrast and compare*. Sometimes I was convinced they forgot I was a girl.

"We can talk about tits if you prefer, that's more my area of expertise." Joey laughed, Max and Rusty joining him. The whole I'm-sleeping-with-the-guy-in-the-other-band glossed over in favor of anatomy.

"So are you guys okay with me *seeing* Jason? I mean, nothing is going to change with the band. I'm not leaving or anything and it doesn't affect the tour."

The band was my family, and while other people's opinions didn't matter to me, theirs did. It was important. Next to my dad, Rusty and the guys were all I had.

"Angie, see, date, fuck or whatever it is you want to call it, whoever you want. We know you're with us." Max's warm smile said more than his words. There was no judgment here.

"Yeah, there is no breaking up this band." Joey tossed a stick before catching it midair, his goofy grin putting me at ease.

"Rus?" I knew he had his reservations, knowing better than anyone how bad this could potentially end up, but his endorsement was the one I craved the most.

"Whatever makes you happy, babe." His eyes meeting mine as he shot me a wink. "But I'm not calling him dad."

His wisecrack earned him enthusiastic laughter from the others. They were so easily amused.

"You're all assholes." More guitar picks were thrown at them. The endless supply of picks and strings was a very cool perk of playing with the big boys. Thanks Power Station.

"Yeah, but you love us." Rusty deflected the plastic shrapnel with very little effort. He was right—I loved them.

"Yeah I do. Now let's do this sound check before the audio guy gets any angrier. He's been giving us a stare down for the last ten minutes."

'17 Jason

THERE WAS A DEFINITE THEME WITH THE SONGS. THE ONES ANGIE would chose for her colorful finales. Last night's effort had been "Black Widow" By *Iggy Azeala.* Not very subtle.

It was so obvious I wasn't sure how I'd missed it. Each song, a new hidden message. It was kind of adorable but mostly sexy. Impressive too. That her band was able to churn out a new tune every night. Sure, occasionally they messed up, a dropped note that hardly anyone would even pick up, but for the most part they nailed it. And Angie—was flawless.

If her renditions were supposed to piss me off or offend me, she'd failed. It just made me want her more. If that could even be possible, considering I'd pretty much wanted her all the fucking time.

Not sure what kind of death wish I was rocking by making Angie and me a regular thing, but it was one I didn't have any intention in changing. The fact she didn't kiss my ass just made it better. Safer almost. Less chance of it ending in tears. Which is exactly what I needed to avoid.

Our time in Boston was over, with a new show—and no doubt new song—awaiting us at our next destination.

New Haven was next.

My fingers mindlessly ran across the keys, playing some tune that had been stuck in my head for days. The messed up bed served as an impromptu stand. It wasn't even a song I'd been working on, just noise, but I kept playing it anyway.

"Is that Chopin?" Angie walked in from the bathroom, towel wrapped tightly around her body, another twirled around her head.

"Nope, just noise." I stopped playing, flexing my fingers as I lifted them off the keys.

"Well it was good. I liked it." She sat in my lap, her hands moving my fingers back to the keys. "Play for me."

"Maybe later." My fingers found a better place to be as they wrapped around Angie's waist.

"Fine, be a spoilsport." Her hands went down to the keyboard as she tried unsuccessful to make something sound musical. "I'm pretty sure I remember it."

"I know what you're doing each night." I figured having the conversation while she was half-naked on my lap meant less chance she'd be able to pull a dodge and run.

"Blowing your mind with my amazing sex moves? I didn't think I was trying to hide it." She didn't look up from her fingers, bung notes flying left, right and center.

"*Sex moves* isn't a thing, Angie."

"Sure it is, and if its not then I'm copyrighting that tomorrow. Because it should be. It's okay Jase, you've got them too, just not as impressive as mine."

"That's not what I meant, but your diversion tactics are also impressive." My hands moved on top of hers, no longer able to suffer the torture of her rendition. My assist meant at least her fingers were hitting the right keys even if the timing was jacked-up.

"So what *did* you mean?" She ditched the playing altogether, her body twisting toward me. Those eyes I loved so much sent a shiver right down to my cock as they gave me their full attention.

"I know what you are doing with the songs. It's cute." My fingers picked up where hers had bailed, the notes ringing out despite the distraction.

"Cute? Cute?" she scoffed. "Take it back before I start playing again and prove how uncute I am." Her hands T-rex'd in front of her ready to assault my keyboard.

"Fine, it's not cute," I conceded, not wanting the ebonies and ivories to be subjected to her wrath. Or my ears for that matter. As a keyboard player, she made an excellent guitarist. "Clever then. Inventive." My offered replacements.

"Those adjectives are much better. Your instrument is safe." She lowered her hands and settled back into my lap, appeased.

"*And* sexy as hell," I added, no longer interested in the bullshit I was playing.

"Really?" She didn't even try and hide how pleased she was. "Tell me more about how sexy it is." The smile it earned me worth every second.

"Very sexy." I leaned in closer. "You need visual demonstration?" My hand moved to her thigh, sliding under her towel.

"Nope. Not right now." She sprung up out of my lap, grabbing the phone off the nightstand. "I'm ordering room service. I'm hungry."

"Yeah, I don't think you're going to find what you want on the menu." I leaned back into my chair and watched her bite her lip as she waited to order.

"Fine," She tossed the phone to the side as she settled again in my lap. "Just wait until my encore tonight, buddy. We'll see who wants what from the menu." Her mouth fusing to mine as my hands got busy.

We eventually did order food, but only after we'd both had our fill of each other. Which didn't leave much time for anything else. Not a problem as far as I was concerned.

So when I found myself a few hours later in my usual spot stage side while she sang, I couldn't help but grin at her song choice.

"Buttons." By *Pussy Cat Dolls*. And *loosening up her buttons* was not a fucking problem at all.

East Rutherford, New Jersey.

"So, why the Army?" Angie leaned over the front of my treadmill; the only part of her body currently getting a workout was her mouth.

"Give me two miles and I'll tell you." My head tilted to the treadmill beside me that could use some feet on the belt.

"How about you run them for me and I'll give you a blowjob." She smirked.

"Jesus, Angie."

"Is that a yes? Talk and run, you'll be rewarded later." She leaned over the display and cranked up the speed slightly. "And feel free to take your shit off at any time"

Had to hand it to her. She made an excellent case.

My past wasn't something that was publicized. Lawyers, NDA's and a lot of coin kept the shit buried. That, coupled with the fact most people who knew anything about it weren't the most reliable sources, meant People magazine would be running another feature on Kim Kardashian's ass before they'd get anything on me. Plus—for the cheap seats—I was the keyboard player. Fucks given, total of none.

"I got into trouble as a teenager, more so than most because I was running with a bunch of morons whose future looked set to include orange jumpsuits. And my moving in the wrong circles saw me making some choices that weren't the best for my personal growth. So it was either serve jail time or enlist."

My chest burned from having to talk while my feet kept moving, my neck starting to prickle with sweat.

"You were a criminal?"

Cue the wide-eyes and open jaw that I was one hundred percent expecting.

BACK STAGE

"I had a juvie record, it's sealed. Breaking and entering, petty larceny, destruction of property, getting into fights. Nothing huge but enough to get me on the wrong side of the law. But I got a DUI when I was seventeen, almost killed myself by wrapping my car around a tree. So I made the change."

"Wow. Jason. Um."

"Not what you thought I was going to say, right?"

"No."

"See, not so honorable am I?"

She didn't answer, her hand reaching over and pulling the emergency stop key, the belt underneath my feet grinding to a sudden stop.

"Fuck me." Her eyes spelling out exactly what those words meant, her lips parted in invitation.

"We're in a hotel gym, Angie. Security cameras. People." Not to mention I was slick with sweat and smelled like yesterday's gym socks. "You don't need to prove a point."

"I'm not trying to prove a point. Fuck me anyway."

I didn't bother trying to talk her out of it. Partly because as I said, I wasn't honorable, and partly because talking about my backstory made me edgy. And sex is one hell of an equalizer.

We settled on a compromise. Taking the *fucking* back up to my hotel room, where I pushed her up against a wall and fucked her so hard she had small bruises on her ass where my hands had been.

That night's song was "Bad Romance." By *Lady GaGa*. Never had a song been more fucking appropriate.

Philadelphia, PA

The traveling schedule was brutal. Usually it was only a couple of days in one place and then packing up and rolling into the next town. Nights on stage, mornings sleeping late. And as for free time, there wasn't a lot, but what we had I usually spent with Angie.

We weren't always naked either, spending a large chunk of the daylight hours actually just hanging out. We were even able to talk without her hurling insults at me. Wonders would never cease. There was definitely more to her that met the eye and damn if I didn't want to know more about her.

"So, why not go to college? It can't be that you didn't have the grades?" I dipped a fry in ketchup before shoving it in my mouth.

"Money." She picked at her salad, looking at my plate with envy. She'd convinced herself her ass was getting bigger which was utter shit. And I should know considering I stared at every inch of it, every single night.

"When my mom died, things got tight at home. Small business. Medical bills. Funeral expenses." She shook her head as I inched my plate closer, offering her a reprieve from her miserable dinner. "Besides, my dad needed me."

"He's lucky to have you." I took a bite of my burger, the size of my ass not being a concern, and enjoyed the mouthful. Then chased it down with another bite.

She caved, snagging a fry off my plate and popping it into her mouth, the smile that spread across her lips validation enough it was better than the rabbit food she'd been chowing down on.

"Can I ask you a question?" She stole another fry before taking a sip of her soda, and I had to stop from staring at her mouth so I could concentrate on what she was saying.

"What is that?" I pushed my plate toward her, more than happy to give her the other half of my dinner. Hers was just too sad to even be called a meal.

She didn't take much convincing, picking up half the burger that was on the plate and taking a small bite. "So you've fed me the line about the no girlfriends, but I know it hasn't always been like that, right?"

"Angie."

"C'mon Jase, we're just talking, right? Just talk to me."

BACK STAGE

"No, it wasn't always like that."

"There was one girl in particular. In your past, who messed you up."

If she had meant to ask a question, she didn't. Instead she nailed exactly why I was happy to keep doing my solo routine.

"You want to have sex?" I pushed away from the table, wiping my mouth with a napkin. "Let's go do that."

Pulling at her hand I yanked her out of her chair, my mission to get her naked sooner than later. She squeaked as her body hit mine, fries still in her hand as I went to scoop her up. To bed. That's where I wanted her and the conversation.

"No. I want to talk." She wiggled out of my hold, escaping just as I was about to throw her over my shoulder.

"Yes, fine. There was one girl in particular in my past." My hand raked through my hair in frustration.

"She cheated on you, right? That's why you are so against it. Because she hurt you and you don't want to do that to someone else."

"Fuck. Yes, she cheated on me. I thought I was in love with her and she slept with my best friend. It's over. I'm not going to be part of that again, in any capacity." My voice bounced off the walls and I was fucking thankful we were in my hotel room and not having this conversation somewhere else.

"Don't yell." She stood her ground. "Look at me." She pulled my face into her hands. "I'm sorry she was a bitch and did that, but don't yell at *me*."

Now it was my turn to give the goldfish impression.

The apology I was working on got stuck between I'm-sorry-I'm-an-asshole and I'm-sorry-where-would-you-like-my-balls?

"What was her name?" She ignored me and took another bite of our shared burger.

"Why, you going to look her up? Swap recipes?" I laughed, but at myself not at the questions themselves. Because I'd been delusional in thinking I had any control over anything when it came to Angie. Including the topic of conversation.

"No. I just need to rename my voodoo doll." She gave me a smile that just about knocked me on my ass. "The old name isn't working for me anymore seeing as it's the same name I'm screaming most nights. Besides, I think I've punished you enough."

She pulled me from rage to amazement with a flash of a grin. It was more than just seduction that those dark-brown eyes were packing.

"Em."

It burnt my lips saying it, but I volunteered it anyway. The additional information about how she stole my car, my money and most of all, my fucking sanity was conveniently left out.

"Em." Angie's lips moved as they pushed out the sound. The chill jacked-up my spine hearing her say that name, knowing I'd do whatever I had to so she wouldn't ever say it again.

"Don't say her name, Angie." It was halfway between a plea and a warning. "I don't want something so ugly ever coming out of your mouth."

"You've heard the way I talk and you think the ugliest thing I could say is her name?" Angie's eyes widened in disbelief as the blast of leave-it-alone I was throwing hopefully hit its mark.

"Trust me on this, even when you are swearing like a sailor it's still more beautiful than those two fucking letters." And I meant every word.

"Even when I call you an asshole?" her voice moving from serious to playful. That was the place I wanted her to be, and where I wanted to keep her.

"Especially when you call me an asshole."

My smile was back, as was my absolute awe of the woman in front of me. The memories of the evil got shoved back where they belonged as I focused on the only thing that mattered right now—her.

"Thanks." She moved closer, her head rested on my shoulder, my hands finding their mark on her body. "For telling me. About her."

The song that night had to be a coincidence because there is no way she could have predicted the conversation. "You know I'm no good." By *Amy Winehouse*.

BACK STAGE

And later, when we had our own private encore, she had screamed my name so loud I wasn't sure we were going to have the cops knocking at my hotel door.

I started waking up early, my internal clock jerking me awake without the need for an alarm. My prize for my early bird ritual was watching her sleep beside me. It was addictive; me living for those quiet moments where I could just look at her, and be awed by her perfection. It never got old.

The other thing I hadn't been able to shake was my inability to sleep until I knew she was safely inside dream world. The need for my own Z's taking a back seat until I'd felt her breathing even out and her body relax beside mine.

"Ugh."

The moan coming from Angie's lips wasn't the good kind, not like the ones she'd been giving me earlier. Her head was tilted away from me, the room still pitch black thanks to the early hour of the morning.

"Angie?" I lifted my head off the pillow as my hand reached for the bedside lamp.

"No," she all but screamed, the light flicking on for only a second before I killed it again. "Don't turn on the light." Her body scrunched into a ball, rolling to the far side of the bed.

"What the fuck?" I moved closer to her, my hands finding her in the dark. "You want to tell me what's going on?"

"Head. Bad," she stuttered. "Headache. It hurts." Her body rocked in the dark as I massaged her back. More moans following after.

"Do I need to call someone?" I fumbled in the dark for my phone while trying to keep my hands on her. Calling 9-1-1 for a headache was overkill, right? Still, this didn't seem like the run of the mill kind that was going to be killed by a couple of Tylenols.

"No, it's okay. I get them from time to time. Stress. Fatigue. My dad gets them too. It's nothing major; trust me, I even had my head scanned a couple of years back ... you know ... just to make sure," she mumbled while she kept her back to me, her body still tightly coiled as the pain griped her.

There was no need to elaborate on what the scan might have been for, and I was surprised by how relieved I felt that there wasn't more to it. Just the thought of something serious being wrong making me swallow, hard.

Uh-hum. Yeah.

So maybe instead of sitting there like an emotional dumbass with no clue, I should actually do something to help her.

"Okay, give me a second." I moved off the bed and went to the bathroom, doing my walk in the dark so not to make the shit any worse for her than it already was. My hands managed to locate the ibuprofen while I rummaged through my toiletry bag before I made my way to the mini bar, grabbing a couple cans of Coke.

"Here." I crouched down beside her side of the bed, the hiss of the can making her wince as I opened it. "Take some pills and drink the Coke."

"What? That's crazy. It will make it worse," she argued, her hands holding her head like it was going to explode.

"Trust me. It works. I can Google the science behind it later, but trust me, it works." My hand moved to her back and gently lifted her. "Take them." My fingers brought the pills to her mouth, her lips reluctantly opening for me.

"That's it, good girl." I snagged the opened Coke from the nightstand and lifted it to her mouth, easing the can slightly so she could take a drink. "Drink." I repeated the action, giving her a little.

When she had a few more sips that I was satisfied with, I lowered her back on the bed. Leaving the open can sitting on the nightstand beside her.

"I'll be right back." I gave her a kiss on the forehead and grabbed the other can of Coke and went back into the bathroom. This time I shut the door so I could hit the lights, my vision needed for the next part of playing doctor Jase.

My eyes blinked as they tried to adjust to the bright overhead light, the attack brutal, making me glad I'd shut the door. I placed the can on the sink before sinking to my knees in front of the tub, reaching out and turning on the faucet. I adjusted the water so it was running a little on the hot side; the water level in the tub rose as the bathroom started to steam.

While I waited I grabbed a couple of towels and stuck them on the edge, wanting to make it as comfortable as possible.

Didn't need a full tub, so was able to cut the water pretty soon after, hitting the light before opening the door. My eyes once again had a minute or two of black and white dots before being operational. The door back to the bedroom was pulled open as my vision started to return.

"Ugh," Angie moaned again, her body rocking slowly in the bed.

"Angie." My arms moved under her, lifting her body off the mattress. "Come with me, sweetheart."

She didn't fight me. There was no backchat or asking what-are-we-doing, with her willingly flinging her arms around my neck as I carried her into the bathroom. I kept it dark even though it meant making the journey harder. If anyone was stubbing their toe, it was only going to be me so my care factor was low.

Her breath heaved against my neck, her whimpering not as loud as I moved her feet into the tub. Her ass gently lowered onto the towel-covered tub edge as I eased her further down.

"Ah, it's hot." She pulled her feet out of the water, the splashes hitting both of us.

"It feels hotter than it is. Just give it a minute." I felt her body ease as she lowered her feet back in. The telltale splash told me her toes had hit the water. "That's it. Doing awesome." My hand rubbed small circles on her back as I sunk down to my knees beside her.

My fingers fumbled around in the dark and snared the other can of Coke. I cradled it against the base of her neck, the cold metal hitting her skin making her jump.

"Easy," I laughed. "Just relax. I've got you." My hand kept contact with her skin while I balanced the can against her neck. The contrast in temperature between her feet and the base of her head supposed to help.

We didn't talk, just sat there in the dark. My knees were not doing so hot on the tile but I didn't dare move. My comfort not a priority right now as I made sure she had what she needed.

It took a while but finally her body eased a little, her shoulders relaxing with her breathing a little less rapid. Either the ibuprofen with the Coke chaser had kicked in or the temperature remedy was responsible, but I was glad she was no longer sounding like she was wounded.

"Better?" I lifted the Coke can that wasn't so cold anymore away from her neck and put back on the sink.

"Yes, it's still there but not as bad. How did you know all that?" Her head stayed tilted forward as my fingers moved to massaging her neck.

"Just stuff I've picked up here and there, you'd be surprised what other skills I have." My hands worked the base of her skull.

"Oh yeah, was the massage the next step? Like after the other two?"

"Nope, step three my fingers do a different kind of rubbing. Orgasm, if the blood is rushing to other parts of your body, it can't be giving you headache."

She laughed, her body gently shaking as the noise escaped her lips.

"Whatever. Who wants sex when they have a headache? I'm calling bullshit."

"You know, I'm going to prove you wrong." I pushed up off my knees, my body coming to full height. "Let's go." I didn't give her much of a chance to protest as I lifted her off the edge of the tub, her feet wet and dripping on the floor as we made our back to the bed.

Lucky for me—and her as the case may be—she was already naked. It's not that I hadn't noticed earlier, it had just been other shit that had my attention i.e. doing whatever I had to do to make her feel better. But now, as I laid her down on the mattress, her legs spread out in front of me, it was hard not to notice.

BACK STAGE

"Jason—"

"Relax, we're not having sex."

My hands travelled up her thighs, my fingers going to where they needed to be as I lowered myself down on the bed in between her legs. And what a beautiful sight it was. So much so, that I gave up on letting my hands have all the fun. My mouth lowered onto her pussy, my tongue giving her clit all the attention while my finger gently slid inside of her. Which she seemed to enjoy. My tongue and my hands working together like a team as her breathing, which had been all settled a few minutes ago, kicking back up in tempo. This time for the right reasons.

"Jason."

Unlike the first time she had said my name, there wasn't any hesitation. Her hands finding themselves in my hair as I stayed where I needed to be—in between her legs, my mouth alternating between licking and sucking. Of course now my face was getting most of the action, so I upped the ante with my hand, adding another finger to the one I already had buried inside of her. Both of them got busy finding a good rhythm.

It didn't take long. A lot less time than I would have liked to be honest. My hands and tongue happy to continue on this prescribed course of therapy a little longer, but it seems Angie's body had other plans.

"Yes." Her body bowed off the bed, moving closer to my mouth as I picked up the pace and made sure every single inch of her pussy was getting that lovin' feeling.

"Yes." She grabbed my hair, her legs moving restlessly while I worked to bring her undone. One last flick of my tongue was all it took.

Watching her come never got old. Her eyes were tightly shut as her body stilled, even though everything I was doing didn't stop. The crest coming like a wave before she finally exploded on my mouth and hand. Both happy to have been of service as they teased every last inch of pleasure out of her.

"I liked your third solution the best." Her breath rushed out between her lips.

"Yeah, I bet you did." I lifted my mouth away from her but not before one last pass with my tongue, her body shaking in appreciation.

"Now, go to sleep." I pulled up the covers over her beautiful skin.

"But what about you?"

"Don't worry about me. This was about you."

I didn't bother to mention the hard-on that had developed the minute I'd lowered her onto the bed and spread her legs. Best that piece of information stayed on the backburner, my dick cursing me out for the hell I'd condemned it to.

"No, I can ..." Her hands reached for me on the mattress.

"You can do whatever you want to me in the morning if you still feel inclined. How's that for a deal?"

"Okay. Her voice and her hands settled, my body not sharing the same sentiment. So juiced up, just the brush of the covers probably enough to set me off.

"Awesome." I watched her body relax on the bed, her eyes closing. "We'll play in the morning."

It was going to be a hell of a long night.

18
Angie

FATIGUE. ROAD WEARY WAS AN ACTUAL THING, MY EYES DROOPING slowly as the plane came into land. It was midmorning, though unlike the cheery airline staff, I hadn't the five liters of coffee that would get me to their shared state of happy. It wasn't just lack of sleep, it had been physical fatigue too with my body more sore from the after show performances than my bouncing on stage.

"Hey, guys, over here."

Security pushed and pulled us in different directions, moving us through the arrivals section at Chicago's O'Hare. My feet trudged slow down the walkway as I hit a wall of bodies, a few die-hard Power Station fans slowing up the process by trying to get the band's attention. They went first—Power Station. Their band with their significant others more alert than us in what I can only assume was an acquired tolerance.

"Hey are you, Angie Morelli?" A short, dark-haired girl who was wearing more eye makeup than clothes stopped in front of us.

My eyes dipped down to the front of my shirt to check if I was wearing some kind of nametag. Nope, nothing there. Unless my name had been changed over night to The Ramones.

"Ummm, yeah," I answered, not wanting to be rude.

"Oh. My. God. I love you. Your band is amazing." She grabbed a hold of my arm and started to shake uncontrollably. "I love you so much."

"Err, thanks?"

Doing something—anything—would have been the smart thing to do. But I was kind of frozen. The surprise of someone I didn't know knowing me, had my feet glued to the floor. No one had ever stopped me before, not outside my neighborhood. And even then, it was usually someone I had already met.

The girl attached to my arm had a friend, who grabbed my other arm and between the two of them roughly played a tug of war with my body. Not hard, but enough that I was starting to feel a little freaked out. More hands touched me and I had to remember to breathe. The overwhelming urge to run burned through my body yet my feet wouldn't respond.

I watched in slow motion as the rest of my group moved further away, everyone too consumed with conversations to notice I was stuck. The faces I recognized blurring in the distance as my pulse started to race.

"You need to keep moving." Jason's hand circled my waist, having appeared miraculously by my side and pulled me forward. The girls attached to my arms, still holding on. Neither of them doing much more than babbling—I heard *I love you* a few times too.

"Thanks, see you at the show." Jason peeled the girls from my body in what seemed to be very little effort. "One foot in front of the other," he whispered in my ear, his hands on my hips encouraging me to perform the simply function, which apparently was too hard for me to do on my own.

"Is that what it's like for you?" His body slipped into step beside mine, his hands directing me forward to where everyone was filing into cars.

"Yeah, most of the time they just want to say hello. Are you okay?"

BACK STAGE

He stopped, his face on me despite others waiting for him.

"I'm fine, you should go."

The impatient security guard held the door open for the one Power Station member not currently sitting in one of their assigned idling SUV's, his jaw tightening more by each second. Me, not necessarily being at the top of his list of concerns given a crowd was starting to gather.

"I'm riding with, Angie." Jase waved off Mr. tight-jaw and pulled me into one of the not so flashy vans that had been designated for us. The topic of conversation not open for discussion as he pulled closed the door.

"I'm fine." I pulled across my seat belt, my body settling into the cloth seat. My racing pulse disagreed with my assessment of me being *fine*.

"Yeah, I know you are." Jase fastened his seatbelt, my other band members giving me the why-is-Jason-in-our-car look. "Your windows aren't tinted." He knocked on the glass. "I'll be able to see more of the city going in."

That excuse was bullshit if ever I heard one, but I didn't argue because having him in the car with me actually made me feel better. And right now I wasn't going to stop something that made me feel good.

The car ride was filled with the usual chatter—talking and laughing, and my pulse finally returning to normal. Jase reached over, his hand brushing over mine. His eyes stayed on me despite him saying he wanted to see the view, the landscape whizzing past.

The hotel was the same as they all were, big and impersonal. Jase's hands didn't move from my body as we traveled through the lobby and then up to his room. The discussion on where were going, not had, at least not verbally.

It was huge.

The room, the bed and the window. All of it, big and fancy, which by now shouldn't be surprising, but it was.

Jason and the view distracted me from my mild freak out, and with his hands shoved into his pockets, he joined me at the glass.

What had been happening with us, with him—there was no denying things had changed. He was being kind, sensitive, caring ... he was acting like—yeah, that word neither of us would say.

Boyfriend.

Even my subconscious whispered it.

So instead of bringing it up, I focused on the landscape in front of me. My eyes unable to be peeled away from the view.

"Wow, the city looks great from here." I leaned my body against the floor-to-ceiling window, the sunlight hitting the tops of each of the buildings, making the skyline sparkle.

"I don't really look anymore." He moved beside me, mimicking me by pressing his nose to the glass. "You're right, the view is impressive. Not sure why I don't take the time anymore to appreciate it when we travel. I guess it's all become second hand now, more of the same."

"You're so fucking jaded." I laughed stepping away from the window. "If I start talking like that, I'm going to kick my own ass."

"Is that what you want to do? Kick my ass?" He grinned; the prospect of me doing just that seeming to excite him.

"Ah, if only there was time." I wrapped my arms around his neck, knowing that while today my schedule was wide open, the keyboard player who I was canoodling with had places to be. In bed, with me, not at the top of the list.

"Yeah, well I have a surprise for you."

"Is it a vibrator to keep me busy while you're gone? If not, that's cool. I bet the shower head in this place is five-star."

Staying with Jason hadn't been discussed. But seeing as my bags usually found their way into his room, and I spent most nights in his bed it was a fairly safe bet this is going to be my room too. Besides, there was that view, and having him screw me up against the window was quickly added to my list of requests.

"It's not a vibrator." He pulled me from the window and I hit the wall of flesh that was his body. Well hello, pectoral muscles. It's nice to see

BACK STAGE

you again.

"I'll take care of anything that needs to be taken care of when I get back." His hand floated down to my ass which he then squeezed. Fair, seeing as my hands were doing the same to him. "But until then, you've got company. I figured it might be a good distraction. At least until I get back to give you a better one."

The company, I found out about five minutes later, was in the form of Ash and Megs. Apparently he'd texted them on the car ride over assuming I'd need the comfort. Not that he said as much, selling it like it was them who wanted to spend time with me. But I guessed he was worried about leaving me alone after the airport. His busy day meant it couldn't be him.

And as the bubbly duo bounced into the room, the sexy considerate guy who promised to wow me with plentiful orgasms left.

As much as I hate to admit it, I was really going to miss those two. They were so friendly and while our time had been limited over the past two weeks, their company on the tour had been one of the highlights. Other than playing on proper stages, and the mind-blowing sex.

Lexi and Hannah were great. Both had earned their commendations of greatness and my hero worship. Juggling jobs, husbands and kids all the while looking flawless. Unlike me, who looked like hot mess on a nine a.m. flight with no excuse except an active libido and willing partner. But they just didn't have the same dynamic the other two did.

Ash and Megs were different. Smashing through uninvited and welcoming me into their group, my usual feelings of inadequacy not getting a second thought. And they probably should have because these girls were perfect, and imperfect in the most amazing way. They might have been the first *real* girlfriends I'd had. Ones I didn't worry about stabbing me in the back, or judging me. And in a complete flip in my usual character, I trusted them. Blindly, even though I had no reason to.

It was while Megs was giving me a manicure—trust me, arguing was futile with that girl, red flag and bulls being what they were and all—that the I casually steered the conversation in the direction I wanted.

"So ... did you ever meet any of Jason's *girlfriends*?" My contribution to our *girlie chat* was thrown into the ring.

Casually.

Like a grenade.

I was going to need more practice.

"No, not really. He doesn't really date," Ash volunteered, my lack of finesse either overlooked or politely ignored. I *really* liked these girls.

"Other than you, we mean," Megs added, twisting the lid off the fire engine red nail polish that apparently I *needed* to be wearing.

"It's okay." I nodded, my fingers spread out, ready for the assault. "I know we're not *really* dating."

Not in the real sense of the word. At least not on his side of the equation, my side had been pretty blurry lately. Hence the sudden curiosity into Jason's past, and the jealousy that seemed to accompany it.

"Of course you are." Megs threw me a look of utter disbelief. "He's crazy about you." Her voice rose with enthusiasm.

"No, we're both crazy but not about each other, which is great because it works out." My mouth did that thing where it spat out words without properly processing them. It was right about one thing, both of us were certifiably crazy. Me, tipping the scales a little higher in my effort to be an overachiever.

"Well you're wrong." Megs held down my hands, red brush in between her fingers ready to do her worst. "Whatever you *want* to call it. It's most definitely dating."

"I'll let it slide 'cause you're knocked up." And because very few people lost an argument when it came to Megs. "But I don't want you to be disappointed by the lack of save the date cards we'll be mailing. Jase made it pretty clear he doesn't do commitment."

For the first time I heard the disappointment in my own voice. Well look at that. I think I may have developed feelings.

Well. Fuck.

"Plleeeeeaaasssseeee," Megs almost screamed. "That man is head over heels for you. I don't know why he's saying that bullshit, but I can tell you that he's never looked at a girl the way he's looked at you. And there have been plenty around."

"Did you guys ever meet Em?"

There I went, another grenade. Because the first one hadn't exploded in my face, I needed to tempt fate and throw another. My need to know obviously worth the risk of a possible messy fall out.

Of course neither of them had. The bitch-face troll—my new name for her—was well before their time with the guys.

"I think she was a big bitch anyway." Megs continued with my nails, the shiny red beacons shimmering like a stop sign, or the light out front of a whorehouse. "Broke his heart. Why anyone would want to do that to Jase? I just don't understand. He's a sweetheart."

"He totally is," Ash agreed. "Such a nice guy."

"And he's really good looking." Megs nodded, the shopping list of how wonderful Jason Irwin was growing.

"Super good looking." Ash nodded, her smile not even close to being discreet.

"And have you seen him with his shirt off?" Megs took to fanning herself dramatically. "Wow. Muscles for days."

"You can stop now."

The virtues coming thick and fast weren't actually needed. I was already falling in love with him. Yeah. There was that *word*. Not one I would be repeating, even to myself.

"Why, we're just talking about Jase." Ash shrugged naïvely.

"Yes, telling me how awesome he is."

"Megs, I don't think either of us used the word *awesome*, did we?" Ash looked to Megs, blowing across her freshly painted nails.

"No, Ash." Megs smiled with satisfaction. "I don't recall saying awesome at all."

"You are both so transparent. We are not a couple." I waved my hands in the air to prove my point.

"But you like him right, you called him awesome." Ash didn't give me a chance to retract.

"Yes, I like him. He is awesome, but—" I tried in vain to stop all talk of Jason and I all kissing-up-a-tree.

"No, you can't put a *but* on there. You like him. He's awesome. That's all." Megs gave me no chance to take back my Freudian slip.

"Just don't get your hopes up. I'm not expecting anything." And by anything I meant reciprocation. Because what I was definitely expecting was disappointment; that was a bona fide certainty.

So in one afternoon I had discovered that I was capable of two things I didn't think were possible. Number one, develop two beautiful friendships with these amazing women. And number two, fall in love with the same guy twice.

Both had been surprising, with only the second scaring the ever living hell out of me.

That night I sang "Supermassive Black Hole" by *Muse*. No explanation was needed.

'19 Jason

"**Good to see you diversifying your insults, Angie. I** especially liked tonight's efforts." I held her hands above her head, with my lips at her throat, driving her crazy. And crazy was what she was making me so it was only fair to share.

"That's me, so versatile." She laughed as she tried to kiss me back. I didn't let her, she could do what she wanted on stage but in bed, she was mine.

Tonight's effort had been "So What" by *P!nk* with her enthusiasm higher than usual while singing the word *tool* in the lyrics. She sang that line directly at me with a smirk on her face.

"Call me whatever you want on stage, sweetheart, but you have no problem remembering my name when I make you come." My mouth moved lower, this time her nipples getting my attention. Her body bowed off the bed in appreciation. And didn't that make me just want to do it more.

"Fame has made you so conceited, Jason. I think my next song should be You're so Vain." She closed her eyes as I continued the assault on her body with my mouth. The words she was trying to say barely coming out of her mouth convincingly.

Her list of songs had been extensive. As were her list of insults. And to the outside spectator were nothing more than a random collection of eclectic tunes. Different bands, different genres—all of them given her personal brand of flair as she showcased them on stage.

"Vanity isn't my problem." My mouth kissed the base of her stomach, my hands parting her thighs.

"What's your problem?" She all but begged as my mouth moved further south. Her hand that pulled at my hair to direct where she wanted me, not needed.

"My addiction to making you come apart." My tongue lapped at her thigh, getting close with every pass. "Watching you come, knowing it's because of me."

"That's ... that's ... " she stuttered, unable to finish her sentence as my lips gently closed around her clit, sucking it.

"That's exactly what you are going to get, Angie. When you're with me. I'm going to make you come each and every time." I slid in a finger to go along with the tongue attention I was giving her.

"Jason," she moaned as her fingers gripped at my hair. Her need to hold me in place unnecessary because there wasn't anything that would have stopped me.

"Yes." My mouth vibrated against her hot, wet pussy. My lips and tongue taking turns in making her feel good. Jury was still out as to which one was giving her the most pleasure.

"Don't stop." Her eyes flew open as she nailed me with a look, hovering somewhere between euphoria and desperation.

"Wasn't planning on it." I added an extra finger, pumping in and out of her as my mouth went back to being busy.

"Yes, Yes." Her body writhed underneath me as I felt her explode on my mouth, my fingers getting a treat as her pussy pulsed around them.

Unfortunately my dick wasn't so pleased, thinking my hand didn't deserve the praise Angie was giving it and demanding a chance to even the score.

"I'm going to need you to do that again." I shifted from my position between her thighs and moved higher up the bed.

The rip of the condom packet prompted her to open her eyes, her change in view coming just in time to see me smooth the latex down my shaft.

"Every time I see it, it gets no less impressive." She licked her lips, her eyes fixated on what I had in my hand.

"My cock impresses you? Or what I do with it?" I asked, regaining my lost position, her legs widening to accommodate me.

"Both." She sighed as I rubbed the head of dick at her opening, the bastard desperate to get inside.

"I told you." I pushed inside of her quickly, the sharp breath she drew hinting she hadn't been expecting it. "I'm not here to impress you, sweetheart. I'm here to make you come."

"Jase." She moved her lips to mine, her mouth begging for everything I had to give her. "I need you."

"And I need you." The words were automatic, my brain obviously suffering a loss of oxygen on account my dick was taking it all. Bad idea, and yet in that moment, I wasn't about to take it back.

I did *need* her. In every sense of the word, and the thought of losing her wreaked havoc on my nervous system. The fear of not being with her every day was only superseded by the fear of hurting her.

"Please," she begged, thankfully not hearing what I'd said. Or showing me how smart she was by ignoring it. "Please, don't stop." Her fingers dug so deep into my shoulders I could feel the skin bruise underneath. Did I care I'd be rocking bruises for the next few days? Not a fucking chance.

The kick of pain only served to juice me up higher as I slid in and out of her. The slow and controlled pace I'd been keeping not anywhere close to what I was desperate to give her.

"Fuck, Angie." I grabbed her legs as she pushed up against me, her hips thrusting against mine in a rebellious attempt to control the tempo.

She should have known better. She could have her turn later, but right now, it was me who was doing the *fucking*.

"I want—"

I slapped her ass, not giving her a chance to finish as every inch I had filled her; her pussy fisting me as she came on my hard-on. Her thighs pressed against me as her body shook.

"That's it." I kept moving, teasing every last shudder of pleasure from her. Mine. Every single tremble, every whimper, every ounce of pleasure had been all mine.

"That's it," I repeated, trying to slow down as a battle of wills between my mind and my balls went all out warfare in my body. "I know what you need, Angie. And I'll always give it you." Each drag of my hips made it harder and harder to maintain control.

Her lips crushed mine as she pulled me down onto her. My body smothering her while my hips kept pumping.

Need.

There was that word again. My mind giving up its fight as my body took over.

There was no holding back.

I couldn't stop even if I had wanted to, and I sure as hell didn't want to. My cock pounded in and out of her at an alarming pace. Over and over again, my body invaded hers. Harder and faster each time, as I struggled to get deep enough into her. Her tight pussy gripped me as I filled her with each thrust. Her breath labored as it pushed past my ear, my own bordering on hyperventilation.

"Stop," she almost screamed. The single word enough to make me put on my brakes and for my mind to kick back in.

I was hurting her, crushing her under my weight as I hammered into her. Any common sense I'd had, left as the desperation kicked in, controlling my body in a way that was bordering on possession.

We'd been rough before, but not like this. With my movements no longer being dictated by want, but by that sick and sadistic *need* I had been trying to suppress, taking me over.

BACK STAGE

It had been dominating my thoughts the whole time since I'd said it, but I'd pushed it down, thinking it was something I could control. But I was delusional if I thought I had a chance, and that stupid word had no business rattling around in my head.

I was a fucking animal. The lowest form of life, and I sure as hell didn't deserve her, let alone the fucking honor of being inside of her.

"No." She held me, preventing me from pulling out, her arms wrapping around me like a chain weighing me down. "No," she said again, more forceful this time and showing no signs of letting go.

"Angie, we need to stop. I was hurting you." Hearing the words made me want to throw up. That I had gone there, treated her like that. Never again.

"You weren't hurting me, you just scared me a little." Her arms remained locked around my body, her eyes trained on me despite mine refusing to meet hers.

"That doesn't make it fucking better." I buried my head into the curve of her neck, the scent of her skin and her shampoo making my insides twist.

"Just look at me, please." One of her arms released its death grip from around my torso, her hand tugging at my hair hard enough to lift my head. I welcomed the pain. I deserved it.

"I can't do that to you again." As hard as it was to own what I'd done, I manned up. My eyes locked on hers. "I won't do that to you again." I'd sooner die.

"And I trust you." Her hand moved from my hair and touched my face, giving me affection I knew I didn't deserve. Her other arm had refused to relinquish its hold, her tiny frame holding on with everything it had. "But I also need you and you promised me you would always give that to me."

The same words I had spoken to her minutes ago smacked me in the face. The stupid, arrogant promise I'd made before my brain checked out and my body had gone rogue.

"Angie, it's not the time to be cute." My head shook, not in the mood for the word games we used to play. Not in the mood for *any* games any more.

"I'm not being cute, Jason." There was no laugh, no smile, no sarcasm—her voice demanding my attention. "Look at me. *Really* look at me."

I couldn't have looked away if I'd tried. Not after that. She owned every single cell in my fucking body, and there wasn't anything I wouldn't have done if she'd asked. Jump of a cliff? Thanks, it's been nice knowing you.

"God you're fucking beautiful." My eyes committed to memory every single curve of her face. I could've gone blind tomorrow and I'd have every line and every dip burned into my mind. She was more than beautiful; she was perfection. And I was so freaking undeserving, it fucking hurt. "What the hell are you doing here with me?"

"It's where I want to be." Her answer simple and uncomplicated, with zero doubt. "Be with me. Slow. With me." She paused between each word, adding more weight to what she was asking me to do.

"I can't believe you still want to after that." My lips fell to her forehead, her skin on my mouth more precious than the air in my fucking lungs.

"What, and give up that impressive cock?" She smiled, every inch of her face lighting up with amused delight. "Not a freaking chance."

While my cock was on board with giving her whatever she wanted—we'd already established she owned me—the rest of me wasn't sold this was a smart decision. Check that. Probably motherfucking dumb if I was honest.

"Are you sure?" This was no longer about the sex, and everything to do with her. "You can say no at any time."

"I know, but I'm not saying no." She lifted her head and pressed her lips on mine, not wanting to take the out I was giving her. "Just go slow."

"Slow," I repeated, my mouth kissing her neck while my hands got reacquainted with her body.

BACK STAGE

Her hand moved down my back as she pulled me closer to her body. "Slow."

20

Angie

THAT NIGHT CHANGED EVERYTHING.

Something had happened in that room. A shift where he'd morphed into something else, *someone* else and I'd lost him. The level of anger and aggression wasn't something I'd seen before. He'd always had it all together. Cool, calm, collected. I'd never seen him lose control. Especially during sex. He had such a tight handle on it, that now, I wasn't sure if he had been holding back this whole time.

Something inside of him had become unhinged, and he was no longer Jason. His eyes dark, void, soulless. Like his spirit just got up and left. Gone. Done.

It scared me.

Not because I thought he would hurt me, but because I no longer knew the man I was in bed with. He was a stranger. He was uninvited and cold, his body mechanical, aggressive and being used for punishment. And I wasn't sure which one of us the punishment was intended for. Honestly, I didn't think it had been directed at me—and that scared me even more.

BACK STAGE

It would have been easy to walk out. To leave, but I just couldn't go. And he came back.

Slowly, at first. It had been almost impossible to get him to touch me again but he did. But it wasn't like it had been. I wondered if that was part of the reason he'd kept his distance, why his relationship ban was in play. He'd been holding back. It was something just below the surface, and I wasn't sure if I should scratch just a little bit further. Or if either of us was ready to face it.

It didn't happen again.

Every night Jason was not only gentle but incredibly considerate. That control was back, but it was different. He was slower, more deliberate and less aggressive. The edges had softened as we'd moved somewhere else.

We didn't talk about the R word, because it wasn't important. The label on what we were, unnecessary. This was more than what I had with anyone else, but I knew he was still holding back. Rocking the boat wouldn't work.

"Hey, Pops." My hand gripped the phone tighter, missing him like crazy. "I'm in Atlanta."

"Hey, sweetheart. You having a good time?" His voice sounded weary and I knew it wasn't fatigue. The date that so blatantly displayed itself on the calendar marked the anniversary of my mom's death and it was the first time ever that I hadn't been home for it.

Talking with him, thinking about my mom, being away from home, fatigue and all the other emotions of the past few weeks washed over me in a huge rush. And while I tried to keep it together, I knew if I didn't get off the phone soon, it was going to be more than just a few stray tears I was going to have to deal with. I didn't often cry but sometimes your eyes didn't give you the choice. Stupid leaky eyes.

I ended the call, shoving my phone into the pocket of my jeans. My head lifted high and my shoulders pushed back as I prepared to deal with the world. Today that wasn't going to be easy.

Jase and his band were going to be doing press all day. My morning and afternoon free and clear to do whatever I wanted, and while Rusty and the guys weren't too far away, I didn't want anyone to be dragged down with my mood.

The elevator was my new destination. Where I was going to be headed hadn't been decided yet but it at least it got me out of my room—the room I never slept in anymore. Besides, its not like the day could get any worse.

"Hey, are you crying?"

The metal elevator doors opened to reveal something that *could* make it worse.

"Why are you crying?"

Dan fucking Evans.

"I'm fine. It's not a big deal." My hands quickly wiped my eyes as I cursed the freaking universe. Really? You sent me Dan? Sometimes there really weren't enough variations of the word fuck.

"Bullshit. Girls don't cry for no reason. Especially you." He stepped out of the elevator and moved closer toward me.

"Don't be an ass, Dan. I'm allowed to be sad sometimes." My traitorous eyes letting go another fucking tear as if on cue. Goddamn it. Now I didn't know who I was more pissed off with, him or me.

"No. No you're not. There's no crying on tour." His head shook, affirming his stance.

Really, the man was begging to die.

"Dan, please. Just leave me."

"No. Not until you tell me what's wrong." He disregarded my telepathic urging that he shut-the-fuck-up and continued. "I can't have you crying on tour, it messes up my mojo. Like for real, epic bad shit could happen so you need to stop."

He was officially public enemy number one.

"Look at the fucking date, asshole."

Dan stopped as his eyes widened in recognition.

"Oh. Fuck. I'm sorry."

The penny finally dropped.

He, like Troy, had been with me the day my mother had died. Cynthia Morelli had been battling cancer for years, and when all the chemo and surgery hadn't worked she did what she always did. Held her head high and left on her own terms. I'd held her hand until the last moment before they took her away. The Harris family and their "adopted" son, Dan, had stayed with me while Pops went and did whatever adults needed to do when they lost the love of the life.

"Okay, you need to come with me." Dan reached into his pocket and pulled out his cell, his fingers furiously texting.

"What?" My feet unconsciously took a step back. "No, I don't want to go anywhere with you."

"Yeah, well put *want* in one hand and *shit* in the other and see which one fills up faster. You're still coming."

With his texting session apparently over and his phone shoved back into his pocket, his hand was free to grab me and pull me into the elevator, which at the touch of the button opened on command. Of course it did. That elevator was an instrument of the devil that clearly had a personal vendetta against me.

"You know kidnapping is a crime, right?" I tried to pull my arm out of his grasp with no success. Wow, he was stronger than he looked. "Even you can't smooth talk yourself out of unlawful detainment."

"Blah, Blah. Big fancy words blah." Dan mocked me, his free hand pressing the button for the top floor while the other stayed clamped around my arm.

"I hate you, Dan." I pouted and short of head butting or kicking him in the nuts I was going wherever he had designated.

"Nah, you love me." He smiled. Arrogant asshole. "All that shit we did to each other in the past was classic brother and sister stuff. You didn't have one, so I had to pick up the slack."

"Um, I'm pretty sure my *brother* wouldn't have tried to sleep with me when I was sixteen, Dan."

"Yeah, that was a moment of weakness. You got hot. Couldn't be helped." He shrugged like it had been no big deal.

The metal box from hell finally pinged, opening its doors and freeing us from its demonic clutches. Dan didn't give me a chance to hesitate, dragging me out with him into the foyer that lead to the penthouse apartments.

"Got the message, what's the emergency?" Jason appeared from another door, his phone still in his hand. "Hey." Jason stepped closer, his eyes on me and the arm that was being held ransom by Douchebag Evans. "Let her go."

"Relax, asswipe. I didn't hurt her, but your girl needs attention." Dan all but pushed me at Jason. "Oh, and I'm telling the guys we're cancelling all our shit today. We're all taking a day off."

He walked off, cell at his ear, planning our scheduled day off without any further argument.

"We can't just take a day off, we're in the middle of a tour." My eyes turned to Jason.

"We can do whatever we want, Angie." His thumbs gently wiping away any remaining tears. "We're not cancelling shows, and that is all anyone is going to care about. Now, talk to me."

My mouth opened ready to spill. And I do mean spill, as everything washed through me. It wasn't one thing, it was all of them heaped together and I needed someone. But like always, I just couldn't ask. My mouth closed just as quickly as it had opened with no words coming out. It was stuck. And so was I.

Jase didn't wait for the answer as he pulled me out of the foyer and into his room. His arms moved around my body, pulling me close to his chest and whispering, "Hey, I'm sorry I didn't notice the date. I'm an asshole, remember?"

I didn't want to smile but my mouth had its own ideas, spreading into a grin at the sound of Jason calling himself an asshole, and that he'd remember something about me that happened so long ago.

"Yeah you are." My head nodded against his shirt, wondering if it was bad karma that something sad had facilitated this moment.

I was completely in love with him.

BACK STAGE

Again.

With his asshole status decided, we didn't talk anymore, which was okay because his mouth found something better to do. Which was great because my mouth was right there with his, not talking and doing other things … with each other.

It would have been easy for it to dissolve into sex. It seemed to be a pattern where we used it to deal with the other emotions—both of us guilty of it. But for some strange reason it didn't go that way with the action staying pretty tame and our lips being the only things that got busy. It was kind of nice.

But just because there was no sex on the horizon, it didn't mean we didn't make it to the bed. Jason pulled me down with him onto the pillowy mattress as he continued to kiss me. My mind completely scrambled like the eggs I hadn't been able to eat for breakfast.

And then it hit me. The words Dan had used when he not so subtly threw me at Jase. *His Girl,* and Jason hadn't set him straight and I had no idea what that meant. I needed to know. Because if he didn't feel the same way then this had already gone too far—I had already gone to far.

"Jase?" My head pulled away from his mouth, my brain and my mouth having an internal war.

"Yes," he said tipping my chin up toward his face, his lips not stopping despite mine now doing less kissing and more talking.

"Douchebags." The knock at the door stopped any further conversation. "Whatever you're doing in there, wrap it up in thirty. I hired helicopters and we're going to Disneyworld. Oh and I'm a motherfucking genius 'cause the idea about going to the happiest place on earth was totally mine. Yeah, I'm that badass. Go back to fucking." His voice trailing as he walked away.

"You want to kill him, or should I?" Jase kissed my neck.

"It should be a collaboration." I tried to smile, the interruption totally killing my nerve.

It could wait until tomorrow. Maybe the day after. It didn't have to be today. The words just needed to be said, and I would say them. I totally would. Just not now. Not here, and not now.

I nuzzled back against Jason's chest, the heart that I so desperately wanted to be mine thumped strong and steady against my cheek as his hands played with my hair. Thump, Thump. Thump, Thump. And just being able to breathe proved difficult.

"You good?" Jason asked, his lips giving me another kiss on my forehead as he pulled away to look at me.

"Yeah," I lied, the word almost getting stuck in my throat. "I'm going to Disneyworld with freaking Power Station. What could be wrong?"

21
Jason

THE SEPARATE HOTEL ROOMS WERE REDUNDANT.

We ended up together every night anyway, unable to keep our hands off each other and needing the release. So in my bed was where she had to be. And if she ended tucked up by my side when she fell asleep, well that was a fucking bonus.

Shit had changed between us. There was no denying that. The fact she was still here was something I marveled at every single day.

I'd fucked up.

Lost control, with my handle on things no longer steady.

The rage wasn't a new thing; me and my inner demon had been kicking it together for a while. It was at least part of the reason why I kept the sex casual, and the girlfriends, non-existent. It was better for everyone concerned. Case in point, me losing my motherfucking mind.

Those lines I had worked so hard to keep neat and tidy were no longer straight. I knew it, and yet, I couldn't make myself stop. I didn't want to stop. Craving every little bit of whatever it was we were doing, to continue.

"Why are you awake?" The dark-brown eyes that should have been closed stared back at me. Her tired smile giving me the best good morning a man could ever ask for.

"I was watching you," she confessed, hijacking my daily habit.

"Creepy. I like it." I pulled her closer toward me, wanting to feel more of her skin on mine. "Go back to sleep, it's early."

"Okay." Her voice pushed out a breath but her eyes didn't close.

"Do you need me to help you get back to sleep?" My hand slid up her side, finding its mark as it palmed one of her breasts. My cock stirred at the prospect of getting some morning attention.

"Okay," she said, but her body didn't give the usual reaction despite what my hands were doing.

"Angie, what's wrong?"

Last night I had comforted her in the only way I knew how. Having her underneath me, screaming my name never got old but lately going slow was becoming a new favorite. I still made her scream—that was not negotiable.

"You thinking about your mom?"

"No," she answered with zero hesitation.

"Then what's on your mind?" I scooted up on to my elbow to get a better look at her. God she was beautiful, the view never got old.

"The tour ending, things going back to normal."

"The tour? Sure it will eventually end, but the band has done well. The crowds love you. I would be surprised if there isn't a recording contract waiting for you in New York when you get back."

"I wasn't talking about the band," she said slowly.

"You were talking about us."

"Is there an *us*? I mean we're here, in this bubble and it feels like a relationship but it's not really, is it?"

There was that word. The one I had been fighting so hard to avoid. Anytime I had attached a fucking label to it, the fucking thing went down the tubes. This wasn't a relationship; it was something else.

"What do you want me to tell you?"

BACK STAGE

There was no way I could explain to her what was going on in my head when it didn't even make sense to me.

She sighed slowly, like she'd been holding a breath for too long and then closed her eyes, the conversation shutting down with them.

I swallowed, refusing to move the hand that was glued to her side, keeping her close even if I wasn't sure it's what she wanted. "What do you *want* to happen?"

"I want us to be together." She said it slow, letting each word fully ring out before she said the next.

"Aren't we together now?" My hand around her tightening, bringing her even closer so her face was inches from mine.

"I'm serious, Jase." She pushed away from me, her hands straining against my chest. "This all ends tomorrow. We both go home. What happens?"

"I don't know." She was asking me questions I had no answers for. "Let's not worry about it for now."

"Then *when* do we worry about it?" She shuffled up against the headboard, pulling up the sheets to cover her body.

"Jesus, did you want to fight? Is that what you want?" I sat up, flicking on the lamp on the nightstand.

"No, I don't want to fight but I also need to know that when we go back home there is going to be a place for me." Her voice louder than it'd been before.

"There's a place for you, we'll work something out."

"What's there to work out?" She laughed, and not in a funny cute way. Condescending was more the vibe she was rocking. "Are you going to work me into a rotation? Do I get you on weekends or when I can come visit you in the city? Or am I like the alternate for when you feel like slumming?"

"That was a cheap shot, even for you."

"No, it's reality. It's my reality and I need to know what I mean to you."

"Angie, this is the closest I've come to anything real in a long time.

Just please don't push it."

That handle on things I was struggling to keep, wasn't doing so hot under the current conditions. My need for control also extended to this conversation. The one where the good stuff we had going on between us, distanced itself like Angie had, moving herself as far away from me on the mattress as possible.

"Would it be so terrible to be in a relationship? It's not so different to what we are doing now. It doesn't have to be a big deal." She pushed her hair back from her face in frustration.

"Why are you worrying about hypotheticals when we don't have to? Like I said, it's months away. We'll work it out." My voice had more edge to it than I would have liked.

She didn't back down, her tone matching mine. "You're not sleeping with anyone else, neither am I. We don't use words like girlfriend or boyfriend, but what are we?"

"We're here, in the moment. So let's enjoy that." My hand slammed down on the mattress in frustration.

She flinched as her eyes nailed me from the other side of the bed as I pushed back the covers and grabbed my boxers from the floor. The conversation had entered into fucking territory I no longer wanted to be in.

Things had been fine. Why couldn't we just leave things the way they were? I wasn't sure who I was madder at—her for pushing, or me for being unable to give her what she obviously wanted from me. Like she'd said from the beginning, I was an asshole. And we'd rehashed that so many fucking times, it had its own soundtrack. No shit, and I had to listen to it every fucking night.

Her voice had stayed level despite me ejecting from the bed. "Do you remember what you said to me the first time you left?" She reached out and touched my arm trying to pull me back onto the mattress.

"Of course, I said we'd made a mistake." I answered without turning around to look at her. My body giving the wall some face time even with her hand on me. My feelings jacked up.

BACK STAGE

My not turning around didn't help the situation, with the thud of her feet hitting the floor soon after. The rustling that followed I assumed was her getting dressed. But it didn't change anything. My heart beating so fast I wasn't sure it wasn't going to explode.

Stopping her and talking about it probably should have happened, but I didn't think anything was going to be solved tonight. And the last thing I wanted to do was say shit I didn't mean, because I felt backed into a corner.

She stepped in front of me, mostly dressed; the hurt on her face evident. Her eyes on me demanded that I look at her and I wasn't surprised she was ready to leave. The bed beside us wasn't going to be getting any more attention tonight.

"But you didn't ask me, you just told me you made a mistake and you left. I didn't get a say. No right of reply, nothing. I had barely got my clothes back on."

"How many times can I say sorry?" My fist punched against the headboard in frustration, my hand hitting the wood hard. It hurt but I didn't care. Hating myself was an understatement, I hated *everything* about this situation. "I'm sorry. It was a mistake."

"I was in love with you." The first tear fell.

It all stopped. Noise. Movement. I couldn't feel or hear anything. The words she had said hanging there, between us.

"What?" I asked like a dumbass, not because I hadn't heard her but because it didn't seem real.

"I was in love with you," she repeated, her eyes wide. "I was young, but it didn't make it less real. I hung on your every word. Every single time you showed me the slightest bit of interest it would make my world turn. And then you slept with me and left. I felt like a whore, Jason. Used. I was *in love* with the guy who treated me like that. I would have given up everything for you. Just to be with you, and you didn't even care."

There was lots I knew about that girl she'd been back then. She was beautiful, she was smart and she was full of attitude. Same as she was now, and for some unknown reason would give me all kinds of time. Loving me was not one of the things I knew.

"Angie, I didn't know. I thought it was a crush, I wouldn't have done that if I had known."

Never. I would have been stronger, put my dick in a fucking blender before I would have used her like that.

"You mean you wouldn't have slept with me or you wouldn't have used me?" The pain in her eyes floored me as she waited for my answer. "Actually." She raised her hand as she looked away. "Don't answer that."

"I'm no good at this. I've tried to tell you from the start, but you didn't want to listen."

Every single muscle in my body screamed to touch her and yet my fists stayed white-knuckled at my side, neither my hands nor my feet able to move.

"You're wrong." Her voice shook, unsteady. "I listened, but not to *you*. I listened to my fucking heart instead." Another tear fell. "And I'm in love with you again."

I couldn't breathe. It felt like a hundred pound weight was sitting on my chest as I tried to suck in air.

"Angie."

"I know, I know." She wiped her eyes as she gave me a weak smile. "Dumb, right? Who makes the same mistake twice?"

The pain in her eyes was real. Like someone had just punched her in the face. And it was there because of yours truly. Me. Well done, asshole, take a motherfucking bow. Those fucking tears she was crying had my name all over them. I had done that.

"Then this has to stop." My mouth said the words as I wanted to rip out my own fucking heart. "I don't want to hurt you again."

"Too late for that, dumbass. You already have."

"Which is why it has to stop." I fished around for my T-shirt, pulling it over my head in an effort to move away from her.

"So you're just going to dump me? You're not even going to try?"

BACK STAGE

Her face contorted, horrified.

I was the last thing she needed. She needed someone who was going to be there in every capacity, not some asshole with commitment issues. I couldn't change who I was. I couldn't be what she needed me to be.

"I can't *do* what you are asking me to *do*," I fired back, wondering why the hell she wasn't listening to me.

"Are you fucking serious?" She coughed in disbelief. Like actual bewilderment flashed across her face. "You can say whatever you want to fucking say but we have *been* in a relationship. I wasn't your whore. We shared other things besides bodily fluids. Nothing bad happened." Her rage kicked up a notch as she continued. "I understand some *bitch* from your past fucked you up, but for fuck's sake, get over it!"

The mention of Em wasn't a slap in the face, it was an explosion. That control I thought I'd lost a few minutes ago not even close to what was happening now as I struggled not to put my fist through the fucking drywall. *Get over it?* Like I hadn't been trying for the last ten years?

"Get out." I didn't recognize the voice that flew out of my mouth. The words distorted I'd screamed them so loud.

Angie flinched, her voice not as confident as when we started. "No. I deserve an explanation. I'm not Em—"

"Don't fucking bring her into this. Don't you fucking dare do it." I cut her off, my nerves juiced up at the mention of that motherfucking whore's name.

"You don't get to walk out on me twice," she screamed, her fists flying at my chest. "You don't get to break my fucking heart twice. That's not fair."

"Life isn't fucking fair, Angie." I took every hit in the chest she gave me as I watched the tears bleeding out of her eyes. "And I'm all out of explanations. I warned you. I told you what I was like." I stepped forward, the edge in my tone making her slowly back away. "You didn't fucking listen because you know everything." Her back hit the wall, her effort to get away from me running out of room. There was a moment of panic that flashed through her eyes when she realized she had nowhere else to go as I got real close to her and sneered. "Why don't you take your own advice and *get over it*."

Evil. Pure evil was pouring out of me and I couldn't stop it. This is why I couldn't be with her; right fucking there was the evidence. She wanted to see it; she wanted to know how much I could hurt her. Well, there you fucking go. Rinkside seats, right on the motherfucking ice.

"Why are you so cruel?" She wrapped her hands around her chest, looking like a wounded animal. "God, I hate you so much right now." Her voice was barely a hum.

"Good." I got closer to her, no doubt scaring the hell out of her as I measured each word. "Remember that, and walk the hell away. We're done. Now leave."

22

Angie

THE HARSH REALITY WAS WORSE THAN A SCREAMING MATCH. HIS words had felt like barbed-wire, stinging just as much when he hurled them at me as when he ripped them out.

The unrelenting pain consumed me. Swallowing me whole. My heart, my mind and soul completely shredded. My body empty, like something inside me had just gotten up and left.

And the depth of how cruel he was chilled me to my very core. He had cut me so deep I wasn't sure I'd ever stop bleeding. I was so fucking raw I didn't even want to go on stage. Rusty and the band the reasons for me getting in front of that mic.

I still cried myself to sleep though.

Every. Single. Night.

It was over.

Really, finally and truly over.

The one thing I hadn't been able to do was the finale. What was usually the highlight of my evening made me want to dry heave. I wasn't strong enough, not even to give him the *fuck you* he deserved.

Did he deserve it though? Maybe he was right, and I just liked playing the role of the doormat. He had warned me. He had spelled it out in the beginning that he did not want my love nor would he be giving me any in return.

I was the one who had changed the rules.

So instead of bouncing around on stage, tricking up some pop song and laughing at the irony of the lyrics, I walked off. Rusty and Max took over and sang the old *Beastie Boy's* song "Hey, Fuck You." And wasn't that appropriate. Yep. Fuck you. It wasn't just directed at Jason. There were plenty of *fucks* that were directed squarely at me. Not in the song, but in my own head. Which just made me cry harder.

Avoiding Jason was surprisingly easier than I thought. It seemed that all our past interaction had been intentional, with there being no need for the bands to even cross over. We did sound check at different times, our rooms were on different floors, traveled in separate vehicles and when we flew we were in coach. It was better that way; it's where we belonged.

Show after show I sang. My body and my voice gave the audience a hundred and ten percent, even though my heart wasn't in it. And the performances were amazing despite my soul being crushed. The accolades I had dreamed of finally getting thrown at my feet, and yet I couldn't enjoy the ride.

At least my career was on the incline—rave reviews coming in after each performance—even though my love life was in the toilet.

The set list changed as well. The colorful finales—done. We kept it simple and wrapped with one of our more upbeat originals, took a group bow and walked off stage. Then left the stadium before Power Station even hit their first note. Better to be safe than sorry.

"Where are we?" I laughed as I finished my sixth beer for the night. I knew the laugh was alcohol-induced and yet, even though it was manufactured I didn't care. It still felt good and it had been a while since I'd laughed.

"Phoenix." The bartender took the empty bottle from in front of me and wiped down the condensation on the bar. His hand movement so efficient and I couldn't help staring. Whoa. Look at that. Fascinating.

"Awesome, I like the desert," I responded, not peeling my eyes from his hand and the bar.

"Hey." His voice snapped me from my daze and called me to attention. "I'm going to have to cut you off."

"But why?" I whined, annoyed that I was just starting to feel the buzz and Mr. No Fun wanted to cut-me-off. It was a total power play, making the big man feel good by telling me no. I bet he probably hadn't gotten laid in a while either. There was no way I was that drunk.

"I know I sound drunk, but I'm just happy." I tried to stand up but had to hold onto the bar to steady myself. "See." By some miracle I was able to stop swaying and lifted my hands triumphantly. Look, barman, no hands. "Just happy and I'm staying in the hotel so it's not like I have to drive."

"Even still, you've had enough for one night." He folded his arms across his chest, the international sign for we're-done-discussing. Was poking my tongue out an acceptable response?

"Fine." I sunk back onto the bar stool, my need to show my sobriety no longer valid. "Ruin my life even more." My dramatic flair usually increased the drunker I got, and while I wasn't going to be winning any *Oscars*, I would have definitely been a shoe-in for a daytime soap.

It was late. We'd—by we, I meant the band—come off stage sometime around eight and I'd—by I, I meant me, solo, lone wolf—come straight to the bar. It's not that I'd turned into an alcoholic, but I was spending more downtime with a synthetic high than not. It beat facing reality, which was that I was a dumbass. *Give me a D, give me a U, give me a M and B, give me an A, give me a S, give me another S—what does it spell? Dumbass. Hurray.* All I needed was the pom poms and the fucking ability to do a backflip. I'd have to work on my cheer though, not smooth at all.

"Rough night?" A tall athletic guy in a nice suit sat down beside me. He smelled nice. And he had nice eyes. All four of them.

"Pfft. When did everyone get so fucking sensitive about public intoxication?" I slurred at the four-eyed-man. "I mean it's not like I took my top off and flashed my tits." My eyes rolled so hard I almost saw my brain. Not really. I meant, mentally. Because I was being sarcastic. Oh, never mind.

"Maybe that would improve the bartenders disposition. Who can say no to a beautiful, topless woman?" My suited companion laughed beside me.

Wow, look at that. Boom. He grew another head. Two heads. At least he's good looking. Not that I really was in any condition to judge.

"I bet *he* would still say no." I pointed to the bartender who was doing his best to ignore me. "Besides, I'm not beautiful." I scoffed as I stood up to illustrate my point. "I'm too short and my ass is too big. Plus I have these fucking childbearing hips." My hand moved around my body like a game show model. "Look at this. It's like the trunk of a Cadillac."

Newsflash. I was not my biggest fan.

"I think you're beautiful," the two headed, four-eyed and obviously delusional man responded.

"Then you my friend, must be drunker than I am."

I'd meant to think it but it came out of my mouth anyway. Meh. I'm not sober enough to care and hopefully drunk enough not to remember.

"Actually this is my first beer, so maybe *you're* the one who is wrong." He lifted his mostly full beer as he stared at me amused.

Great, now I was the sideshow.

"Didn't your momma tell you to never tell a woman she's wrong?" I laughed not having a more coherent or intelligent argument.

"My mother's been gone for a long time, so I must have missed out on all those words of wisdom." He took a sip of his beer before placing it on the bar.

Awesome. Hey foot, meet mouth. Get acquainted, it's going to be a long night I feel.

"I'm sorry. I don't have a mom either." I fumbled my apology, the over share of me having lost my mom not intentional.

BACK STAGE

"Well I guess we have something in common then." He moved his hand to where my fingers were and gently rubbed them. It felt wrong but I didn't move my hand.

"Yeah, I guess." I'd stopped laughing, my eyes following his thumb moving over my knuckles.

Crap. He was hitting on me. Well, that was just great.

"So seeing as I don't think you are going to get anymore service here, you want to come up to my room?" He edged in closer, that nice cologne he was wearing tickling my nose. "I have a full stocked mini bar and a credit card that is begging to get maxed out."

The last time I'd had sex, was with Jason. Actually, that wasn't sex; we'd made love. Because I'd loved him. The fact he didn't love me back didn't change what it had been. But that was over. Done. Finished. Kaput. And I was single, and free to have sex with whomever I pleased. But no one pleased me enough to want to. I mean, I wasn't pleased enough to try. I mean, I wasn't having sex because I still wanted Jason and was in love with him. Ah. Fuck. I hope I wasn't saying any of this out loud.

My eyes glanced up; the two-headed beautiful man with his astonishing four eyes was still waiting patiently for my response. The one that wasn't about a drink, but about whether or not I was willing to get naked and have sex. Because that's what he was asking me, right?

"Sure." The word left my mouth before I'd even really decided. "Why the hell not." My backup statement concurred with my first. It's not like I needed to be holding out for anyone. Besides, casual hook-ups are the *thing* right now. Sex and no commitment, why not. Surely that's what Jason has been doing, returning to his old habits.

"But I won't drink bourbon. Anything but that." I shook my head at the thought.

That's what he drank and if I was going to do this then anything that reminded me of him was out. God, I hoped I didn't cry. That wouldn't be cool and not very sexy either. The first time would be the hardest and then I would see that I was okay, so it was better to get it over with.

"No bourbon. I think we can work with that." The man I was about to have a drink with, aka have sex with, stood up and threw some money on the bar.

"Hey Angie, I was about ready to send out a search party." Rusty circled his arms around my body and pulled me off my barstool. His warm smile almost made me want to cry. It seemed to be my usual response lately. I was so leaky it was pathetic.

"Rusty! Oh I missed you." I swayed on my feet as I hugged him back fiercely. "Hey, meet my friend." Ummm what did he say his name was? Did I even ask him his name? Shit, was I about to sleep with some guy whose name I didn't even know?

"Sorry, what was your name?" I asked my *friend* the question I probably should have opened with.

"Jason." He nodded, adding a wink and a smile.

I'm sorry, excuse me? Jason? There's like five billion—okay, maybe not that many—names in the world and he has to have *that* one. Fuck you! I'm not sure to who that fuck you was directed at, but someone sure as hell deserved it.

"Wow, really?" I tried not to cringe, his nod confirming his name. "Well that's unfortunate. Anyway, Jason, this is my bestest friend in the whole wide world, Rusty." I wasn't sure if that came out exactly right. I didn't mean to say the unfortunate part. I had nothing against the name. Or maybe I did. Not that it was the name's fault. Oh for god's sake. His name was Jason? Who does that?

"Okay baby, let's get you up to bed." Rusty pulled me close to his body, my feet stumbling unsteadily under my weight. Standing up was hard work.

"He your boyfriend?" Jason—not the Power Station one, the bar one—tipped his head to the man who was currently keeping me vertical. Rusty, my knight in shining armor.

"Who Rusty?" I laughed. I didn't mean to but it was just that so many people assumed. Hell even Jason—the Power Station one, not the bar one—had.

BACK STAGE

"No. We tried to have sex once, it didn't work out." My mouth once again spewed things it hadn't meant to say.

"And on that note, you've had enough." Rusty, wrapped both his arms around me, caging me in. Oh, look. I'm in a Rusty cage. I laughed out loud at my private joke.

"Oh come on, Rusty, don't be such a buzz kill." I wriggled unsuccessfully trying to free myself. "Jason is going to take me to his room where we are going to drink everything in his mini bar. Except the bourbon."

Because *he* likes bourbon and I refuse to even touch anything that *he* likes. I reminded myself, in case I'd forgotten.

"Who is *he*?" Jason asked, my private reminder having not been so private.

"Nobody. I mean literally nobody." I meant to say it confidently but it came out as a whisper. Maybe because I wasn't convinced he was a nobody, maybe because I knew I was lying.

"Hey Jason." Rusty scooped me into his arms and lifted me off the floor. "Thanks for looking after my girl, but I've got it from here."

And before my brain registered what was happening we were out of the bar and into the elevator. I didn't even say goodbye. Goodbyes and Jasons didn't have a good track record it seemed.

"Rus, put me down." My legs kicked in his arms as he held me close to his chest. The elevator had already started to move.

He didn't answer, instead waiting until the door slid open on the floor where our rooms were situated.

"Rusty." I protested again.

Nope, still nothing.

With what I can only describe as an amazing amount of skill, Rusty was able to wiggle his key out of his pocket and pressed it against the lock. The amazing skill did not extend to being able to holding me and open the door, which meant he had to put me down.

"No. I don't want to go to bed. I'm not a fucking child." I stomped my foot exactly like the child that I was not.

"Then stop acting like one." With a flick of the wrist, the door was open and Rusty had pushed me into his hotel room. "What the hell are you doing, Angie, this isn't you."

"What?" I asked naïvely pretending I didn't know what he was talking about. Duh. Like I didn't know.

He tossed his keycard onto the coffee table, leaning against the back of the couch. "You mean to tell me that you weren't about to go to some strange man's room for sex?"

"So what if I was? Maybe I just wanted to have sex. You have sex with lots of girls you don't know. I don't fucking judge you, all high and mighty."

I wasn't sure if I was mad that he was right or mad at myself for actually considering it.

"I'm not judging you." His voice didn't rise, nor did eyes move from mine. "I would never judge you, but don't tell me this is about sex. It's about *him*."

"Not everything is about Jason. The band one, not the bar one. Sometimes it's just about sex." My voice yelled where his hadn't.

I wasn't convincing, tears threatening to spill at any moment at just the mention of his name.

"Fine, then you can wait until you are sober and then you can have sex with as many random guys as you like," he yelled back.

"I'm not that drunk." More yelling, this time, me.

"Yes you are, you can barely stand." Yelling again, Rusty's turn.

"I don't want to wait until I'm sober. I want to have sex now, damn it." My voice was raised, as was my temper. Are you seeing a pattern yet?

"Fine, then have sex with me."

Oh I must be loaded because I could have sworn that Rusty just asked me to have sex with him. And that would be ridiculous.

I burst into hysterical laughter, taking a minute to catch my breath. "Oh my God, Rusty. I'm dying here." Well at least we weren't yelling anymore.

"I'm serious. You want to be on top or the bottom?" He slowly unbuttoned his shirt, the fabric slipping off his shoulders and onto the floor. His toned chest displaying his crazy detailed dragon tattoo that flexed as he went to unbutton his jeans.

Holy shit, he was serious. He was actually, serious.

"Have you lost your fucking mind?"

"Why? It's just sex, right?" He kicked off his boots, cool, calm and collected. "No big deal. You want sex so let's just fuck, take care of that urge for you."

He moved closer pushing aside my hair and looked me in eyes.

"No." I pulled away, my world feeling like it had been turned on its head.

"Why, no, Angie?" He didn't yell this time, pulling me into his arms and kissed my hair. "Didn't you just finish telling me how much you wanted it?"

"We can't have sex because it would be … a mistake," I answered, knowing that everything we had, would change. I'd already lost one man I loved, I couldn't lose a second. Not my best friend.

"Yeah it would." He nodded, his hands holding me still as I started to shake. "It would be a huge mistake, and still not as big as the one you would make if you went and fucked that other guy."

The point.

And there it was. And there I was. Completely unraveled. And the only one who hadn't seen it had been me.

"I'm a mess, Rus."

I tried not to cry. I mean really tried, but I couldn't stop. The pain, the hurt—I'd lost Jason, twice. And this time, it was so much worse.

"Yeah you are." Rusty, slowly rocked me. My fat ugly tears falling over his beautiful ripped chest. And yet, there wasn't one thing that was sexual about it. "Lucky for you I like my friends messy." He laughed. "It makes me feel more normal."

"Thank you." The palms of my hands wiped away my tears. The stain of mascara smudges all over my skin, both under my eyes and on my hands. Lucky I wasn't trying to be seductive because my latest effort would have most definitely failed.

"You know, usually the girl thanks me *after* the sex but sure." He shrugged, giving me a kiss on the cheek.

"We're not having sex." I shook my head. Rusty still standing there with his jeans unbuttoned, wearing no shirt wasn't going to convince me otherwise. As fine as the man was, what we had was better.

"Fine." His arms fell dramatically to his side as he sighed. "Let's be boring and *not* fuck." He flashed his amazing smile, the one that usually sent the panty population into overdrive. Well, all except for the ones I was currently wearing.

"I'm probably going to need some coffee. And an exorcist." My reflection stared back at me from the obnoxious mirror across the room. What I saw—wasn't pretty.

"Coffee I can do." Another hug. Another kiss. "The other part—I think we just get you showered and into bed and see where we land in the morning."

23
Jason

BIGGEST CLUSTERFUCK OF ALL TIME.

Of all the dumbest, most monumentally stupidest shit I'd ever done, this has to take the cake. And what made it even worse was I saw it coming a mile away and still, it didn't stop me.

Angie was right. I was an asshole.

She loved me.

Those words confused me so much I couldn't breathe. I'd heard them before, and the last time, they didn't bring good things.

I couldn't expect her to understand. There were the things she was asking of me that I wasn't able to give. Not because I didn't want, but because I couldn't. And if I pretended, it would have just made it worse—for me and for her.

In the crystal ball department I had come up empty. And who knows what forever even fucking meant. Did she want a promise? Say I'd never leave, that she'd do the same? Like words actually meant something. My actions were stronger than any words I'd ever spoke, and it hadn't been enough. She owned me, I wasn't going anywhere but she had to push.

It was always going to end up the same way. Both of us were delusional if we'd thought there'd be any other outcome. She deserved better. And not because I didn't love her—yeah, there was that word I'd promised I'd never fucking say—but because I was too fucked up to give her what she needed.

Well done, Jason. The minute you meet a girl worth a damn, you fucking run like a pussy. Because that's what I was doing. *I* let her walk out the door. *I* didn't stop her.

Table for miserable asshole, party of one? Yep. I had the standing reservation.

Every time there was a knock at the door I wanted it to be her. I wanted it all—her rage, her fury, her fists flying at my face. Except, the knock—and her rage—didn't come.

Her nightly *dedications* to me had stopped. Finished. No more. Nothing about what a cock I was. No odes to my death. No tributes to my demise. Just nothing. Radio fucking silence. That, ladies and gentleman, was the worst kind of hell. Because I knew—I'd broken her.

I'd done that. Me. Well done, motherfucker, you are a real champion.

I saw her even though she didn't see me. My messed up stalker routine not taking a breather even though we were done. Just hoping to catch a glimpse of her here or there when she didn't know I was watching. That light in her eyes? Gone. The firecracker attitude? Gone. And there wasn't a second out of every fucking day after it that I didn't fucking hate myself more. Dan was right. I was the gift that kept on giving.

"Hey, asswipe." Speak of the devil. "You want to get in on a game? Troy's shuffling the deck."

My zero fucks policy had extended to my door. Which had meant it was open. Which allowed the cocksucker to come in. Mental note, close the fucking door.

"Nope. I have this thing going on where I'm busy being a miserable fuck. It's taking up all of my time." My arms stretched out behind my head. My mind firmly cemented on hanging out in my hotel room, on my

BACK STAGE

couch. Preferably, alone. "Thanks for the offer though."

It was nice to be asked, even if he knew the answer. Same answer as it had been the last night, and the night before that. The whole *sharing is caring* rule didn't apply to me. I wasn't sharing jack.

"Hey look at this way, at least she is no longer telling most of the continental United States what a dick you are." He parked his ass on the sofa beside me, his eyes scooting around looking to see if there was a bottle. There wasn't. The drinking myself into a stupor had already gotten old. Besides, getting on stage with a hangover wasn't giving me a case of the warm and fuzzies. Neither was acting like an obnoxious dick. Other than what I already was. You could only fight nature so much.

"I know you are trying to help." My thanks-but-no-thanks coming thick and fast. "But you're not. So don't."

"Okay, okay." He raised his hands, hopefully throwing in the towel on operation cheer up Jase. "I'm not Troy, and I don't always know the right thing to say. But misunderstandings happen. You fuck up, you say sorry and you move on. That's the way it works. You obviously give a shit about this girl, because I don't notice dick usually and even *I* could see that."

Of all the fucking times for Dan to be perceptive, now was not that time. It just added another layer to the shit that was already piled on there. *Hey, we all noticed you loved her, yet you still let her go. Bravo. Dick.*

"Is there a point somewhere in there, or you just trying to contribute to my misery?"

Not that it mattered. The misery was pretty maxed out, so an extra helping here or there wasn't going to make a difference. Still, I hoped leaving was going to be featuring on his agenda soon. Misery most definitely did *not* love company, and who ever coined that phrase needed to go eat a big bag of dicks.

"What I'm saying is." I prepared myself for the *awesome* that was Dan logic. That was sarcasm in case you didn't know. "If you care about her just go back and get her. You'll work it out."

Sure, because shit is just that easy. *Sorry* wasn't a fucking cure-all and exactly what had changed in the last few days? I had no more to offer her than I did before I ended us. A heart to heart over a box of Kleenex wasn't going to cut it.

"There are some things that can't be worked out, Dan. But thanks."

I admired his commitment. The bastard had shown real growth of late. A world away from the selfish, arrogant dude he used to be.

"So you're just going to sit here and be fucking miserable?" Dan's session offering pearls of wisdom was obviously not over. "Newsflash, it doesn't work out, asshole. When Ash left me, I tried to convince myself I'd just find someone else. But there wasn't anyone else. She was it. Troy—he came to the same fucking conclusion. His girl didn't even ditch him; he just had his head too far up his ass that he couldn't see what was right in front of him. James and Hannah, they broke up and guess what, they got back together. Alex and Lexi, same fucking thing. Those two were more dramatic about it because let's face it—they are both fucking drama queens, but in the end, there was no keeping them apart."

No words. Which is exactly what you have to say when Dan starts making sense. My silence gave Dan the floor once more, to wow me again with his astounding attempt at being friend of the year.

"I'm not going to put words in your mouth, but it looks to me like you might love this girl and if you don't go after her, you're going to regret it."

"I already regret it." My clipped response shot out of my mouth like a bullet out of a gun. Regret rocked the number two position on my list when it came to Angie. Right after how much I fucking loved her.

Well … Fuck.

"So why are you sitting here talking to me?" He punched me in the arm, the leather of the couch creaking under his ass as he moved. "She's in the same fucking building and I've seen her, she looks like shit. That's not me being a douchebag about it because it's Angie, I mean she looks sad. She's miserable without you too."

But she'd be more miserable with me. "I can't go get her back."

"Why the fuck not?" The I-don't-understand face came right after the sentence. "I take back what I said about Lexi and Alex, *you're* the fucking drama queen."

"Because I'm the fucking one who ended it, asshole." The voice boomed, making the bastard sit up in his seat. "It was me." I shook my head, the gravity of the situation hitting me, as I owned it. "I'm the one who told her we were done."

"Well why the hell did you do that, loser?" Dan stared in disbelief, finally seeing I wasn't the dude who had his shit all together. "Aren't you supposed to be smart?"

"Because I fucking love her." My head fell into my clenched fists. It was the first time I'd said out loud. The word hung in the air for a second before I was able to continue. "Because I fucking know that if she is with me, I'm going to hurt her."

"What the *fuck* are you talking about?" Dan continued on his trail of disbelief, the big picture not being drawn for him yet. "Are you fucking moonlighting as a serial killer? How the fuck are you going to hurt her? Unless you count dating a jerk-off like you as a personal injury, what the hell could you fucking do? You're the sensible one. The reliable one." He listed all the things I was *supposed* to be, not the things I actually was. Broken, should have topped out the list.

"No. I'm a fucking fraud," I yelled, no longer giving a shit with the pretense. "You see what you want to fucking see. But I'm not a good guy. You've seen the real me, dude. You've seen me so drunk that I couldn't stand up. You've seen me break some guy's nose I didn't know because I was so angry I couldn't take it. And I think even you know how many women I've fucked in the past in an effort just to keep myself from going over the edge. That shit doesn't go away, it's still there just waiting to fucking come out and play. You want to put her on the crash course? And even if by some kind of walk-on-water miracle I can be guaranteed that someday my shit isn't going to be jacked-up, what can I fucking give her? Marriage? Kids? What am I going to tell her if she wants to have that conversation?"

Dan stared at me, his mouth wide open; the outburst not the first he'd seen, but it had been a while since he'd been up close and personal with my crazy.

"Em wasn't just some high school crush who just screwed my best friend. I had my life together. I stopped all that shit, and she dragged me right back to hell. I know Angie is not Em. But the shit that bitch put me through just about ruined me. Straight up, I wanted to kill her. Not pretend kill. Like actually do it. And the thought of being in a relationship again scares the fuck out of me. That someone could make me go that fucking crazy, or that I'd hand over the keys to my sanity again."

So there it was. On the table. All of it, and I hadn't held anything back. Never in a million years did I ever think I would fess up to being afraid of anything, but I'd said it anyway. I was scared. Scared as fuck of breaking Angie's heart. Scared she would break mine. But most of all scared that I was so fucking defective that I didn't have the capacity to be normal. To have a normal relationship where I could be with her. Trust issues. Giving over a power. None of it simmered well with me.

"I can't tell her that *love will conquer all* bullshit when I don't believe it myself."

Fuck knows what I believed anymore, my reality had twisted so much in my head I was convinced that maybe it hadn't been true. That all that shit from the past was a bad dream. Drama queen, like Dan said. And then I realize, it all happened. And I live that hell all over again.

"It's not because I don't want to, it's because I can't."

"Fuck me, Jason." For the first time since he walked in Dan wasn't wearing his shit-is-going-to-be-ok glasses. "This is really fucked up."

"Yes. It is."

My coming clean, now full circle. It wasn't going to change, we could pretend it was different and wrap it up with a freaking bow but it was always going to be the same.

"I am fucked up and I am not going to fucking bring that down on her." The thought of any of it touching her, ripped the rage right back to where I knew I could be dangerous. "Do you get that? I left because I loved her, because I'm in love with her, and *not* because I didn't care enough."

"I don't know what to say." Well, someone call Guinness. Dan was speechless. "Like legit, I have no words right now."

"Yep, so you see a bunch of roses and a *sorry* isn't going to cut it." I laughed. Not because it was funny, because really, what else was there to do? Yep. World of fucking shit—population one.

"Maybe we should get Troy, he's better at this shit than I am." Dan conceded that he was in over his head.

"Nope, we get no one else involved. I will deal with this my way. I'm good, really." First came the nod. "Give me a few more days, let the sting wear off and then I'll move on." Then I moved on to the forced smile. Fake-it-till-you-make-it was going to be featuring heavily in my repertoire for a while. The bullshit about moving on was thrown in for good measure.

"Do you really think you can?" Dan took about a second before he called me on it. "You said you loved her. I don't know many men who can just walk away from a girl they're in love with."

Surely there was some catastrophic event about to take place. Like the end of the world or something. Because there we were, Dan being responsible, and me being the recipient of the advice. It was my time to step up.

"Yeah, well I'm not *many men*." I swallowed, hard. "I'm me, and I can walk away because I know it's the right thing to do." It *was* the right thing to do.

"Stop being so fucking perfect, douchebag." Dan punched me in the arm, his grin unsteady. "You're going to make me look bad."

"Only *you* can hear what I just told you and still think I could make you look bad. Trust me, Dan. I'm far from fucking perfect." I shook my head in disbelief.

"You're a lot more than you think. If it's one thing Ash taught me, it's that perception is subjective." Dan slapped me on the shoulder.

"Wow dude, big words and everything. That beautiful wife of yours use flash cards when she taught you that?" I laughed. No seriously, someone needed to check the date. When did those Mayans say the end of the world was coming?

"Go fuck yourself." He flipped me off, big ass grin of his face.

"Thanks." The *for everything* that I didn't attach to the end of the sentence was unnecessary. The eyeball exchange we had going on said more than that word anyway.

"Anytime. And for the record, my wife *is* fucking beautiful." The smugness was back as was the smile he got when he spoke about his wife. "And if I weren't such an arrogant asshole, I'd admit she's way better than I deserved. But whatever her reason was for giving me a chance, I'll take it. In fact, I applaud her lack of judgment. Maybe give *that* some thought."

"Dan, stop, dude. You are freaking me out with all this maturity." It was my turn to punch him in the arm.

"Ok loser, I'm going to go call my beautiful wife. Hopefully she'll talk dirty to me so I can jerk off. This long distance thing blows, I think my balls might actually explode." Dan stood up, pulling at the crotch of his jeans.

So much for Dan and his maturity, I've got to admit, it was starting to make me more than just a little uncomfortable. "And everything is once again right with the world." I laughed as I watched him walk out the door.

24

Angie

THE NIGHT IN THE HOTEL ROOM WITH RUSTY WAS MY BOTTOM. MY low. There was nowhere further to go. The drinking, the idea of sleeping with some man I didn't even know—punishment, because I was stupid enough to fall in love with the same man twice. Have my heart broken by the same man, twice.

So, I'd been an idiot. Dumb beyond belief. But I needed to start healing and love myself. Not in the narcissistic way Dan Evans loved himself, although he wasn't as conceited as he used to be. But in a way where I accepted that what happened wasn't a personal flaw.

I loved. That's who I was.

I would never be perfect, my ass would always be bigger than I'd want it to be. My hair wasn't going to suddenly be shiny, blonde and perfect. And I was probably always going to be the girl who said the word *fuck* too much and didn't wear the right kind of clothes. It was okay, because I'm me. And rather than try and worry about what I couldn't do or what I didn't have, I would focus on the fact that I had so very much. A band that was more like family than friends, a father who loved me enough for the mom I missed, and friends new and old who accepted me for who I was. Fuck Jason Irwin. He didn't deserve me.

"I hear Megs and Ash are coming in this afternoon. We going to lose you to the *Sisterhood of the Traveling Pants*?" Rusty nudged my shoulder, taking a seat beside me. His grin proved he wasn't anywhere near annoyed.

"You'd never lose me, but I'm glad they are spending the weekend with us. I miss those two so much." My own grin widened. And my smile was totally not faked.

"So is that why you called this band meeting? You're worried about my defection to my own sex?"

Rusty had sent a message early this morning saying we needed to discuss the rest of the tour. While it wasn't completely out of character, it seemed way too structured for him. He was more a let's-get-a-beer-and-discuss, not the-first-point-on-the-agenda-is. Which is why the four of us had gathered in my hotel room, the venue for our makeshift meeting.

"Yeah, about that." Rusty rubbed the back of neck awkwardly. "Just remember how much you love me and how much your life would suck without me." His sentence punctuated by a knock at the door.

"What did you do?" My eyes widened as they darted from the door back to him. Bodily harm hadn't been ruled out.

"I'll get it." Max stood up, apparently bored with Joey and talk of his newfound fame. His face not showing surprise led me to believe he was in on whatever was about to go down. Bastards. Screw them and their unflagging loyalty to each other.

"Rusty, who is on the other side of that door?" I demanded, watching Max move to the door and pull it open. My heart had suddenly started beating so fast I was convinced I was going to have a heart attack.

"Hey." Troy walked in, the rest of Power Station behind him. Jason being that he was part of that band was included in the people who entered the room. "Good to see everyone could make it." He looked around and nodded to Rusty, some secret telepathic exchange taking place.

It was all rather inconvenient. Not the meeting part, whose purpose

BACK STAGE

hadn't been ascertained yet, it was the having to find another guitarist part that concerned me. It wouldn't be easy to replace Rusty, as his death catapulted to the top of my to-do list. Of course I'd make sure he was properly mourned, it would be the least I could do.

"What's all this about?" Jason's eyes flared as they came to rest on me.

The asshole still looked good, wearing the hell out of the jeans and T-shirt that had been lucky enough to grace his body. I had given up hope that was going to change, obviously asking too much of the universe that he suddenly become grotesquely ugly. His body was also a problem. He needed to stop working out so much too. Thank god, he was still wearing a shirt. And why the hell was I even thinking about *him* and any of that? My to-do list was going to need an amendment. Shaking myself had now taken the number one position.

"Relax, brother. Take a seat." James patted him on the back. By him I meant Jason, the guy who was currently staring at me. This I knew because I happened to be staring back. Awesome. It couldn't get more awkward if we tried. At least I wasn't the only one in the dark, the good-looking asshole I was currently eyeballing also seeming to not have received the memo.

"So anyone else chilly?" Rusty shivered, before nodding to Max and Joey. "Yeah, think we should move this meeting to the pool. Boys, follow me."

"What, where are you going?" My stare match with Jason took a backseat to the threat of being deserted. Being alone with him never worked out well and my feelings were still very much off kilter. As much as I was planning Rusty's demise, I needed him to stay. We needed a buffer; the Rocky Mountains would have been good, but at this stage I'd settle for the substitute that was my band.

"Angie, just know we love you. We'll be back later." His hand rubbed my arm in reassurance, his eyes spelling out that he wouldn't be far.

My head nodded that I would be okay even though I didn't believe it, which allowed Rusty to turn his attention to Troy. "Troy, you better know what you are doing. This goes bad, you'll be finding yourself a new support band."

"I've got it from here," Troy reassured him, the *it* that he *had* still very much a mystery to me. The prospect of finding out wasn't automatically filling me with excitement.

"You guys better come with us too." Rusty glanced over at Power Station and jerked his head to the door. I almost fell to my knees in relief that the meeting just would be Troy and me. While not ideal, but just the two of us, I could handle.

"Looks like our cue to leave too, Dan and Alex." James rounded up only two of the three band members who were supposed to leave. "I think the pool sounds like a good idea." My relief short lived.

Great. We were being sandbagged.

"Is this some fucked up intervention?" Jason echoed my very thought. He'd obviously not been informed of the plan either, the two of us apparently the only ones in the dark.

"Jase, just listen to Troy." Dan clapped him over the shoulder. "Sorry brother, but you're both fucking miserable. This shit can't go on."

There was no further discussion, with both my band and Power Station leaving. And then there were three. Three was never a good number unless you were into threesomes, which I wasn't so I could only expect bad things to follow.

"Troy, I know what you are trying to do but it's unnecessary." My voice finally found itself as I tried to reason my way out of it. The *it* still undefined. "There isn't anything that we need to talk about." We'd said it all before. Back to front and sideways. Nothing was going to change.

"Have to agree with Angie, nothing to discuss here." Jase joined the party, his tone clipped and annoyed. Which just annoyed me more. In case anyone forgot, he was an asshole.

"Oh, so *now* you agree with me." I couldn't help the sarcasm as it leaped out of my throat before I had a chance to stop it. Honestly, not sure I would have anyway. "Allow me a minute to bask in the wonder that is Jason Irwin's approval." The eye roll was unnecessary but once again, couldn't be helped.

"I'm not engaging in this, Angie. You want to talk shit, go right ahead." His stare was fierce but not of hate—like mine—but of something else. Resolve? Intent?

"God forbid you engaged in *anything*." I couldn't help myself pushing it further with the hurt subsiding, as anger became my new best friend. "How's life on asshole island?"

"Original. Still not interested." He was so cold.

How could anyone be so unfeeling? We'd had tender moments, it hadn't been just sex, but it was like a switch had been flicked and we were back to where we'd started. The weeks erased, with the Jason standing in front of me being the same one who was with the band when they'd asked me to first join the tour.

"Fuck you and your *not interested*—"

"Okay, both of you. Sit down and stop talking," Troy exploded, the vein on the side of his neck doing the thing it did when he got angry. Which he seemed to be right now. "You are both giving me a headache."

"Troy, thanks but it's obvious neither of us want to talk to each—"

"I said, sit down." Troy repeated, calmer than the first but no less intense. My butt hit the chair without any further encouragement.

Jase stayed standing, defiantly.

"That wasn't a fucking request." Troy paused after each word incase Jase was not reading the scary vibe he was rocking. That vein bulging at the side of his neck, threatening to explode.

"Fine." He conceded and took a seat opposite me, which incidentally was as far as he could get while still satisfying Troy's urge to have us both sit down. I was both offended by his conspicuous distance and relieved by the comfort of the safeness.

"You know what, you are both acting like fucking dumbasses." Troy didn't back down, holding his ground even though Jason didn't look pleased. "And you both need your asses kicked as far as I'm concerned. You don't want to sort this shit out? Well guess what, neither of you have a say in it anymore." He eyed us both hard and I had no doubt that no one would be leaving the room until some sort of resolution was in place. Who needed a negotiator, scary Troy was enough of an incentive.

"There is nothing to be sorted." My throat got tighter as emotions jostled for position.

"No, you need to hear something first." While Troy's voice was directed at me, his eyes were solely focused on Jase. Whoa. Scary Troy sounded like he had some insider knowledge. Here was the loop, and here I was—completely out of it.

"Troy, don't." Jase gained an understanding in their wordless exchange that clearly I didn't. "This isn't any of your business."

"Is that how you see it? That this is none of my business?" Troy shook his head in disbelief. "You are so fucking wrong. That day you joined us—the band, you became fucking family. Doesn't matter you weren't there from the start, it doesn't mean shit. You're my brother, same as Dan, Alex or James and I don't sit around when I see my *family* doing something I know they will regret. So you are wrong, it is very much *my* business."

The urge to wave my hand and say *umm ... hello, I'm still here* was overwhelming. Instead I went with sitting silently. Less attention that way.

"Em—" Troy started.

"Don't. Don't you fucking dare," Jason warned, up out of his chair, almost lunging for Troy. Holy shit. I think he might actually hit him.

"You wanna take a swing?" Troy stretched out his arms, his eyes welcoming it. "Fucking do it. Because the only way this isn't happening is if you lay me out. So you better make that first fucking hit count, because I'm only giving you one shot."

The fists clenched by Jason's sides were white and ready to take a swing. Troy's face absolutely ready to take it to that level if that's where it needed to go.

"Troy." My voice wavered as I stepped in between the two heavyweights. Getting in the middle of a fistfight wasn't smart, but I wasn't going to sit by and watch them duke it out either.

"Angie, you need to know." A ripple of calmness cracked through as Troy flicked his eyes down on me. "There is a lot of shit that you don't know about. Jason's past, before you knew him. Things that will fucking mess a man up."

"He told me." I nodded, hoping the situation had been defused. Not that his reasoning made complete sense to me, and not that it made it hurt any less. In fact it made it hurt more, that I was paying for the sins of someone else. "His girlfriend cheated on him. I get it. He has trust issues."

"That's what you told her?" Troy's head whipped around to Jason.

"That's what happened." Jason's words barely audible through his tight jaw.

"Look, it doesn't matter. He had a girlfriend who betrayed him and—"

"Em was his fucking wife." The words echoed off the walls.

Silence.

No one spoke.

Wife.

I heard it over and over again. It hadn't been a girlfriend. It had been his wife.

"What? You were married?" My mouth dropped open in total disbelief. "You told me she was your girlfriend." I scaled my memory to make sure I hadn't heard incorrectly. Nope. Wife was something I would have remembered. The *Oh, hey I was married* never having been mentioned.

"No, I told you I was with a girl and she cheated. You assumed she was my girlfriend. I didn't correct you." Jase's eyes focused on me, his tone unapologetic.

"Are you fucking with me?" My voice almost choked in disbelief. No seriously, was he fucking kidding?

"I've been divorced for longer than I was married. It is not important."

The man I had known was a complete and utter lie.

"You." Troy pointed to Jase, his gaze enough to level a ten-story building without the use of dynamite. "If you were going to tell her anything, you should have told her the whole fucking story. And you," his attention turned back to me, "you shouldn't just automatically jump to conclusions that it was just *a girl* fucking around that has made him so detached. No one is that much of a fucking pussy."

I was stunned. Troy had never yelled at me like that. In fact, I'd never seen him lose his cool. The words I had planned to say lost their way from my brain to my mouth as I stared, wide-eyed and mute.

With both Jase and I subtly silenced, either from shock or the I-have-no-idea-what to say, Troy took a seat. Jase encouraged by his friend's ass-in-chair position decided to replicate it and also sat down.

"So you know about his past."

I nodded as sorrow and possibly regret flicked through Jase's beautiful brown eyes. If I hadn't been so mad and hurt I may have wanted to hold him.

"Problem was, while he left his delinquent buddies behind, his evil bitch of a girlfriend tracked him down," Troy continued. The mention of the evil bitch enough to make Jase flinch. "Military life didn't suit her by all accounts."

"Why did you marry her if she was a bitch? And why so young? If you were trying to make a change, why keep her?"

"Originally because it was habit. I thought I cared about her and when I tried to break up with her, she got pregnant. As much as I didn't want to be with her, I didn't want my kid growing up without a dad."

The news of his marriage was nothing. It just got a hundred times worse.

"Holy shit. You have a kid too?" My hands moved up to my throat as I struggled to breathe. "Did I know anything about you? Like at all?"

It felt like the walls were closing in on me, as the lies continued to unravel.

"Yes, you did." His eyes refused to leave mine, pleading with me to believe him "You know me *now*. Who I am, now. I didn't want you to know the other stuff. I'm not proud of who I was. My life was a mess; I'd made shitty choices. I put my family through hell and they never deserved any of it, they are good people." He swallowed hard, as if fighting an internal battle as to whether or not to continue. "I was turning it around. I figured I could help her do that too, and we could raise our kid together. I take care of what's mine."

I continued to freak out over the current downloading of information I was receiving. Asking if it could get any worse would be surely tempting fate. Troy was the one who first broke through the current silence.

"I'm going to let you guys talk it out." He nodded to both of us, seeking permission before leaving. "But I'm going to be outside, so if either of you get out of control expect me to be coming right back in. We clear?"

"Yes." Both Jason and I answered simultaneously. In truth, the horror would be better *without* the audience.

"So where is your kid now? With your ex-wife?" I asked Jason as Troy closed the door behind him.

"I assume so," he answered, very non-committal.

"You assume?" I said louder than I intended. "You don't know where your own kid lives?" The whole I-take-care-of-what's-mine argument still ringing in my ears.

"I don't have any rights anymore." The words seeming to sting as he spoke them. "So *no*, I don't know."

"What do you mean you don't have any rights? You just signed over your kid?"

"He wasn't mine!" he shouted, the sound exploding through the room. His face a mix of pain and anger as his body seemed to struggle with remaining still. "She came clean just before his first birthday. I'd come home from working a twelve-hour day and found her passed out drunk on the floor. Thomas was crying in his crib wearing the same fucking diaper for who knows how long. I threatened to divorce her, told her that if she didn't sober up I would leave and I'd take our son with me. She just laughed and told me he wasn't my kid. Bragged that she didn't know whose he was." His eyes blinked rapidly, as his voice tightened. "I watched him be born, fucking held him for months. Was up late while he cried. *I* was his father."

There was nothing I could say, the pain ripping through him enough to tear out my own heart. My own tears threatening to spill as he continued.

"I thought she was full of shit, that the booze was talking. So we got the tests done. For the first time ever, Em had told the truth. He wasn't mine." He shook his head, as he seemed to struggle to go on. "And even knowing all of that, I stayed. Because I loved Thomas more than I hated Em. I didn't care he didn't have the same blood type, that kid was mine."

"So what happened?" My voice was barely a whisper, not wanting to contribute to more of his pain.

"We tried to make it work but we couldn't. The drinking didn't stop and my enlistment was almost up. Honestly, the thought of signing up again scared the fuck out of me. Knowing I could be shipped away and leaving Thomas with only his mother. So I decided to get out, and just before I separated from the Army, she left. Cleared out my bank account and took my car while I was at work one day. Didn't say goodbye. No note explaining why, and she had taken Thomas with her."

"Did you try and find them?"

"Of course I fucking tried to find them." The hurt visible in his eyes. "I was granted leave and went looking for them. She kept moving and it wasn't until she got into trouble and her mother was awarded temporary custody of Thomas that I tracked them down. She had been doing drugs and sleeping around, not far from our hometown; she didn't even care about him. So consumed with herself, she didn't even give a shit." His jaw tightened with rage, seemingly reliving his hell with the telling of his past. My heart ached for him and the pain I knew he must have endured.

"I fought for him." He shook his head and he rubbed his eyes. "I used every single cent I had left to fight for a kid that wasn't even mine, and I lost. I had no rights, no say. Apparently loving a kid for the first twelve months of his life doesn't mean shit to judges." He coughed out a laugh of disbelief.

"Can you believe she sat in that courtroom and laughed? She thought it was funny that I knew she had slept around, knew that Thomas wasn't my son and that I was still willing to raise him anyway. She laughed her ass off; confessed Thomas was my best friend's kid. Said she never loved me, that she just said the words. Because I was convenient."

"I can't believe someone could do that to another human being. Be so cruel." *I'm so sorry* I finished in my head, overwhelmed by the desire to hold him. My hands, like the rest of me, didn't try, scared that my touch wouldn't be welcomed. The back-off his body was screaming, loud and clear.

"Needless to say, the day of the court case I bought a used car and left town. Canada seemed far enough, so I sat in a bar and got messed up. Lucky for me it was the same bar the guys were playing in. Not sure if it was fate or some higher power that they found me, but they took me in and gave me a reason not to go home. Which was a plus, or I'd probably still be doing jail time right now.

"So yeah, it wasn't *just* that she cheated on me. It's not just something I can just get over. That vile excuse for a woman almost destroyed me. I gave her that power, married her and handed over my fucking heart. She used me so many times I lost count. So, yeah. I have a bunch of issues. Commitment and trust in relationships not a good experience for me."

"Jason, why didn't you tell me?" I struggled not to cry, wanting desperately to make it better, say something to change it.

"Why Angie, so I could have your fucking pity?" He stared at me with emotions I couldn't even define burning through his eyes. "You think it would have made it easier to be around me knowing how fucked up I was? You didn't need all that extra baggage in your life. I saw the way you looked at me. Like I was a decent guy, and I wanted you to believe the lie. I didn't want you to know any of this."

"But you *are* a decent guy." I finally stopped fighting the urge, my hand reaching out and touching his. "You fought for a kid that wasn't even yours."

"I should never have been with her." He pulled his hand out of mine and got up out of his chair. "Do you know how many people warned me about her? I didn't listen. The shit I put my family through, because of my *friends*, because of *her*. That's not a decent person. Open your eyes, Angie; I am *not* a decent person. She fucking destroyed me but I've owned what I've become. And that is not someone you should be around. You are too fucking perfect, and even on my best day I wouldn't deserve you."

It killed me. Jason unable to see what an amazing man he was, for him to feel like his past defined him. For him to think that he was undeserving of love.

"I'm not perfect." My head shook as the tears started to fall. It was too late, my leaky eyes deciding they had waited long enough. "You are all I ever wanted. I just wanted *you*."

"Oh hell, Angie." He kneeled down in front of me and wiped away my tears with his thumbs. "Well that's dumb." He gave me a sad smile. "Why would you want an asshole like me?"

"Because I love you, asshole. I tried not to, but that didn't work out so well." The tears continued to fall, any hope I had of stopping them long gone.

"Angie, all I seem to do is hurt you." He pulled me in close to his chest, his thumping heartbeat pounding just as fast as mine. "What if I can't change? What if I can't be anything other than this? I don't know that I can ever get married again. Kids? I just don't know that I can do that. It killed me to lose him, for me to say goodbye to a child I thought was mine. I can't ask someone I love to hang around on a maybe. I won't do that to you." His hand gently stoked my hair as my tears wet the front of his T-shirt.

"You love me?" My head jerked back in shock, the words almost knocking the wind out of me. My eyes tried desperately to focus despite the tears.

"Yeah, I love you. I always knew you were something special, Angie. Which is why I resisted sleeping with you for so long. I didn't want you to be just another girl for me. There was something so inherently good about you; I could tell that just in the time we spent together. And I just wanted to feel that, just once. I was selfish for wanting that, but I couldn't stop myself."

"But I'm not perfect. I'm not as good as you think I am. And I wanted to be with you."

"You are perfect. In every single way. That fact you can't see that makes me want to punch a hole in a wall. Look at you, you're beautiful. But that isn't even the half of it. You're so fucking talented, it's ridiculous. And so freaking smart. And that mouth of yours … " He gentled thumbed my lips. "I love every single word that comes out of it."

"Then be with me. Take a chance with me."

I'd never begged a man in my life. In fact, begging for anything wasn't in my nature. It wasn't who I was; the idea frowned upon in my family. It wasn't in my make up to sit and hope something happened, I either made it happen or I moved on. And the only other time I begged for anything was for my mom not to die. For her to stay just a little longer with us. But I knew that my Pops had begged for the exact same thing so that made it okay. But, as Jason held me in his arms, I was begging. Begging that he gave us that chance. That I wouldn't lose the only man I'd ever really loved other than my dad. That he wouldn't walk out on me again.

"You deserve better. You deserve so much better." He kissed the top of my head, his arms tightly wrapped around me.

"No, you do."

It was as if my mouth had a mind of its own—which to be honest, it usually did—and it stopped talking and started kissing him. I knew the kiss wouldn't solve anything. It wouldn't take away his pain or mine. It wouldn't change the wasted years, the misunderstanding. But I needed to anyway. I needed to connect with him, to be closer to him than I already was. And right now, the only way I could do that was with my kiss. And I was going to kiss him for as long as he would let me.

25

Jason

"ANGIE, SWEETHEART." I PULLED AWAY FROM HER MOUTH, MY LIPS cursing me for the distance the minute I'd moved away. "You're making it hard for me to stop."

Sex shouldn't have even been on my radar. Hell, walking out and making sure I never made her cry the way she just did should have been my only priority. But her kissing me like that threw whatever ideas I had out the window. My cock didn't give a shit how inappropriate the timing was; it wanted her and only her.

"Then don't stop." She pulled me back against her. "Be with me and don't stop." She sucked against the skin at my throat as my hard-on kicked at the front of my jeans.

"Sex won't solve anything." By some miracle I was able to say something other than get your clothes off and let me bury myself inside of you. "I can't use you; I can't do it just because it feels good." My hands not listening to my mouth as they palmed her tits.

"Don't be with me because it solves anything; be with me because you want me." She clawed at my shirt, the fucking thing following her

BACK STAGE

every command as she ripped it off my body.

"Angie, Troy is right outside that door. And it's not locked." My eyes flicked to the door the big guy was no doubt still standing behind. His words crystal clear that he wasn't going to be far in case we needed a referee.

"Then lock the door, but I don't care what he sees or hears. I want you, and I want you to be with me, now." Her fingers fumbled with the front of my jeans, my suggestion that we put the brakes on not even getting airtime.

"Look at me." I tipped her chin toward me so I could get a good look into those drop-dead gorgeous eyes. "No one gets to see or hear you like that. And there is nothing I want more than to be with you right now, but I can't do it and hurt you again."

"You aren't going to hurt me. I'm not asking you to give me forever, just be with me now."

Walk away is what my mind screamed. *Kiss her goodbye and leave her the fuck alone.* But I couldn't. It wasn't in me.

"Hell, I can't ever say no to you. I know I should, but I just can't." I grabbed her T-shirt and tore it from her body. "I want you. I've always wanted you." My mouth sucked against her skin, her bra getting in the way of what I wanted.

"Good, then take me because I want you, too." She rubbed her body against the front my jeans, my cock ready to give her whatever the hell she demanded.

The unlocked door got my attention for about a minute, and then I settled myself knowing if anyone came through that door I'd tear them limb from limb. No one would get to see her the way I did, naked and exposed with nothing but that fancy ink to cover her body. That was mine, and even though I had no claim to it, I wanted it tonight.

"Take them off." Her fingers clawed at my jeans, her effort to get them off not getting them further than my hips.

"Not here." I stood up, grabbing her ass and hauling her up with me. "I want you on the bed, so I can lay you out and look at you properly."

She didn't protest, just a quiet little moan as I ground my cock in that sweet spot between her legs before lifting her higher so I could carry her to her bed.

Unlike our hotel rooms, hers was basic. Which was convenient being that I only had to take five steps from the couch where we'd been situated, to her bed, which is where I needed us to be. The sheets were still unmade, the comforter hanging half way off the bed as I tossed her down on the mattress.

"This bra is pretty but it's blocking my view." My fingers got busy releasing the clasp from the back, the lace getting tossed aside the minute I was able.

"I want you naked, too." She pulled me down on the bed, scrambling up onto her knees before I had a chance to have any more play time.

"You wear the fuck out of these jeans, but I need you out of them." She yanked at the denim, encouraging me to lift my ass as she moved them down my legs.

"Now what's your grand plan, beautiful?" I lifted my head off the pillow and studied the bunched up jeans pooled at my feet, their journey off me and onto the floor being stopped by a pair of heavy, black boots.

"You think that's going to stop me from getting what I want?" She smirked, her eyes going straight to the bulge being housed in my boxers. "Mmm, I like to see you hard and know it's because of me."

"Christ, Angie, I just have to look at you and I get hard. You touching me just accelerates the process." My pulse worked overtime as I watched her lean down and lick the front of my boxers. "Fuck me." The words poured out of my mouth as she pulled down the fabric and swirled her tongue around the head of my cock. I had no hope of stringing together anything more coherent than cuss words and heavy breathing.

My hands fisted her hair as she sucked my shaft deeper into her mouth, her tongue tracing around my length before allowing it to pass between her lips. The action of licking and sucking driving me so crazy my lungs were having problems remembering how to function.

"Jesus, Angie. Slow down." I yanked on her hair, needing her to ease off the award winning blowjob or I was going to spill my load right into her mouth.

"You having a problem with control, asshole?" She flicked her tongue against the head of my dick one last time. "My mouth tempting you to come already?"

"Yes. I've told you how much I love that dirty fucking mouth."

It was my turn, my back jacking up off the mattress as I grabbed her waist. My mouth claimed hers while I toed off my boots and kicked off my jeans. My hands got busy with her jeans, Angie getting on the same page as she kicked off her heels and wriggled out of her pants. It felt like shit was moving in slow motion as we stripped down to just our underwear.

"You're still wearing too much." My eyes went from her beautiful naked tits to the lace that was still covering her pussy. "So unless you want me to tear them from your body, I suggest you get them off." My plan was for her panties to be off any way possible. Her way or mine, didn't faze me either way.

"You aren't naked either, smartass." Her short fingernails grazed just enough of my skin to sting, her attention not being on the material covering her body, but on the one covering mine.

Any thoughts I had went out the window, with just one remaining.

Her.

And I needed her in every sense of the word.

"That's better." She pushed the boxers far enough down my thighs that my cock was able to spring free, my hard-on hitting my stomach.

"Following instructions isn't a strong point for you, is it?" I finished the job of getting naked, getting rid of the boxers and tossed them to the floor.

"We were getting you naked." I grabbed at the side of those delicate panties and pulled, the fabric easily tearing away from her body. "Don't say I didn't warn you." The shredded panties swung playfully off one of my fingers before she even had a chance to realize she was bare.

"You're paying for those." She grinned and snatched them out of my hands.

"I'm just giving you what you wanted, and I'm not paying for shit." I grinned back, pushing her body down on the mattress so she was stretched out in front of me.

Every single curve of her body was a work of fucking art. The color that covered it just enhanced an already perfect canvas and I wanted to kiss every square inch of it. So rather than stare at her like a creepy asshole, my mouth got busy doing just that. Starting with her neck, then to the swell of her tits and then further down to her flat stomach. She mewled with approval as my mouth got creative, kissing or licking parts of her skin, my hands parting her thighs so I could see just how much she was ready for me.

"Jesus, Angie." My tongue moved along her pussy, her body more than ready to take me. "You get this wet from sucking my dick?"

"Yes," she moaned arching her back and lifting her body closer to my mouth.

"I want to taste you so bad but my cock is getting jealous." My fingers plunged into her as my lips moved to sucking her clit. "Very jealous." My mouth hummed against her skin as I continued to lick in between her legs.

"Yes." Her fingers dug into my shoulders as I watched her come apart, getting her there not taking very long with the finger and tongue combo I was working.

"That feel good, Angie?" I kissed the inside of her thigh while her pussy tightened against my fingers. "That what you needed?" I couldn't bring myself to stop, seeing her writhe underneath me as the orgasm I provided echoed through her body.

"You want more validation, you egomaniac, or you finally going to take me?"

There was no more thinking involved. The game I had been playing, teasing the pleasure out of her, was no longer fun as I moved up her body and sunk my cock into her. It was automatic, our bodies coming together like they belonged. I'd been fighting it for so long that the minute she'd given me permission I couldn't stop. Her lips kissing my throat while I slid into her, dragging my length out before pushing back inside of her. It was heaven.

It felt so good.

Too good.

Which is exactly what made me stop, my body freezing mid stroke as I realized I wasn't wearing a condom.

"Fuck." My elbows dug into the mattress as I scrambled to pull out. "Angie, I'm not wearing anything."

"It's ok. I have that thing in my arm. I can't get pregnant." She locked her legs around me, stopping me from pulling out all the way.

"I don't think it's a good idea." The thought of accidently getting her pregnant enough to make me break out into a cold sweat.

"Look." She stretched out her arm and wriggled her fingers around on it. "You can see it just below my skin. Jason, I'm not going to trap you. I'm not her." Her hand reached up and gently stroked the edge of my jaw.

The fact she felt she had to prove it just about broke my heart. That I had moved her to a place where she thought I questioned her motives. I trusted her completely—big call coming from me— and deep down, I knew that Angie would never do what Em had done. But going bare wasn't just about me; it was about protecting her as well. And that right there was more important to me than anything.

More important than protecting myself—both physically and mentally.

"I know you aren't, I just don't want to do anything you don't want to." My brain not convinced we shouldn't be pulling out and getting suited up before continuing down this road.

"Look at me. I'm clean and you get tested, right?" Her hand moved down my neck and across my shoulder. Her fingertips tingling my skin in their wake.

"Yes of course, I've never had sex without a condom except ... well except for her and you." I couldn't bring myself to say her name. She had gotten enough of a mention.

"Let go, Jase." Angie strained her neck to kiss me, her lips only making it as far as my pecs. "I promise nothing bad will happen. Trust me." She kissed my skin trying to coax me back.

"It's me I don't trust." My body took over from my brain as I slowly slid back inside of her. "It's me."

There was no more talking; the fast paced fucking had also stopped. Our bodies found a slower rhythm as I moved against her, feeling every inch of my length fill her before pulling out again. The skin-on-skin contact making it harder to hold out while my body welcomed the delicious torture.

She tilted her hips, joining me in every thrust as I watched myself sliding inside of her bare. It wasn't going to last much longer, her tight pussy fisting me each time I slid inside her wet, hot center. Every second seemed to drag out, and yet not nearly long enough.

Her hand reached down between us, alternating between touching herself and cupping my balls, the sensation sending me so close to the edge I couldn't see straight.

"I'm coming," she breathed as her body convulsed underneath me, my ability to hold back voided as the pulsing sensation traveled against the length of my cock. Her orgasm chasing down mine as she came apart while I watched.

"Angie." My body shook as I erupted, my load spilling into her as my arms gave way and I all but collapsed onto her. My out of control breathing matched hers as I kissed her neck and tried to push myself back onto my elbows.

"No, stay like that." Her arms wrapped around me, holding me against her body. Her arms strained in the effort to stop me from lifting off.

"I'll crush you." I pulled away, worried I was going to hurt or break her, her tiny frame dwarfed by my massive body.

"You already did, and I survived." She blinked, her arms trying to coax me back. "I need to feel you on me. To make sure this is real."

BACK STAGE

Hearing her say that just made me hate myself even more. Knowing what I put her through, knowing what I continued to put her through, made me want to drive a knife through my own heart.

"I'm sorry." I buried my head against the curve of her neck.

"Don't be sorry, just please don't leave me right now. I promise I won't pressure you, but don't run from me, Jase." Her hands gently strummed my back.

"I can't make promises, Angie. I want to, but I can't." My voice vibrated against her skin and I wished to God I had something better to offer her than that. I wouldn't lie to her though, never again would I do that. Even if the truth wasn't pretty.

I lifted my head, and while my lips were pissed off they were no longer on her skin, my eyes were treated to the most spectacular view of her smile. There was no hesitation in her voice as she looked up at me.

"Then don't. I don't need promises, I just need you."

26

Angie

"WHAT DID HE SAY?" MY BODY AUTOMATICALLY NUZZLED against Jason's the minute he'd climbed back into my bed. It's where we both wanted to be—my body and I—my brain still wasn't convinced any of what we were doing was a good idea.

"I think the towel around my waist was a tip-off we weren't trying to kill each other. He also mentioned that if he didn't hear my name screamed by you ever again, it would be too soon. But he didn't say much else other than giving me a don't-fuck-this-up look or two. He's probably just glad he doesn't have to jump in between us." His arms wrapped around me as he kissed my forehead. Those kisses I hoped would never stop.

Things had been said. Things that would forever change the way I saw Jason. But not in the way he thought they would. He was worried about how I would have reacted to the news. But all his past did was prove to me what a remarkable man he was, and validated what I had always known. It's why I loved him, and why I knew I would love him forever. He was a fighter. He was exactly the man for me.

BACK STAGE

The sex hadn't been the plan, but my body took over and it was a connection we both seemed to need. Who was I to argue?

Troy waiting for us had been unfortunate. Some prior planning before we got naked would have been better, to let the poor guy off the hook. Maybe give him a heads up that we were all good now, and were going to have sex so he didn't have to stand outside and wait. That would have been the polite thing to do. Sadly, manners were the furthest thing from our minds.

"I could have gone out and told him, you know." My lips showered his arms with kisses. They were such strong, capable arms. They definitely deserved their own Tumblr.

"If you think there was any chance of me letting you get out of this bed and talk to Troy naked, you're even more delusional than I first thought." He pulled me closer to his body, and I felt his smile against my skin.

"Firstly, you don't get to *let me* do anything." I poked him in the chest for good measure. "If you think you, or anyone else, has any control over me then you are the one who is *delusional*." My fingers did the little air quotes for delusional just for extra effect. "Secondly, Troy is like a brother to me. He would never look at me that way even if he wasn't happily married with a baby on the way, which he is. So. Yeah. You're wrong." My arms folded across my chest as I smiled.

"So quick to be defensive," Jason laughed. "Firstly, I would never tell you what you can *or* can't do. I'm not feeling suicidal. Well, at least not today. And secondly, I wasn't worried about Troy seeing you that way. I was worried about myself. Seeing you stride to that door naked, no way in hell I wouldn't have my hands all over you. I didn't think Troy would appreciate the show. So my statement was less about *you*, and more about my self-preservation." He pulled me closer, nipping at my shoulder.

I promised I wouldn't push, not when I knew why Jason had been so resistant in the first place. And as far as reasons go, his were pretty good ones. Even though I would never do what *she* had done, I wasn't going to start demanding stuff either.

I was going to let him go.

If he came back to me, then I would know. If he didn't then it's not because he didn't want me but because he couldn't be with anyone.

It would still be the most epic of heartaches but that was old news for me. I'd been through it once or twice before. For me, it was worth the risk.

So I kicked him out of my room, telling him I needed to get ready for Megs and Ash's arrival. Which was the truth. But also gave us that time away too.

Here I was, letting him go.

"Hey you!" Megs grabbed me and pulled me into a hug, her belly noticeably bigger. "In the interest of full disclosure, I know everything. But I'm going to need to hear it again because Troy Harris sucks when it comes to gossip. I love the man, but he isn't great with details. Oh well, it's my reassurance that he is still human." She barely took a breath as she pulled away from me and gave me a look over. "You look thinner. Ash, has she lost weight, or is it just because I'm like gigantacon now?"

"Megs, gigantacon isn't a word and even if it was, you aren't." Ash smiled before taking her turn to hug me. "Hey Angie, ignore her. Megs is getting crazier with each passing month."

"I've missed you both, and all your crazy." My arms wrapped around both of them. Happily accepting the affection. It wasn't even weird that I welcomed it.

"So," Megs smiled, her eyebrow arching in question, "you still having accidents with his penis?" She slowly eased into a chair.

"Yeah, but were taking things slow. I'm not expecting anything. There is a lot that he went through, shit I will never understand and he needs time. Maybe we won't make it anyway, but I'm not walking away and not pressuring him."

"What do you mean you're not expecting anything? Like he's not making a commitment, and you are just going to hang around and wait? Get Jason down here right now so I can kick his ass." Megs tried unsuccessfully to leap out of the chair, with her attempt ending up a weird wiggling display. "The minute I get up, I'm going to kick his ass." She pushed against the armrest of the chair and slowly righted herself on her feet.

"You don't need to do that. I'm fine with the way things are." A calm floated over me in a way it hadn't before. Either way, this time I knew I was going to be fine.

"Well that's the most important thing, right, Megs?" Ash tried her best to play peacekeeper, even if she didn't seem to buy it herself.

"I know you don't understand; I don't expect you to. And maybe when this is all said and done, I will totally regret this." I took a deep breath. I'd said it all in my head a million times, and if ever I was going to talk about this with someone other than Jase, these two were who I'd confide in. "But I know that I can't walk away. I've tried unsuccessfully for years to forget him and I keep coming back. It's where I need to be, and hopefully, he'll come to the same conclusion. If not, well at least we tried, right? That has to be better than nothing at all."

"Sounds to me like he doesn't know how lucky he is." Megs slunk back into the chair she had so passionately tried to get out of, hopefully shelving all ideas of confronting Jase and attempting to kick his ass. Pregnant or not, I didn't doubt she would do it.

"We're both lucky."

This wasn't just about Jason. It was about me and my own unhealthy outlook. My idea that loving meant desertion, and that I'd deny myself the chance. It didn't matter if he left. If there were a hundred men that left after him. I wanted to love and I wanted to be loved, and I wasn't going to be scared of it anymore. I would stand out on the edge of the cliff and whatever was going to happen would happen. And it would be enough.

"You know, *all* relationships have their ups and downs." Ash gently touched my hand. "And if it's the right one, it's worth fighting for."

"Thanks. I know this is the right one." In fact I'd never been surer of anything in my life. "I love him and he loves me too. And I'm going to play this out, and if it all ends in tears, I'll still have you two, Rusty and the band."

And most importantly myself.

I am woman, hear me roar, right?

"Hey, we should find Rusty a nice girl." Megs immediately got distracted at the mention of Rusty. "He doesn't have a girlfriend, does he? He's gorgeous too. I can't believe you've never gone there with him."

"Megs, don't." Ash laughed, neither of us holding much hope of convincing Megs no one needed a relationship doctor.

"Fine. You people spoil all my fun."

I was going to wait. And while I waited, I was going to love him beyond measure and let him love me, too. Because I'd rather love him now and have an uncertain forever, than give up now for definite heart break.

The road.

No matter what happened with us, some things didn't stop. The revolving door of cities and stadiums were constant. Planes, buses, cars and hotel rooms, they were also on high rotation. And we continued to exist in the snow globe of the insanity, every day a new shake up yet still things stayed the same.

I watched him from the bathroom. His keyboard splayed on the bed as he played that tune he sometimes did. It was simple and beautiful even though he said it was nothing special. To my ears, there was nothing more perfect.

BACK STAGE

"I thought the *watching* thing was mine?" His head twisted to see me in the doorway. "You want to come sit in my lap and help me play?" His fingers didn't stop moving even though he wasn't looking at them.

"Ha. Too much going on there for my liking. I'll stick to the guitar, I like an instrument I can get my hand around." The double entendre intentional.

My body moved away from the doorway and found itself in his lap. A place my body often liked to be.

"Really? You're going to say that to me when there is a bed in the vicinity?" His eyes darted to the mussed up sheets, his response completely predictable.

I flipped him off which was also predictable, but I did it with a grin. Service with a smile was in such a decline, I felt it was my duty to do my part. You know, so he knew I cared.

Of course this earned me a flashing smile in return, which I loved. Jason had always had such a great smile, and I was glad we'd seen more of it these days.

"So, you given any more thought to your encores? I miss your little odes to me." One of his hands continued to play while the other tiptoed up my arm, his grin getting bigger.

"Aww. You feeling neglected, Jase? Missing me calling you an asshole?"

Despite our situation going back to sort of normal, my finale songs had stayed sidelined. Firstly, because there was no further need for the fuck you's and secondly, it was really fucking hard learning a different new song every night. Even if they were usually easy, over-played pop songs that didn't usually have more than four chord progressions, it was still a feat. It had been fun while it lasted, but we had both moved on, its purpose well and truly served. We, like the songs, had moved to another place and going back wasn't an option.

"You know." His arm moved causing my body to dip, my mouth spontaneously letting out a squeak as my head flew back. "You could sing songs about all the orgasms I'm giving you. That might be fun. I'll even help you compile the list."

His head bowed down to meet mine, kissing my exposed neck.

"Nope, no one wants to hear about that." I wiggled in his arms. "Besides, why tell the people about all the orgasms *you* won't be giving *them*. Think Jason, that's just plain mean." His laugh matching mine while he continued to kiss me.

I loved him like this. Playful, happy—mine. The edginess was still there but it had evened out, and for the most part he was different. And he was either trying really hard or he'd changed, either way massive progress had been made.

"I love you," he whispered in my ear, both his hands completely given up on the keyboard as they solely focused on me. My body still tilted, the angle making the blood rush to my head.

"I love you, too," I whispered back, my hand tracing the line of his jaw.

And that's where it would usually end, the conversation about us or love.

Most of the time it would go back to playful, a throwback to our earlier days of name calling and mild teasing, the bad intentions completely gone.

Sometime I'd catch him studying me, like he was now. His eyes scanning my entire face, like he was waiting for me to say something. What for, I wasn't sure. So I'd usually just whisper another I love you and it would usually be enough.

And it was enough.

27
Jason

I'D EXPECTED AN ULTIMATUM.
The *we're-either-together-or-I'm-done*, but it never came.
A week.
It had been a whole week since the showdown in Angie's room and I'd told her everything. Told her about Em, told her about Thomas. Told her how fucked up I had been.
She hadn't left.
She hadn't demanded shit.
She hadn't tried to push the issue.
Not even a little, which blew my freaking mind. Buttons and Angie, they were like a done deal. But this one just didn't happen.
Then the next week came, and the week after that. Same thing. Status quo was maintained. We were as together as we ever were going to get. Back to spending our nights together, back to me being unable to be away from her. It was a sickness and one I didn't want a cure from.
Still, not a fucking word.
It had to be killing her. The limbo, wondering if all of a sudden I was

going to turn around and bail. Who sticks around on a possibility? No one. Except the one girl who said that's what she was going to do, and regardless of how difficult it was, she was keeping her word. And if she could do that, then I knew whatever fucked up crap I had rolling around in my head wasn't going to land with us.

I loved Angie. I loved her enough to know there was never going to be another girl. And I sure as hell wasn't letting her go and have some other guy take her. Not freaking happening. It wasn't even about marriage; it was knowing that I couldn't be without her.

Forever.

It was the first time I'd been able to think about that word and not need a fifth of vodka chaser. And I wanted the forever with her. I wanted her to be my wife, for that word to mean something for the first time in my life. I'd been running a really long time and I didn't want to run anymore. I wanted to stand still with her. And I wanted to have a million fucking kids, too. But only if she was their mother. I just knew it would be different, and I would take that jump if she was willing to go with me.

She was still too good for me, but like Dan had said not so long ago—if she was willing to give me that chance, then I'd applaud her lack of judgment. I was going to marry her and I was going to spend the rest of my days loving her the way she deserved.

"Hey." I took a seat at the table, everyone already situated and waiting. My message had been ambiguous. The let's-meet-to-discuss-a-new-tune usually came from Alex or James, still they all showed up ready to hear me out.

"Hey." Troy gave me a nod, the bastard losing sleep over the fact his wife was getting close to popping out a baby soon.

The other hey's or hi's came soon after, each of the guys giving me a tip of the chin, ready to get this show on the road.

"I'm going to need a favor."

There was no point dragging it out more than it had to be. Asking for help wasn't something that came easy for me, but this was something that I couldn't do on my own.

BACK STAGE

"Of course, brother. Whatever you need." James tapped me on the shoulder, his unwavering support not unexpected but still floored me.

"All good here." Alex agreed before even hearing what I was asking.

"Yep, same goes with me." Troy nodded, throwing his stamp of approval on my ask just like the other two.

"I'm down as well." Dan's smile settled in as he folded his arms across his chest. "Looks like we're all on the same page."

"You've all agreed without even knowing what I need?"

"Doesn't matter what it is, you're asking for it. If it's something you need, that's enough." Troy tapped on the table, affirmative grunts coming from the others.

If there were ever any doubts that my life had been saved that day in the bar, they had very much been put to bed. Total game changer. That I got to work with these men was an honor—that I got to call them friends … fuck, that was a lottery win. That knowing them led me to Angie, yeah. Some guys just get more than their fair share of luck. And looking around this room, knowing the girl I have waiting on me, I've more than exceeded my share.

"Our last song, I need it to be this." I handed them each a sheet of paper with the title and artist of what I wanted our finale to be. It wasn't one of ours.

"Um, okay," James laughed. "We haven't done a cover in years but yeah, I'm cool."

"Ha. Nice," Alex agreed. "Yep. That isn't a hard ask."

"Your sudden need to do a cover have anything to do with a certain front woman?" Troy smirked cupping the back of my neck. "Guess we're playing a cover."

"What?" Dan looked up from the paper I'd handed him. "No fucking way. Pick something else." The paper dropped from his hands to the table like the thing was carrying a disease. "We're not playing that."

"Dan, it has to be this," I insisted, bending on the song choice not an option. I'd play it and sing it myself if I had to, but it had to be that one song.

"Why the hell would we want to play that?" Dan screwed up his face in disgust. "Did you leave your fucking balls in a purse somewhere? Or did you fucking hit your head on the way over, because there will be a cold day in Hell before I will ever play *that.*" The paper got his attention again as he pointed at it accusingly. Seemed Dan wasn't going to be so down with my plan after all.

"The song isn't that bad, Dan," Alex weighed in, no doubt hoping to try and smooth things over.

"Not that bad of a song?" Dan shot Alex a horrified look like the dude had suddenly grown another head. "Fuck me, sideways. Someone get Lexi on the horn right now and tell her that her husband has dumbass disease."

"Dan, c'mon. It's for Angie."

The full reason of why we'd be rocking a tune that wasn't our own being spotlighted in case everyone hadn't already joined the dots. "She used the covers at the end of her set as a message, and as fucked up as they sometimes used to be, it's the only way I know how to say what I need to say. This is the way I need to say it."

She might have started it, her game of musical clues, but I was most definitely finishing it. There were things I needed to say and this was a way I knew she would understand.

"Well say it with some other fucking song. What about that Bruno Mars, he's a smooth motherfucker. Choose something of his. Better yet, we'll write one for her. James, get a piece of paper and let's knock something out real quick. What can be better than getting her own song? She'll cream her pants for sure." Dan pushed back, the song choice unorthodox because we were a rock band.

The minutes ticked over. Dan glaring at the page like it was going to suddenly spit in his eye while I reinforced there wasn't a back-up plan. This was it.

"It's not about her creaming her pants, and it can't be another song." My finger drummed nervously on the desk. "Just this. Dan, I need to do this."

"You look at me, you fucking tell me you love that girl." Dan reached across the table and got up in my grill, his face fucking fierce. "Then you tell me there will never be another girl for you. Because I can tell you right now, you're only getting a pass like this one fucking time."

"I love her," I said with zero hesitation.

Absolutely none. She was it and I wasn't afraid to fess to it either. Angie was mine and I was hers even without the formalities, but it was about time we took care of them anyway. "There will never be anyone else. It's her. I need her." I took a swallow as I met each of my brothers in the eye. "And I'm going to ask her to marry me and hopefully, if I'm lucky enough, she'll say yes. Because there is no way I can live without her."

Dan blew out a breath as he weighed my words. "Motherfucker."

"Yep." I nodded, meaning every single word I'd said.

No one talked, my intentions for Angie just hanging there in the air. Me ever getting married again was a bet that no one would ever take. They'd assumed I'd eventually settle down with someone and do the living in sin thing. But me putting a ring on someone's finger, again—that was the equivalent to an apocalyptic prediction. Funny that me getting married was once rated on par with the end of the world, and in my eyes—used to be one in the same.

"I love her. I need her to be my wife. And this is the way I need to ask," I repeated. Not because I thought they hadn't heard me but because I couldn't stop saying it. I may have been late to the party but I sure as hell was here now. Going anywhere else wasn't happening any time soon.

"One time." Dan broke the silence first, clocking me with a look I knew meant business. "We do this song, one fucking time, so you better make sure she's watching." He shook his head as he agreed, giving my plan the final green light.

"One time." I met his eyes, my smile finally making an appearance. "I promise it's all I need."

Dan bucked out a laugh, the bastard slamming his fist down onto the table. "Well, hold on to your fucking hats boys because Power Station are about to play Taylor fucking Swift."

I'd never been nervous about a show. Not even close. And yet with every song that we got closer to the end, I felt like I was going to puke. Public displays of affection weren't my thing either; as for putting my ass on the line in front of thousands of people, let's chalk that up to never. But tonight wasn't about me. Thank Christ the audience wouldn't know the whole story, other than Power Station losing their minds and playing a pop song. The headlines it was no doubt going to attract—epic. The care factor on that—nonexistent.

"Yo, you ready to do this thing?" Dan leaned over my keys, his fingers glued to his fret board ready to play.

"As ready as I'll ever be." I looked over to the side of the stage where Angie was standing, her appearance there guaranteed by Rusty. "Let's do it."

"You realize if she says no, we just played Taylor Swift for nothing. I'm pretty sure I'm going to have to insist she says yes just on principle." Dan smirked, his eyes looking over to an amused Angie who had no idea why glances were suddenly being shot in her direction.

"I'm hoping she won't say no, but if she does, you'll shut your mouth and be grateful I'm not making you play Miley Cyrus." I mouthed I love you to Angie as James hit the mic, ready to announce the song.

"We have a special request tonight." His voice barely audible over the noise from the crowd. "But before we play this last song we want to thank you for being on this road with us. We never thought we'd be lucky enough to still be here so many years later, doing what we love and getting to call it a job. We're here because you put us here and it's a fucking honor to play for you. So as we wrap up tonight, know this isn't goodbye but see you later. We love you and you'll always be with us."

BACK STAGE

The thunderous applause reached ear-bleeding proportions.

"So here we go; this song goes out to a special someone. You know who you are." James looked to Troy who counted us in with the sticks.

The opening notes of "Love Story" started and the crowd hushed into a confused calm of silence. Like Angie had done with her renditions, we had put our own spin on it, but there was no denying what the song was. The words James was singing slightly changed so he didn't sound like he was looking to seduce a dude. Dan's insistence, and I didn't disagree.

It was a song, written by a teenage girl comparing her first love to one of the greatest stories of all time.

Romeo and Juliet.

The words were cheesy and not at all my speed. In fact, I hated it. But it told a story of how the young couple tried to keep away and couldn't. And unlike the Shakespearian play, those two lovebirds didn't end up with matching headstones, which is always a plus. Instead Romeo pops the question, down on one knee after asking her daddy's blessing. Just like I had. Only I wasn't on one knee on account I still need to play.

Angie's mouth dropped open as the significance of those lyrics hopefully came to light. Either that or she really hated Taylor Swift, in which case I was SOL. It didn't matter, whether she said yes or no, I needed to say what I needed to say.

We'd been trying to keep away long enough. Fighting a love that had threatened to break us both, but the only real love either of us ever had known. It was where we both belonged; we'd just taken the scenic route to get there.

It got to the part of the song I was waiting for, my chance. And as James screamed out the lyrics, I mouthed, "Marry me, Angie." My eyes nailed directly on hers as she watched, her tears already flowing thick and fast.

There was no indication on how she was going to respond, the rest of the song playing out as she stood on the side of the stage and cried. Rusty held her so she didn't fall, her body seeming to have trouble staying vertical. And I wanted off that stage and her in my arms more than I wanted my next breath.

As the last cord sung through the amp, we took our place on the stage and waved a quick good bye. Usually I'd stay a little longer and bask in the adulation, but there was only one person whose approval I needed and that was the girl who I was heading toward.

"Angie." I ignored Rusty completely and pulled her out of his arms. "I love you, marry me."

She didn't answer, her beautiful eyes flooded with tears as she looked back at me. The fear crept up on me slowly that maybe I'd missed my chance.

"It doesn't have to be right now. Fuck knows you waited long enough for me. I'll wait forever if I have to. And that is a promise that I have no problem making. Forever, Angie. That's what I want. That's what I'm asking you for." My mouth couldn't stop talking, needing to tell her how dumb I had been.

"My baggage still exists, and I'm still fucked up. But I know that if I don't have you then me being destroyed again is a certainty. I'd rather have twelve months of happiness with you and the most epic breakup of all mankind than go the next twelve years without you. And I swear I will never hurt you again, I'll —"

"Shut up, asshole." She covered my mouth with her hands, stopping it from spewing words that it needed to say. "I love you." She slowly moved her hand away and smiled. "Yes. I'll marry you, but on one condition."

"Anything, name it." The words couldn't shoot out of my mouth fast enough. "Whatever it is. You've got it."

"Neither of us ever play another Taylor Swift song again." The smile slowly spread across her lips.

"Halle-fuckin-luiah!" Dan called from behind us, the fact that I'd been doing this with an audience just now coming to light.

I laughed, looking around at the people around us. Their faces an easy read on how happy they were for us. Even Angie's band seemed fucking ecstatic, Rusty shaking my free hand while the other was still around my girl. That was the other thing, my girl. Looking into her eyes I knew I'd been saved all over again. Not because this was a relationship, because it wasn't. She was more than that, just like the band wasn't just a band. Both of them were so much more.

This was my family.

"Yeah, let's stick to originals from here on out." My mouth found its mark on hers. "It's time for a new soundtrack."

EPILOGUE

Angie

"Look at you, bare foot and pregnant. I'm still reeling from the shock." Rusty wrapped his arms around me, my swollen belly stopping him from giving me a proper hug.

"We're sitting beside a pool, dumbass, of course I'm going to be in bare feet." My hand playfully slapped him across the chest. It had only been a couple of weeks since we'd seen each other, but somehow in that time I'd ballooned to waddle size. That there was a tiny human growing in my body was still a sense of wonderment.

"Rusty, you better not be upsetting my wife. I like you, and I don't want to have to rearrange your face." Jase's arms found their way around me; it's where they usually were when he was around. Which he was a lot since our wedding fourteen months ago.

"Easy there, *GI Joe*. I've told you people a million times, I'm a lover not a fighter." Rusty reached out his hand to Jase, the handshake evolving into some manly hug.

"Hey, Rus." James lifted a cold beer from the cooler and handed it to Rusty. "Good of you to make it."

"Well it's not often I'm summoned to the Power Station compound."

BACK STAGE

Rus looked around at the lofty Bowden mansion, kids squealing in the pool beside us. "Besides, I haven't met Briana yet. Figure two birds, one stone and all of that." The easy smile spread across his face.

"Ha, you think Dan is going to let you anywhere near his daughter? Oh this I've got to see." Troy wandered over, his year-old son, Evan, hanging off his dad's arm like he was a jungle gym. "Hey buddy, how about you let daddy say hi to Uncle Rusty?" He reached down and scooped up the boy who had somehow managed to win the genetic lottery of both his mother's and his father's good looks. "Mama," Evan demanded, missing Megs, who was already back to work and would be joining us for dinner later.

"I've been around kids before. It's not like I'd drop her or anything." Rusty shrugged, not having seen Dan in action since his little girl had come into the world two months ago.

"Drop her?" Alex laughed, adjusting Grace's goggles so she could cannon ball into the pool with Noah and Jesse. "The only way anyone gets to hold that kid is if he is either out of the country or sedated. It's hysterical; I cannot wait until she starts dating." He laughed, kissing the top of his daughter's head as she ran off to join her mother in the pool. Lexi and I were sporting matching bumps, her due date three weeks before mine.

"Yeah, well as long as you keep recording, you can pop out as many kids as you want. Although Jase, I hope you give my front woman a break every now and again, we're going to need her for a tour in six months." Rus took his seat on the poolside chair, Hannah waving to him as she carried out a huge platter of cut fruit.

"Yep, tour still goes ahead." Jason smiled, "I'm going to enjoy being backstage for a change." He took his seat on the huge patio couch, pulling me into his lap as he did so. The fact that I could barely fit obviously escaping his attention.

"So, what's the deal? Other than the reunion, you must have a reason for calling me out here." Rusty eased back into his chair, his smile fixed on Troy who was still wrestling with Evan, and took a slow slip of his beer. "I have to admit, I'm more than a little curious."

"Rus, they have a proposition for us. I know Joey and Max will agree to anything as long as they get to play, but I wanted to talk it over with you before we took it to the band." My nerves had been shot all morning, James and Alex's suggestion still tossing around in my head.

"Angie, last time Power Station had a proposition for us we ended up on a massive tour and you came home with a husband. Seeing as you're already knocked up, not sure how much more they can offer us. I'm not having anyone's baby if that's what's on the table."

"Hey, did I miss anything?" Dan waltzed in, baby sling wrapped tightly around his chest, his arms free to carry a diaper bag in one hand and hold his wife's waist with the other. It was multitasking at its finest.

"Nope, just about to start." James directed him to an empty chair.

"Hey, Angie." Ash gave me a wave. "Hey babe, why don't you give me Briana so you can have your meeting." She turned her attention to Dan who had already taken his seat, the sleeping kid attached to him not seeming to hinder him in anyway.

"Got it, babe. She's fine with me. Go relax, I'll call you if she needs to be fed."

"You know you are going to eventually have to loosen up your grip, right? You can't hold her forever." Ash laughed, her smile hinting it was probably not the first time she'd argued the point.

"Ash, stop saying stuff you know is going to upset me." He waved off his wife, his hand instinctively wrapping around his daughter.

"She's pretty." Rusty peered over the swaddling at a sleeping Briana. "Definitely takes after her mother."

"Yeah she sure does." Dan looked down at her and smiled. "Which is why I'm letting no one near her. I'm actually going to build a bunker. I saw some shit on Doomsday Preppers. They are all batshit crazy, but some of their ideas I can work with."

"Okay, so other than certifying Dan for an institution, why am I here again?" Rusty looked around confused. The circus that was Power Station a lot crazier than our own band.

BACK STAGE

"They want to sign us," I blurted out, not able to hold back any longer. The fact it had been suggested days ago and I still hadn't said anything was a miracle in itself.

"We got a deal, weren't those fancy papers we signed twelve months ago a record contract? I know I'm not as smart as you, but I seemed to remember reading record label somewhere on them." Rusty rubbed his chin, the sarcasm dripping from his voice.

"Yes, we signed a deal but you said it yourself, the control they had was a pain in the ass. You hate that they choose which singles get released. You even hate the cover they made us shoot." The romantic notion of being signed didn't live up to the hype. As an unknown quantity we had very little control over much. We were able to fight any creative changes but other than that, it was sit down, shut up and let the big boys do what they needed to do. We didn't do so well with the directive, but the paycheck they'd already paid us meant we had to at least pretend to play nice.

"Well yeah, I hated it. Other than getting our shit out to a wider audience. It blows donkey's balls. So what exactly are you suggesting?"

"We're starting our own label," James interrupted, itching to get Rusty on board. "We're all married with kids, and while we aren't ready to hang it all up just yet, we're looking to the future. Music is always going to be our thing and we've learned a thing or two about what to do and what not to do. What better way to help promote emerging talent than to produce it and help get it out there—the right way. Without all the suit and tie bullshit."

"So how are *you* going to be different to the New York heavyweights we're dealing with now? No offense dude, but it's been a while since you were *emerging*." Rusty took another swallow of his beer, in no hurry to sign another deal.

"Because we'll give you creative control. Ash is coming on board as our business manager. Lexi will deal exclusively with our clients. Hannah will work with client relations. This will be a family-run set up, and we know how important family is. We'll buy out your current deal, you sign to us and we work with you, not you working for us."

"Why? It can't be for the money." Rusty asked the exact same questions I asked. The sudden shift from musicians or businessmen not immediately clear.

"The band was never about the money for us, we just wanted to do what we did." Alex nodded to James, taking his opportunity to turn on the charm. "But if it's one thing we learned from the last tour—and having you guys on the road with us—Trust, loyalty, integrity—that is shit you can't buy, and it's missing from our industry in a big way. Thankfully not everyone has sold out. We're going to find those guys and pay it forward."

"This is a good thing, Rusty. Our next album could be our own." The baby in my belly kicked, obviously concurring with my decision. "They are giving us the keys to the car, we drive it how we want."

"Alright," Rusty nodded looking around at the mayhem that was surrounding us. "Yeah, let's drive."

It was a stark difference from the boardroom we'd been in when we signed our first deal. The impersonal handshakes and cookie-cutter secretaries, a world away from five guys who had a dream and made it happen. And that's what it all came down too, having a dream and seeing it through, even if you tripped along the way.

"You okay?" Jase asked, his hand going to the part of my belly where junior was practicing field goals. The tiny kicks making me marvel at how far we'd all come.

"Yeah, it took us a while but I think everything is finally okay."

ACKNOWLEDGEMENTS

Thank you to my amazing family—Gep, Jenna, Liam and Woodley, who undoubtedly suffer along with me with the long hours while I am hammering away at the keyboard. If I don't say it enough, I love and appreciate your love and support always.

Thank you to the girls who remind me daily that superheroes exist. Sadly, capes are frowned upon so they stick to civilian clothes most of the time. **Mini, Nat, Juzzie, Sam, Shell, Grace, Bec, Kirsty** and **Jo**, you keep my wheels turning even when I want to stop.

To my beta team who read and give me feedback so that the book I write is the best it can be. **Amy, Terri** and **Maz**, thank you all for your work and your time. I appreciate it more than you know.

Special thanks to **Maz, Andie** and **Nichole** (my editor), who talked me down from the ledge over this book.

Thank you to the amazing group of peers who I am luck enough to call my friends. Humbled to be in your company and honored to be alongside you in the "trenches." **Lili Saint Germain, JB Hartnett, Skyla Madi, CJ Duggan, Lilliana Andersen, Rachael Brookes, JD Nixon, JD Chase, Natasha Preston, Kirsty Mosely, Ker Dukey, LA Casey, Jill Patten, Callie Hart, Andie Long, Abbi Glines, Chantal Fernando, Penelope Louleas, Jay Crownover, Kim Karr, SC Stephens, Joanna Wylde** and **Kylie Scott**. I might give you crazy eyes, but that's only because I love you. P.S I still feel like the dork that somehow weaseled their way into a group of cool kids, and seeing as no one has wised up, I'm staying!

Thank you to *my* **Hang Le**. I know she is loved by many, but as far as I'm concerned she is ALL mine. She makes me feel like a rock star every single time. Best graphic designer ever! My back cover, teasers and other amazing graphic stuff wouldn't be the same. You're stuck with me, lady.

Thank you to **Gian** for another amazing cover. Sadly this will be our last one, but I'll never forget your contribution. People *do* judge books by their covers and you gave me some stunning ones.

Thanks to **Angelique Ehlers** for front cover photography.

Thank you to the bloggers and blogs who have supported me. **Helen S-** Kinky Book Klub, **Kelly O-** Kelly's Kindle Konfessions, **Marie M-** Surrender to Books, **Jodie O-** Fab Fun and Tantalizing Reads, **Rebecca** and **Nicole** – Author Groupies, **Tammy M-** A Slice of Fiction, The Book Nuts and The SubClub, **Francessca W** – Francessca's Romance Reviews, **Sam** -Forever Me Romance, **Debbie O-** Hard Rock Romance, **Tash D-** Book Lit Love, **Stephanie G** – The Lemon Review, **Kristine B-** Glass Paper Ink Bookblog, **Karen H-** A Thousand Lives Book Blog, **Belinda** and **Lily-** Hopelessly Devoted 2 Books, **Amy J** – The SubClub, **Paige** and **Kylie** –Give me Books, **Sian D** - Rauchy, Rude and Readers blog, **Laurie F** – Book Fancy, **Jo W-** Four Brits and a Book, **Erin-** Read and Ramble, **Sarez-** Talk Supe, **Bianca** – Martini Times Romance blog, **Rosarita** - iScream Books, **Kimmy**, **Paige**, **Claire**, **Steph** – Fictional Men's Room for Ho's, **Kelly** – Perusing Princess, and sorry to anyone I have forgotten. I love you all.

Thanks to the **T Gephart Entourage**, I like that you have all embraced my crazy. Best group ever!

Thank you to **Jemina Venter** at BookNerdFanGirl Designs—you rock lady.

Thanks to my Fictionally Yours, Melbourne team- **Penny** and **Simone** and our Bloggers, **Trish**, **Angela**, **Erin** and **Tash**. It's been a wild ride.

Thank you to my editor, **Nichole Strauss**, from Perfectly Publishable. I love that you get me despite my excessive profanity, dropped words, spoilers and periodic freak-outs. You know just the right way to tease more out of me using the kindest of touches. (Not in a dirty Dan way either)

Thanks to **Max Henry** from Max Effect for my amazing formatting. You take my words and make them beautiful.

And a massive thanks **to all my readers**. Knowing you are with me makes this sometimes difficult journey worthwhile.

Lastly, to The Power Station boys and their ladies—you have given me more laughs and tears than most "real" people. Hope to see you again sometime in the future. You will always be in my heart.

ABOUT THE AUTHOR

T GEPHART IS AN INDIE AUTHOR FROM MELBOURNE, AUSTRALIA.
T's approach to life has been somewhat unconventional. Rather than going to University, she jumped on a plane to Los Angeles, USA in search of adventure. While this first trip left her somewhat underwhelmed and largely depleted of funds it fueled her appetite for travel and life experience.

With a rather eclectic resume, which reads more like the fiction she writes than an actual employment history, T struggled to find her niche in the world.

While on a subsequent trip the United States in 1999, T met and married her husband. Their whirlwind courtship and interesting impromptu convenience store wedding set the tone for their life together, which is anything but ordinary. They have lived in Louisiana, Guam and Australia and have traveled extensively throughout the US. T has two beautiful young children and one four legged child, Woodley, the wonder dog.

An avid reader, T became increasingly frustrated by the lack of strong female characters in the books she was reading. She wanted to read about a woman she could identify with, someone strong, independent and confident and who didn't lack femininity. Out of this need, she decided to pen her first book, A Twist of Fate. T set herself the challenge to write something that was interesting, compelling and yet easy enough to read that was still enjoyable. Pulling from her own past "colorful" experiences and the amazing personalities she has surrounded herself with, she had no shortage of inspiration. With a strong slant on erotic fiction, her core characters are empowered women who don't have to sacrifice their femininity. She enjoyed the process so much that when it was over she couldn't let it go.

T loves to travel, laugh and surround herself with colorful characters.

This inevitably spills into her writing and makes for an interesting journey - she is well and truly enjoying the ride!

Based on her life experiences, T has plenty of material for her books and has a wealth of ideas to keep you all enthralled.

CONNECT WITH T

Webpage
http://tgephart.com/bio/4579459512

Facebook
https://www.facebook.com/pages/T-Gephart/412456528830732

Goodreads
https://www.goodreads.com/author/show/7243737.T_Gephart

Twitter
@tinagephart

BOOKS BY T GEPHART

THE LEXI SERIES
Lexi

A Twist of Fate

Twisted Views: Fate's Companion

A Leap of Faith

A Time for Hope

THE POWER STATION SERIES
High Strung

Crash Ride

Back Stage

Made in the USA
Charleston, SC
31 May 2016